THE WIMBOURNE BOOK OF VICTORIAN GHOST STORIES
Volume 1

Alastair Gunn is a writer, musician and professional astrophysicist based in the UK. Alastair writes a regular column for *BBC Science Focus* magazine, has written for *The Daily Telegraph*, *The Independent* and *The Guardian* and is a contributor to many astronomy magazines including *Astronomy Now* and *BBC Sky at Night Magazine*. His fiction includes a collection of supernatural stories called *Ballymoon* and his debut novel, *The Bergamese Sect*. He is the editor of the successful anthology series entitled *The Wimbourne Book of Victorian Ghost Stories*.

By Alastair Gunn

BALLYMOON
THE BERGAMESE SECT
THE WIMBOURNE BOOK OF VICTORIAN GHOST STORIES

THE WIMBOURNE BOOK OF

Victorian Ghost Stories

Volume 1

Edited and with an Introduction by

ALASTAIR GUNN

Wimbourne Books 2018

THE WIMBOURNE BOOK OF
VICTORIAN GHOST STORIES
(Volume 1)

First Publication Worldwide
Published by Wimbourne Books 2018

Copyright © Wimbourne Books 2018

ISBN 978-0-9929828-4-3

A CIP catalogue record for this book is available from the British Library.

Cover illustration: An 1887 portrait of author Dinah Maria Craik [née Mulock] (1826-1887) by Sir Hubert von Herkomer (1849-1914).

Typeset in Palatino Linotype by Wimbourne Books, UK.

Contents

THE WIMBOURNE BOOK OF

Victorian Ghost Stories

Volume 1

Wimbourne Books 2018

Introduction

Alastair Gunn

My library shelves are literally bursting with dirty, dusky volumes; long out-of-print first editions, loose-leaved penny-dreadfuls and leather-bound Victorian periodicals; time-capsules from an era now no longer held in living memory. And most of them have been gathering dust on my shelves for one reason — they contain something of the *macabre*. Having been an avid collector and devourer of Victorian supernatural fiction for over thirty years, I have accrued an often-frowned-upon collection of yellowing pages. Each page, though, holds a particular charm for me. Some I may have discovered at the bottom of an unsorted box of papers hidden beneath the shelves of a forgotten recess in an Edinburgh second-hand book shop. Others may have stood proud but unnoticed among the fiction section of an open-air store in Hay-on-Wye, next to the sodden cardboard honesty box. Yet more may have required haggling with the erudite purveyor of literary goods in a certain shop in Alnwick, Northumberland. All of them, whatever their provenance, hold a childish fascination for me; for their ragged beauty, for their material existence, for the history they have lived through, for the characters who have owned them, but most of all for the strange words and tales they relate.

So, imagine my delight when Wimbourne Books asked if I would be interested in compiling and editing a collection of Victorian ghost stories. I relished the opportunity. First, it gave me an excuse to peruse these forgotten treasures once again; to blow the dust from their yellowing pages; to rediscover what it was that enthralled me as a child, and enthrals me still; to reconnect with that slightly sinister Victorian predilection for everything occult, deathly and mysterious. But also, it gave me the chance of bringing this popular genre to an even wider audience. I hope the tales between these pages, and I expect in the pages of further volumes in this series, will enthral you too and that you will discover what I have discovered among these fading printed words. I especially wish that readers new to this genre will discover its pleasures; the Victorian quaintness, the sometimes shocking difference in social norms, the almost comical politeness and structured etiquette, the archaic and precise language, but mostly the Victorians' skill at stoking our fears and trepidations, our insecurities and doubts.

Even if you are already an aficionado of the ghostly tale I hope there is much within these pages to interest you. Many collections are available, for single authors, or as multi-author anthologies, but not all tales are easy to come by, or are available only in print at exorbitant cost. The decision of Wimbourne Books to produce this series in both print and e-book formats should be applauded. It means the cost can be minimised, a wider audience on numerous devices can be accommodated and now these tales are forever recorded digitally for subsequent generations. So, it is my hope that as the series progresses even the die-hard Victorian supernatural fiction fan will find tales to savour — even ones they have not come across before.

The great tradition of the Victorian ghost story grew out of a far older tradition; that of the Gothic tale. Inspired by the Germanic tradition — foreboding mountains, mythical beasts, perched castles, medieval taverns, ancestral curses, dark forests and the fear of the unknown — the Gothic tale grew in popularity, particularly in England, after the publication of Horace Walpole's *The Castle of Otranto* (1764). Some of the classics of Gothic literature are classics still, such as Mary Shelley's *Frankenstein* (1818) and the much later *Dracula* (1897) by Bram Stoker. But in the late 18th and early 19th century the Gothic novel was paramount; novels such as Clara Reeve's *The Old English Baron* (1778), Friedrich Schiller's *The Ghost-Seer* (1789), Ann Radcliffe's *The Mysteries of Udolpho* (1794), and Matthew Gregory Lewis's *The Monk* (1796) were all extremely successful. Other more obscure gothic novels have been thankfully republished in the twentieth century (such as William Beckford's *Vathek*, 1786, and John Polidori's *The Vampyre*, 1819) and I urge the reader to seek them out. These novels were a rich source of catalysis for the development of the traditional 'ghost' story which became in many ways standardised by the Victorians.

By the start of the Victorian era, the Gothic framework was giving way to a more historical and 'realistic' depiction of the supernatural, free of romanticism. An early exponent of this style was the American author Edgar Allan Poe, whose short story *The Fall of the House of Usher* (1839) is an excellent example of the melding of the Gothic tradition with Victorian realism. Other authors who similarly blended the now-outdated Gothic subtext with urban or domestic themes were G. W. M. Reynolds (cf. *Wagner the Wehr-wolf*, 1847), G. P. R. James (cf. *The Castle of Ehrenstein*, 1847) and Emily Brontë (cf. Cathy's ghost at the window scene in *Wuthering Heights*, 1847). It is this backdrop in the first decade of Queen Victoria's rule which allowed the short, 'other-worldly realism' of the ghost story to develop from the longer, darker, sensationalist novel full of Gothic tropes.

But what were the factors which led to the establishment of such an easily-recognisable genre and why were ghost stories so popular in the Victorian era? There are no plain answers to these questions and it is clear that the Gothic inspiration for the ghost story, long though it was in the making, and crucial, was not the only catalyst.

We should first deal with a common misconception. It has often been said that Charles Dickens created the Victorian obsession with the ghost story. But this is only partly true. The genre was already born in the penny-dreadfuls of the late Regency era, long before Dickens achieved the heights of his fame. What Dickens did do, however, was to meld together the traditions of Christmas with the traditions of story-telling, particularly the telling of spooky or gruesome tales of the macabre. And that connection has never since been broken. His 1843 novella, *A Christmas Carol,* was an instant bestseller, and remains so to this day, having been adapted many times for film, TV, stage and opera. The story was not only a spooky yarn, it was allegorical, nostalgic and yet full of contemporary themes such as poverty, social injustice and redemption. In effect, *A Christmas Carol* explored many of the prevalent social and philosophical ideologies of the early 1840s — it was extraordinarily timely — and the Victorians lapped it up.

But actually the tale is inspired by Dickens's own childhood and his own longing for a lost Christmas tradition, which may never have existed, except in his own writing. Three years before the novella was published, Queen Victoria had married Prince Albert. A German style of celebrating Christmas, which Albert had brought to the family home, was immediately popular — the sending of Christmas cards, the giving of gifts (which had hitherto been associated with Epiphany in January) and the decorating of Christmas trees. Dickens himself seems to be responsible for our association of snow-covered landscapes with Yuletide celebrations. Even though the UK, for example, only saw seven white Christmases in the 20th century, our Christmas cards often depict a snowy Christmas scene. Admittedly, it may be that Dickens had lived his own childhood through some particularly harsh winters (six of his first nine Christmas's had been white) and he had carried this association with him through adulthood — and into his prose. In *Sketches by Boz* (1833) and *The Pickwick Papers* (1837) Dickens had already alluded to this idealised Christmas tradition, a secular tradition, full of song, snow and candles, which was later to be born fully-formed in *A Christmas Carol*.

In his novella Dickens had written of his own nostalgia as well as the pivotal issues of the era in which he lived. He thus presented to the Victorian palate a sense of community, a great humanitarian yarn, with some ghosts thrown in for good measure. It crystallised a picture of Christmas which has never left us. Dickens would continue to bolster the claim that Christmas was a time for telling ghostly stories. Many of the greatest spooky tales of the Victorian era are to be found in the Christmas editions of popular periodicals; including but not limited to Dickens's *All The Year Round* and *Household Words*. So, as important as Dickens was in the popularisation of the ghost story, he did not create the obsession for the Victorian reader. There were other, much more influential factors which allowed the development of the genre.

The profound social and technological changes which post-industrial Victorian society ushered in allowed easier and cheaper printing, increased literacy and resulted in more of what we now call 'disposable income'. It saw the birth of the middle classes eager for entertainment. Thus the weekly or monthly periodical became extremely popular and the macabre tales they peddled likewise grew in popularity. It is not surprising that many of the tales in this volume first appeared in these periodicals — *Cornhill Magazine*, *Fraser's Magazine*, *The Argosy*, *The Illustrated London News*, *Bentley's Miscellany*, *Welcome Guest*, *Belgravia*, *Blackwood's Edinburgh Magazine*, *New Quarterly Magazine*, *MacMillan's Magazine*, *Longman's Magazine* as well as Dickens's own *Household Words* and *All The Year Round*. The list goes on. With the explosion in the publishing market, editors needed large amounts of copy to satisfy weekly demand, and the short ghost story became a valuable commodity.

We could ask the question whether the market created the demand or the demand created the market. It seems the latter is more likely. Spiritualism, the belief that the departed can communicate with the living, coincidentally had its origins in New York State in the 1840s. Soon, the practice of séances, automatic writing and the like became hugely popular and allowed mediums to earn a tidy income. By the 1850s, in England, the séance, or table-turning parties, were the height of fashion. The subjects of apparitions and ghostly visitations were not given the degree of scepticism common today and the Victorians were naturally disposed to the themes of death, the occult and mysticism. Ghost and ghouls and mysterious tappings at night were ubiquitous, so much so that by 1887 we find Mary Louisa Molesworth's narrator in her story *The Story of the Rippling Train* (reproduced in this volume) asking "aren't you tired of them? One hears nothing else nowadays". It is surely no coincidence that ghostly fiction, produced *en masse* by the popular press, peaked at the same time as the interest in spiritualism.

Some have pointed out that this mystic tendency of the Victorians is apparently at variance with their technological and scientific renaissance. However, the huge changes in industry, communications and science were actually the catalyst of a longing for past simplicity. For all their modernity, their advances still could not *explain*. The abysmal mortality rate, the perceived dichotomy between science and religion, the mysteries of nature – all these required explanation. Within their rapidly changing world the Victorians reached out for answers to a more 'understandable' and convenient plane — the mystical itself. It coloured their entire view of life and death as well as the realms beyond. So, Victorian practices such as *post-mortem* photography (also called *memento mori*), Ouija boards, Tarot cards, mediums, hypnotism, mesmerism, the summoning of the dead, things which are these days treated with some cynicism and occasionally distaste, were perfectly normal and accepted in Victorian society. The Victorians were in many ways obsessed with death and, by implication, what lay beyond. Hardly surprising then that some of their most popular fiction of the day concerned the ghostly realms.

A scholar of ghostly fiction, Richard Dalby, once proposed that more than half of the best British supernatural short fiction was penned by female authors. Furthermore, according to Jessica Amanda Salmonsen, of all the ghost stories published in the Victorian era in British and American magazines, about 70% were by women. This prevalence of the female writer in this genre means that for this first volume in the Wimbourne series, I have decided to concentrate solely on female writers.

In an era when women were far from emancipated it is important to consider why ghostly fiction attracted female writers. It was previously suggested that the draw was often monetary — that widowed, educated women could easily support themselves and their families financially because of the demand for short supernatural fiction. But this is a gross oversimplification. Author Michael Cox contends that the supernatural genre allowed women the freedom to explore ideas and concepts beyond the normal social constraints of the time — indeed, darker, more intimate and even erotic overtones would be less likely frowned upon in the supernatural setting. Hence, female authors are often found exploring thoughts of love, death, marriage and even sexuality in the pages of Victorian periodicals — conversations that would clearly be shocking if expounded at the dinner table.

Another factor is perhaps that Victorian rationality itself promoted the female as an authority on the quasi-scientific, or, as one writer says, as 'repositories of residual instincts and intuitions'. Women were also held in esteem (mostly) as upholders of the moral high-ground and thus permitted to explore the themes of retribution, betrayal and misguided avarice – themes which appear often in the ghostly tale. But the female-penned ghost story also reveals some of the frustrations of the author and often deals with pre-suffrage themes such as dispossession of property, the patriarchal society, unhappy marriage, the dominant father-figure and economic bondage — as well as the common resentments and anxieties of the Victorian woman. There is no doubt also that many of their stories continue the tradition of the Victorian 'sensation fiction' — a genre more often than not dominated by women writers. In many ways, then, Victorian women writers used the traditional ghost story, like the sensation novel, to highlight the cultural inequalities of the era.

So, who were these extraordinary women who did so much to bring the ghostly genre to the forefront of Victorian literature? In this volume I have included stories from a wide range of female authors; English, Irish, Scottish, Welsh and American. I have ordered them chronologically, spanning the years 1852 to 1901, if only to show the changing style in both language and material. I have not been too strict on the definition of a 'ghost story'. Not all require someone with a sheet over their head — thus we may encounter unseen apparitions, mysterious goings-on or even a simple stranger with a large nose. But they are all stories of the supernatural that present or imply a force or apparition beyond our worldly realms. I should also point out that I have rarely edited the following texts to reflect modern spelling or usage — they appear as they do in the original publications (with the exception of a few obvious typographical errors to aid understanding). However, certain Victorian peculiarities *have* been changed, for example the hyphenation of 'to-day' and 'to-night', and the propensity of Victorians to separate words like 'anyone', 'sometimes', 'everywhere', etc., into their component parts. These corrections are simply because the originals tend to trip up the modern eye. In what follows I present some basic biographical and bibliographical details for each of our authors and encourage the reader to seek out more of their works (some of which will undoubtedly appear in further volumes of this series).

Elizabeth Cleghorn Gaskell (1810-1865) was an English novelist and short story writer popular during the early Victorian period. She was born in Chelsea but on the death of her mother when she was only thirteen months old, her father sent her to live with her aunt in the picturesque Cheshire town of Knutsford. This town was the inspiration for the fictional 'Cranford' that featured in much of her later writing, including her best remembered novel *Cranford* which was first serialised in Dickens's magazine *Household Words* between 1851 and 1853. Having married and settled in Manchester in 1832, it was the death of her only son, William, in 1845 from scarlet fever, which led her to writing; on her husband's suggestion that it might ease her grief. Her writing was much respected, even within her own time, and is characterised by realistic portraits of Victorian life within all classes of society, particularly the struggling lower echelons of the labouring community. Living within one of the most industrialised cities in England, but also surrounded by renowned cultural and intellectual institutions, Elizabeth Gaskell produced relevant and insightful literature concerning the social issues of the time. Her success brought her into contact with many important writers of the day. She formed a strong friendship with Charlotte Brontë and would later write, on the request of Charlotte's father Patrick, the first biography of her dear friend; *The Life of Charlotte Brontë* (1857). Her other notable novels include *North and South* (1854-55) and *Wives and Daughters* (1865). Elizabeth Gaskell was also a master of supernatural fiction in the best Victorian tradition. In fact, her very first publication (*Clopton Hall*, 1840) was a gothic description of a haunted ancestral home. She wrote many ghostly or macabre stories that originally appeared in Dickens's periodicals *Household Words* and *All the Year Round*. These include *Disappearances*, *The Scholar's Story*, *The Squire's Story*, *The Ghost in the Garden Room*, *The Doom of the Griffiths*, *The Poor Clare*, *Lois the Witch*, *Curious*, *If True* and *The Grey Woman*. For this collection I have chosen the ever-popular *The Old Nurse's Story* which first appeared in the special Christmas edition of *Household Words* in 1852 and later in the collection *Lizzie Leigh and Other Tales* (1855). Elizabeth Gaskell died suddenly at only 55 years old whilst secretly trying to purchase a house in Holybourne, Hampshire as a retirement gift for her husband and family.

Dinah Maria Mulock (1826-1887), more commonly known under her married name of Craik, was born in Stoke-on-Trent, England. After the death of her mother in 1845 her father abandoned her and her siblings, and so aged nineteen she set off for London in the hope of becoming an author. Perhaps not coincidentally, since her evangelist father was reputedly known to Byron (due to his vitriolic letter-writing addressed to the poet), Dinah fell in with just the right crowd; Alexander MacMillan, founder of the MacMillan publishing house, Charles Edward Mudie, the instigator of one of the world's first public lending libraries, and the writer and essayist Camilla Toulmin. Dinah's first novel was a children's book, *Cola Monti* (1849), but she is best remembered for *John Halifax, Gentleman* (1857), a tale of a lowly orphan's rise to middle-class success. Her other novels include *The Ogilvies* (1849), *Olive* (1850), *The Head of the Family* (1851), *Agatha's Husband* (1853), *A Life for a Life* (1859), *Mistress and Maid* (1863), *Christian's Mistake* (1865), *The Little Lame Prince* (1874) and the posthumously published *An Unknown Country* (1887). Although not widely remembered for her ghostly or supernatural writings, Dinah Mulock produced several excellent tales of the macabre. I have selected for this volume Dinah's tale *The Last House in C—— Street* which first appeared in *Fraser's Magazine* in October 1856, but also featured in her 1857 collection titled *Nothing New*. The story takes some concentration due to Mulock's story-within-a-story technique and the reader is left wondering whether there ever was a ghost involved in the strange circumstances related by Mrs. McArthur. Dinah Mulock died just weeks before the marriage of her adopted foundling daughter, Dorothy, reportedly exclaiming on her death bed "Oh, if I could live four weeks longer! But no matter, no matter!"

Catherine Ann Crowe (née Stevens) was born in Kent in 1790. She was home-educated, married in 1822 but then separated from her husband (John Crowe) after the birth of their son in 1823. Moving to Edinburgh she made the acquaintance of some prominent authors, including William Makepeace Thackery and Hans Christian Anderson. She was an early advocate of women's educational rights and had a deeply-rooted interest in the occult; at one time being considered a leading spiritualist. She is best remembered for her crime novel *The Adventures of Susan Hopley* (1841) which was adapted into a play by George Dibdin Pitt and ran for eight years (and 343 performances) at London's Royal Victoria Theatre. Her other novels, which often detailed the plight of women in Victorian society, include *Men and Women* (1844), *The Story of Lily Dawson* (1847), *The Adventures of a Beauty* (1852), and *Linny Lockwood* (1854). She turned later to occult themes and produced a hugely successful volume called *The Night-side of Nature* in 1848 which concerned popular subjects of the time; ghost-seeing, mesmerism, parapsychology, poltergeists and phrenology. Dickens was a huge admirer of her work and described *The Night-side of Nature* as 'one of the most extraordinary collections' of ghost stories ever published. Already having a reputation as a bit of an outlandish sort, Catherine was caught up in a controversy in 1854 after reports surfaced that she had run stark naked down an Edinburgh street. Apparently, she had been informed by spirits that if she went out wearing "only her chastity" but clutching a handkerchief and a calling card, she would be invisible. The "hopelessly insane" woman was reportedly committed to Hanwell Asylum for a brief period. This story was well-known in the literary and paranormal communities of the time, including by Charles Dickens, but the details of the episode are unclear (Crowe herself denied it had ever happened). On balance though, the contemporary accounts suggest something untoward involving Crowe clearly took place and it is almost certain that she suffered some form of breakdown. After the "insanity" incident Crowe's popularity waned somewhat and she ended up selling all her copyrights in 1861. She eventually moved to London then returned to Kent in 1871, the year before her death. For this volume I have chosen the tale entitled *My Friend's Story* which first appeared in Crowe's collection of fifteen ghostly tales *Ghosts and Family Legends: A Volume for Christmas* in 1859.

Mary Elizabeth Braddon (1835-1915) is best remembered for her novel *Lady Audley's Secret* which caused quite a stir on its publication in 1862 and made the author a fortune. It was neatly summarised by critic Elaine Showalter in the following terms; "Braddon's bigamous heroine deserts her child, pushes husband number one down a well, thinks about poisoning husband number two and sets fire to a hotel in which her other male acquaintances are residing". She was the Victorian era's most accomplished 'sensation' novelist, her sales outstripping even Charles Dickens! Braddon was born in London and supported herself and her estranged mother by becoming an actress before striking up a relationship with the publisher John Maxwell. Maxwell's wife is often described as "living in an asylum in Ireland" but it seems she was actually estranged from her husband and living with her family. Nevertheless, Mary lived with Maxwell for over a decade as a surrogate mother to his five children. They married after Maxwell's wife died in 1874, but not before their irregular relationship had caused a minor scandal and all their domestic staff had resigned. Together they had a further six children. Braddon died in 1915 in Richmond and is interred in Richmond Cemetery. She was a prolific writer, having published over 80 novels, most of them in the 'sensation novel' category, including *Aurora Floyd* (1862), *John Marchmont's Legacy* (1861) and *The Doctor's Wife* (1864). Her supernatural fiction includes the short stories *Eveline's Visitant, At Chrighton Abbey, John Grainger, The Shadow in the Corner* and the tale chosen for this volume, *The Cold Embrace*, which first appeared in the weekly periodical *Welcome Guest* in September 1860 and later in Braddon's collection *Ralph the Bailiff and Other Stories* (1862).

Born in London, Amelia Ann Blanford Edwards (1831-1892) became a significant authority on Egypt and a vocal campaigner for the preservation and study of Egyptian relics. In 1882, she co-founded the Egypt Exploration Fund (now the Egypt Exploration Society) and later founded the Edwards Chair of Egyptology at University College London. Her fame for advocating the protection of ancient antiquities came after she had already built a substantial career as an authoress; her first novel, *My Brother's Wife*, having been published in 1855. Her other works included *Barbara's History* (1864), *The Days of My Youth* (1873), and the hugely successful *Lord Brackenbury* (1880). Edwards was accomplished as a writer of ghostly fiction (having been selected on numerous occasions to write for Dickens's famously spooky Christmas periodicals). These tales include *Monsieur Maurice, An Engineer's Story, The Four-Fifteen Express, My Brother's Ghost Story, The Story of Salome* and *Sister Johanna's Story*. Edwards's most famous and often anthologised ghost story is *The North Mail* (*The Phantom Coach*) but here we have presented her lesser-known tale *How the Third Floor Knew the Potteries* which first appeared (uncredited) in the Christmas edition of Charles Dickens's periodical *All the Year Round* in 1863. The tale was also reprinted in Edwards's anthology *Miss Carew* under a different title, *Number Three*, in 1865.

Rosa Mulholland (1841-1921) was an Irish writer who received the welcome patronage of Charles Dickens. Born in Belfast, she married (at age 50) the antiquarian John Thomas Gilbert and later became Lady Gilbert after her husband's knighthood in 1897. Originally she studied art at South Kensington, wishing to become a painter, but after several rejections, soon turned to literature — her first novel, *Dumana*, appearing in 1864 (under the pseudonym Ruth Murray). Her writing was decidedly Irish and often depicted the sorry state of the peasantry in her native country — based on personal experience as she had lived for many years in the remote west of Ireland after the death of her father. After publishing Rosa's short story *No Thoroughfare* in his periodical *All the Year Round*, Dickens asked her to contribute a full-length tale to the magazine. He even chose the title for her; *The Late Miss Hollingford*. Dickens continued to encourage Rosa in all her literary pursuits. Some of her best-known novels were *The Wicked Woods of Toobereevil* (1872), *Hetty Gray* (1883), *The Wild Birds of Killeevy* (1883), *The Mystery of Hall-In-The-Wood* (1893) and *Banshee Castle* (1895). Although not a masterly teller of the ghost story, Rosa produced some notable examples of the genre throughout her career. For this collection I have chosen Rosa's tale *The Haunted Organist of Hurly Burly* which first appeared in *All the Year Round* in November 1866 and which later formed the title story of an 1890 collection of spooky tales. Her other supernatural stories include *Not to be Taken at Bed-Time*, *The Ghost at Wildwood Chase*, *The Ghost at the Rath*, *The Mistery of Ora* and *A Strange Love Story*. Rosa died at the family home, *Villa Nuova*, in Blackrock, County Dublin, in 1921.

Isabella Banks (also sometimes known under her maiden-name, Isabella Varley, and most often as Mrs. G. Linnaeus Banks) was born in Manchester, England, in 1821. She came from a politically-minded family (her father at various times being an alderman and a magistrate), was an early campaigner for women's rights and had a keen fascination for the history of her home city and its surroundings. She married George Banks (a journalist and poet from Birmingham) in 1846 and altł they had eight children together only three surviveʉ ʟʊ adulthood. Afflicted by an alcoholic husband, who twice sold all the family possessions to pay for his habit, she turned to writing at a late age. Although she began publishing at a young age (she was sixteen when the *Manchester Guardian* published her poem entitled *A Dying Girl To Her Mother*), it was the death of her eldest child in the early 1860s which apparently inspired her to write her first novel. *God's Providence House* (1865) was a tale of intrigue and romance set in and around the city of Chester at the time of the plague. She is best remembered, however, for her novel *The Manchester Man* (1870), the tale of Jabez Clegg, a lowly apprentice who makes good in the industrial revolution sweeping the north of England in the early 19th century. Between 1865 and 1894 she published twelve novels, three volumes of poetry, and three volumes of stories, and was rarely out of the critic's columns during those years. She died in London in 1897. Isabella Banks was by no means prolific in supernatural literature but the tale included here, *Wraith-Haunted*, first appeared in the Christmas 1869 edition of the *Belgravia Annual* and was later included in the collection *Through the Night: Tales of Shades and Shadows* (1882).

American author Harriet Beecher Stowe (1811-1896) was famous for her anti-slavery novel *Uncle Tom's Cabin*, first published in 1852 and still in print today. It was (and still is) a bastion of the abolitionist agenda and broke all publishing records of the time. She wrote over thirty books, some novels, but others including advice on housekeeping, travel memoirs, religious studies and biographies. Harriet was born in 1811 in Lichfield, Connecticut, the sixth of eleven children, all of whom became ministers or were active in education or women's rights. Harriet started writing at an early age; her first publication being a textbook on geography for children. In 1832 the family moved to Cincinnati and there she met Calvin Stowe, a widower who was a professor at the local seminary, and they married in January 1836. The couple later moved to Brunswick, Maine, where Calvin was appointed a lecturer at Bowdoin College. Harriet and Calvin had seven children together. It was the death of one of these, Samuel Charles Stowe, of cholera, at only eighteen months of age, which inspired Harriet to begin the novel which made her famous. She later explained: "Having experienced losing someone so close to me, I can sympathize with all the poor, powerless slaves at the unjust auctions". With the financial security that *Uncle Tom's Cabin* brought her, Harriet embarked on a literary career that lasted over 50 years. Other notable works include *The Minister's Wooing* (1859), *The American Woman's Home* (1869, co-authored with her sister Catharine), *Lady Byron Vindicated* (1871) and *Pogunuc People* (1878). Harriet produced some excellent ghostly fiction in short-story form, including *The Ghost in the Mill* and *Tom Toothacre's Ghost Story*, most appearing in the collection *Sam Lawson's Oldtown Fireside Stories* (1870). The tale reproduced here, *The Ghost in the Cap'n Brown House*, is also in that collection but first appeared in *The Atlantic Monthly* for December 1870.

Rhoda Broughton was born in Denbigh, north Wales, in 1840, a granddaughter of the eighth baronet of Broughton, and a niece to the famous Irish publisher and novelist Joseph Sheridan Le Fanu; whose work in Victorian supernatural fiction is in many ways unparalleled. Rhoda took her first efforts at writing to her uncle in Dublin and he published them in serial form in his *Dublin Magazine*. Her novels garnered a reputation for containing 'fast' female characters of questionable morals, and the occasional homoerotic undertone, a reputation which remained with her throughout her life and may have led to a decline in her popularity in later years. It is even reported that Lewis Carroll declined an invitation to a gathering because he knew she would be present, but whether this was because of her reputation is not recorded. The eminent writer Margaret Oliphant (whose story *The Secret Chamber* appears in this volume) was reportedly scandalised by Miss Broughton's 'uncleanly suggestions' and she was even said to have intimidated the sensibilities of Oscar Wilde. Later, the residents of Headington Hill, near Oxford, where Broughton moved in old age, were concerned by her presence, but only because they had confused her with the scandalous Mary E. Braddon (see above). Broughton's most successful novels include *Cometh Up as a Flower* (1867), *Nancy* (1873), *Belinda* (1883), *Alas!* (1890), *A Beginner* (1893) and *A Waif's Progress* (1905). Perhaps inspired by the reputation of her uncle, Rhoda dipped occasionally into supernatural fiction. Her collection, *Tales for Christmas Eve* (1873) contained five ghost stories that have been described as 'skilfully wrought'. For this volume I have chosen the strange tale *The Man with the Nose* from that volume, but which was first published in *Temple Bar* in October 1872. Rhoda Broughton never married and lived much of her life with her sister. She died at her home near Oxford in 1920.

Ellen Wood (née Price) was born in Worcester in 1814 and until the age of seven was brought up by her paternal grandparents. In 1836 she married Henry Wood (and was hence better-known by her writing name of Mrs. Henry Wood). Henry was the proprietor of a banking and shipping firm in France and it was whilst living in Dauphiné that Ellen began to publish sporadically in the *New Monthly Magazine* and *Bentley's Miscellany* (although she had written from a young age). After her husband's business failed around 1856 the family returned to live in Upper Norwood near London. Short of money, Ellen stepped up her writing career by winning a competition for a 'temperance novel' called *Danesbury House* (1860), which she had written in only a few weeks. Her next novel, *East Lynne* (1861), became hugely successful after a favourable review in *The Times*. Her career took off and she published a further twelve novels in the next four years, chief amongst them being *A Life's Secret* (1862), *Oswald Cray (1864)*, *Mrs. Halliburton's Troubles* (1862), *The Channings* (1862), *Lord Oakburn's Daughters* (1864) and *The Shadow of Ashlydyat* (1863). Ellen's husband died in 1866. That same year, after suffering a severe backlash by publishing a scandalous tale of bigamy, the owner of *The Argosy* magazine, Alexander Strahan, sold the publication to Ellen Wood. She remained its editor (and chief contributor) until her death, serialising most of her novels within its pages. Her later works include *Anne Hereford* (1868), *Within the Maze* (1872), *Adam Grainger* (1876) and *The House of Halliwell* (published posthumously in 1890). Wood's supernatural fiction is known to extend to three novellas, nine short stories and several stand-alone chapters in novels. Some of her best short ghostly fiction includes *The Parson's Oath, A Mysterious Visitor, Reality or Delusion?* and *A Curious Experience*. For this volume I have chosen *Seen in the Moonlight*, first published in *The Argosy* magazine in December 1875 and later collected in Wood's *Johnny Ludlow Stories: Second Series* in 1880. Ellen Wood died in February 1887 after a long bronchial infection and is buried alongside her husband in Highgate Cemetery, London.

Margaret Oliphant was a prolific Scottish writer whose life was beset with grief and sorrow. Born near Mussleburgh, East Lothian, in April 1828, her childhood was spent near Dalkeith, then in Glasgow and Liverpool. Margaret began writing in 1844 and her first novel, *Passages in the Life of Margaret Maitland*, appeared in 1849. She would go on to publish over 130 works (including 100 novels) and reputedly became one of Queen Victoria's favourite authors. Her most successful novels include *Merkland* (1850), *Caleb Field* (1851), *The Chronicles of Carlingford* (in six separate novels), *Squire Arden* (1871), *A Beleaguered City* (1879), *Hester* (1883) and *Kirsteen* (1890). In 1851 she met William Blackwood, publisher of the popular *Blackwood's Edinburgh Magazine* and she became a life-long contributor to its varied pages. Margaret married her cousin, Frank Wilson Oliphant, an artist, in 1852 and settled in London. Frank's health was poor, mainly from tuberculosis, causing the family to relocate to sunnier climes, first in Florence and then to Rome. Frank died in Rome in 1859 leaving Margaret with three surviving children; Maggie, Cyril and Francis. Having lost three children in infancy and her husband at a very young age, Margaret returned distraught and destitute to England — only to then endure the later deaths of her children Maggie (in 1864), Cyril (in 1890) and Francis (in 1894). She also ended up supporting her alcoholic brother, Willie, whose business in Canada had been declared bankrupt, and her brother Frank and his three children. Notwithstanding this emotional turmoil, Margaret pursued a very successful literary career and managed to send her two surviving sons to Eton. She died from cancer of the colon during the Jubilee celebrations for Queen Victoria in June 1897 and was buried in Eton cemetery alongside her two sons. In later life, perhaps becoming interested in the 'life hereafter' due to her outliving all her children and husband, she turned to writing supernatural tales. These writings (actually spanning the years 1857 to 1897) appeared in, among other publications, *Blackwood's*

Edinburgh Magazine, New Quarterly Magazine, Fraser's Magazine, MacMillan's Magazine and *Longman's Magazine.* Her ghost stories were highly regarded by M. R. James who wrote that "the religious ghost story, as it may be called, was never done better than by Mrs. Oliphant in *The Open Door* and *A Beleaguered City*". In the current volume I have included *The Secret Chamber*, one of Margaret's very first eerie tales, which appeared in *Blackwood's Edinburgh Magazine* in December 1876.

Charlotte Riddell (née Cowan) was born into a well-to-do family in Carrickfergus, Ireland, in 1832. As a child she had a voracious appetite for learning and literature and later recalled writing her first full-length novel by moonlight at age fifteen. The family moved to London in 1855 after the death of her father — a move she later confessed had broken her heart. Her first year in London was spent traipsing the cold streets looking for a publisher for her first novel (now exceedingly scarce), called *Zuriel's Grandchild* (1856). She found one and then, a year later, published her first successful novel, *The Moors and the Fens* (1857). But, her joy was severely tempered by the death of her mother before the book had even appeared in print. Left utterly alone, but on the verge of fame, it wasn't long before she married — to Joseph Hadley Riddell, a civil engineer. In her subsequent long writing career, at first using the *nom-de-plume* F. G. Trafford, she produced 56 books. She is perhaps best remembered for her 'city novels' such as *City and Suburb* (1861), *The Senior Partner* (1881) and others, novels which minutely depicted life in the City of London. Her most successful novel, and the one for which she received the most favourable terms, was *George Geith of Fen Court* (1864), which was later dramatised for the stage. In 1867 Charlotte acquired part ownership of the renowned literary publication *St. James's Magazine* and served as one of its editors for many years. Her final days were spent in 'genteel poverty, loneliness, depression, and terrible pain' in her house in Harlington, Middlesex (nowadays right next to London's Heathrow Airport). She died in 1906 and is buried in nearby Heston Church cemetery. Charlotte enjoyed weaving a supernatural tale and indeed five of her full-length novels are ghostly in nature; *Fairy Water* (1872), *The Uninhabited House* (1875), *The Haunted River* (1877), *The Disappearance of Mr. Jeremiah*

Redworth (1878) and *The Nun's Curse* (1888). But her greatest ghostly contributions are to be found in her collection called *Weird Stories* (1882). The volume contains six tales; *Walnut-Tree House, The Open Door, Nut Bush Farm, The Old House in Vauxhall Walk, Sandy the Tinker* and *Old Mrs. Jones*. For this volume I have included the excellent tale entitled *The Open Door*.

The identity of our next author, Mary E. Penn, is a complete enigma. Scholars of the macabre have been unable to discern any details of her person, origin or character (assuming she was indeed female). We only know that from the 1870s to the 1890s this author published several stories in late-Victorian periodicals, most commonly in *The Argosy* (Ellen Wood's monthly publication). Many of her contributions were unattributed and her name only appears from 1878 onwards. Her final ghost story appeared in 1893, although she continued to write crime thrillers until 1897. When *The Argosy* finally went under in 1901 Mary E. Penn disappeared from the literary world completely, as mysteriously as she had first appeared. Penn's ghost stories were collected together in 1999 for the first time by the eminent ghost-story scholar Richard Dalby (volume 2 of the *Mistresses of the Macabre* series produced by Sarob Press). The volume contained eight short stories; *Snatched from the Brink* (1878), *Desmond's Model* (1879), *How Georgette Kept Tryst* (1879), *Old Vanderhaven's Will* (1880), *The Tenant of the Cedars* (1883), *The Strange Story of Our Villa* (1893), *At Ravenholme Junction* (published anonymously but ascribed to Penn by Dalby on stylistic grounds), and *In the Dark* (first appearing in *The Argosy* in June 1885). It is this last tale, a spooky story of bumps and screams in the night that appears in this volume.

Mary Louisa Molesworth (née Stewart), daughter of a Scottish merchant, was born in Rotterdam in 1839 but spent most of her childhood in the northern English city of Manchester. She became a prolific writer of children's novels although her first publications (under the pen name Ennis Graham) were romances. It was her writings for older children that brought her success; aimed at, mainly girls, too old for fairy-tales but not mature enough for the Brontë-esque fashions of the day. Although overly moralistic for today's taste, Molesworth's works are interesting in that they began a trend of phonetically spelling children's speech in order to convey character. Her most popular books were *Tell Me a Story* (1875), *Carrots* (1876), *The Cuckoo Clock* (1877), *The Tapestry Room* (1879), and *A Christmas Child* (1880). In later life Molesworth took an interest in supernatural writing and produced two volumes of very fine ghostly tales; *Four Ghost Stories* (1888) and *Uncanny Stories* (1896). These stories are *Lady Farquhar's Old Lady*, *Witnessed by Two*, *Unexplained*, *The Story of the Rippling Train*, *The Shadow in the Moonlight*, *The Man With the Cough*, *Half-way Between the Stiles*, *At the Dip of the Road*, "—— *Will Not Take Place*" and *The Clock that Struck Thirteen*. In addition, a ghost story called *Old Gervais* appeared in her collection *Studies and Stories* (1893). Mary Molesworth died in 1921 and is buried in Brompton Cemetery, London. Here we have reproduced *The Story of the Rippling Train* which first appeared in *Longman's Magazine* in October 1887.

Vernon Lee was the pseudonym of British writer Violet Paget (1856-1935). Born in France, and living mostly in continental Europe, she was a renowned writer of supernatural fiction as well as an accomplished scholar of aesthetics, art, the Italian renaissance, music and travel. She was fluent in French, Italian and German and published in these languages as well as English. She formed passionate relationships with three women during her life, one of whom, Kit Anstruther-Thomson, collaborated with her on a theory of psychological aesthetics and art appreciation. Lee's writing is often cerebral, liberally interspersed with her knowledge of the arts and history and often conveys places and events in a descriptive, atmospheric prose. This style is, of course, ideally suited to supernatural fiction and her stories are regarded by aficionados as some of the best examples of the genre. Her first publication in this vein was *A Culture-Ghost; or, Winthrop's Adventure*, which appeared in *Fraser's Magazine* in January 1881 (although it had been written in 1874). She later reworked this story under a new title, *A Wicked Voice*, which appeared in her first collection called *Hauntings* (1890), and which is included in the present collection. Lee died near Florence on the 13th February 1935 and is interred in the Agli Allori Cemetery.

Like Mary E. Penn, the author Lettice Galbraith is somewhat of an enigma. Despite extensive research by some of the most eminent aficionados of the genre, no historical or biographical details of this mysterious writer have ever been found. However, I have recently found references in the Society of Authors collections which indicate that Lettice Galbraith was an alias for Miss L. Gibson. This name is given in correspondence (1889-1893) between the author and the Society concerning her "case against" W. G. B. Page of Hull, who appears to have been the sub-librarian of the Hull Subscription Library. What this "case" was and the identity of Miss L. Gibson may one day be discovered on closer inspection of the archives. Perhaps Miss Galbraith is actually Lettice Susan Gibson (b. 1859) author of four novels; *The Freemasons* (1905), *Burnt Spices* (1906), *Ships of Desire* (1908) and *The Oakum Pickers* (1912), the second of which is an occult novel. Whatever her provenance Lettice Galbraith first appears in print in 1892 with a story titled *The Spin of the Coin* in *Beeton's Christmas Annual*. Then, the following year, two small collections appeared, *Pretty Miss Allington and Other Stories*, and *New Ghost Stories*, which was to become one of the most popular (and most reprinted) ghostly collections of the final decade of the 19th century. It included the stories *The Case of Lady Lukestan*, *The Trainer's Ghost*, *The Ghost in the Chair*, *In the Séance Room*, *The Missing Model* and *The Ghost's Revenge*. These tales, together with *The Blue Room* (which first appeared in *Macmillan's Magazine* in October 1897) were collected as *The Blue Room and Other Stories* by Sarob Press in 1999. All in all, the enigmatic Lettice Galbraith produced eight ghostly tales, and all of them are excellent, if typical, Victorian fantasies. This volume reproduces the story *The Trainer's Ghost*.

Louisa Baldwin (1845-1925) was one of eleven children of Wesleyan minister George Brown McDonald (1805-1868). Three of her sisters married successful men; Alice (1837-1910) married John Lockwood Kipling and was the mother of Rudyard Kipling, Georgiana (1840-1920) married the pre-Raphaelite painter Edward Burne-Jones and Agnes married future president of the Royal Academy Edward Poynter. Louisa herself married the industrialist Alfred Baldwin and was the mother of prime minister Stanley Baldwin (the only British prime minister to serve under three monarchs; George V, Edward VIII and George VI). An apocryphal story tells that as a child Louisa attempted to contact her deceased sisters at a séance and that this led to a lifelong obsession with the occult. It is also told that she turned to writing during an unexplained illness six weeks after marrying; and in fact she seems to have suffered from various mysterious ailments throughout her life. Louisa was not a prolific writer by any stretch of the imagination. She produced novels, including *A Martyr to Mammon* (1886), *The Story of a Marriage* (1889), *Richard Dare* (1894), *The Pedlar's Pack* (1910) and *Afterglow* (1911), as well as children's books and poetry, but none of her works were well-received or successful. Her debut supernatural tale, *The Weird of the Walfords*, first appeared in *Longman's Magazine* in November 1889 and a tale called *The Shadow on the Blind* (which first appeared in *The Cornhill Magazine* in September 1894) became the title story for a collection published in 1895. Other stories in that collection were *The Uncanny Bairn*, *Many Waters Cannot Quench Love*, *How He Left the Hotel*, *The Real and the Counterfeit*, *My Next Door Neighbour*, *The Empty Picture Frame*, *Sir Nigel Otterburne's Case* and *The Ticking of the Clock*. Here we have included the tale *How He Left the Hotel* which first appeared in *The Argosy* in October 1894.

Katharine Tynan (1859-1931) was an acclaimed Irish writer and staunch nationalist from Clondalkin, near Dublin. She married the English writer and barrister Henry Albert Hinkson in 1898 and spent most of her life in England, dying in Wimbledon, near London in April 1931. She was the occasional friend of the poets William Butler Yeats (who may even have proposed to her) and Gerard Manley Hopkins and the Irish nationalist politician Charles Parnell. In her autobiography she claimed never to have had a yearning for the literary life until aged seventeen she had a few verses published in a Dublin newspaper. Within a few years she had achieved some success for her poetry and had become a recognised figure within the Dublin literary circle. She would go on to become an extremely prolific writer, publishing over 100 novels, twelve collections of short stories and more than a dozen collections of poetry. She is best remembered for her poetry and as an early exponent of the Irish Literary Revival, as well as her views on nationalism, feminism, the suffrage movement, Catholicism and the effect of World War I. Tynan wrote the occasional macabre tale, the best of which is probably that presented here, *The Picture on the Wall*, which first appeared in *The English Illustrated Magazine* in December 1895.

Our next author was from an eminent American family. (Sarah) Madeleine Vinton Dahlgren (1825-1889) was the only daughter of US Congressman Samuel F. Vinton and was born in Gallipolis, Ohio. After being widowed with two children, in 1865 Madeleine married Admiral John Adolphus Bernard Dahlgren (1809-1870), himself a widower, and had three further children. Admiral Dahlgren was a US Navy officer who developed advances in naval weapons and founded the Navy's Ordnance Department. Madeleine's writing career began around 1859, in order to support herself after her first husband's death, with various press articles, often under the pseudonyms "Corinne" or "Cornelia". Extremely erudite, she would later write not only novels but also poetry and non-fiction books on female suffrage (in fact, she was an anti-suffragist), social etiquette (concerning which she was considered an expert) and biography, as well as translations of French, Spanish and Italian texts. Her novels include *South Sea Sketches* (1881), *South-Mountain Magic* (1882), *The Lost Name* (1886), *Divorced* (1887) and *Lights and Shadows of a Life* (1887). She is perhaps best remembered for the novel *A Washington Winter* (1883) a tongue-in-cheek depiction of polite Washington society. Madeleine Dahlgren founded the *Washington Literary Society* in 1873, for which she was vice-president and often acted as host for the Society's meetings at her home at Thomas Circle, Washington. She was also a president of the *Ladies Catholic Missionary Society*. Mrs. Dahlgren died on 28th May 1898 and was buried on South Mountain, Maryland. A collection of Madeleine's short fiction, called *The Woodley Lane Ghost and Other Stories* was first published posthumously in 1899. It contained twenty-four stories, but only nine of these had a supernatural theme. For the present volume I have included the title story, *The Woodley Lane Ghost*. Others spooky tales in the collection were *Who Was She?*, *The Amulet Ring*, *A Reminiscence*, *Earth-Bound*, *The Fatal Boots*, *My First Patient*, *A Murder Mystery* and *The Judge's Dream*.

Not much is known about our final author in this collection. Lilian Giffen (1872-1946) was born in New Orleans in 1872, lived much of her life in the Baltimore area, and later Massachusetts, and was known as an artist, writer and lecturer. Although not achieving much success at these pursuits, she regularly exhibited her artworks in the Baltimore area. The story included here is the title tale from her only known volume of fiction, *The Ghost of the Belle-Alliance Plantation, and Other Stories*, a small volume printed privately in 1901. Lilian Giffen died in 1946.

Having concluded our biographical sketches of these eminent purveyors of the occult, I encourage you now to wait until the dark of the stormy night, lock the doors, shutter the windows, light the fire, sit with your back to the wall and bury yourself in the Victorian macabre. Try not to let the creaking floorboards, the distant howl of a dog, the chill breeze that caresses the candle, the shadows in the far recesses of your room, disturb your concentration. Enjoy!

The Old Nurse's Story

Elizabeth Gaskell

You know, my dears, that your mother was an orphan, and an only child; and I dare say you have heard that your grand-father was a clergyman up in Westmoreland, where I come from. I was just a girl in the village school, when, one day, your grandmother came in to ask the mistress if there was any scholar there who would do for a nurse-maid; and mighty proud I was, I can tell ye, when the mistress called me up, and spoke to my being a good girl at my needle, and a steady, honest girl, and one whose parents were very respectable, though they might be poor I thought I should like nothing better than to serve the pretty, young lady, who was blushing as deep as I was, as she spoke of the coming baby, and what I should have to do with it. However, I see you don't care so much for this part of my story, as for what you think is to come, so I'll tell you at once. I was engaged and settled at the parsonage before Miss Rosamond (that was the baby, who is now your mother) was born. To be sure, I had little enough to do with her when she came, for she was never out of her mother's arms, and slept by her all night long; and proud enough was I sometimes when missis trusted her to me. There never was such a baby before or since, though you've all of you been fine enough in your turns; but for sweet, winning ways, you've none of you come up to your mother. She took after her mother, who was a real lady born; a Miss Furnivall, a granddaughter of Lord Furnivall's, in Northumberland. I believe she had neither brother nor sister, and had been brought up in my lord's family till she had married your grandfather, who was just a curate, son to a shopkeeper in Carlisle — but a clever, fine gentleman as ever was — and one who was a right-down hard worker in his parish, which was very wide, and scattered all abroad over the Westmoreland Fells. When your mother, little Miss Rosamond, was about four or five years old, both her parents died in a fortnight — one after the other. Ah! that was a sad time. My pretty young mistress and me was looking for another baby, when my master came home from one of his long rides, wet, and tired, and took the fever he died of; and then she never held up her head again, but lived just to see her dead baby, and have it laid on her breast before she sighed away her life. My mistress had asked me, on her death-bed, never to leave Miss Rosamond; but if she had never spoken a word, I would have gone with the little child to the end of the world.

The next thing, and before we had well stilled our sobs, the executors and guardians came to settle the affairs. They were my poor young mistress's own cousin, Lord Furnivall, and Mr. Esthwaite, my master's brother, a shopkeeper in Manchester; not so well to do then, as he was afterwards, and with a large family rising about him. Well! I don't know if it were their settling, or because of a letter my mistress wrote on her death-bed to her cousin, my lord; but somehow it was settled that Miss Rosamond and me were to go to Furnivall Manor House, in Northumberland, and my lord spoke as if it had been her mother's wish that she should live with his family, and as if he had no objections, for that one or two more or less could make no difference in so grand a household. So, though that was not the way in which I should have wished the coming of my bright and pretty pet to have been looked at — who was like a sunbeam in any family, be it never so grand — I was well pleased that all the folks in the Dale should stare and admire, when they heard I was going to be young lady's maid at my Lord Furnivall's at Furnivall Manor.

But I made a mistake in thinking we were to go and live where my lord did. It turned out that the family had left Furnivall Manor House fifty years or more. I could not hear that my poor young mistress had ever been there, though she had been brought up in the family; and I was sorry for that, for I should have liked Miss Rosamond's youth to have passed where her mother's had been.

My lord's gentleman, from whom I asked as many questions as I durst, said that the Manor House was at the foot of the Cumberland Fells, and a very grand place; that an old Miss Furnivall, a great-aunt of my lord's, lived there, with only a few servants; but that it was a very healthy place, and my lord had thought that it would suit Miss Rosamond very well for a few years, and that her being there might perhaps amuse his old aunt.

I was bidden by my lord to have Miss Rosamond's things ready by a certain day. He was a stern proud man, as they say all the Lords Furnivall were; and he never spoke a word more than was necessary. Folk did say he had loved my young mistress; but that, because she knew that his father would object, she would never listen to him, and married Esthwaite; but I don't know. He never married at any rate. But he never took much notice of Miss Rosamond; which I thought he might have done if he had cared for her dead mother. He sent his gentleman with us to the Manor House, telling him to join him at Newcastle that same evening; so there was no great length of time for him to make us known to all the strangers before he, too, shook us off; and we were left, two lonely young things (I was not eighteen), in the great old Manor House. It seems like yesterday that we drove there. We had left our own dear parsonage very early, and we had both cried as if our hearts would break, though we were travelling in my lord's carriage, which I thought so much of once. And now it was long past noon on a September day, and we stopped to change horses for the last time at a little, smoky town, all full of colliers and miners. Miss Rosamond had fallen asleep, but Mr. Henry told me to waken her, that she might see the park and the Manor House as we drove up. I thought it rather a pity; but I did what he bade me, for fear he should complain of me to my lord. We had left all signs of a town, or even a village, and were then inside the gates of a large, wild park — not like the parks here in the south, but with rocks, and the noise of running water, and gnarled thorn-trees, and old oaks, all white and peeled with age.

The road went up about two miles, and then we saw a great and stately house, with many trees close around it, so close that in some places their branches dragged against the walls when the wind blew; and some hung broken down; for no one seemed to take much charge of the place; — to lop the wood, or to keep the moss-covered carriage-way in order. Only in front of the house all was clear. The great oval drive was without a weed; and neither tree nor creeper was allowed to grow over the long, many-windowed front; at both sides of which a wing projected, which were each the ends of other side fronts; for the house, although it was so desolate, was even grander than I expected. Behind it rose the Fells, which seemed unenclosed and bare enough; and on the left hand of the house, as you stood facing it, was a little, old-fashioned flower-garden, as I found out afterwards. A door opened out upon it from the west front; it had been scooped out of the thick dark wood for some old Lady Furnivall; but the branches of the great forest trees had grown and overshadowed it again, and there were very few flowers that would live there at that time.

When we drove up to the great front entrance, and went into the hall I thought we should be lost — it was so large, and vast, and grand. There was a chandelier all of bronze, hung down from the middle of the ceiling; and I had never seen one before, and looked at it all in amaze. Then, at one end of the hall, was a great fireplace, as large as the sides of the houses in my country, with massy andirons and dogs to hold the wood; and by it were heavy, old-fashioned sofas. At the opposite end of the hall, to the left as you went in — on the western side — was an organ built into the wall, and so large that it filled up the best part of that end. Beyond it, on the same side, was a door; and opposite, on each side of the fire-place, were also doors leading to the east front; but those I never went through as long as I stayed in the house, so I can't tell you what lay beyond.

The afternoon was closing in and the hall, which had no fire lighted in it, looked dark and gloomy, but we did not stay there a moment. The old servant, who had opened the door for us bowed to Mr. Henry, and took us in through the door at the further side of the great organ, and led us through several smaller halls and passages into the west drawing-room, where he said that Miss Furnivall was sitting. Poor little Miss Rosamond held very tight to me, as if she were scared and lost in that great place, and as for myself, I was not much better. The west drawing-room was very cheerful-looking, with a warm fire in it, and plenty of good, comfortable furniture about. Miss Furnivall was an old lady not far from eighty, I should think, but I do not know. She was thin and tall, and had a face as full of fine wrinkles as if they had been drawn all over it with a needle's point. Her eyes were very watchful to make up, I suppose, for her being so deaf as to be obliged to use a trumpet. Sitting with her, working at the same great piece of tapestry, was Mrs. Stark, her maid and companion, and almost as old as she was. She had lived with Miss Furnivall ever since they both were young, and now she seemed more like a friend than a servant; she looked so cold, and grey, and stony, as if she had never loved or cared for anyone; and I don't suppose she did care for anyone, except her mistress; and, owing to the great deafness of the latter, Mrs. Stark treated her very much as if she were a child. Mr. Henry gave some message from my lord, and then he bowed good-bye to us all, — taking no notice of my sweet little Miss Rosamond's outstretched hand — and left us standing there, being looked at by the two old ladies through their spectacles.

I was right glad when they rung for the old footman who had shown us in at first, and told him to take us to our rooms. So we went out of that great drawing-room, and into another sitting-room, and out of that, and then up a great flight of stairs, and along a broad gallery — which was something like a library, having books all down one side, and windows and writing-tables all down the other — till we came to our rooms, which I was not sorry to hear were just over the kitchens; for I began to think I should be lost in that wilderness of a house. There was an old nursery, that had been used for all the little lords and ladies long ago, with a pleasant fire burning in the grate, and the kettle boiling on the hob, and tea things spread out on the table; and out of that room was the night-nursery, with a little crib for Miss Rosamond close to my bed. And old James called up Dorothy, his wife, to bid us welcome; and both he and she were so hospitable and kind, that by and by Miss Rosamond and me felt quite at home; and by the time tea was over, she was sitting on Dorothy's knee, and chattering away as fast as her little tongue could go. I soon found out that Dorothy was from Westmoreland, and that bound her and me together, as it were; and I would never wish to meet with kinder people than were old James and his wife. James had lived pretty nearly all his life in my lord's family, and thought there was no one so grand as they. He even looked down a little on his wife; because, till he had married her, she had never lived in any but a farmer's household. But he was very fond of her, as well he might be. They had one servant under them, to do all the rough work. Agnes they called her; and she and me, and James and Dorothy, with Miss Furnivall and Mrs. Stark, made up the family; always remembering my sweet little Miss Rosamond! I used to wonder what they had done before she came, they thought so much of her now. Kitchen and drawing-room, it was all the same. The hard, sad Miss Furnivall, and the cold Mrs. Stark, looked pleased when she came fluttering in like a bird, playing and pranking hither and thither, with a continual murmur, and pretty prattle of gladness. I am sure, they were sorry many a time when she flitted away into the kitchen, though they were too proud to ask her to stay with them, and were a little surprised at her taste; though to be sure, as Mrs. Stark said, it was not to be wondered at, remembering what stock her father had come of. The great, old rambling house was a famous place for little Miss Rosamond. She made expeditions all over it, with me at her heels; all, except the east wing, which was never opened, and whither we never thought of going. But in the western and northern part was many a pleasant room; full of things that were curiosities to us, though they might not have been to people who had seen more. The windows were darkened by the sweeping boughs of the trees, and the ivy which had overgrown them: but, in the green gloom, we could manage to see old China jars and carved ivory boxes, and great, heavy books, and, above all, the old pictures!

Once, I remember, my darling would have Dorothy go with us to tell us who they all were; for they were all portraits of some of my lord's family, though Dorothy could not tell us the names of every one. We had gone through most of the rooms, when we came to the old state drawing-room over the hall, and there was a picture of Miss Furnivall; or, as she was called in those days, Miss Grace, for she was the younger sister. Such a beauty she must have been! but with such a set, proud look, and such scorn looking out of her handsome eyes, with her eyebrows just a little raised, as if she wondered how anyone could have the impertinence to look at her; and her lip curled at us, as we stood there gazing. She had a dress on, the like of which I had never seen before, but it was all the fashion when she was young: a hat of some soft, white stuff like beaver, pulled a little over her brows, and a beautiful plume of feathers sweeping round it on one side; and her gown of blue satin was open in front to a quilted, white stomacher.

"Well, to be sure!" said I, when I had gazed my fill. "Flesh is grass, they do say; but who would have thought that Miss Furnivall had been such an out-and-out beauty, to see her now?"

"Yes," said Dorothy. "Folks change sadly. But if what my master's father used to say was true, Miss Furnivall, the elder sister, was handsomer than Miss Grace. Her picture is here somewhere; but, if I show it you, you must never let on, even to James, that you have seen it. Can the little lady hold her tongue, think you?" asked she.

I was not so sure, for she was such a little, sweet, bold, open-spoken child, so I set her to hide herself; and then I helped Dorothy to turn a great picture, that leaned with its face towards the wall, and was not hung up as the others were. To be sure, it beat Miss Grace for beauty; and, I think, for scornful pride, too, though in that matter it might be hard to choose. I could have looked at it an hour, but Dorothy seemed half frightened at having shown it to me, and hurried it back again, and bade me run and find Miss Rosamond, for that there were some ugly places about the house, where she should like ill for the child to go. I was a brave, high-spirited girl, and thought little of what the old woman said, for I liked hide-and-seek as well as any child in the parish; so off I ran to find my little one.

As winter drew on, and the days grew shorter, I was sometimes almost certain that I heard a noise as if someone was playing on the great organ in the hall. I did not hear it every evening; but, certainly, I did very often; usually when I was sitting with Miss Rosamond, after I had put her to bed, and keeping quite still and silent in the bed-room. Then I used to hear it booming and swelling away in the distance. The first night, when I went down to my supper, I asked Dorothy who had been playing music, and James said very shortly that I was a gowk to take the wind soughing among the trees for music: but I saw Dorothy look at him very fearfully, and Agnes, the kitchen-maid, said something beneath her breath, and went quite white. I saw they did not like my question, so I held my peace till I was with Dorothy alone, when I knew I could get a good deal out of her. So, the next day, I watched my time, and I coaxed and asked her who it was that played the organ; for I knew that it was the organ and not the wind well enough, for all I had kept silence before James. But Dorothy had had her lesson I'll warrant, and never a word could I get from her. So then I tried Agnes, though I had always held my head rather above her, as I was even to James and Dorothy, and she was little better than their servant. So she said I must never, never tell; and if I ever told, I was never to say *she* had told me; but it was a very strange noise, and she had heard it many a time, but most of all on winter nights, and before storms; and folks did say, it was the old lord playing on the great organ in the hall, just as he used to do when he was alive; but who the old lord was, or why he played, and why he played on stormy winter evenings in particular, she either could not or would not tell me. Well! I told you I had a brave heart; and I thought it was rather pleasant to have that grand music rolling about the house, let who would be the player; for now it rose above the great gusts of wind, and wailed and triumphed just like a living creature, and then it fell to a softness most complete; only it was always music, and tunes, so it was nonsense to call it the wind I thought at first, that it might be Miss Furnivall who played, unknown to Agnes; but, one day when I was in the hall by myself, I opened the organ and peeped all about it and around it, as I had done to the organ in Crosthwaite Church once before, and I saw it was all broken and destroyed inside, though it looked so brave and fine; and then, though it was noon-day, my flesh began to creep a little, and I shut it up, and run away pretty quickly to my own bright nursery; and I did not like hearing the music for some time after that, any more than James and Dorothy did. All this time Miss Rosamond was making herself more and more beloved. The old ladies liked her to dine with them at their early dinner; James stood behind Miss Furnivall's chair, and I behind Miss Rosamond's all in state; and, after dinner, she would play about in a corner of the great drawing-room, as still as any mouse, while Miss Furnivall slept, and I had my dinner in the kitchen. But she was glad enough to come to me in the nursery afterwards; for, as she said, Miss Furnivall was so sad, and Mrs. Stark so dull; but she and I were merry enough; and, by-and-by, I got not to care for that weird rolling music, which did one no harm, if we did not know where it came from.

That winter was very cold. In the middle of October the frosts began, and lasted many, many weeks. I remember, one day at dinner, Miss Furnivall lifted up her sad, heavy eyes, and said to Mrs. Stark, "I am afraid we shall have a terrible winter," in a strange kind of meaning way. But Mrs. Stark pretended not to hear, and talked very loud of something else. My little lady and I did not care for the frost; not we! As long as it was dry we climbed up the steep brows, behind the house, and went up on the Fells, which were bleak, and bare enough, and there we ran races in the fresh, sharp air; and once we came down by a new path that took us past the two old, gnarled holly-trees, which grew about half-way down by the east side of the house. But the days grew shorter, and shorter; and the old lord, if it was he, played away more, and more stormily and sadly on the great organ. One Sunday afternoon, — it must have been towards the end of November — I asked Dorothy to take charge of little Missey when she came out of the drawing-room, after Miss Furnivall had had her nap; for it was too cold to take her with me to church, and yet I wanted to go. And Dorothy was glad enough to promise, and was so fond of the child that all seemed well; and Agnes and I set off very briskly, though the sky hung heavy and black over the white earth, as if the night had never fully gone away; and the air, though still, was very biting and keen.

"We shall have a fall of snow," said Agnes to me. And sure enough, even while we were in church, it came down thick, in great, large flakes, so thick it almost darkened the windows. It had stopped snowing before we came out, but it lay soft, thick and deep beneath our feet, as we tramped home. Before we got to the hall the moon rose, and I think it was lighter then, — what with the moon, and what with the white dazzling snow — than it had been when we went to church, between two and three o'clock. I have not told you that Miss Furnivall and Mrs. Stark never went to church: they used to read the prayers together, in their quiet, gloomy way; they seemed to feel the Sunday very long without their tapestry-work to be busy at. So when I went to Dorothy in the kitchen, to fetch Miss Rosamond and take her up-stairs with me, I did not much wonder when the old woman told me that the ladies had kept the child with them, and that she had never come to the kitchen, as I had bidden her, when she was tired of behaving pretty in the drawing-room. So I took off my things and went to find her, and bring her to her supper in the nursery. But when I went into the best drawing-room, there sat the two old ladies, very still and quiet, dropping out a word now and then, but looking as if nothing so bright and merry as Miss Rosamond had ever been near them. Still I thought she might be hiding from me; it was one of her pretty ways; and that she had persuaded them to look as if they knew nothing about her; so I went softly peeping under this sofa, and behind that chair, making believe I was sadly frightened at not finding her.

"What's the matter, Hester?" said Mrs. Stark sharply. I don't know if Miss Furnivall had seen me, for, as I told you, she was very deaf, and she sat quite still, idly staring into the fire, with her hopeless face. "I'm only looking for my little Rosy-Posy," replied I, still thinking that the child was there, and near me, though I could not see her.

"Miss Rosamond is not here," said Mrs. Stark. "She went away more than an hour ago to find Dorothy." And she too turned and went on looking into the fire.

My heart sank at this, and I began to wish I had never left my darling. I went back to Dorothy and told her. James was gone out for the day, but she and me and Agnes took lights and went up into the nursery first, and then we roamed over the great large house, calling and entreating Miss Rosamond to come out of her hiding place, and not frighten us to death in that way. But there was no answer; no sound.

"Oh!" said I at last. "Can she have got into the east wing and hidden there?"

But Dorothy said it was not possible, for that she herself had never been in there; that the doors were always locked, and my lord's steward had the keys, she believed; at any rate, neither she nor James had ever seen them: so, I said I would go back, and see if, after all, she was not hidden in the drawing-room, unknown to the old ladies; and if I found her there, I said, I would whip her well for the fright she had given me; but I never meant to do it. Well, I went back to the west drawing-room, and I told Mrs. Stark we could not find her anywhere, and asked for leave to look all about the furniture there, for I thought now, that she might have fallen asleep in some warm, hidden corner; but no! we looked, Miss Furnivall got up and looked, trembling all over, and she was nowhere there; then we set off again, everyone in the house, and looked in all the places we had searched before, but we could not find her. Miss Furnivall shivered and shook so much, that Mrs. Stark took her back into the warm drawing-room; but not before they had made me promise to bring her to them when she was found. Well-a-day! I began to think she never would be found, when I bethought me to look out into the great front court, all covered with snow. I was up-stairs when I looked out; but, it was such dear moonlight, I could see quite plain two little footprints, which might be traced from the hall door, and round the corner of the east wing. I don't know how I got down, but I tugged open the great, stiff hall door; and, throwing the skirt of my gown over head for a cloak, I ran out. I turned the east corner, and there a black shadow fell on the snow; but when I came again into the moonlight, there were the little footmarks going up - up to the Fells. It was bitter cold; so cold that the air almost took the skin off my face as I ran, but I ran on, crying to think how my poor little darling must be perished, and frightened. I was within sight of the holly-trees, when I saw a shepherd coming down the hill, bearing something in his arms wrapped in his maud. He shouted to me, and asked me if I had lost a bairn; and, when I could not speak for crying, he bore towards me, and I saw my wee bairnie lying still, and white, and stiff, in his arms, as if she had been dead. He told me he had been up the Fells to gather in his sheep, before the deep cold of night came on, and that under the holly-trees (black marks on the hill-side, where no other bush was for miles around) he had found my little lady — my lamb — my queen — my darling — stiff, and cold, in the terrible sleep which is frost-begotten. Oh! the joy, and the tears, of having her in my arms once again! for I would not let him carry her; but took her, maud and all, into my own arms, and held her near my own warm neck, and heart, and felt the life stealing slowly back again into her little, gentle limbs. But she was still insensible when we reached the hall, and I had no breath for speech. We went in by the kitchen door.

"Bring the warming-pan," said I; and I carried her up-stairs and began undressing her by the nursery fire, which Agnes had kept up. I called my little lammie all the sweet and playful names I could think of, — even while my eyes were blinded by my tears; and at last, oh! at length she opened her large, blue eyes. Then I put her into her warm bed, and sent Dorothy down to tell Miss Furnivall that all was well; and I made up my mind to sit by my darling's bedside the live-long night. She fell away into a soft sleep as soon as her pretty head had touched the pillow, and I watched by her till morning light; when she wakened up bright and clear — or so I thought at first — and, my dears, so I think now.

She said, that she had fancied that she should like to go to Dorothy, for that both the old ladies were asleep, and it was very dull in the drawing-room; and that, as she was going through the west lobby, she saw the snow through the high window falling — falling — soft and steady; but she wanted to see it lying pretty and white on the ground; so she made her way into the great hall; and then, going to the window, she saw it bright and soft upon the drive; but while she stood there, she saw a little girl, not as old as she was, "but so pretty," said my darling, "and this little girl beckoned to me to come out; and oh, she was so pretty and so sweet, I could not choose but go." And then this other little girl had taken her by the hand, and side by side the two had gone round the east corner.

"Now, you are a naughty little girl, and telling stories," said I. "What would your good mamma, that is in heaven, and never told a story in her life, say to her little Rosamond, if she heard her — and I dare say she does — telling stories!"

"Indeed, Hester," sobbed out my child, "I'm telling you true. Indeed I am."

"Don't tell me!" said I, very stern. "I tracked you by your foot-marks through the snow; there were only yours to be seen: and if you had had a little girl to go hand-in-hand with you up the hill, don't you think the foot-prints would have gone along with yours?"

"I can't help it, dear, dear Hester," said she, crying, "if they did not; I never looked at her feet, but she held my hand fast and tight in her little one, and it was very, very cold. She took me up the Fell-path, up to the holly trees; and there I saw a lady weeping and crying; but when she saw me, she hushed her weeping, and smiled very proud and grand, and took me on her knee, and began to lull me to sleep; and that's all, Hester — but that is true; and my dear mamma knows it is," said she, crying. So I thought the child was in a fever, and pretended to believe her, as she went over her story — over and over again, and always the same. At last Dorothy knocked at the door with Miss Rosamond's breakfast; and she told me the old ladies were down in the eating parlour, and that they wanted to speak to me. They had both been into the night-nursery the evening before, but it was after Miss Rosamond was asleep; so they had only looked at her — not asked me any questions.

"I shall catch it," thought I to myself, as I went along the north gallery. "And yet," I thought, taking courage, "it was in their charge I left her; and it's they that's to blame for letting her steal away unknown and unwatched." So I went in boldly, and told my story. I told it all to Miss Furnivall, shouting it close to her ear; but when I came to the mention of the other little girl out in the snow, coaxing and tempting her out, and her up to the grand and beautiful lady by the holly-tree, she threw her arms up — her old and withered arms — and cried aloud, "Oh! Heaven, forgive! Have mercy!"

Mrs. Stark took hold of her; roughly enough, I thought; but she was past Mrs. Stark's management, and spoke to me, in a kind of wild warning and authority.

"Hester! keep her from that child! It will lure her to her death! That evil child! Tell her it is a wicked, naughty child." Then, Mrs. Stark hurried me out of the room; where, indeed, I was glad enough to go; but Miss Furnivall kept shrieking out, "Oh! have mercy! Wilt Thou never forgive! It is many a long year ago —"

I was very uneasy in my mind after that. I durst never leave Miss Rosamond, night or day, for fear lest she might slip off again, after some fancy or other; and all the more, because I thought I could make out that Miss Furnivall was crazy, from their odd ways about her; and I was afraid lest something of the same kind (which might be in the family, you know) hung over my darling. And the great frost never ceased all this time; and, whenever it was a more stormy night than usual, between the gusts, and through the wind, we heard the old lord playing on the great organ. But, old lord, or not, wherever Miss Rosamond went, there I followed; for my love for her, pretty, helpless orphan, was stronger than my fear for the grand and terrible sound. Besides, it rested with me to keep her cheerful and merry, as beseemed her age. So we played together, and wandered together, here and there, and everywhere; for I never dared to lose sight of her again in that large and rambling house. And so it happened, that one afternoon, not long before Christmas day, we were playing together on the billiard-table in the great hall (not that we knew the right way of playing, but she liked to roll the smooth ivory balls with her pretty hands, and I liked to do whatever she did); and, by-and-by, without our noticing it, it grew dusk indoors, though it was still light in the open air, and I was thinking of taking her back into the nursery, when, all of sudden, she cried out, —

"Look, Hester! look! there is my poor little girl out in the snow!"

I turned towards the long, narrow windows, and there, sure enough, I saw a little girl, less than my Miss Rosamond dressed all unfit to be out-of-doors such a bitter night — crying, and beating against the window-panes, as if she wanted to be let in. She seemed to sob and wail, till Miss Rosamond could bear it no longer, and was flying to the door to open it, when, all of a sudden, and close upon us, the great organ pealed out so loud and thundering, it fairly made me tremble; and all the more, when I remembered me that, even in the stillness of that dead-cold weather, I had heard no sound of little battering hands upon the window-glass, although the Phantom Child had seemed to put forth all its force; and, although I had seen it wail and cry, no faintest touch of sound had fallen upon my ears. Whether I remembered all this at the very moment, I do not know; the great organ sound had so stunned me into terror; but this I know, I caught up Miss Rosamond before she got the hall-door opened, and clutched her, and carried her away, kicking and screaming, into the large, bright kitchen, where Dorothy and Agnes were busy with their mince-pies.

"What is the matter with my sweet one?" cried Dorothy, as I bore in Miss Rosamond, who was sobbing as if her heart would break.

"She won't let me open the door for my little girl to come in; and she'll die if she is out on the Fells all night. Cruel, naughty Hester," she said, slapping me; but she might have struck harder, for I had seen a look of ghastly terror on Dorothy's face, which made my very blood run cold.

"Shut the back kitchen door fast, and bolt it well," said she to Agnes. She said no more; she gave me raisins and almonds to quiet Miss Rosamond: but she sobbed about the little girl in the snow, and would not touch any of the good things. I was thankful when she cried herself to sleep in bed. Then I stole down to the kitchen, and told Dorothy I had made up my mind I would carry my darling back to my father's house in Applethwaite; where, if we lived humbly, we lived at peace. I said I had been frightened enough with the old lord's organ-playing; but now that I had seen for myself this little, moaning child, all decked out as no child in the neighbourhood could be, beating and battering to get in, yet always without any sound or noise — with the dark wound on its right shoulder; and that Miss Rosamond had known it again for the phantom that had nearly lured her to her death (which Dorothy knew was true); I would stand it no longer.

I saw Dorothy change colour once or twice. When I had done, she told me she did not think I could take Miss Rosamond with me, for that she was my lord's ward, and I had no right over her; and she asked me, would I leave the child that I was so fond of, just for sounds and sights that could do me no harm; and that they had all had to get used to in their turns? I was all in a hot, trembling passion; and I said it was very well for her to talk, that knew what these sights and noises betokened, and that had, perhaps, had something to do with the Spectre-Child while it was alive. And I taunted her so, that she told me all she knew, at last; and then I wished I had never been told, for it only made me more afraid than ever.

She said she had heard the tale from old neighbours, that were alive when she was first married; when folks used to come to the hall sometimes, before it had got such a bad name on the country side: it might not be true, or it might, what she had been told.

The old lord was Miss Furnivall's father — Miss Grace, as Dorothy called her, for Miss Maude was the elder, and Miss Furnivall by rights. The old lord was eaten up with pride. Such a proud man was never seen or heard of; and his daughters were like him. No one was good enough to wed them, although they had choice enough; for they were the great beauties of their day, as I had seen by their portraits, where they hung in the state drawing-room. But, as the old saying is, "Pride will have a fall"; and these two haughty beauties fell in love with the same man, and he no better than a foreign musician, whom their father had down from London to play music with him at the Manor House. For, above all things, next to his pride, the old lord loved music. He could play on nearly every instrument that ever was heard of: and it was a strange thing it did not soften him; but he was a fierce, dour, old man, and had broken his poor wife's heart with his cruelty, they said. He was mad after music, and would pay any money for it. So he got this foreigner to come; who made such beautiful music, that they said the very birds on the trees stopped their singing to listen. And, by degrees, this foreign gentleman got such a hold over the old lord, that nothing would serve him but that he must come every year; and it was he that had the great organ brought from Holland, and built up in the hall, where it stood now. He taught the old lord to play on it; but many and many a time, when Lord Furnivall was thinking of nothing but his fine organ, and his finer music, the dark foreigner was walking abroad in the woods with one of the young ladies; now Miss Maude, and then Miss Grace.

Miss Maude won the day and carried off the prize, such as it was; and he and she were married, all unknown to anyone; and before he made his next yearly visit, she had been confined of a little girl at a farm-house on the Moors, while her father and Miss Grace thought she was away at Doncaster Races. But though she was a wife and a mother, she was not a bit softened, but as haughty and as passionate as ever; and perhaps more so for she was jealous of Miss Grace, to whom her foreign husband paid a deal of court — by way of blinding her — as he told his wife. But Miss Grace triumphed over Miss Maude, and Miss Maude grew fiercer and fiercer, both with her husband and with her sister; and the former who could easily shake off what was disagreeable, and hide himself in foreign countries — went away a month before his usual time that summer, and half-threatened that he would never come back again. Meanwhile, the little girl was left at the farm-house, and her mother used to have her horse saddled and gallop wildly over the hills to see her once every week, at the very least — for where she loved, she loved; and where she hated, she hated. And the old lord went on playing — playing on his organ; and the servants thought the sweet music he made had soothed down his awful temper, of which (Dorothy said) some terrible tales could be told. He grew infirm too, and had to walk with a crutch; and his son — that was the present Lord Furnivall's father — was with the army in America, and the other son at sea; so Miss Maude had it pretty much her own way, and she and Miss Grace grew colder and bitterer to each other every day; till at last they hardly ever spoke, except when the old lord was by. The foreign musician came again the next summer, but it was for the last time; for they led him such a life with their jealousy and their passions, that he grew weary, and went away, and never was heard of again. And Miss Maude, who had always meant to have her marriage acknowledged when her father should be dead, was left now a deserted wife — whom nobody knew to have been married — with a child that she dared not own, although she loved it to distraction; living with a father whom she feared, and a sister whom she hated. When the next summer passed over and the dark foreigner never came, both Miss Maude and Miss Grace grew gloomy and sad; they had a haggard look about them, though they looked handsome as ever. But by-and-by Miss Maude brightened; for her father grew more and more infirm, and more than ever carried away by his music; and she and Miss Grace lived almost entirely apart, having separate rooms, the one on the west side, Miss Maude on the east — those very rooms which were now shut up. So she thought she might have her little girl with her, and no one need ever know except those who dared not speak about it, and were bound to believe that it was, as she said, a cottager's child she had taken a fancy to. All this Dorothy said, was pretty well known; but what came afterwards no one knew, except Miss Grace, and Mrs. Stark, who was even then her maid, and much more of a friend to her than ever her sister had been. But the servants supposed, from words that were dropped, that Miss Maude had triumphed over Miss Grace, and told her that all the time the dark foreigner had been mocking her with pretended love — he was her own husband; the colour left Miss Grace's cheek and lips that very day for ever, and she was heard to say many a time that sooner or later she would have her revenge; and Mrs. Stark was for ever spying about the east rooms.

One fearful night, just after the New Year had come in, when the snow was lying thick and deep, and the flakes were still falling — fast enough to blind anyone who might be out and abroad — there was a great and violent noise heard, and the old lord's voice above all, cursing and swearing awfully, — and the cries of a little child, — and the proud defiance of a fierce woman, — and the sound of a blow, — and a dead stillness, — and moans and wailing's dying away on the hill-side! Then the old lord summoned all his servants, and told them, with terrible oaths, and words more terrible, that his daughter had disgraced herself, and that he had turned her out of doors, — her, and her child, — and that if ever they gave her help, — or food, — or shelter, — he prayed that they might never enter Heaven. And, all the while, Miss Grace stood by him, white and still as any stone; and when he had ended she heaved a great sigh, as much as to say her work was done, and her end was accomplished. But the old lord never touched his organ again, and died within the year; and no wonder! for, on the morrow of that wild and fearful night, the shepherds, coming down the Fell-side, found Miss Maude sitting, all crazy and smiling, under the holly-trees, nursing a dead child, — with a terrible mark on its right shoulder. "But that was not what killed it," said Dorothy: "it was the frost and the cold. Every wild creature was in its hole, and every beast in its fold, while the child and its mother were turned out to wander on the Fells! And now you know all! and I wonder if you are less frightened now?"

I was more frightened than ever; but I said I was not. I wished Miss Rosamond and myself well out of that dreadful house for ever; but I would not leave her, and I dared not take her away. But oh! how I watched her, and guarded her! We bolted the doors, and shut the window-shutters fast, an hour or more before dark, rather than leave them open five minutes too late. But my little lady still heard the weird child crying and mourning; and not all we could do or say, could keep her from wanting to go to her, and let her in from the cruel wind and the snow. All this time, I kept away from Miss Furnivall and Mrs. Stark, as much as ever I could; for I feared them — I knew no good could be about them, with their grey hard faces, and their dreamy eyes, looking back into the ghastly years that were gone. But, even in my fear, I had a kind of pity — for Miss Furnivall, at least. Those gone down to the pit can hardly have a more hopeless look than that which was ever on her face. At last I even got so sorry for her — who never said a word but what was quite forced from her — that I prayed for her; and I taught Miss Rosamond to pray for one who had done a deadly sin; but often when she came to those words, she would listen, and start up from her knees, and say, "I hear my little girl plaining and crying very sad - Oh! let her in, or she will die!"

One night — just after New Year's Day had come at last, and the long winter had taken a turn, as I hoped — I heard the west drawing-room bell ring three times, which was the signal for me. I would not leave Miss Rosamond alone, for all she was asleep — for the old lord had been playing wilder than ever — and I feared lest my darling should waken to hear the spectre child; see her I knew she could not. I had fastened the windows too well for that. So, I took her out of her bed and wrapped her up in such outer clothes as were most handy, and carried her down to the drawing-room, where the old ladies sat at their tapestry work as usual. They looked up when I came in, and Mrs. Stark asked, quite astounded, "Why did I bring Miss Rosamond there, out of her warm bed?" I had begun to whisper, "Because I was afraid of her being tempted out while I was away, by the wild child in the snow," when she stopped me short (with a glance at Miss Furnivall), and said Miss Furnivall wanted me to undo some work she had done wrong, and which neither of them could see to unpick. So, I laid my pretty dear on the sofa, and sat down on a stool by them, and hardened my heart against them, as I heard the wind rising and howling.

Miss Rosamond slept on sound, for all the wind blew so; and Miss Furnivall said never a word, nor looked round when the gusts shook the windows. All at once she started up to her full height, and put up one hand, as if to bid us listen.

"I hear voices!" said she. "I hear terrible screams — I hear my father's voice!"

Just at that moment, my darling wakened with a sudden start: "My little girl is crying, oh, how she is crying!" and she tried to get up and go to her, but she got her feet entangled in the blanket, and I caught her up; for my flesh had begun to creep at these noises, which they heard while we could catch no sound. In a minute or two the noises came, and gathered fast, and filled our ears; we, too, heard voices and screams, and no longer heard the winter's wind that raged abroad. Mrs. Stark looked at me, and I at her, but we dared not speak. Suddenly Miss Furnivall went towards the door, out into the ante-room, through the west lobby, and opened the door into the great hall. Mrs. Stark followed, and I durst not be left, though my heart almost stopped beating for fear. I wrapped my darling tight in my arms, and went out with them. In the hall the screams were louder than ever; they sounded to come from the east wing — nearer and nearer — close on the other side of the locked-up doors — close behind them. Then I noticed that the great bronze chandelier seemed all alight, though the hall was dim, and that a fire was blazing in the vast hearth-place, though it gave no heat; and I shuddered up with terror, and folded my darling closer to me. But as I did so, the east door shook, and she, suddenly struggling to get free from me, cried, "Hester! I must go! My little girl is there; I hear her; she is coming! Hester, I must go!"

I held her tight with all my strength; with a set will, I held her. If I had died, my hands would have grasped her still, I was so resolved in my mind. Miss Furnivall stood listening, and paid no regard to my darling, who had got down to the ground, and whom I, upon my knees now, was holding with both my arms clasped round her neck; she still striving and crying to get free.

All at once, the east door gave way with a thundering crash, as if torn open in a violent passion, and there came into that broad and mysterious light, the figure of a tall, old man, with grey hair and gleaming eyes. He drove before him, with many a relentless gesture of abhorrence, a stern and beautiful woman, with a little child clinging to her dress.

"Oh Hester! Hester!" cried Miss Rosamond. "It's the lady! the lady below the holly-trees; and my little girl is with her. Hester! Hester! let me go to her; they are drawing me to them. I feel them — I feel them. I must go!"

Again she was almost convulsed by her efforts to get away; but I held her tighter and tighter, till I feared I should do her a hurt; but rather that than let her go towards those terrible phantoms. They passed along towards the great hall-door, where the winds howled and ravened for their prey; but before they reached that, the lady turned; and I could see that she defied the old man with a fierce and proud defiance; but then she quailed — and then she threw her arms wildly and piteously to save her child — her little child — from a blow from his uplifted crutch.

And Miss Rosamond was torn as by a power stronger than mine, and writhed in my arms, and sobbed (for by this time the poor darling was growing faint).

"They want me to go with them on to the Fells — they are drawing me to them. Oh, my little girl! I would come, but cruel, wicked Hester holds me very tight." But when she saw the uplifted crutch she swooned away, and I thanked God for it. Just at this moment — when the tall, old man, his hair streaming as in the blast of a furnace, was going to strike the little, shrinking child — Miss Furnivall, the old woman by my side, cried out, "Oh, father! father! spare the little, innocent child!" But just then I saw — we all saw — another phantom shape itself, and grow clear out of the blue and misty light that filled the hall; we had not seen her till now, for it was another lady who stood by the old man, with a look of relentless hate and triumphant scorn. That figure was very beautiful to look upon, with a soft, white hat drawn down over the proud brows, and a red and curling lip. It was dressed in an open robe of blue satin. I had seen that figure before. It was the likeness of Miss Furnivall in her youth; and the terrible phantoms moved on, regardless of old Miss Furnivall's wild entreaty, and the uplifted crutch fell on the right shoulder of the little child, and the younger sister looked on, stony and deadly serene. But at that moment, the dim lights, and the fire that gave no heat, went out of themselves, and Miss Furnivall lay at our feet stricken down by the palsy — death-stricken.

Yes! she was carried to her bed that night never to rise again. She lay with her face to the wall, muttering low, but muttering always: "Alas! alas! what is done in youth can never be undone in age! what is done in youth can never be undone in age!"

The Last House in C—— Street

Dinah Maria Craik

I am not a believer in ghosts in general; I see no good in them. They come — that is, are reported to come — so irrelevantly, purposelessly — so ridiculously, in short — that one's common sense as regards this world, one's supernatural sense of the other, are alike revolted. Then nine out of ten "capital ghost stories" are so easily accounted for; and in the tenth, when all natural explanation fails, one who has discovered the extraordinary difficulty there is in all society in getting hold of that very slippery article called a fact, is strongly inclined to shake a dubious head, ejaculating, "Evidence! it is all a question of evidence!"

But my unbelief springs from no dogged or contemptuous scepticism as to the possibility — however great the improbability — of that strange impression upon, or communication to, spirit in matter, from spirit wholly immaterialised, which is vulgarly called "a ghost". There is no credulity more blind, no ignorance more childish, than that of the sage who tries to measure "heaven and earth and the things under the earth", with the small two-foot rule of his own brains.

The presumption of mere folly alone would argue concerning any mystery of the universe, "It is inexplicable, and therefore impossible."

Premising these opinions, though simply as opinions, I am about to relate what I must confess seems to me a thorough ghost story; its external and circumstantial evidence being indisputable, while its psychological causes and results, though not easy of explanation, are still more difficult to be explained away. The ghost, like Hamlet's, was "an honest ghost". From her daughter — an old lady, who, bless her good and gentle memory! has since learned the secrets of all things — I heard this veritable tale.

"My dear," said Mrs. MacArthur to me — it was in the early days of table-moving, when young folk ridiculed and elder folk were shocked at the notion of calling up one's departed ancestors into one's dinner-table, and learning the wonders of the angelic world by the bobbings of a hat or the twirlings of a plate; — "My dear," continued the old lady, "I do not like trifling with spirits."

"Why not? Do you believe in them?"

"A little."

"Did you ever see one?"

"Never. But once, I heard one."

She looked serious, as if she hardly liked to speak about it, either from a sense of awe or from fear of ridicule. But it was impossible to laugh at any illusions of the gentle old lady, who never uttered a harsh or satirical word to a living soul. Likewise the evident awe with which she mentioned the circumstance was rather remarkable in one who had a large stock of common sense, little wonder, and no ideality.

I was very curious to hear Mrs. MacArthur's ghost story.

"My dear, it was a long time ago, so long that you may fancy I forget and confuse the circumstances. But I do not. Sometimes I think one recollects more clearly things that happened in one's teens — I was eighteen that year — than a great many nearer events. And besides, I had other reasons for remembering vividly everything belonging to this time, — for I was in love, you must know."

She looked at me with a mild deprecating smile, as if hoping my youthfulness would not consider the thing so very impossible or ridiculous. No; I was all interest at once.

"In love with Mr. MacArthur," I said, scarcely as a question, being at that Arcadian time of life when one takes as a natural necessity, and believes in as an undoubted truth, that all people, that is, good people, marry their first love.

"No, my dear; not with Mr. MacArthur."

I was so astonished, so completely dumbfounded — for I had woven a sort of ideal round my good old friend — that I suffered Mrs. MacArthur to knit in silence for full five minutes. My surprise was not lessened when she said, with a gratified little smile — "He was a young gentleman of good parts; and he was very fond of me. Proud, too, rather. For though you might not think it, my dear, I was actually a beauty in those days."

I had very little doubt of it. The slight lithe figure, the tiny hands and feet, — if you had walked behind Mrs. MacArthur down the street you might have taken her for a young woman still. Certainly, people lived slower and easier in the last generation than in ours.

"Yes, I was the beauty of Bath. Mr. Everest fell in love with me there. I was much gratified; for I had just been reading Miss Burney's *Cecilia*, and I thought him exactly like Mortimer Delvil. A very pretty story, *Cecilia*; did you ever read it?"

"No." And, to arrive quicker at her tale, I leaped to the only conclusion which could reconcile the two facts of my good old friend having had a lover named Everest, and being now Mrs. MacArthur. "Was it his ghost you saw?"

"No, my dear, no; thank goodness, he is alive still. He calls here sometimes; he has been a faithful friend to our family. Ah!" with a slow shake of the head, half pleased, half pensive, "you would hardly believe, my dear, what a very pretty fellow he was."

One could scarcely smile at the odd phrase, pertaining to last-century novels and to the loves of our great-grandmothers. I listened patiently to the wandering reminiscences which still further delayed the ghost story.

"But, Mrs. MacArthur, was it in Bath that you saw or heard what I think you were going to tell me? The ghost, you know?"

"Don't call it that; it sounds as if you were laughing at it. And you must not, for it is really true; as true as that I sit here, an old lady of seventy-five, and that then I was a young gentlewoman of eighteen. Nay, my dear, I will tell you all about it.

"We had been staying in London, my father and mother, Mr. Everest, and I. He had persuaded them to take me; he wanted to show me a little of the world, though even his world was but a narrow one, my dear, — for he was a law student, living poorly and working hard.

"He took lodgings for us near the Temple; in C—— street, the last house there, looking on to the river. He was very fond of the river; and often of evenings, when his work was too heavy to let him take us to Ranelagh or to the play, he used to walk with my father and mother and me up and down the Temple Gardens. Were you ever in the Temple Gardens? It is a pretty place now

— a quiet, grey nook in the midst of noise and bustle; the stars look wonderful through those great trees; but still it is not like what it was then, when I was a girl."

Ah! no; impossible.

"It was in the Temple Gardens, my dear, that I remember we took our last walk — my mother, Mr. Everest, and I — before she went home to Bath. She was very anxious and restless to go, being too delicate for London gaieties. Besides, she had a large family at home, of which I was the eldest; and we were anxiously expecting another baby in a month or two. Nevertheless, my dear mother had gone about with me, taken me to all the shows and sights that I, a hearty and happy girl, longed to see, and entered into them with almost as great enjoyment as my own.

"But tonight she was pale, rather grave, and steadfastly bent on returning home.

"We did all we could to persuade her to the contrary, for on the next night but one was to have been the crowning treat of all our London pleasures: we were to see Hamlet at Drury-lane, with John Kemble and Sarah Siddons! Think of that, my dear. Ah! you have no such sights now. Even my grave father longed to go, and urged in his mild way that we should put off our departure.

"But my mother was determined.

"At last Mr. Everest said — I could show you the very spot where he stood, with the river — it was high water — lapping against the wall, and the evening sun shining on the Southwark houses opposite. He said — it was very wrong, of course, my dear; but then he was in love, and might be excused —

"'Madam,' said he, 'it is the first time I ever knew you think of yourself alone.'

"'Myself, Edmond?'

"'Pardon me, but would it not be possible for you to return home, leaving behind, for two days only, Dr. Thwaite and Mistress Dorothy?'

"'Leave them behind — leave them behind!' She mused over the words. 'What say you, Dorothy?'

"I was silent. In very truth, I had never been parted from her in all my life. It had never crossed my mind to wish to part from her, or to enjoy any pleasure without her, till — till within the last three months. 'Mother, don't suppose I —'

"But here I caught sight of Mr. Everest and stopped.

"'Pray continue, Mistress Dorothy.'

"No, I could not. He looked so vexed, so hurt; and we had been so happy together. Also, we might not meet again for years, for the journey between London and Bath was then a serious one, even to lovers; and he worked very hard — had few pleasures in his life. It did indeed seem almost selfish of my mother.

"Though my lips said nothing, perhaps my sad eyes said only too much, and my mother felt it.

"She walked with us a few yards, slowly and thoughtfully. I could see her now, with her pale, tired face, under the cherry-coloured ribbons of her hood. She had been very handsome as a young woman, and was most sweet-looking still — my dear, good mother!

"'Dorothy, we will discuss this no more. I am very sorry, but I must go home. However, I will persuade your father to remain with you till the week's end. Are you satisfied!'

"'No,' was the first filial impulse of my heart; but Edmund pressed my arm with such an entreating look, that almost against my will I answered 'Yes.'

"Mr. Everest overwhelmed my mother with his delight and gratitude. She walked up and down for some time longer, leaning on his arm — she was very fond of him; then stood looking on the river, upwards and downwards.

"'I suppose this is my last walk in London. Thank you for all the care you have taken of me. And when I am gone home — mind, oh, mind, Edmond, that you take special care of Dorothy.'

"These words, and the tone in which they were spoken, fixed themselves on my mind — first, from gratitude, not unmingled with regret, as if I had not been so considerate to her as she to me; afterwards — But we often err, my dear, in dwelling too much on that word. We finite creatures have only to deal with 'now' — nothing whatever to do with 'afterwards'. In this case, I have ceased to blame myself or others. Whatever was, being past, was right to be, and could not have been otherwise.

"My mother went home next morning, alone. We were to follow in a few days, though she would not allow us to fix any time. Her departure was so hurried that I remember nothing about it, save her answer to my father's urgent desire — almost command — that if anything went amiss she would immediately let him know.

"'Under all circumstances, wife,' he reiterated, 'this you promise?'

"'I promise.'

"Though when she was gone he declared she need not have said it so earnestly, since we should be at home almost as soon as the slow Bath coach could take her there and bring us back a letter.

"And besides, there was nothing likely to happen. But he fidgeted a good deal, being unused to her absence in their happy wedded life. He was, like most men, glad to blame anybody but himself, and the whole day, and the next, was cross at intervals with both Edmond and me; but we bore it — and patiently.

"'It will be all right when we get him to the theatre. He has no real cause for anxiety about her. What a dear woman she is, and a precious — your mother, Dorothy!'

"I rejoiced to hear my lover speak thus, and thought there hardly ever was young gentlewoman so blessed as I.

"We went to the play. Ah, you know nothing of what a play is, nowadays. You never saw John Kemble and Mrs. Siddons. Though in dresses and shows it was far inferior to the Hamlet you took me to see last week, my dear — and though I perfectly well remember being on the point of laughing when in the most solemn scene, it became clearly evident that the Ghost had been drinking. Strangely enough, no after events connected therewith ever were able to drive from my mind the vivid impression of this my first play. Strange, also, that the play should have been Hamlet. Do you think that Shakespeare believed in — in what people call 'ghosts?'"

I could not say; but I thought Mrs. MacArthur's ghost very long in coming.

"Don't, my dear — don't; do anything but laugh at it."

She was visibly affected, and it was not without an effort that she proceeded in her story.

"I wish you to understand exactly my position that night — a young girl, her head full of the enchantment of the stage — her heart of something not less engrossing. Mr. Everest had supped with us, leaving us both in the best of spirits; indeed my father had gone to bed, laughing heartily at the remembrance of the antics of Mr. Grimaldi, which had almost obliterated the Queen and Hamlet from his memory, on which the ridiculous always took a far stronger hold than the awful or sublime.

"I was sitting — let me see — at the window, chatting with my maid Patty, who was brushing the powder out of my hair. The window was open half-way, and looking out on the Thames; and the summer night being very warm and starry, made it almost like sitting out of doors. There was none of the awe given by the solitude of a closed room, when every sound is magnified, and every shadow seems alive.

"As I said, we had been chatting and laughing; for Patty and I were both very young, and she had a sweetheart, too. She, like every one of our household, was a warm admirer of Mr. Everest. I had just been half scolding, half smiling at her praises of him, when St. Paul's great clock came booming over the silent river.

"'Eleven,' counted Patty. 'Terrible late we be, Mistress Dorothy: not like Bath hours, I reckon.'

"'Mother will have been in bed an hour ago,' said I, with a little self-reproach at not having thought of her till now.

"The next minute my maid and I both started up with a simultaneous exclamation.

"'Did you hear that?'

"'Yes, a bat flying against the window.'

"'But the lattices are open, Mistress Dorothy.'

"So they were; and there was no bird or bat or living thing about — only the quiet summer night, the river, and the stars. I be certain sure I heard it. And I think it was like — just a bit like — somebody tapping.

"'Nonsense, Patty!' But it had struck me thus — though I said it was a bat. It was exactly like the sound of fingers against a pane — very soft, gentle fingers, such as, in passing into her flower-garden, my mother used often to tap outside the school-room casement at home.

"'I wonder, did father hear anything. It — the bird, you know, Patty — might have flown at his window, too?'

"'Oh, Mistress Dorothy!' Patty would not be deceived. I gave her the brush to finish my hair, but her hand shook too much. I shut the window, and we both sat down facing it.

"At that minute, distinct, clear, and unmistakable, like a person giving a summons in passing by, we heard once more the tapping on the pane. But nothing was seen; not a single shadow came between us and the open air; the bright starlight.

"Startled I was, and awed, but I was not frightened. The sound gave me even an inexplicable delight. But I had hardly time to recognise my feelings, still less to analyse them, when a loud cry came from my father's room.

"'Dolly, — Dolly!'

"Now my mother and I had both one name, but he always gave her the old-fashioned pet name, — I was invariably Dorothy. Still I did not pause to think, but ran to his locked door and answered.

"It was a long time before he took any notice, though I heard him talking to himself, and moaning. He was subject to bad dreams, especially before his attacks of gout. So my first alarm lightened. I stood listening, knocking at intervals, until at last he replied.

"'What do 'ee want, child?'

"'Is anything the matter, father?'

"'Nothing. Go to thy bed, Dorothy.'

"'Did you not call? Do you want anyone?'

"'Not thee. O Dolly, my poor Dolly,' — and he seemed to be almost sobbing, 'why did I let thee leave me?'

"'Father, you are not going to be ill? It is not the gout, is it? (for that was the time when he wanted my mother most, and, indeed, when he was wholly unmanageable by anyone but her.)'

"'Go away. Get to thy bed, girl; I don't want 'ee.'

"I thought he was angry with me for having been in some sort the cause of our delay, and retired very miserable. Patty and I sat up a good while longer, discussing the dreary prospect of my father's having a fit of the gout here in London lodgings, with only us to nurse him, and my mother away. Our alarm was so great that we quite forgot the curious circumstance which had first attracted us, till Patty spoke up from her bed on the floor.

"'I hope master beant going to be very ill, and that noise — you know — came for a warning. Do 'ee think it was a bird, Mistress Dorothy?'

"'Very likely. Now, Patty, let us go to sleep.'

"But I did not, for all night I heard my father groaning at intervals. I was certain it was the gout, and wished from the bottom of my heart that we had gone home with mother.

"What was my surprise when, quite early, I heard him rise and go down, just as if nothing was ailing him! I found him sitting at the breakfast-table in his travelling coat, looking very haggard and miserable, but evidently bent on a journey.

"'Father, you are not going to Bath?'

"'Yes, I be.'

"'Not till the evening coach starts,' I cried, alarmed. 'We can't, you know?'

"'I'll take a post-chaise, then. We must be off in an hour.'

"An hour! The cruel pain of parting — (my dear, I believe I used to feel things keenly when I was young) — shot through me — through and through. A single hour, and I should have said good-bye to Edmond — one of those heart-breaking farewells when we seem to leave half of our poor young life behind us, forgetting that the only real parting is when there is no love left to part from. A few years, and I wondered how I could have crept away and wept in such intolerable agony at the mere bidding good-bye to Edmond — Edmond, who loved me!

"Every minute seemed a day till he came in, as usual, to breakfast. My red eyes and my father's corded trunk explained all.

"'Dr. Thwaite, you are not going?'

"'Yes, I am,' repeated my father. He sat moodily leaning on the table — would not taste his breakfast.

"'Not till the night coach, surely? I was to take you and Mistress Dorothy to see Mr. Benjamin West, the king's painter.'

"'Let king and painters alone, lad; I am going home to my Dolly.'

"Mr. Everest used many arguments, gay and grave, upon which I hung with earnest conviction and hope. He made things so clear always; he was a man of much brighter parts than my father, and had great influence over him.

"'Dorothy,' he whispered, 'help me to persuade the Doctor. It is so little time I beg for, only a few hours; and before so long a parting.' — Ay, longer than he thought, or I.

"'Children,' cried my father at last, 'you are a couple of fools. Wait till you have been married twenty years. I must go to my Dolly. I know there is something amiss at home.'

"I should have felt alarmed, but I saw Mr. Everest smile; and besides, I was yet glowing under his fond look, as my father spoke of our being 'married twenty years'.

"'Father, you have surely no reason for thinking this? If you have, tell us.'

"My father just lifted his head, and looked at me woefully in the face.

"'Dorothy, last night, as sure as I see you now, I saw your mother.'

"'Is that all?' cried Mr. Everest, laughing: 'why, my good sir, very likely you did; you were dreaming about her.'

"'I had not gone to sleep.'

"'How did you see her?'

"'Coming into my room, just as she used to do in our bedroom at home, with the candle in her hand and the baby asleep on her arm.'

"'Did she speak?' asked Mr. Everest, with another and rather satirical smile; 'remember, you saw Hamlet last night. Indeed, sir — indeed, Dorothy — it was a mere dream. I do not believe in ghosts; it would be an insult to common sense, to human wisdom — nay, even to Divinity itself.'

"Edmond spoke so earnestly, justly, and withal so affectionately, that perforce I agreed; and even my father began to feel rather ashamed of his own weakness. He, a sensible man and the head of a family, to yield to a mere superstitious fancy, springing probably from a hot supper and an over-excited brain! To the same cause Mr. Everest attributed the other incident, which somewhat hesitatingly I told him.

"'Dear, it was a bird; nothing but a bird. One flew in at my window last spring; it had hurt itself, and I kept it, and nursed it, and petted it. It was such a pretty gentle little thing, it put me in mind of Dorothy.'

"'Did it?' said I.

"'And at last it got well and flew away.'

"'Ah! that was not like Dorothy.'

"Thus, my father being persuaded, it was not hard to persuade me. We settled to remain till evening. Edmond and I, with my maid Patty, went about together chiefly in Mr. West's Gallery, and in the quiet shade of our favourite Temple Gardens. And if for those four stolen hours, and the sweetness in them, I afterwards suffered untold remorse and bitterness, I have entirely forgiven myself, as I know my dear mother would have forgiven me, long ago."

Mrs. MacArthur stopped, wiped her eyes, and then continued — speaking more in the matter-of-fact way that old people speak in, than she had been lately doing.

"Well, my dear, where was I?"

"In the Temple Gardens."

"Yes, yes. Then we came home to dinner. My father always enjoyed his dinner, and his nap afterwards; he had nearly recovered himself now: only looked tired from loss of rest. Edmond and I sat in the window, watching the barges and wherries down the Thames; there were no steam-boats then, you know.

"Someone knocked at the door with a message for my father, but he slept so heavily he did not hear. Mr. Everest went to see what it was; I stood at the window. I remember mechanically watching the red sail of a Margate hoy that was going down the river, and thinking with a sharp pang how dark the room seemed to grow, in a moment, with Edmond not there.

"Re-entering, after a somewhat long absence, he never looked at me, but went straight to my father.

"'Sir, it is almost time for you to start;' (oh! Edmond). 'There is a coach at the door; and, pardon me, but I think you should travel quickly.'

"My father sprang to his feet.

"'Dear sir, wait one moment; I have received news from Bath. You have another little daughter, sir, and —'

"'Dolly, my Dolly!' Without another word my father rushed away, leaped into the post-chaise that was waiting and drove off.

"'Edmond!' I gasped.

"'My poor little girl — my own Dorothy!'

"By the tenderness of his embrace, less lover-like than brother-like — by his tears, for I could feel them on my neck — I knew, as well as if he had told me, that I should never see my dear mother any more. — 'She had died in childbirth' continued the old lady after a long pause — 'died at night, at the same hour and minute that I had heard the tapping on the window-pane, and my father had thought he saw her coming into his room with a baby on her arm."

"Was the baby dead, too?"

"They thought so then, but it afterwards revived."

"What a strange story!"

"I do not ask you to believe in it. How and why and what it was I cannot tell; I only know that it assuredly was as I have told it."

"And Mr. Everest?" I inquired, after some hesitation.

The old lady shook her head. "Ah, my dear, you may perhaps learn — though I hope you will not — how very, very seldom things turn out as one expects when one is young. After that day I did not see Mr. Everest for twenty years."

"How wrong of him — how —"

"Don't blame him; it was not his fault. You see, after that time my father took a prejudice against him — not unnatural, perhaps; and she was not there to make things straight. Besides, my own conscience was very sore, and there were the six children at home, and the little baby had no mother: so at last I made up my mind. I should have loved him just the same if we had waited twenty years. I told him so: but he could not see things in that light. Don't blame him, my dear, don't blame him. It was as well, perhaps, as it happened."

"Did he marry?"

"Yes, after a few years; and loved his wife dearly. When I was about one-and-thirty, I married Mr. MacArthur. So neither of us was unhappy, you see — at least, not more so than most people; and we became sincere friends afterwards. Mr. and Mrs. Everest come to see me still, almost every Sunday. Why, you foolish child, you are not crying?"

Ay, I was — but scarcely at the ghost story.

My Friend's Story

Catherine Ann Crowe

"I don't know how often you have promised to tell me a remarkable thing in the ghostly line, that happened to yourself," said I, the other day to my friend; "but something has always come in the way; now I shall be very much obliged to you for the particulars, if you have no objection to my printing the story."

"None," she said, "but as regards names of persons and places; the circumstances are so singular that I think they deserve to be recorded. That part of the affair which happened to myself I vouch for; and I can only say that I have most entire confidence in the truth of the rest, and that all the enquiries I made, tended to confirm the story.

"I remember your asking me once, why I so seldom visited our place in S——, and I told you it was because it was so dreadfully *triste* that I could not inhabit it. You will perhaps suppose that what I am going to relate happened there, but it did not, for the house has not even the recommendation of being haunted — that would at least give it an interest — but I am sorry to say the sole interest it possesses is, that it happens to be ours. Dull as it is, however, we lived there shortly after I was married, for some time. I had no children then, which made it all the duller, particularly when my husband was called away; and on one of these occasions, some acquaintances I had, who were living at a place called the Bellfry, about two miles distant, invited me to visit them for a few days.

"The Bellfry is a common place square house, just such as the doctor or lawyer would inhabit in a provincial town; a little white swing gate, a round grass plot, with a few straggling dahlias, a gravel road leading to the small portico, and a terrible loud bell to ring, when you want to be admitted. So much for the exterior. The interior is not at all more suggestive to the fancy. On the ground floor, there is the usual parlour on one side, and drawing-room on the other, with a long passage leading to the offices at the back; upstairs, a sort of corridor, with dingy bedrooms opening into it. Decidedly not lively, but perfectly prosaic, it was by no means calculated to inspire ghostly terrors; and, indeed, I must confess the supernatural, as it is called, was a subject that, at that time, had never engaged my attention. I mention all this to show you that what happened was not 'the offspring of my excited imagination,' as the learned always tell you these things are. Moreover, I was young; and, to the best of my belief, in very good health.

"The room they gave me was the best. It was plainly but comfortably furnished, with a large four-post bed, and it looked into the churchyard; but this is not an uncommon prospect in country towns, and I thought nothing about it. Now that we understand these things better, I should think it not ghostly, but unhealthy.

"The first two or three nights I slept there, nothing particular occurred; but on the fourth or fifth night, soon after I had fallen asleep, I was awoke by a noise which appeared very near me, and on listening attentively, I heard a rustling sound, and footsteps on the floor. I forgot for the moment that I had locked my door, and concluding it was the housekeeper, who sometimes looked in when I was going to bed, to ask if I was comfortable, I said, 'Is that you, Mrs. H?' But there was no answer, upon which I sat up and looked around; and seeing nobody, though I heard the sound still, I jumped out of bed. Then I observed, for it was a bright moonlight night, that there was a large tree in the churchyard, which grew very close to the window, and I concluded that a breeze had arisen, and caused the branches to touch the glass; so I got into bed again quite satisfied, and settled myself to sleep. But scarcely had I closed my eyes, when the footsteps began again, much too distinct this time to be mistaken for anything else; and whilst I was listening in amazement, I heard a heavy, heavy sigh. I had raised myself on my elbow, in order to have my ears freer to listen, and presently I saw the curtains at the foot of the bed, which were closed, slowly and gently opened. I saw no figure, but they were held apart, apparently by the two hands of someone standing there. I bounded out of bed, and rushed out of the room into the corridor, screaming for help. All who heard me, got up and came out of their rooms, to enquire what had happened; but I had not courage to tell the truth, I was afraid of giving offence, or incurring ridicule, and I said I had been awakened by a noise in my room, and I was afraid somebody was concealed there. They went in with me and searched; of course, nobody was found; and one suggested that it was a mouse, another that it was a dream, and so forth. But then, and still more the next morning, I fancied, from their manner, they were better acquainted with my midnight visitor than they chose to say. However, I changed my room, and soon after quitted the Bellfry, which I have never slept at since, so there concludes the story, so far as I am concerned; but there is a sequel to the tale.

"I must tell you that I never mentioned these circumstances, because I knew I should only be laughed at; besides I thought it might annoy my hosts, as they had an idea of going abroad for some time, and it might have interfered with their letting the house.

"Now to my sequel.

"Two or three years after this occurrence, I fell desperately ill; first I was confined of an infant which did not survive; and then I was attacked with typhus fever, which raged in the neighbourhood. I was at death's door for eleven weeks, and not expected to recover; but you see, I did, *nonobstant messrs. les medicins*; but I was so long regaining my strength, that I was recommended to try the effects of a sea voyage. Even then, I could not sit up, and was lifted about like a baby; and as a fine lady's maid would have been of no use on board the yacht, a sailor's daughter from the coast was engaged to attend me; a strong, healthy young woman, to whom my weight was a feather. She tended me most faithfully, and I found her simple, truthful, and straightforward; insomuch, that I had thoughts of engaging her in my service permanently. With this view, and also because it helped to pass the time, I questioned her about her family, and the manner of life of her class, in the out of the way part of the country from which she came.

"'I suppose, Mary, you've never been away from home before?'

"'Oh, yes, Ma'am; I was in service as housemaid for a short time at the Bellfry, not far from your place, Ma'am; but I soon left that, and I have never been out again.'

"'But why did you leave? Didn't you like the place?'

"'No, Ma'am.'

"'But why? Perhaps you'd too much to do?'

"'No, Ma'am, it wasn't a hard place; but unpleasant things happened, and so I left.'

"'What sort of unpleasant things?' said I, my own adventure there suddenly recurring to my memory.

"She hesitated, and said, that perhaps it would alarm me; she had also made a sort of promise to her master and mistress not to talk about it, and she never had mentioned what happened except to her parents, in order to account for leaving so suddenly. I assured her that I should not be alarmed, and overcame her scruples, and then she told me what follows.

"It appeared that she was engaged as housemaid at the Bellfry about two years before my visit there. Shortly after her arrival, her mistress being taken very unwell, her master went to sleep at the other side of the house, whilst Mary made her bed in the dressing-room, in order to be near at hand if the invalid required any assistance in the night. She had directions to keep some refreshment ready in case it was wanted, and towards two o'clock in the morning, her mistress saying she should like a little broth, Mary rose, and half drest, proceeded down stairs with a candle in her hand, to fetch some which she had left simmering on the kitchen fire. As she descended the last flight of stairs, she was a good deal startled at seeing a bright light issuing from the kitchen — the door of which was open — much brighter than could possibly proceed from the fire, for the whole passage was illuminated by it. Her first and very natural idea was that there were thieves in the house; and she was about to rush upstairs again to her master's room, when it occurred to her that one of the servants might be sitting up for some object of her own, and she stopt to listen, but there was not the least sound — all was silent. It then occurred to her that possibly something might have caught fire; so half-frightened, she advanced on tip-toe and peeped in, when, to her surprise, she saw a lady dressed in white, sitting by the fire, into which she was sadly and thoughtfully gazing. Her hands were clasped upon her knees, and two large greyhounds — beautiful dogs, said Mary — sat at her feet, both looking up fondly in her face.

Her dress seemed to be of cambric or dimity, and from Mary's description, was that worn by ladies in the seventeenth century.

"The kitchen was as bright as if illuminated by twenty candles, but this did not strike her she said, till afterwards; so quite reassured by the appearance of a lady instead of a band of robbers, it did not occur to her to question who she was or how she came there; and saying, 'I beg your pardon ma'am', she entered the kitchen, dropt a curtsey, and was going towards the fire, but as she advanced the vision retreated, till, at last, lady, chair, and dogs, glided through the closed window; and then the figure appeared standing erect in the garden, with its face close to the panes, and the eyes looking sorrowfully and earnestly on poor Mary.

"'And what did you do then, Mary?' said I.

"'Oh, ma'am, then I *fared* to feel very queer, and I fell upon the floor with a scream.'

"Her master heard the cry, and came down to see what was the matter. When she told him what she had seen, he endeavoured to persuade her it was all fancy; but Mary said she knew better than that; however, she promised not to talk of it, as it might frighten her sick mistress.

"Subsequently, she met the same melancholy apparition pacing the corridor into which the room that I had slept in opened; and not liking these rencontres she gave warning and left the place.

"She knew nothing more, for her home was at some distance from the Bellfry, which she had not since revisited: but when I had recovered my health and returned to that part of the country, I found, on enquiry, that this apparition was believed to haunt not only the house, but the neighbourhood; and I conversed with several people who affirmed they had seen her, generally alone, but sometimes accompanied by the two dogs.

"One woman said she had no fear, and that she had determined if she met the ghost, to try and touch her, in order to ascertain if it was positively an apparition; she did meet her in the dusk of the evening on the path that runs by the high road between the Bellfry and G—— and put out her arm to take hold of her dress. She felt no substance, but she described the sensation as if she had plunged her hand into cold water.

"Another person saw her go through the hedge, and he observed, that he could see the hedge through the figure as she glided into the field.

"It is whispered that this unfortunate lady was an ancestress of the original proprietor of the place, who married a man she adored, contrary to the advice of her friends; and too late she discovered that he had taken her only for her money, which was needed to repair his ruined fortunes; he, the while being deeply enamoured of her younger sister, whose portion was too small for his purpose.

"The sister came to live with the newly married couple; and suspecting nothing, the bride was some time wholly unable to account for her husband's mysterious conduct and total alienation. At length she awakened to the dreadful reality, but unable to overcome her passion, she continued to live under his roof, suffering all the tortures of jealousy and disappointed love. She shunned the world; and the world, who soon learnt the state of affairs, shunned her husband's society; so she dragged on her dreary existence with no companionship but that of two remarkable fine greyhounds, which her husband had given her before marriage. Riding or walking, she was always accompanied by these animals — they and their affection were all she could call her own on earth.

"She died young; not without some suspicions that her end was hastened — at least, passively, by neglect, if not by more active means.

"When she was gone, the husband and the sister married; but the tradition runs, that the union was anything but blest. It is said that on the wedding night, immediately after her attendant had left her, screams were heard proceeding from the bridal chamber; and that on going upstairs, the bride was found in hysterics, and the groom pale, and apparently horror-stricken. After a little while, they desired to be left alone, but in the morning it was evident that no heads had prest the pillows. They had past the night without going to bed, and the next day they left their home — she never to return. She is supposed to have gone out of her mind, and to have died abroad in that state, carefully tended by him to the last. After her decease, he returned once to the Bellfry, a prematurely aged, melancholy man; and after staying a few days, and destroying several letters and papers, to do which appeared the object of his visit, he went away, and was seen no more in that county."

Alas, for poor human nature! How we are cursed in the realisation of our own wishes! How we struggle and sin to attain what we are never to enjoy!

The Cold Embrace

Mary Elizabeth Braddon

He was an artist — such things as happened to him happen some-times to artists.

He was a German — such things as happened to him happen sometimes to Germans.

He was young, handsome, studious, enthusiastic, meta-physical, reckless, unbelieving, heartless.

And being young, handsome and eloquent, he was beloved.

He was an orphan, under the guardianship of his dead father's brother, his uncle Wilhelm, in whose house he had been brought up from a little child; and she who loved him was his cousin — his cousin Gertrude, whom he swore he loved in return.

Did he love her? Yes, when he first swore it. It soon wore out, this passionate love; how threadbare and wretched a sentiment it became at last in the selfish heart of the student! But in its golden dawn, when he was only nineteen, and had just returned from his apprenticeship to a great painter at Antwerp, and they wandered together in the most romantic outskirts of the city at rosy sunset, by holy moonlight, or bright and joyous morning, how beautiful a dream!

They keep it a secret from Wilhelm, as he has the father's ambition of a wealthy suitor for his only child — a cold and dreary vision beside the lover's dream.

So they are betrothed; and standing side by side when the dying sun and the pale rising moon divide the heavens, he puts the betrothal ring upon her finger, the white and taper finger whose slender shape he knows so well. This ring is a peculiar one, a massive golden serpent, its tail in its mouth, the symbol of eternity; it had been his mother's, and he would know it amongst a thousand. If he were to become blind tomorrow, he could select it from amongst a thousand by the touch alone.

He places it on her finger, and they swear to be true to each other for ever and ever — through trouble and danger — sorrow and change — in wealth or poverty. Her father must needs be won to consent to their union by and by, for they were now betrothed, and death alone could part them.

But the young student, the scoffer at revelation, yet the enthusiastic adorer of the mystical, asks:

"Can death part us? I would return to you from the grave, Gertrude. My soul would come back to be near my love. And you — you, if you died before me — the cold earth would not hold you from me; if you loved me, you would return, and again these fair arms would be clasped round my neck as they are now."

But she told him, with a holier light in her deep-blue eyes than had ever shone in his — she told him that the dead who die at peace with God are happy in heaven, and cannot return to the troubled earth; and that it is only the suicide — the lost wretch on whom sorrowful angels shut the door of Paradise — whose unholy spirit haunts the footsteps of the living.

The first year of their betrothal is passed, and she is alone, for he has gone to Italy, on a commission for some rich man, to copy Raphaels, Titians, Guidos, in a gallery at Florence. He has gone to win fame, perhaps; but it is not the less bitter — he is gone!

Of course her father misses his young nephew, who has been as a son to him; and he thinks his daughter's sadness no more than a cousin should feel for a cousin's absence.

In the meantime, the weeks and months pass. The lover writes — often at first, then seldom — at last, not at all.

How many excuses she invents for him! How many times she goes to the distant little post-office, to which he is to address his letters! How many times she hopes, only to be disappointed! How many times she despairs, only to hope again!

But real despair comes at last, and will not be put off any more. The rich suitor appears on the scene, and her father is determined. She is to marry at once. The wedding-day is fixed — the fifteenth of June.

The date seems to burn into her brain.

The date, written in fire, dances for ever before her eyes.

The date, shrieked by the Furies, sounds continually in her ears.

But there is time yet — it is the middle of May — there is time for a letter to reach him at Florence; there is time for him to come to Brunswick, to take her away and marry her, in spite of her father — in spite of the whole world.

But the days and the weeks fly by, and he does not write — he does not come. This is indeed despair which usurps her heart, and will not be put away.

It is the fourteenth of June. For the last time she goes to the little post-office; for the last time she asked the old question, and they give her for the last time the dreary answer, "No; no letter."

For the last time — for tomorrow is the day appointed for the bridal. Her father will hear no entreaties; her rich suitor will not listen to her prayers. They will not be put off a day — an hour; tonight alone is hers — this night, which she may employ as she will.

She takes another path than that which leads home; she hurries through some by-streets of the city, out on to a lonely bridge, where he and she had stood so often in the sunset, watching the rose-coloured light glow, fade, and die upon the river.

He returns from Florence. He had received her letter. That letter, blotted with tears, entreating, despairing — he had received it, but he loved her no longer. A young Florentine, who has sat to him for a model, had bewitched his fancy — that fancy which with him stood in place of a heart — and Gertrude had been half-forgotten. If she had a rich suitor, good; let her marry him; better for her, better far for himself. He had no wish to fetter himself with a wife. Had he not his art always? — his eternal bride, his unchanging mistress.

Thus he thought it wiser to delay his journey to Brunswick, so that he should arrive when the wedding was over — arrive in time to salute the bride.

And the vows — the mystical fancies — the belief in his return, even after death, to the embrace of his beloved? O, gone out of his life; melted away for ever, those foolish dreams of his boyhood.

68

So on the fifteenth of June he enters Brunswick, by that very bridge on which she stood, the stars looking down on her, the night before. He strolls across the bridge and down by the water's edge, a great rough dog at his heels, and the smoke from his short meerschaum-pipe curling in blue wreaths fantastically in the pure morning air. He has his sketch-book under his arm, and attracted now and then by some object that catches his artist's eye, stops to draw: a few weeds and pebbles on the river's brink — a crag on the opposite shore — a group of pollard willows in the distance. When he has done, he admires his drawing, shuts his sketch-book, empties the ashes from his pipe, refills from his tobacco-pouch, sings the refrain of a gay drinking-song, calls to his dog, smokes again, and walks on. Suddenly he opens his sketch-book again; this time that which attracts him is a group of figures: but what is it?

It is not a funeral, for there are no mourners.

It is not a funeral, but a corpse lying on a rude bier, covered with an old sail, carried between two bearers.

It is not a funeral, for the bearers are fishermen — fishermen in their everyday garb.

About a hundred yards from him they rest their burden on a bank — one stands at the head of the bier, the other throws himself down at the foot of it.

And thus they form the perfect group; he walks back two or three paces, selects his point of sight, and begins to sketch a hurried outline. He has finished it before they move; he hears their voices, though he cannot hear their words, and wonders what they can be talking of. Presently he walks on and joins them.

"You have a corpse there, my friends?" he says.

"Yes; a corpse washed ashore an hour ago."

"Drowned?"

"Yes, drowned. A young girl, very handsome."

"Suicides are always handsome," says the painter; and then he stands for a little while idly smoking and meditating, looking at the sharp outline of the corpse and the stiff folds of the rough canvas covering.

Life is such a golden holiday for him — young, ambitious, clever — that it seems as though sorrow and death could have no part in his destiny.

At last he says that, as this poor suicide is so handsome, he should like to make a sketch of her.

He gives the fishermen some money, and they offer to remove the sailcloth that covers her features.

No; he will do it himself. He lifts the rough, coarse, wet canvas from her face. What face?

The face that shone on the dreams of his foolish boyhood; the face which once was the light of his uncle's home. His cousin Gertrude — his betrothed!

He sees, as in one glance, while he draws one breath, the rigid features — the marble arms — the hands crossed on the cold bosom; and, on the third finger of the left hand, the ring which had been his mother's — the golden serpent; the ring which, if he were to become blind, he could select from a thousand others by the touch alone.

But he is a genius and a metaphysician — grief, true grief, is not for such as he. His first thought is flight — flight anywhere out of that accursed city — anywhere far from the brink of that hideous river — anywhere away from remorse — anywhere to forget.

He is miles on the road that leads away from Brunswick before he knows that he has walked a step.

It is only when his dog lies down panting at his feet that he feels how exhausted he is himself, and sits down upon a bank to rest. How the landscape spins round and round before his dazzled eyes, while his morning's sketch of the two fishermen and the canvas-covered bier glares redly at him out of the twilight.

At last, after sitting a long time by the roadside, idly playing with his dog, idly smoking, idly lounging, looking as any idle, light-hearted travelling student might look, yet all the while acting over that morning's scene in his burning brain a hundred times a minute; at last he grows a little more composed, and tries presently to think of himself as he is, apart from his cousin's suicide. Apart from that, he was no worse off than he was yesterday. His genius was not gone; the money he had earned at Florence still lined his pocket-book; he was his own master, free to go whither he would.

And while he sits on the roadside, trying to separate himself from the scene of that morning — trying to put away the image of the corpse covered with the damp canvas sail — trying to think of what he should do next, where he should go, to be farthest away from Brunswick and remorse, the old diligence coming rumbling and jingling along. He remembers it; it goes from Brunswick to Aix-la-Chapelle.

He whistles to the dog, shouts to the postillion to stop, and springs into the *coupé*.

During the whole evening, through the long night, though he does not once close his eyes, he never speaks a word; but when morning dawns, and the other passengers awake and begin to talk to each other, he joins in the conversation. He tells them that he is an artist, that he is going to Cologne and to Antwerp to copy Rubenses, and the great picture by Quentin Matsys, in the museum. He remembered afterwards that he talked and laughed boisterously, and that when he was talking and laughing loudest, a passenger, older and graver than the rest, opened the window near him, and told him to put his head out. He remembered the fresh air blowing in his face, the singing of the birds in his ears, and the flat fields and roadside reeling before his eyes. He remembered this, and then falling in a lifeless heap on the floor of the diligence.

It is a fever that keeps him for six long weeks on a bed at a hotel in Aix-la-Chapelle.

He gets well, and, accompanied by his dog, starts on foot for Cologne. By this time he is his former self once more. Again the blue smoke from his short meerschaum curls upwards in the morning air — again he sings some old university drinking song — again stops here and there, meditating and sketching.

He is happy, and has forgotten his cousin — and so on to Cologne.

It is by the great cathedral he is standing, with his dog at his side. It is night, the bells have just chimed the hour, and the clocks are striking eleven; the moonlight shines full upon the magnificent pile, over which the artist's eye wanders, absorbed in the beauty of form.

He is not thinking of his drowned cousin, for he has forgotten her and is happy.

Suddenly someone, something from behind him, puts two cold arms round his neck, and clasps its hands on his breast.

And yet there is no one behind him, for on the flags bathed in the broad moonlight there are only two shadows, his own and his dog's. He turns quickly round — there is no one — nothing to be seen in the broad square but himself and his dog; and though he feels, he cannot see the cold arms clasped round his neck.

It is not ghostly, this embrace, for it is palpable to the touch — it cannot be real, for it is invisible.

He tries to throw off the cold caress. He clasps the hands in his own to tear them asunder, and to cast them off his neck. He can feel the long delicate fingers cold and wet beneath his touch, and on the third finger of the left hand he can feel the ring which was his mother's — the golden serpent — the ring which he has always said he would know among a thousand by the touch alone. He knows it now!

His dead cousin's cold arms are round his neck — his dead cousin's wet hands are clasped upon his breast. He asks himself if he is mad. "Up, Leo!" he shouts. "Up, up, boy!" and the Newfoundland leaps to his shoulders — the dog's paws are on the dead hands, and the animal utters a terrific howl, and springs away from his master.

The student stands in the moonlight, the dead arms around his neck, and the dog at a little distance moaning piteously.

Presently a watchman, alarmed by the howling of the dog, comes into the square to see what is wrong.

In a breath the cold arms are gone.

He takes the watchman home to the hotel with him and gives him money; in his gratitude he could have given the man half his little fortune.

Will it ever come to him again, this embrace of the dead?

He tries never to be alone; he makes a hundred acquaintances, and shares the chamber of another student. He starts up if he is left by himself in the public room of the inn where he is staying, and runs into the street. People notice his strange actions, and begin to think that he is mad.

But, in spite of all, he is alone once more; for one night the public room being empty for a moment, when on some idle pretence he strolls into the street, the street is empty too, and for the second time he feels the cold arms round his neck, and for the second time, when he calls his dog, the animal shrinks away from him with a piteous howl.

After this he leaves Cologne, still travelling on foot — of necessity now, for his money is getting low. He joins travelling hawkers, he walks side by side with labourers, he talks to every foot-passenger he falls in with, and tries from morning till night to get company on the road.

At night he sleeps by the fire in the kitchen of the inn at which he stops; but do what he will, he is often alone, and it is now a common thing for him to feel the cold arms around his neck.

Many months have passed since his cousin's death — autumn, winter, early spring. His money is nearly gone, his health is utterly broken, he is the shadow of his former self, and he is getting near to Paris. He will reach that city at the time of the Carnival. To this he looks forward. In Paris, in Carnival time, he need never, surely, be alone, never feel that deadly caress; he may even recover his lost gaiety, his lost health, once more resume his profession, once more earn fame and money by his art.

How hard he tries to get over the distance that divides him from Paris, while day by day he grows weaker, and his step slower and more heavy!

But there is an end at last; the long dreary roads are passed. This is Paris, which he enters for the first time — Paris, of which he has dreamed so much — Paris, whose million voices are to exorcise his phantom.

To him tonight Paris seems one vast chaos of lights, music, and confusion — lights which dance before his eyes and will not be still — music that rings in his ears and deafens him — confusion which makes his head whirl round and round.

But, in spite of all, he finds the opera-house, where there is a masked ball. He has enough money left to buy a ticket of admission, and to hire a domino to throw over his shabby dress. It seems only a moment after his entering the gates of Paris that he is in the very midst of all the wild gaiety of the opera-house ball.

No more darkness, no more loneliness, but a mad crowd, shouting and dancing, and a lovely Débardeuse hanging on his arm.

The boisterous gaiety he feels surely is his old light-heartedness come back. He hears the people round him talking of the outrageous conduct of some drunken student, and it is to him they point when they say this — to him, who has not moistened his lips since yesterday at noon, for even now he will not drink; though his lips are parched, and his throat burning, he cannot drink. His voice is thick and hoarse, and his utterance indistinct; but still this must be his old light-heartedness come back that makes him so wildly gay.

The little Débardeuse is wearied out — her arm rests on his shoulder heavier than lead — the other dancers one by one drop off.

The lights in the chandeliers one by one die out.

The decorations look pale and shadowy in that dim light which is neither night nor day.

A faint glimmer from the dying lamps, a pale streak of cold grey light from the new-born day, creeping in through half-opened shutters.

And by this light the bright-eyed Débardeuse fades sadly. He looks her in the face. How the brightness of her eyes dies out! Again he looks her in the face. How white that face has grown! Again — and now it is the shadow of a face alone that looks in his.

Again — and they are gone — the bright eyes, the face, the shadow of the face. He is alone; alone in that vast saloon.

Alone, and, in the terrible silence, he hears the echoes of his own footsteps in that dismal dance which has no music.

No music but the beating of his breast. The cold arms are round his neck — they whirl him round, they will not be flung off, or cast away; he can no more escape from their icy grasp than he can escape from death. He looks behind him — there is nothing but himself in the great empty *salle*; but he can feel —

cold, deathlike, but O, how palpable! — the long slender fingers, and the ring which was his mother's.

He tries to shout, but he has no power in his burning throat. The silence of the place is only broken by the echoes of his own footsteps in the dance from which he cannot extricate himself. Who says he has no partner? The cold hands are clasped on his breast, and now he does not shun their caress. No! One more polka, if he drops down dead.

The lights are all out, and, half an hour after, the *gendarmes* come in with a lantern to see that the house is empty; they are followed by a great dog that they have found seated howling on the steps of the theatre. Near the principal entrance they stumble over —

The body of a student, who has died from want of food, exhaustion, and the breaking of a blood-vessel.

How the Third Floor Knew the Potteries
(a.k.a. "Number Three")

Amelia B. Edwards

I am a plain man, Major, and you may not dislike to hear a plain statement of facts from me.

Some of those facts lie beyond my understanding. I do not pretend to explain them. I only know that they happened as I relate them, and that I pledge myself for the truth of every word of them.

I began life roughly enough, down among the Potteries. I was an orphan; and my earliest recollections are of a great porcelain manufactory in the country of the Potteries, where I helped about the yard, picked up what halfpence fell in my way, and slept in a harness-loft over the stable. Those were hard times; but things bettered themselves as I grew older and stronger, especially after George Barnard had come to be foreman of the yard.

George Barnard was a Wesleyan — we were mostly dissenters in the Potteries — sober, clear-headed, somewhat sulky and silent, but a good fellow every inch of him, and my best friend at the time when I most needed a good friend. He took me out of the yard, and set me to the furnace-work. He entered me on the books at a fixed rate of wages. He helped me to pay for a little cheap schooling four nights a week; and he led me to go with him on Sundays to the chapel down by the river-side, where I first saw Leah Payne. She was his sweetheart, and so pretty that I used to forget the preacher and everybody else, when I looked at her. When she joined in the singing, I heard no voice but hers. If she asked me for the hymn-book, I used to blush and tremble. I believe I worshipped her, in my stupid ignorant way; and I think I worshipped Barnard almost as blindly, though after a different fashion. I felt I owed him everything. I knew that he had saved me, body and mind; and I looked up to him as a savage might look up to a missionary.

Leah was the daughter of a plumber, who lived close by the chapel. She was twenty, and George about seven or eight-and-thirty. Some captious folks said there was too much difference in their ages; but she was so serious-minded, and they loved each other so earnestly and quietly, that, if nothing had come between them during their courtship, I don't believe the question of disparity would ever have troubled the happiness of their married lives. Something did come, however; and that something was a Frenchman, called Louis Laroche. He was a painter on porcelain, from the famous works at Sèvres; and our master, it was said, had engaged him for three years certain, at such wages as none of our own people, however skilful, could hope to command. It was about the beginning or middle of September when he first came among us. He looked very young; was small, dark, and well made; had little white soft hands, and a silky moustache; and spoke English nearly as well as I do. None of us liked him; but that was only natural, seeing how he was put over the head of every Englishman in the place. Besides, though he was always smiling and civil, we couldn't help seeing that he thought himself ever so much better than the rest of us; and that was not pleasant. Neither was it pleasant to see him strolling about the town, dressed just like a gentleman, when working hours were over; smoking good cigars, when we were forced to be content with a pipe of common tobacco; hiring a horse on Sunday afternoons, when we were trudging a-foot; and taking his pleasure as if the world was made for him to enjoy, and us to work in.

"Ben, boy," said George, "there's something wrong about that Frenchman."

It was on a Saturday afternoon, and we were sitting on a pile of empty seggars against the door of my furnace-room, waiting till the men should all have cleared out of the yard. Seggars are deep earthen boxes in which the pottery is put, while being fired in the kiln. I looked up, inquiringly.

"About the Count?" said I, for that was the nickname by which he went in the pottery.

George nodded, and paused for a moment with his chin resting on his palms.

"He has an evil eye," said he; "and a false smile. Something wrong about him."

I drew nearer, and listened to George as if he had been an oracle. "Besides," added he, in his slow quiet way, with his eyes fixed straight before him as if he was thinking aloud, "there's a young look about him that isn't natural. Take him just at sight, and you'd think he was almost a boy; but look close at him — see the little fine wrinkles under his eyes, and the hard lines about his mouth, and then tell me his age, if you can! Why, Ben boy, he's as old as I am, pretty near; ay, and as strong, too. You stare; but I tell you that, slight as he looks, he could fling you over his shoulder as if you were a feather. And as for his hands, little and white as they are, there are muscles of iron inside them, take my word for it."

"But, George, how can you know?"

"Because I have a warning against him," replied George, very gravely. "Because, whenever he is by, I feel as if my eyes saw clearer, and my ears heard keener, than at other times. Maybe it's presumption, but I sometimes feel as if I had a call to guard myself and others against him. Look at the children, Ben, how they shrink away from him; and see there, now! Ask Captain what he thinks of him! Ben, that dog likes him no better than I do."

I looked, and saw Captain crouching by his kennel with his ears laid back, growling audibly, as the Frenchman came slowly down the steps leading from his own workshop at the upper end of the yard. On the last step he paused; lighted a cigar; glanced round, as if to see whether anyone was by; and then walked straight over to within a couple of yards of the kennel. Captain gave a short angry snarl, and laid his muzzle close down upon his paws, ready for a spring. The Frenchman folded his arms deliberately, fixed his eyes on the dog, and stood calmly smoking.

He knew exactly how far he dared go, and kept just that one foot out of harm's way. All at once he stooped, puffed a mouthful of smoke in the dog's eyes, burst into a mocking laugh, turned lightly on his heel, and walked away; leaving Captain straining at his chain, and barking after him like a mad creature.

Days went by, and I, at work in my own department, saw no more of the Count. Sunday came — the third, I think, after I had talked with George in the yard. Going with George to chapel, as usual, in the morning, I noticed that there was something strange and anxious in his face, and that he scarcely opened his lips to me on the way. Still I said nothing. It was not my place to question him; and I remember thinking to myself that the cloud would all clear off as soon as he found himself by Leah's side, holding the same book, and joining in the same hymn.

It did not, however, for no Leah was there. I looked every moment to the door, expecting to see her sweet face coming in; but George never lifted his eyes from his book, or seemed to notice that her place was empty. Thus the whole service went by, and my thoughts wandered continually from the words of the preacher. As soon as the last blessing was spoken, and we were fairly across the threshold, I turned to George, and asked if Leah was ill?

"No," said he, gloomily. "She's not ill."

"Then why wasn't she —?"

"I'll tell you why," he interrupted, impatiently. "Because you've seen her here for the last time. She's never coming to chapel again."

"Never coming to the chapel again?" I faltered, laying my hand on his sleeve in the earnestness of my surprise. "Why, George, what is the matter?"

But he shook my hand off, and stamped with his iron heel till the pavement rang again.

"Don't ask me," said he, roughly. "Let me alone. You'll know soon enough."

And with this he turned off down a by-lane leading towards the hills, and left me without another word.

I had had plenty of hard treatment in my time; but never, until that moment, an angry look or syllable from George. I did not know how to bear it. That day my dinner seemed as if it would choke me; and in the afternoon I went out and wandered restlessly about the fields till the hour for evening prayers came round. I then returned to the chapel, and sat down on a tomb outside, waiting for George. I saw the congregation go in by twos and threes; I heard the first psalm-tune echo solemnly through the evening stillness; but no George came. Then the service began, and I knew that, punctual as his habits were, it was of no use to expect him any longer. Where could he be? What could have happened? Why should Leah Payne never come to chapel again? Had she gone over to some other sect, and was that why George seemed so unhappy?

Sitting there in the little dreary churchyard with the darkness fast gathering around me, I asked myself these questions over and over again, till my brain ached; for I was not much used to thinking about anything in those times. At last, I could bear to sit quiet no longer. The sudden thought struck me that I would go to Leah, and learn what the matter was, from her own lips. I sprang to my feet, and set off at once towards her home.

It was quite dark, and a light rain was beginning to fall. I found the garden-gate open, and a quick hope flashed across me that George might be there. I drew back for a moment, hesitating whether to knock or ring, when a sound of voices in the passage, and the sudden gleaming of a bright line of light under the door, warned me that someone was coming out. Taken by surprise, and quite unprepared for the moment with anything to say, I shrank back behind the porch, and waited until those within should have passed out. The door opened, and the light streamed suddenly upon the roses and the wet gravel.

"It rains," said Leah, bending forward and shading the candle with her hand.

"And is as cold as Siberia," added another voice, which was not George's, and yet sounded strangely familiar. "Ugh! what a climate for such a flower as my darling to bloom in!"

"Is it so much finer in France?" asked Leah, softly.

"As much finer as blue skies and sunshine can make it. Why, my angel, even your bright eyes will be ten times brighter, and your rosy cheeks ten times rosier, when they are transplanted to Paris. Ah! I can give you no idea of the wonders of Paris — the broad streets planted with trees, the palaces, the shops, the gardens! — it is a city of enchantment."

"It must be, indeed!" said Leah. "And you will really take me to see all those beautiful shops?"

"Every Sunday, my darling — Bah! don't look so shocked. The shops in Paris are always open on Sunday, and everybody makes holiday. You will soon get over these prejudices."

"I fear it is very wrong to take so much pleasure in the things of this world," sighed Leah.

The Frenchman laughed, and answered her with a kiss.

"Good night, my sweet little saint!" and he ran lightly down the path, and disappeared in the darkness. Leah sighed again, lingered a moment, and then closed the door.

Stupefied and bewildered, I stood for some seconds like a stone statue, unable to move; scarcely able to think. At length, I roused myself, as it were mechanically, and went towards the gate. At that instant a heavy hand was laid upon my shoulder, and a hoarse voice close beside my ear, said:

"Who are you? What are you doing here?"

It was George. I knew him at once, in spite of the darkness, and stammered his name. He took his hand quickly from my shoulder.

"How long have you been here?" said he, fiercely. "What right have you to lurk about, like a spy in the dark? God help me, Ben — I'm half mad. I don't mean to be harsh to you."

"I'm sure you don't," I cried, earnestly.

"It's that cursed Frenchman," he went on, in a voice that sounded like the groan of one in pain.

"He's a villain. I know he's a villain; and I've had a warning against him ever since the first moment he came among us. He'll make her miserable, and break her heart someday — my pretty Leah — and I loved her so! But I'll be revenged — as sure as there's a sun in heaven, I'll be revenged!"

His vehemence terrified me. I tried to persuade him to go home; but he would not listen to me.

"No, no," he said. "Go home yourself, boy, and let me be. My blood is on fire: this rain is good for me, and I am better alone."

"If I could only do something to help you —"

"You can't," interrupted he. "Nobody can help me. I'm a ruined man, and I don't care what becomes of me. The Lord forgive me! my heart is full of wickedness, and my thoughts are the promptings of Satan. There go — for Heaven's sake, go. I don't know what I say, or what I do!"

I went, for I did not dare refuse any longer; but I lingered a while at the corner of the street, and watched him pacing to and fro, to and fro in the driving rain. At length I turned reluctantly away, and went home.

I lay awake that night for hours, thinking over the events of the day, and hating the Frenchman from my very soul. I could not hate Leah. I had worshipped her too long and too faithfully for that; but I looked upon her as a creature given over to destruction. I fell asleep towards morning, and woke again shortly after daybreak. When I reached the pottery, I found George there before me, looking very pale, but quite himself, and setting the men to their work the same as usual. I said nothing about what had happened the day before. Something in his face silenced me; but seeing him so steady and composed, I took heart, and began to hope he had fought through the worst of his trouble. By-and-by the Frenchman came through the yard, gay and off-hand, with his cigar in his mouth, and his hands in his pockets. George turned sharply away into one of the workshops, and shut the door. I drew a deep breath of relief. My dread was to see them come to an open quarrel; and I felt that as long as they kept clear of that, all would be well.

Thus the Monday went by, and the Tuesday; and still George kept aloof from me. I had sense enough not to be hurt by this. I felt he had a good right to be silent, if silence helped him to bear his trial better; and I made up my mind never to breathe another syllable on the subject, unless he began.

Wednesday came. I had overslept myself that morning, and came to work a quarter after the hour, expecting to be fined; for George was very strict as foreman of the yard, and treated friends and enemies just the same. Instead of blaming me, however, he called me up, and said:

"Ben, whose turn is it this week to sit up?"

"Mine, sir," I replied. (I always called him "Sir" in working hours.)

"Well, then, you may go home today, and the same on Thursday and Friday; for there's a large batch of work for the ovens tonight, and there'll be the same tomorrow night and the night after."

"All right, sir," said I. "Then I'll be here by seven this evening."

"No, half-past nine will be soon enough. I've some accounts to make up, and I shall be here myself till then. Mind you are true to time, though."

"I'll be as true as the clock, sir," I replied, and was turning away when he called me back again.

"You're a good lad, Ben," said he. "Shake hands."

I seized his hand, and pressed it warmly.

"If I'm good for anything, George," I answered with all my heart, "it's you who have made me so. God bless you for it!"

"Amen!" said he, in a troubled voice, putting his hand to his hat.

And so we parted.

In general, I went to bed by day when I was attending to the firing by night; but this morning I had already slept longer than usual, and wanted exercise more than rest. So I ran home; put a bit of bread and meat in my pocket; snatched up my big thorn stick; and started off for a long day in the country. When I came home, it was quite dark and beginning to rain, just as it had begun to rain at about the same time that wretched Sunday evening: so I changed my wet boots, had an early supper and a nap in the chimney-corner, and went down to the works at a few minutes before half-past nine. Arriving at the factory-gate, I found it ajar, and so walked in and closed it after me. I remember thinking at the time that it was unlike George's usual caution to leave it so; but it passed from my mind next moment. Having slipped in the bolt, I then went straight over to George's little counting-house, where the gas was shining cheerfully in the window. Here also, somewhat to my surprise, I found the door open, and the room empty. I went in. The threshold and part of the floor was wetted by the driving rain. The wages-book was open on the desk, George's pen stood in the ink, and his hat hung on its usual peg in the corner. I concluded, of course, that he had gone round to the ovens; so, following him, I took down his hat and carried it with me, for it was now raining fast.

The baking-houses lay just opposite, on the other side of the yard. There were three of them, opening one out of the other; and in each, the great furnace filled all the middle of the room.

These furnaces are, in fact, large kilns built of brick, with an oven closed in by an iron door in the centre of each, and a chimney going up through the roof. The pottery, enclosed in seggars, stands round inside on shelves, and has to be turned from time to time while the firing is going on. To turn these seggars, test the heat, and keep the fires up, was my work at the period of which I am now telling you, Major.

Well! I went through the baking-houses one after the other, and found all empty alike. Then a strange, vague, uneasy feeling came over me, and I began to wonder what could have become of George. It was possible that he might be in one of the workshops; so I ran over to the counting-house, lighted a lantern, and made a thorough survey of the yards. I tried the doors; they were all locked as usual. I peeped into the open sheds; they were all vacant. I called "George! George!" in every part of the outer premises; but the wind and rain drove back my voice, and no other voice replied to it. Forced at last to believe that he was really gone, I took his hat back to the counting-house, put away the wages-book, extinguished the gas, and prepared for my solitary watch.

The night was mild, and the heat in the baking-rooms intense. I knew, by experience, that the ovens had been overheated, and that none of the porcelain must go in at least for the next two hours; so I carried my stool to the door, settled myself in a sheltered corner where the air could reach me, but not the rain, and fell to wondering where George could have gone, and why he should not have waited till the time appointed. That he had left in haste was clear — not because his hat remained behind, for he might have had a cap with him — but because he had left the book open, and the gas lighted. Perhaps one of the workmen had met with some accident, and he had been summoned away so urgently that he had no time to think of anything; perhaps he would even now come back presently to see that all was right before he went home to his lodgings.

Turning these things over in my mind, I grew drowsy, my thoughts wandered, and I fell asleep.

I cannot tell how long my nap lasted. I had walked a great distance that day, and I slept heavily but I awoke all in a moment, with a sort of terror upon me, and, looking up, saw

George Barnard sitting on a stool before the oven door, with the firelight full upon his face.

Ashamed to be found sleeping, I started to my feet. At the same instant, he rose, turned away without even looking towards me, and went out into the next room.

"Don't be angry, George!" I cried, following him. "None of the seggars are in. I knew the fires were too strong, and —"

The words died on my lips. I had followed him from the first room to the second, from the second to the third, and in the third — I lost him!

I could not believe my eyes. I opened the end door leading into the yard, and looked out; but he was nowhere in sight. I went round to the back of the baking-house, looked behind the furnaces, ran over to the counting-house, called him by his name over and over again; but all was dark, silent, lonely, as ever.

Then I remembered how I had bolted the outer gate, and how impossible it was that he should have come in without ringing. Then, too, I began again to doubt the evidence of my own senses, and to think I must have been dreaming.

I went back to my old post by the door of the first baking-house, and sat down for a moment to collect my thoughts.

"In the first place," said I to myself, "there is but one outer gate. That outer gate I bolted on the inside, and it is bolted still. In the next place, I searched the premises, and found all the sheds empty, and the workshop-doors padlocked as usual on the outside. I proved that George was nowhere about, when I came, and I know he could not have come in since, without my knowledge. Therefore it is a dream. It is certainly a dream, and there's an end of it."

And with this I trimmed my lantern and proceeded to test the temperature of the furnaces. We used to do this, I should tell you, by the introduction of little roughly-moulded lumps of common fire-clay. If the heat is too great, they crack; if too little, they remain damp and moist; if just right, they become firm and smooth all over, and pass into the biscuit stage. Well! I took my three little lumps of clay, put one in each oven, waited while I counted five hundred, and then went round again to see the results. The two first were in capital condition, the third had flown into a dozen pieces. This proved that the seggars might at once go into ovens One and Two, but that number Three had been overheated, and must be allowed to go on cooling for an hour or two longer.

I therefore stocked One and Two with nine rows of seggars, three deep on each shelf; left the rest waiting till number Three was in a condition to be trusted; and, fearful of falling asleep again, now that the firing was in progress, walked up and down the rooms to keep myself awake.

This was hot work, however, and I could not stand it very long; so I went back presently to my stool by the door, and fell to thinking about my dream. The more I thought of it, the more strangely real it seemed, and the more I felt convinced that I was actually on my feet, when I saw George get up and walk into the adjoining room. I was also certain that I had still continued to see him as he passed out of the second room into the third, and that at that time I was even following his very footsteps. Was it possible, I asked myself, that I could have been up and moving, and yet not quite awake? I had heard of people walking in their sleep. Could it be that I was walking in mine, and never waked till I reached the cool air of the yard? All this seemed likely enough, so I dismissed the matter from my mind, and passed the rest of the night in attending to the seggars, adding fresh fuel from time to time to the furnaces of the first and second ovens, and now and then taking a turn through the yards. As for number Three, it kept up its heat to such a degree that it was almost day before I dared trust the seggars to go in it.

Thus the hours went by; and at half-past seven on Thursday morning, the men came to their work. It was now my turn to go off duty, but I wanted to see George before I left, and so waited for him in the counting-house, while a lad named Steve Storr took my place at the ovens. But the clock went on from half-past seven to a quarter to eight; then to eight o'clock; then to a quarter-past eight — and still George never made his appearance. At length, when the hand got round to half-past eight, I grew weary of waiting, took up my hat, ran home, went to bed, and slept profoundly until past four in the afternoon.

That evening I went down to the factory quite early; for I had a restlessness upon me, and I wanted to see George before he left for the night. This time, I found the gate bolted, and I rang for admittance.

"How early you are, Ben!" said Steve Storr, as he let me in.

"Mr. Barnard's not gone?" I asked, quickly; for I saw at the first glance that the gas was out in the counting-house.

"He's not gone," said Steve, "because he's never been."

"Never been?"

"No: and what's stranger still, he's not been home either, since dinner yesterday."

"But he was here last night."

"Oh yes, he was here last night, making up the books. John Parker was with him till past six; and you found him here, didn't you, at half-past nine?"

I shook my head.

"Well, he's gone, anyhow. Good night!"

"Good night!"

I took the lantern from his hand, bolted him out mechanically, and made my way to the baking-houses like one in a stupor. George gone? Gone without a word of warning to his employer, or of farewell to his fellow-workmen? I could not understand it. I could not believe it. I sat down bewildered, incredulous, stunned. Then came hot tears, doubts, terrifying suspicions. I remembered the wild words he had spoken a few nights back; the strange calm by which they were followed; my dream of the evening before. I had heard of men who drowned themselves for love; and the turbid Severn ran close by — so close, that one might pitch a stone into it from some of the workshop windows.

These thoughts were too horrible. I dared not dwell upon them. I turned to work, to free myself from them, if I could; and began by examining the ovens. The temperature of all was much higher than on the previous night, the heat having been gradually increased during the last twelve hours. It was now my business to keep the heat on the increase for twelve more; after which it would be allowed, as gradually, to subside, until the pottery was cool enough for removal. To turn the seggars, and add fuel to the two first furnaces, was my first work. As before, I found number Three in advance of the others, and so left it for half an hour, or an hour. I then went round the yard; tried the doors; let the dog loose; and brought him back with me to the baking-houses, for company. After that, I set my lantern on a shelf beside the door, took a book from my pocket, and began to read.

I remember the title of the book as well as possible. It was called *Bowlker's Art of Angling*, and contained little rude cuts of all kinds of artificial flies, hooks, and other tackle. But I could not keep my mind to it for two minutes together; and at last I gave it up in despair, covered my face with my hands, and fell into a long absorbing painful train of thought. A considerable time had gone by thus — maybe an hour — when I was roused by a low whimpering howl from Captain, who was lying at my feet. I looked up with a start, just as I had started from sleep the night before, and with the same vague terror; and saw, exactly in the same place and in the same attitude, with the firelight full upon him — George Barnard!

At this sight, a fear heavier than the fear of death fell upon me, and my tongue seemed paralysed in my mouth. Then, just as last night, he rose, or seemed to rise, and went slowly out into the next room. A power stronger than myself appeared to compel me, reluctantly, to follow him. I saw him pass through the second room — cross the threshold of the third room — walk straight up to the oven — and there pause. He then turned, for the first time, with the glare of the red firelight pouring out upon him from the open door of the furnace, and looked at me, face to face. In the same instant, his whole frame and countenance seemed to glow and become transparent, as if the fire were all within him and around him — and in that glow he became, as it were, absorbed into the furnace, and disappeared! I uttered a wild cry, tried to stagger from the room, and fell insensible before I reached the door.

When I next opened my eyes, the grey dawn was in the sky; the furnace-doors were all closed as I had left them when I last went round; the dog was quietly sleeping not far from my side; and the men were ringing at the gate, to be let in.

I told my tale from beginning to end, and was laughed at, as a matter of course, by all who heard it. When it was found, however, that my statements never varied, and, above all, that George Barnard continued absent, some few began to talk it over seriously, and among those few, the master of the works.

He forbade the furnace to be cleared out, called in the aid of a celebrated naturalist, and had the ashes submitted to a scientific examination. The result was as follows:

The ashes were found to have been largely saturated with some kind of fatty animal matter. A considerable portion of those ashes consisted of charred bone. A semi-circular piece of iron, which evidently had once been the heel of a workman's heavy boot, was found, half fused, at one corner of the furnace. Near it, a tibia bone, which still retained sufficient of its original form and texture to render identification possible. This bone, however, was so much charred, that it fell into powder on being handled.

After this, not many doubted that George Barnard had been foully murdered, and that his body had been thrust into the furnace. Suspicion fell upon Louis Laroche. He was arrested, a coroner's inquest was held, and every circumstance connected with the night of the murder was as thoroughly sifted and investigated as possible. All the sifting in the world, however, failed either to clear or to condemn Louis Laroche. On the very night of his release, he left the place by the mail-train, and was never seen or heard of there, again. As for Leah, I know not what became of her. I went away myself before many weeks were over, and never have set foot among the Potteries from that hour to this.

The Haunted Organist of Hurly Burly

Rosa Mulholland

There had been a thunderstorm in the village of Hurly Burly. Every door was shut, every dog in his kennel, every rut and gutter a flowing river after the deluge of rain that had fallen. Up at the great house, a mile from the town, the rooks were calling to one another about the fright they had been in, the fawns in the deer-park were venturing their timid heads from behind the trunks of trees, and the old woman at the gate-lodge had risen from her knees, and was putting back her prayer-book on the shelf. In the garden, July roses, unwieldy with their full-blown richness, and saturated with rain, hung their heads heavily to the earth; others, already fallen, lay flat upon their blooming faces on the path, where Bess, Mistress Hurly's maid, would find them, when going on her morning quest of rose-leaves for her lady's pot-pourri. Ranks of white lilies, just brought to perfection by today's sun, lay dabbled in the mire of flooded mould. Tears ran down the amber cheeks of the plums on the south wall, and not a bee had ventured out of the hives, though the scent of the air was sweet enough to tempt the laziest drone. The sky was still lurid behind the boles of the upland oaks, but the birds had begun to dive in and out of the ivy that wrapped up the home of the Hurlys of Hurly Burly.

This thunderstorm took place more than half a century ago, and we must remember that Mistress Hurly was dressed in the fashion of that time as she crept out from behind the squire's chair, now that the lightning was over, and, with many nervous glances towards the window, sat down before her husband, the tea-urn, and the muffins. We can picture her fine lace cap, with its peachy ribbons, the frill on the hem of her cambric gown just touching her ankles, the embroidered clocks on her stockings, the rosettes on her shoes, but not so easily the lilac shade of her mild eyes, the satin skin, which still kept its delicate bloom, though wrinkled with advancing age, and the pale, sweet, puckered mouth, that time and sorrow had made angelic while trying vainly to deface its beauty.

The squire was as rugged as his wife was gentle, his skin as brown as hers was white, his grey hair as bristling as hers was glossed; the years had ploughed his face into ruts and channels; a bluff, choleric, noisy man he had been; but of late a dimness had come on his eyes, a hush on his loud voice, and a check on the spring of his hale step. He looked at his wife often, and very often she looked at him. She was not a tall woman, and he was only a head higher. They were a quaintly well-matched couple, despite their differences. She turned to you with nervous sharpness and revealed her tender voice and eye; he spoke and glanced roughly, but the turn of his head was courteous. Of late they fitted one another better than they had ever done in the heyday of their youthful love. A common sorrow had developed a singular likeness between them. In former years the cry from the wife had been, "Don't curb my son too much!" and from the husband, "You ruin the lad with softness." But now the idol that had stood between them was removed, and they saw each other better.

The room in which they sat was a pleasant old-fashioned drawing-room, with a general spider-legged character about the fittings; spinnet and guitar in their places, with a great deal of copied music beside them; carpet, tawny wreaths on the pale blue; blue flutings on the walls, and faint gilding on the furniture. A huge urn, crammed with roses, in the open bay-window, through which came delicious airs from the garden, the twittering of birds settling to sleep in the ivy close by, and occasionally the pattering of a flight of rain-drops, swept to the ground as a bough bent in the breeze. The urn on the table was ancient silver, and the china rare. There was nothing in the room for luxurious ease of the body, but everything of delicate refinement for the eye.

There was a great hush all over Hurly Burly, except in the neighbourhood of the rooks. Every living thing had suffered from heat for the past month, and now, in common with all Nature, was receiving the boon of refreshed air in silent peace. The mistress and master of Hurly Burly shared the general spirit that was abroad, and were not talkative over their tea.

"Do you know," said Mistress Hurly, at last, "when I heard the first of the thunder beginning I thought it was — it was —"

The lady broke down, her lips trembling, and the peachy ribbons of her cap stirring with great agitation.

"Pshaw!" cried the old squire, making his cup suddenly ring upon the saucer, "we ought to have forgotten that. Nothing has been heard for three months."

At this moment a rolling sound struck upon the ears of both. The lady rose from her seat trembling, and folded her hands together, while the tea-urn flooded the tray.

"Nonsense, my love," said the squire; "that is the noise of wheels. Who can be arriving?"

"Who, indeed?" murmured the lady, reseating herself in agitation.

Presently pretty Bess of the rose-leaves appeared at the door in a flutter of blue ribbons.

"Please, madam, a lady has arrived, and says she is expected. She asked for her apartment, and I put her into the room that was got ready for Miss Calderwood. And she sends her respects to you, madam, and she'll be down with you presently."

The squire looked at his wife, and his wife looked at the squire.

"It is some mistake," murmured madam. "Some visitor for Calderwood or the Grange. It is very singular."

Hardly had she spoken when the door again opened, and the stranger appeared — a small creature, whether girl or woman it would be hard to say — dressed in a scanty black silk dress, her narrow shoulders covered with a white muslin pelerine. Her hair was swept up to the crown of her head, all but a little fringe hanging over her low forehead within an inch of her brows. Her face was brown and thin, eyes black and long, with blacker settings, mouth large, sweet, and melancholy. She was all head, mouth, and eyes; her nose and chin were nothing.

This visitor crossed the floor hastily, dropped a courtesy in the middle of the room, and approached the table, saying abruptly, with a soft Italian accent:

"Sir and madam, I am here. I am come to play your organ."

"The organ!" gasped Mistress Hurly.

"The organ!" stammered the squire.

"Yes, the organ," said the little stranger lady, playing on the back of a chair with her fingers, as if she felt notes under them.

"It was but last week that the handsome signor, your son, came to my little house, where I have lived teaching music since my English father and my Italian mother and brothers and sisters died and left me so lonely."

Here the fingers left off drumming, and two great tears were brushed off, one from each eye with each hand, child's fashion. But the next moment the fingers were at work again, as if only whilst they were moving the tongue could speak.

"The noble signor, your son," said the little woman, looking trustfully from one to the other of the old couple, while a bright blush shone through her brown skin, "he often came to see me before that, always in the evening, when the sun was warm and yellow all through my little studio, and the music was swelling my heart, and I could play out grand with all my soul; then he used to come and say, 'Hurry, little Lisa, and play better, better still. I have work for you to do by-and-by.' Sometimes he said, 'Brava!' and sometimes he said 'Eccellentissima!' but one night last week he came to me and said, 'It is enough. Will you swear to do my bidding, whatever it may be?' Here the black eyes fell. And I said, 'Yes'. And he said, 'Now you are my betrothed'. And I said, 'Yes'. And he said, 'Pack up your music, little Lisa, and go off to England to my English father and mother, who have an organ in their house which must be played upon. If they refuse to let you play, tell them I sent you, and they will give you leave. You must play all day, and you must get up in the night and play. You must never tire. You are my betrothed, and you have sworn to do my work.' I said, 'Shall I see you there, signor?' And he said, 'Yes, you shall see me there.' I said, 'I will keep my vow, Signor.' And so, sir and madam, I am come."

The soft foreign voice left off talking, the fingers left off thrumming on the chair, and the little stranger gazed in dismay at her auditors, both pale with agitation.

"You are deceived. You make a mistake," said they in one breath.

"Our son —" began Mistress Hurly, but her mouth twitched, her voice broke, and she looked piteously towards her husband.

"Our son," said the squire, making an effort to conquer the quavering in his voice, "our son is long dead."

"Nay, nay," said the little foreigner. "If you have thought him dead have good cheer, dear sir and madam. He is alive; he is well, and strong, and handsome. But one, two, three, four, five" (on the fingers) "days ago he stood by my side."

"It is some strange mistake, some wonderful coincidence!" said the mistress and master of Hurly Burly.

"Let us take her to the gallery," murmured the mother of this son who was thus dead and alive. "There is yet light to see the pictures. She will not know his portrait."

The bewildered wife and husband led their strange visitor away to a long gloomy room at the west side of the house, where the faint gleams from the darkening sky still lingered on the portraits of the Hurly family.

"Doubtless he is like this," said the squire, pointing to a fair-haired young man with a mild face, a brother of his own who had been lost at sea.

But Lisa shook her head, and went softly on tiptoe from one picture to another, peering into the canvas, and still turning away troubled. But at last a shriek of delight startled the shadowy chamber.

"Ah, here he is! See, here he is, the noble signor, the beautiful signor, not half so handsome as he looked five days ago, when talking to poor little Lisa! Dear sir and madam, you are now content. Now take me to the organ, that I may commence to do his bidding at once."

The mistress of Hurly Burly clung fast by her husband's arm.

"How old are you, girl?" she said faintly.

"Eighteen," said the visitor impatiently, moving towards the door.

"And my son has been dead for twenty years!" said his mother, and swooned on her husband's breast.

"Order the carriage at once," said Mistress Hurly, recovering from her swoon; "I will take her to Margaret Calderwood. Margaret will tell her the story. Margaret will bring her to reason. No, not tomorrow; I cannot bear tomorrow, it is so far away. We must go tonight."

The little signora thought the old lady mad, but she put on her cloak again obediently, and took her seat beside Mistress Hurly in the Hurly family coach. The moon that looked in at them through the pane as they lumbered along was not whiter than the aged face of the squire's wife, whose dim faded eyes were fixed upon it in doubt and awe too great for tears or words. Lisa, too, from her corner gloated upon the moon, her black eyes shining with passionate dreams.

A carriage rolled away from the Calderwood door as the Hurly coach drew up at the steps. Margaret Calderwood had just returned from a dinner-party, and at the open door a splendid figure was standing, a tall woman dressed in brown velvet, the diamonds on her bosom glistening in the moonlight that revealed her, pouring, as it did, over the house from eaves to basement. Mistress Hurly fell into her outstretched arms with a groan, and the strong woman carried her aged friend, like a baby, into the house. Little Lisa was overlooked, and sat down contentedly on the threshold to gloat awhile longer on the moon, and to thrum imaginary sonatas on the doorstep.

There were tears and sobs in the dusk, moonlit room into which Margaret Calderwood carried her friend. There was a long consultation, and then Margaret, having hushed away the grieving woman into some quiet corner, came forth to look for the little dark-faced stranger, who had arrived, so unwelcome, from beyond the seas, with such wild communication from the dead.

Up the grand staircase of handsome Calderwood the little woman followed the tall one into a large chamber where a lamp burned, showing Lisa, if she cared to see it, that this mansion of Calderwood was fitted with much greater luxury and richness than was that of Hurly Burly. The appointments of this room announced it the sanctum of a woman who depended for the interest of her life upon resources of intellect and taste. Lisa noticed nothing but a morsel of biscuit that was lying on a plate.

"May I have it?" said she eagerly. "It is so long since I have eaten. I am hungry."

Margaret Calderwood gazed at her with a sorrowful, motherly look, and, parting the fringing hair on her forehead, kissed her. Lisa, staring at her in wonder, returned the caress with ardour. Margaret's large fair shoulders, Madonna face, and yellow braided hair, excited a rapture within her. But when food was brought her, she flew to it and ate.

"It is better than I have ever eaten at home!" she said gratefully. And Margaret Calderwood murmured, "She is physically healthy, at least."

"And now, Lisa," said Margaret Calderwood, "come and tell me the whole history of the grand signor who sent you to England to play the organ."

Then Lisa crept in behind a chair, and her eyes began to burn and her fingers to thrum, and she repeated word for word her story as she had told it at Hurly Burly.

When she had finished, Margaret Calderwood began to pace up and down the floor with a very troubled face. Lisa watched her, fascinated, and, when she bade her listen to a story which she would relate to her, folded her restless hands together meekly, and listened.

"Twenty years ago, Lisa, Mr. and Mrs. Hurly had a son. He was handsome, like that portrait you saw in the gallery, and he had brilliant talents. He was idolized by his father and mother, and all who knew him felt obliged to love him. I was then a happy girl of twenty. I was an orphan, and Mrs. Hurly, who had been my mother's friend, was like a mother to me. I, too, was petted and caressed by all my friends, and I was very wealthy; but I only valued admiration, riches — every good gift that fell to my share — just in proportion as they seemed of worth in the eyes of Lewis Hurly. I was his affianced wife, and I loved him well.

"All the fondness and pride that were lavished on him could not keep him from falling into evil ways, nor from becoming rapidly more and more abandoned to wickedness, till even those who loved him best despaired of seeing his reformation. I prayed him with tears, for my sake, if not for that of his grieving mother, to save himself before it was too late. But to my horror I found that my power was gone, my words did not even move him; he loved me no more. I tried to think that this was some fit of madness that would pass, and still clung to hope. At last his own mother forbade me to see him."

Here Margaret Calderwood paused, seemingly in bitter thought, but resumed:

"He and a party of his boon companions, named by themselves the 'Devil's Club', were in the habit of practising all kinds of unholy pranks in the country. They had midnight carousings on the tomb-stones in the village graveyard; they carried away helpless old men and children, whom they tortured by making believe to bury them alive; they raised the dead and placed them sitting round the tombstones at a mock feast. On one occasion there was a very sad funeral from the village. The corpse was carried into the church, and prayers were read over the coffin, the chief mourner, the aged father of the dead man, standing weeping by. In the midst of this solemn scene the organ suddenly pealed forth a profane tune, and a number of voices shouted a drinking chorus. A groan of execration burst from the crowd, the clergyman turned pale and closed his book, and the old man, the father of the dead, climbed the altar steps, and, raising his arms above his head, uttered a terrible curse. He cursed Lewis Hurly to all eternity, he cursed the organ he played, that it might be dumb henceforth, except under the fingers that had now profaned it, which, he prayed, might be forced to labour upon it till they stiffened in death. And the curse seemed to work, for the organ stood dumb in the church from that day, except when touched by Lewis Hurly.

"For a bravado he had the organ taken down and conveyed to his father's house, where he had it put up in the chamber where it now stands. It was also for a bravado that he played on it every day. But, by-and-by, the amount of time which he spent at it daily began to increase rapidly. We wondered long at this whim, as we called it, and his poor mother thanked God that he had set his heart upon an occupation which would keep him out of harm's way. I was the first to suspect that it was not his own will that kept him hammering at the organ so many laborious hours, while his boon companions tried vainly to draw him away. He used to lock himself up in the room with the organ, but one day I hid myself among the curtains, and saw him writhing on his seat, and heard him groaning as he strove to wrench his hands from the keys, to which they flew back like a needle to a magnet. It was soon plainly to be seen that he was an involuntary slave to the organ; but whether through a madness that had grown within himself, or by some supernatural doom, having its cause in the old man's curse, we did not dare to say. By-and-by there came a time when we were wakened out of our sleep at nights by the rolling of the organ. He wrought now night and day. Food and rest were denied him. His face got haggard, his beard grew long, his eyes started from their sockets. His body became wasted, and his cramped fingers like the claws of a bird. He groaned piteously as he stooped over his cruel toil. All save his mother and I were afraid to go near him. She, poor, tender woman, tried to put wine and food between his lips, while the tortured fingers crawled over the keys; but he only gnashed his teeth at her with curses, and she retreated from him in terror, to pray. At last, one dreadful hour, we found him a ghastly corpse on the ground before the organ.

"From that hour the organ was dumb to the touch of all human fingers. Many, unwilling to believe the story, made persevering endeavours to draw sound from it, in vain. But when the darkened empty room was locked up and left, we heard as loud as ever the well-known sounds humming and rolling through the walls. Night and day the tones of the organ boomed on as before. It seemed that the doom of the wretched man was not yet fulfilled, although his tortured body had been worn out in the terrible struggle to accomplish it. Even his own mother was afraid to go near the room then. So the time went on, and the curse of this perpetual music was not removed from the house. Servants refused to stay about the place. Visitors shunned it. The squire and his wife left their home for years, and returned; left it, and returned again, to find their ears still tortured and their hearts wrung by the unceasing persecution of terrible sounds. At last, but a few months ago, a holy man was found, who locked himself up in the cursed chamber for many days, praying and wrestling with the demon. After he came forth and went away the sounds ceased, and the organ was heard no more. Since then there has been peace in the house. And now, Lisa, your strange appearance and your strange story convince us that you are a victim of a ruse of the Evil One. Be warned in time, and place yourself under the protection of God, that you may be saved from the fearful influences that are at work upon you. Come —"

Margaret Calderwood turned to the corner where the stranger sat, as she had supposed, listening intently. Little Lisa was fast asleep, her hands spread before her as if she played an organ in her dreams.

Margaret took the soft brown face to her motherly breast, and kissed the swelling temples, too big with wonder and fancy.

"We will save you from a horrible fate!" she murmured, and carried the girl to bed.

In the morning Lisa was gone. Margaret Calderwood, coming early from her own chamber, went into the girl's room and found the bed empty.

"She is just such a wild thing," thought Margaret, "as would rush out at sunrise to hear the larks!" and she went forth to look for her in the meadows, behind the beech hedges and in the home park. Mistress Hurly, from the breakfast-room window, saw Margaret Calderwood, large and fair in her white morning gown, coming down the garden-path between the rose bushes, with her fresh draperies dabbled by the dew, and a look of trouble on her calm face. Her quest had been unsuccessful. The little foreigner had vanished.

A second search after breakfast proved also fruitless, and towards evening the two women drove back to Hurly Burly together. There all was panic and distress. The squire sat in his study with the doors shut, and his hands over his ears. The servants, with pale faces, were huddled together in whispering groups. The haunted organ was pealing through the house as of old.

Margaret Calderwood hastened to the fatal chamber, and there, sure enough, was Lisa, perched upon the high seat before the organ, beating the keys with her small hands, her slight figure swaying, and the evening sunshine playing about her weird head. Sweet unearthly music she wrung from the groaning heart of the organ — wild melodies, mounting to rapturous heights and falling to mournful depths. She wandered from Mendelssohn to Mozart, and from Mozart to Beethoven. Margaret stood fascinated awhile by the ravishing beauty of the sounds she heard, but, rousing herself quickly, put her arms round the musician and forced her away from the chamber. Lisa returned next day, however, and was not so easily coaxed from her post again. Day after day she laboured at the organ, growing paler and thinner and more weird-looking as time went on.

"I work so hard," she said to Mrs. Hurly. "The signor, your son, is he pleased? Ask him to come and tell me himself if he is pleased."

Mistress Hurly got ill and took to her bed. The squire swore at the young foreign baggage, and roamed abroad. Margaret Calderwood was the only one who stood by to watch the fate of the little organist. The curse of the organ was upon Lisa; it spoke under her hand, and her hand was its slave.

At last she announced rapturously that she had had a visit from the brave signor, who had commended her industry, and urged her to work yet harder. After that she ceased to hold any communication with the living. Time after time Margaret Calderwood wrapped her arms about the frail thing, and carried her away by force, locking the door of the fatal chamber. But locking the chamber and burying the key were of no avail. The door stood open again, and Lisa was labouring on her perch.

One night, wakened from her sleep by the well-known humming and moaning of the organ, Margaret dressed hurriedly and hastened to the unholy room. Moonlight was pouring down the staircase and passages of Hurly Burly. It shone on the marble bust of the dead Lewis Hurly, that stood in the niche above his mother's sitting-room door. The organ room was full of it when Margaret pushed open the door and entered full of the pale green moonlight from the window, mingled with another light, a dull lurid glare which seemed to centre round a dark shadow, like the figure of a man standing by the organ, and throwing out in fantastic relief the slight form of Lisa writhing, rather than swaying, back and forward, as if in agony. The sounds that came from the organ were broken and meaningless, as if the hands of the player lagged and stumbled on the keys. Between the intermittent chords low moaning cries broke from Lisa, and the dark figure bent towards her with menacing gestures. Trembling with the sickness of supernatural fear, yet strong of will, Margaret Calderwood crept forward within the lurid light, and was drawn into its influence. It grew and intensified upon her, it dazzled and blinded her at first; but presently, by a daring effort of will, she raised her eyes, and beheld Lisa's face convulsed with torture in the burning glare, and bending over her the figure and the features of Lewis Hurly! Smitten with horror, Margaret did not even then lose her presence of mind. She wound her strong arms around the wretched girl and dragged her from her seat and out of the influence of the lurid light, which immediately paled away and vanished. She carried her to her own bed, where Lisa lay, a wasted wreck, raving about the cruelty of the pitiless signor who would not see that she was labouring her best. Her poor cramped hands kept beating the coverlet, as though she were still at her agonizing task.

Margaret Calderwood bathed her burning temples, and placed fresh flowers upon her pillow. She opened the blinds and windows, and let in the sweet morning air and sunshine, and then, looking up at the newly awakened sky with its fair promise of hope for the day, and down at the dewy fields, and afar off at the dark green woods with the purple mists still hovering about them, she prayed that a way might be shown her by which to put an end to this curse. She prayed for Lisa, and then, thinking that the girl rested somewhat, stole from the room. She thought that she had locked the door behind her.

She went downstairs with a pale, resolved face, and, without consulting anyone, sent to the village for a bricklayer. Afterwards she sat by Mistress Hurly's bedside, and explained to her what was to be done. Presently she went to the door of Lisa's room, and hearing no sound, thought the girl slept, and stole away. By-and-by she went downstairs, and found that the bricklayer had arrived and already begun his task of building up the organ-room door. He was a swift workman, and the chamber was soon sealed safely with stone and mortar.

Having seen this work finished, Margaret Calderwood went and listened again at Lisa's door; and still hearing no sound, she returned, and took her seat at Mrs. Hurly's bedside once more. It was towards evening that she at last entered her room to assure herself of the comfort of Lisa's sleep. But the bed and room were empty. Lisa had disappeared.

Then the search began, upstairs and downstairs, in the garden, in the grounds, in the fields and meadows. No Lisa. Margaret Calderwood ordered the carriage and drove to Calderwood to see if the strange little Will-o'-the-wisp might have made her way there; then to the village, and to many other places in the neighbourhood which it was not possible she could have reached. She made enquiries everywhere; she pondered and puzzled over the matter. In the weak, suffering state that the girl was in, how far could she have crawled?

After two days' search, Margaret returned to Hurly Burly. She was sad and tired, and the evening was chill. She sat over the fire wrapped in her shawl when little Bess came to her, weeping behind her muslin apron.

"If you'd speak to Mistress Hurly about it, please, ma'am," she said. "I love her dearly, and it breaks my heart to go away, but the organ haven't done yet, ma'am, and I'm frightened out of my life, so I can't stay."

"Who has heard the organ, and when?" asked Margaret Calderwood, rising to her feet.

"Please, ma'am, I heard it the night you went away — the night after the door was built up!"

"And not since?"

"No, ma'am," hesitatingly, "not since. Hist! hark, ma'am! Is not that like the sound of it now?"

"No," said Margaret Calderwood; "it is only the wind." But pale as death she flew down the stairs and laid her ear to the yet damp mortar of the newly built wall. All was silent. There was no sound but the monotonous sough of the wind in the trees outside. Then Margaret began to dash her soft shoulder against the strong wall, and to pick the mortar away with her white fingers, and to cry out for the bricklayer who had built up the door.

It was midnight, but the bricklayer left his bed in the village, and obeyed the summons to Hurly Burly. The pale woman stood by and watched him undo all his work of three days ago, and the servants gathered about in trembling groups, wondering what was to happen next.

What happened next was this: When an opening was made the man entered the room with a light, Margaret Calderwood and others following. A heap of something dark was lying on the ground at the foot of the organ. Many groans arose in the fatal chamber. Here was little Lisa dead!

When Mistress Hurly was able to move, the squire and his wife went to live in France, where they remained till their death. Hurly Burly was shut up and deserted for many years. Lately it has passed into new hands. The organ has been taken down and banished, and the room is a bed-chamber, more luxuriously furnished than any in the house. But no one sleeps in it twice.

Margaret Calderwood was carried to her grave the other day a very aged woman.

Wraith-Haunted

Isabella Banks

"Yes, Helen?"

The speaker, a tall, elegant woman, in whose every lineament beauty yet lingered, as if loth to accept from Time his seventy years' notice to quit, looked up interrogatively at her niece, a blooming matron, busy writing invitations for a juvenile party.

"I did not speak, aunt."

"Did you not? Nor you, Mr. Birley?"

Mr. Birley, engrossed in his evening paper, looked up somewhat vaguely.

"Eh, what?"

"Did you call me?"

"What, I? Certainly not."

"Strange!" murmured Mrs. Carson, involuntarily glancing at the ormolu timepiece ere her eyes bent down once more on her interrupted sewing. The fingers pointed to *ten minutes before nine.*

Click, click, went her needle steadily through the seam; Mrs. Birley's pen made a faint sound as it traced the pink paper; and Mr. Birley studied the "share-list" and "markets" with more than ordinary assiduity. A spaniel coiled up on the hearth dozed in a dog's paradise, in the glow of a ruddy fire, which lit up every corner of the crimson room, and was reflected cheerfully by glass, gilding, and polished furniture.

Presently Mrs. Carson's head was raised again.

"Well?" said she, glancing alternately from niece to nephew.

"What?" questioned both in a breath.

"One of you spoke this time — I heard my name distinctly."

"Indeed, Aunt Marianne, I have not uttered a syllable; I have not lifted my eyes from my desk since you addressed me last."

"Nor I from my newspaper. Mrs. Carson," continued the gentleman, "Dash is snoring most melodiously; possibly you mistook his utterance for mine. Not very complimentary if you did, I must say."

"Indeed I did *not*," returned she, with more emphasis than the occasion seemed to warrant. "I certainly heard myself called by my Christian name."

"Nonsense, aunt; I am sure no one spoke. You must be dreaming."

Again Mrs. Carson's eyes sought the timepiece on the mantel-shelf: the index had advanced five minutes.

"May be so; old people do dream sometimes," replied she quietly, resuming work with a sigh as if to dismiss the subject.

With a light laugh Mrs. Birley dipped her pen into the ink, and Mr. Birley sought his lost paragraph.

Had either husband or wife cared to listen, there might have been heard a beating heart keeping time with the sharp click of the needle and the steady tick of the timepiece. But there was only one listener, and she, seemingly occupied with her needle work, sat with lips apart and head bent in mute expectancy.

The hall-clock gave warning. With a first stroke of nine her work dropped; she grasped the arms of her chair and rose. Her face was blanched and rigid, her brown eyes were wild and wandering. For some moments she stood thus, then with a groan sank nerveless in her seat.

Her companions, alarmed, were by her side in an instant.

"My dear aunt, what is the matter?"

"Are you ill, Mrs. Carson?" and Mr. Birley as he spoke made a movement towards the bell.

The old lady, recovering, arrested his hand, "Are you sure neither of you spoke to me?"

"Quite sure," was the simultaneous reply.

"Do you think any of the children called me?"

"Why, Aunt Marianne, what *are* you thinking of? — the children have been in bed two hours."

"Did neither of you hear anything?"

"I heard nothing."

"Nor I, save the scratching of my own pen and the rustle of James's paper."

Mrs. Carson looked from one to the other as if incredulity struggled with a foregone conclusion; then in answer to their inquiries, said seriously, "I distinctly heard my own name,

Marianne, called thrice, with an interval of five minutes between each call, although *I saw nothing!*"

"Saw nothing! Why, what did you expect to see?" asked Helen, much perplexed.

"Bosh!" muttered Mr. Birley between his teeth as he resumed his seat and study.

"*What* I expected to see is not easy to say; but I heard a voice I have not heard for thirty-five years. It is a solemn warning."

"Of what, aunt?"

"Of *death!*" was the low and measured response.

Mr. Birley laughed outright; his wife fidgeted nervously.

"James," said the old lady, "I know you think me a superstitious old fool, and are laughing in your sleeve at my supernatural forebodings; but if you have patience to listen to an old woman's story first, I will then tell you what I believe is foreshadowed now — you can laugh afterwards, if so inclined."

Mr. Birley yawned and compared his watch with the clock; but there was a grave dignity in the speaker's manner which awed him into something like attention. His wife's curiosity was already aroused; she drew her chair to the fire, and with a gesture and grimace meant to call her spouse to order, said—

"Well, aunt, we are listening."

"Well, Helen, I suppose you know, if James does not, that when your grandfather Denton was in business he was for many years his own traveller; and as there were no railroads, few stagecoaches, and those only on main roads, he used to travel with a horse and gig. On one of his journeys he met at a roadside inn a Mr. Lavery, from Bristol, likewise travelling on his own account, although in a different line.

"The two had met before on the road, but on that occasion he found Mr. Lavery not only invalided but crippled by rheumatism. The women of those days were of a different type from the present generation, and your grandmother was not only an excellent nurse but possessed a valuable specific for rheumatism; so being a man of impulse, without even a letter to announce his return — for a letter would have been longer on the road than himself — my father brought Mr. Lavery, wrapped up in blankets, to his own house, and placed him under my mother's care. For months the patient remained an invalid guest, tended by my mother, his wife being sent for after a while.

"Out of these services rendered and accepted grew a very warm friendship, one token of which was Mrs. Lavery's declared inability to dispense with the society of one or other of the Misses Denton. I, however, was the favourite, my visits generally extending over many months.

"I was about two-and-twenty when my last visit to Bristol was made, and — I may say so now without vanity — I was known as the beautiful Miss Denton; perhaps one reason why Mrs. Lavery was so proud to have me with her. Fond of dress and company herself, she was glad to have an attractive companion, and introduced me into much gayer society than my own mother had thought well for her daughters.

"I had been in Bristol nearly nine months, when the first of those peculiar occurrences which have marked my life stamped its indelible impress on my soul and memory.

"Mr. Lavery was away. Mrs. Lavery and myself had been to a card-party, which, as was customary in those days, broke up about ten o'clock. There had been music as well as cards, and I having then a very fine voice—"

"*Then!* You had a fine voice when I knew you first, twelve years ago," interrupted Mr. Birley.

"Well, James, perhaps so; but I *had* a good voice *then,* and naturally was pressed to exercise it. One of the guests, Mr. Carson, whom I saw that night for the first time, apparently had neither ears nor eyes for anyone else; he seemed literally entranced by my singing, and whispered as much to me as he handed me to my sedan-chair when we left.

"Neither admiration nor adulation was new to me, yet at the one compliment of this young Scotchman I flushed with a strange pleasure such as no flattery had ever called up before. The words lingered in my ears all the while I was carried home; even his peculiar intonation had an unwonted fascination for me; and indeed, when I retired to rest, I found myself still dwelling upon those incidents of the evening in which the handsome Mr. Carson had the most prominent place. I am afraid I answered Mrs. Lavery's remarks somewhat at random, and went to bed with this stranger's parting words floating through my mind as I fell asleep.

"I mention this, my dears, merely to show that there was no possible link of connection between my thoughts and that which followed.

"The bed assigned to me was an old-fashioned four-post, with heavy moreen curtains and full valances, the curtains suspended from brass rings which ran upon iron rods. Mrs. Lavery, in her husband's absence, always slept with me.

"I had been asleep some time, when I suddenly awakened with a start, hearing myself called. I sat up in the bed affrighted. The curtains at the foot were slowly undrawn, the rings jingling as they slipped over the iron rods, and there, in the aperture, distinctly visible in the frosty moonlight, stood the form of *my mother* in her night robes. She was thin, and ghastly white; but a smile of ineffable sweetness parted her wan lips, from which issued slowly the words 'Marianne, Marianne, Marianne!' Raising her hand as if in benediction, she melted away, as it were, into the moonbeams.

"Terror for the moment held me fast. When I recovered my self-possession I roused my bedfellow. She had seen nothing, heard nothing, and was therefore sceptical. In vain she strove, like you, to persuade me I had been dreaming; *the still open curtains refuted that,* for she recollected closing them with her own hand as she got into bed. She then suggested that the maid had played me a trick; but we found the door locked, with the key inside, as we had left it.

"'Oh, Mrs. Lavery,' I moaned in an agony of apprehension, 'something is wrong at home—my mother is either ill or in trouble, perhaps dying, and wants me. Oh, that I had never left her!'

"'Now do, my dear child, go to sleep; you have had the nightmare, that is all. It is not much more than a week since you heard from home; all was well then,' said Mrs. Lavery, trying to soothe my distress.

"'Oh, that was ten days ago,' I argued. 'It is a fortnight since the letter was written. What may not have happened since then I must go home at once.'

"There was no response from my friend; sleep had overpowered her sympathy. Neither my terror nor distress had fully roused her.

"For me there was no more sleep that night. I sat up shivering in bed until the piercing cold compelled me to lie down. I watched the still open curtains and the retreating moonbeams as they marked on the wall the passage of the silent hours; but although my mother's pale face and languid voice haunted my memory, the actual presence came no more.

"Night shadows linger long in December, and I was afraid to rise until daylight, but the first streak of dawn found me astir collecting my scattered possessions; and by the time Mrs. Lavery had got up I had almost completed my packing, for I had determined to go home, and knew that the "Royal Mail" coach would start that very day for Manchester, and, if I missed it, I must wait three days for another.

"Mrs. Lavery's astonishment is not describable; the episode of the night had left no impression on her sleep-bound faculties. She tried raillery, banter, persuasion, to induce me to abandon a 'foolish whim, the off-spring of a dream.'

"She changed her tone when the sluggish postman called out to the deaf servant a letter for Miss Denton, and a shilling to pay in a voice which penetrated to the breakfast-table, and my trembling fingers almost refused to unclasp my purse or break the seal, which, however, was *not* black.

"Well I remember the tenor of that letter. It told that during my father's absence from home some rollicking fellow with that in his head which was *not wit* had knocked loudly at our door in the middle of the night when all were asleep, and then run off. My mother, always a light sleeper, had started up under the impression that your grandfather had returned unexpectedly, and in her hurry to reach the door before he, in his irritable impatience, should knock a second time, caught her foot in the coverlet and fell heavily against a carved oak coffer. There she was found in the morning with her collar-bone broken. The fracture was reduced, but she never fairly rallied, and I was summoned home, her symptoms being alarming.

"We were yet discussing these sad tidings when Mr. Carson was announced. He called, he said, not only to inquire after our health, but to offer his services in conveying either message or package to my friends in Manchester, whither he was then bound. (You need not smile, Helen; it was a common practice at that time to burden travellers with friendly letters and parcels, until their delivery at the journey's end became quite a tax.)

"'You have come quite opportunely, Mr. Carson,' Mrs. Lavery answered briskly; you will relieve me from a sore dilemma. Miss Denton's mother having met with a severe injury, our young friend is summoned home hastily. She has never travelled alone in her life, and I was debating how I could trust her so far without a guardian. Will you undertake the charge? I know I can rely upon your care.'

"I saw a flush of pleasure light up his clear eye and handsome face as he answered earnestly, 'If Miss Denton will graciously accept my humble services, I shall only be too proud of the trust.'

"In my eagerness to depart I had lost sight of the dangers and discomforts of the long journey to an unprotected girl, but the picture drawn by Mrs. Lavery to deter me from quitting Bristol, as she then thought, needlessly, had made the prospect something formidable. There was no disguising my satisfaction when a protector offered himself so unexpectedly; and if I thanked him quietly, I know it was sufficiently.

"Mr. Carson's place had been booked the day before — outside. He hastened to the coach-office to secure an inside seat for me, and to transfer his own. A fruitless errand; every inside place was already secured. There only remained the hope that some male passenger would surrender his inside seat in favour of a lady.

"A vain hope. The 'insides' were all long-distance passengers, and to a man resented any infringement on the right of 'number one,' expressing their personal opinions more freely than courteously.

"'Mr. Carson,' I whispered, 'do not let there be any altercation on my account' (he was waxing warm). 'I should dread being penned up with those coarse men for two days; I would much rather sit outside with you.'

"An incautious speech, but the grateful look which answered it sent my blood tingling with very shame to my finger-ends. He answered soberly, 'I do prefer the outside in all seasons; but, then, I am hardy. You are not fitted to brave the inclemency of a midwinter frost. Only the urgency of life and death should tempt you to make the experiment.'

"'It *is* the urgency of life and death,' I answered. 'But I am not afraid of a little cold; my pelisse is warm, and my fur tippet protects my chest.'

"I bade my weeping friend 'good-bye.' Without another word Mr. Carson assisted me to mount the movable ladder to a seat at the back which held two, and fronted the guard's solitary post. Just then a messenger, despatched by Mrs. Lavery, came up laden with a rug and shawl.

"With much care Mr. Carson placed the rug beneath my feet, and adjusted the shawl around my knees. I felt at once that I was in good hands, though in my ignorance I considered the precaution unnecessary.

"The leaders' heads were released, the coachman cracked his long whip, the guard blew his horn, a final 'adieu' was said, and I had started on the most momentous journey of my life.

"Rightly judging that my emotions were not less deep because they did no more than well-up into my eyes, my new protector entered into a conversation with the guard to divert his attention, and left me to my meditations. Sombre enough they were. I could not quit my kind friend without regret; but what weighed heaviest on my heart was the presentiment that my mother was *dead*, and that I had seen her *passing spirit*. More sorrowful and gloomy became my thoughts as one by one the milestones were left behind on the turnpike-road, and notwithstanding my wrappings I began to feel a little chilly.

"I need not weary you with the details of that long and miserable journey, only rendered endurable by the unremitting attention of my protector, for such in truth he was. Not only the scenery, but the weather and temperature varied with the districts through which we rode. From hard black frost we passed to a region where snow lay thick on the distant hills, like a shroud on a dead giant, and in light patches here and there by the roadside or on the trees, which tossed their skeleton arms in the breeze and played at snow-ball with us as the coach swept past. From falling snow we made an advance under a canopy of weeping clouds — first a drizzle, then rain, soaking, persistent, pitiless rain, rain without intermission, rain which would have penetrated a plank.

"No wonder, then, that notwithstanding the plaid which Mr. Carson had stripped from himself to fold round me during the chill of the first evening (using as a substitute, when too late, a horse-rug obtained from an ostler at a fabulous price) — no wonder, I say, that several hours before we reached our destination I was drenched to the skin, and utterly worn out both in body and mind.

"When the steaming horses drew the miry coach up before the Bridgewater Arms, I had lain for some time in a state of insensibility on Mr. Carson's shoulder, utterly unconscious of his supporting arm, or of the anathemas vented by the sympathising guard on the stolid 'insides,' whose victim he clearly considered me to be.

"Uncle Bancroft was fortunately in waiting, for I had to be lifted from the coach-top, and my generous friend was himself too cramped and benumbed to render further assistance. Brandy was poured down my throat, and as soon as a hackney-coach could be found I was conveyed, not to my father's house, but to my uncle's, Mr. Carson never leaving me until I was safe under the roof of my friends and showed some signs of returning animation.

"My shoes, stockings, and upper garments, sodden and saturated, had to be cut from my swollen limbs; but of this I knew nothing, for a fever had supervened and blotted out everything.

"Evasive answers were given to my first inquiries for my mother, as I was too weak to bear the truth; but when I approached convalescence, I was told everything. *She was dead when I commenced my journey — had died on the 23rd of December, close upon midnight.* Her last inquiry had been for me. Glancing feebly around from one weeping relative to another, she had said: *'All here? All! all except Marianne. Marianne, Marianne, Marianne!'*

"Helen, there could be no question that my mother's parting spirit had visited my bedside. The impression made was thenceforth ineffaceable."

"The coincidence was certainly remarkable," said Mr. Birley; "still, I incline to think the whole a dream."

"There was something very awful about it, even if it was a dream; you must own that, James," put in his wife.

"It was *no* dream; but my next revelation took place in broad daylight — *that* could be no dream," said Mrs. Carson sadly. "I have called my journey momentous, and justly. It influenced my life. My friend in his care for me had sacrificed himself. Hardy as he was, inflammation laid its hot hand upon his chest, held him down, and only let him rise with a spot marked like a target for the shaft of death. Gratitude and pity rose to heart and lips when I first saw his altered face. That journey had indeed fused two souls into one. Whatever impressions our first meeting had made, my sufferings and his self-sacrifice had confirmed. What I had found him during our long and miserable ride I found him ever, and loved him as such large-hearted, self-denying men should be loved. There was no talk of marriage between us for at least eighteen months; but there was no doubt whither we were drifting. Every moment he could spare from business was spent with me; and I think it was principally on my account that he induced his uncle in Glasgow, a muslin manufacturer, to engage a traveller and give him a permanent agency in Manchester, opening a ware-room for the sale of their goods.

"Shortly after that I became his wife, with the full approbation of friends, and with every prospect of happiness. He had furnished for me, simply but well, a house in Hanover-street, then a thorough Scotch colony, and my father's house being in Cannon-street, I was not more than a quarter of a mile from home. As was then the custom, we were married on Sunday, it being likewise my birthday, the 21st of December, and at once took possession of our new abode.

"The twenty-third was signalled by one of the fiercest conflagrations Manchester had known for years. A cotton-mill at Ancoats had taken fire whilst the hands were being dismissed. Some were in the upper-stories at the time; the narrow staircase was crowded, and many lives were in danger. Attracted by the glare, Mr. Carson was quickly on the spot, forgetful of all but the duty before him, and to his heroic efforts three girls at least owed their lives. They came to thank him a week later. Alas where was he? His hair was singed, and so was his coat, from which the tails were dangling loose; he had been wetted through alike with perspiration and water from the engine, but he waited until all danger to others was over, and when he reached home his clothes were apparently dry. He kissed me, apologised for keeping me waiting tea, and sat down to describe the incidents of the fire. Of his own exploits he said little; but on the plea of fatigue excused his sitting down to tea in the plight he then was. After the meal, he dozed off, which I attributed to his recent exertions and the heat of our own fire. It was only on going to rouse him that I discovered his clothes had been wetted, and I was too inexperienced to calculate the consequences.

"The following day I had promised to spend with my father and sisters. William was to join me on closing the warehouse. Being a bride, I was, of course, an object of special attention, made more of by my relations than at any other period of my life. I found there a perfect levee of aunts and cousins, discussing the bride's cake and future prospects with equal freedom. In the midst of our lively chat time fled fast. There came a sharp rat-tat-tat at the street-door.

"'Why, that is William's knock; what brings him from the warehouse so early?' exclaimed I, running to anticipate the servant in opening the door. Without another word than 'Marianne,' strangely spoken, he passed me by, never stopping to kiss me, as was his wont.

"I confess he had spoiled me. I pouted, petulant tears welled to my eyes, and I lingered with the fastening of the door before I turned round.

"'Marianne!'

"He was calling me from behind. I dropped the latch and followed him, as I thought, into the room I had just quitted.

"'Where is William?' I asked, looking round but not seeing him.

"'He has not come in here.'

"'Marianne!'

"The voice seemed to come from the room on the opposite side the hall. I ran thither, anticipating the loving embrace he was too reserved to give before strangers.

"*He was not there.*

"'William, dear, where are you? don't hide from me!'

"There was no answer. I ran into the back parlours — upstairs — downstairs, calling his name. *He was nowhere to be seen.*

"By this time the house was in commotion. Sisters and cousins alike had heard the knock, but no one had seen my husband or heard his voice.

"As they looked from me to one another for an explanation of that which is inexplicable, I having protested that Mr. Carson had passed and spoken to me in the hall, a sudden light flashed over and appalled me. I remembered *seeing the hall-panelling through his figure!* With a startling shriek, I rushed bareheaded from the house, tore across Cannon-street, along Sugar Lane, and up Shude Hill, like a mad woman, nor paused till my grasp was on the handle of my own door.

"That was ajar. A bad omen. I found my beloved husband extended on our bed, a doctor by his side vainly trying to bleed him — *the blood would not flow.*

"Inflammation — the result, no doubt, of his over-night's wetting and fatigue — had seized him suddenly.

"On his way home he had called on his doctor, who never left him again in life.

"Before night fell on the earth, the night of Death had fallen on my idolised husband, and my soul was in eclipse.

"Maid, wife, widow in a week, a widow all unconscious of her widowhood. A dumb, dreamy, statuesque automaton. I lived and moved, but that was all.

"I was taken home. When the funeral was over, the house in Hanover-street was given up. I was incapable of managing it.

"In this state I remained until my boy was born. Then the ice at my heart thawed, and tears came to my relief. The babe lived, and I lived for him.

"How I idolised that boy! I watched him night and day with more than a mother's care. He grew up a fine strong youth, the image of his dead father, whose name he bore. His father's uncle would have taken the entire charge of him; but I would not part from Willie, so we were summoned to Glasgow together, and there lived until the death of old Mr. Carson, when Willie was sixteen. The old gentleman left considerable property behind him, much of which was bequeathed to my son.

"Having no ties in Scotland, I came back to the old home, from which two of my sisters had gone away to homes of their own.

"Between myself and his grandfather, Willie stood a fair chance of being spoiled. He grew a tall, athletic man, not overfond of business or study, but much given to all manly sports and pastimes; in which he was encouraged by his grandfather. As for me, I saw no harm in his pursuits, and never dreamed of danger.

"Willie had a friend close by with whom he often put on the gloves, or practised fencing and singlestick.

"One day, towards the close of the year — my sorrows have always come in the midst of other's rejoicing — I sat reading by the fire; my father was playing his favourite game of backgammon with my sister Sarah; you, then a child of three years, nursing a kitten at your mother's feet; she had brought you to spend Christmas with us.

"My father, I must tell you, had then given up business, and our garret was filled with old lumber from the warehouse, several open baskets or 'wiskets' containing waste 'cops,' spindles, and other refuse amongst the rest.

"Our quiet was broken, and the rattling dice drowned by a loud clash and clatter upstairs.

"'Someone has left that garret-window open again, and the cats are making fine havoc with those cops, I know; hark how they rattle!'

"'Go upstairs, Sally, and shut the window,' said my father, pausing in his game.

"Sarah went. All was still.

"'The window is fast enough, and I saw no cats,' said she, as she sat down again to the board.

"Again the clash and clatter, as of metal, clear and distinct.

"'Helen, do you go up. Take my stick, and rout the intruder out; I'd swear the cats are there.'

"Your mother went, and came back with the same report — nothing there; all silent.

"Again the self-same clash and clatter, louder than before. I, haunted by old memories, felt my heart sink.

"'Here, Marianne, lass, lend me thy arm; thou and I'll go up and see what all this din's about; but don't thou look so scared.'

"We mounted the first flight, he leaning on my arm. All at once the clatter ceased.

"'Mother, mother, mother!' came floating like a breath down the stairway, and while we paused to listen — for my father heard it also — the figure of Willie brushed past us, with one hand pressed upon his heart.

"I trembled and grew faint. *I had seen the balustrades through the form.*

"My father chuckled outright. 'Ah, the young dog, so it was Willie playing tricks upon us, after all.'

"I said nothing until I reached the parlour. As I rightly conjectured, no Willie was there.

"'Father,' said I, clasping my hands in anguish, 'that was not Willie, it was his wraith. I have been *wraith-haunted* all my life.'

"My father looked dazed; my sisters, perhaps with a good motive, rallied me on my Scottish superstition, much as you have done; but ere their laughter had well subsided, there was an imperative knock at the street-door.

"We were summoned to our neighbour, Mr. Neale's; an accident had befallen my son.

"He lay on a couch pale and bleeding, wounded in the chest, the room in disorder, foils upon the floor. He had barely strength left to press my hand, and say 'Mother, do not weep; Tom could not help it — the button came off his foil. Mother, forgive —' and I was childless.

"I was spared all the agony of the inquest, for there was another long blank in my memory; and during my mental oblivion your grandfather died, borne down by the double sorrow.

"You see, I have good reasons for saying I am wraith-haunted, and for knowing that the voice I heard tonight is a call from the spirit-world to me."

Mr. Birley and his wife both looked perplexed and serious.

"I do remember something about a ghost in grandfather's garret when I was a very little girl. But how is it I was never told of the warnings you think you have had?"

"They were hushed up lest my grief should be re-awakened. And now let us go to bed — it is late. The issues of life and death are in higher hands than ours."

The morning broke — clear, sparkling, exhilarating. Mrs. Carson made her appearance in her ordinary health, a little paler it might be, but that was all.

Mrs. Birley had hesitated whether to issue her invitations, but finally resolved not to disappoint the children, and so they were sent.

The nursery-doors were thrown open, and all hands, big and little, summoned to the task of decoration with evergreens and holly.

In the midst of it all a carrier brought a large box, inscribed, "Aunt Carson's Gift." The old lady had made her purchases the day before. There was a general rush to wrench open the lid, and make a raid on the contents. Books, dolls, workboxes, a desk, toys noisy and noiseless, were there, each labelled with the fortunate recipient's name. Flushed and elated, the youngsters rushed hither and thither displaying their prizes. Frocks and pinafores filled to repletion dropped their contents, until the little ones might be tracked by straggling Shems and Noahs, cups and saucers, whistles and drumsticks.

The box had been removed, the litter cleared away, the stray waifs collected, when Mrs. Carson descended the stairs after her customary nap. A wee round toy, the colour of the stair-carpet, had been overlooked; she stepped upon it, and fell from top to bottom, striking her head against the balustrades.

There was a rush through the house to where she lay stunned on the oilcloth. Reverently and sadly she was carried into the nearest room, — the one occupied over-night. A messenger was sent on horseback for a surgeon and for Mr. Birley.

Shocked beyond measure, the latter gentleman hastened home in time to hear the fiat pronounced.

"An injured spine — concussion of the brain — no hope whatever."

A physician summoned hastily confirmed the surgeon's decision.

The weeping children were huddled from the room.

"How long may she linger?" was Mr. Birley's question.

"She may go off any moment, the shock to her system is so great; she *may* last two or three hours."

"Do you think she is conscious?"

"I am afraid not."

Mrs. Birley, sobbing, whispered to her husband, "James, do you think aunt did hear anything supernatural last night."

Two days before he would have said, "All bosh!" now he answered, "God only knows! It is most mysterious."

"If she did she will not die until nine o'clock."

"At nine!" murmured the dying woman; "at nine."

She was evidently conscious, and something more she said, but the words were inaudible. Husband and wife watched the clock as intensely as Mrs. Carson had watched it the night before.

Ten minutes to nine! The retreating pulse quickened under the doctor's touch. The lips moved.

"William!" was faintly audible to the bent ear.

Five minutes to nine! The "change" was perceptible.

"Yes, William!"

There was another pause — a burr — the clock's note of warning. There was a rattle in the throat of the dying woman.

"Coming, William!" was gasped out audibly.

NINE!

A last leap of the pulse — a last flicker of the eyelids — the "call" was obeyed.

Mrs. Carson, wraith-haunted, spirit-summoned, was of the dead!

The Ghost in the Cap'n Brown House

Harriet Beecher Stowe

"Now, Sam, tell us certain true, is there any such things as ghosts?"

"Be there ghosts?" said Sam, immediately translating into his vernacular grammar: "wal, now, that are's jest the question, ye see."

"Well, grandma thinks there are, and Aunt Lois thinks it's all nonsense. Why, Aunt Lois don't even believe the stories in Cotton Mather's 'Magnalia.'"

"Wanter know?" said Sam, with a tone of slow, languid meditation.

We were sitting on a bank of the Charles River, fishing. The soft melancholy red of evening was fading off in streaks on the glassy water, and the houses of Oldtown were beginning to loom through the gloom, solemn and ghostly. There are times and tones and moods of nature that make all the vulgar, daily real seem shadowy, vague, and supernatural, as if the outlines of this hard material present were fading into the invisible and unknown. So Oldtown, with its elm-trees, its great square white houses, its meeting-house and tavern and blacksmith's shop and milly which at high noon seem as real and as commonplace as possible, at this hour of the evening were dreamy and solemn. They rose up blurred, indistinct, dark; here and there winking candles sent long lines of light through the shadows, and little drops of unforeseen rain rippled the sheeny darkness of the water.

"Wal, you see, boys, in them things it's jest as well to mind your granny. There's a consid'able sight o' gumption in grandmas. You look at the folks that's alius tellin' you what they don't believe, — they don't believe this, and they don't believe that, — and what sort o' folks is they? Why, like yer Aunt Lois, sort o' stringy and dry. There ain't no 'sorption got out o' not believin' nothin'.

"Lord a massy! we don't know nothin' 'bout them things. We hain't ben there, and can't say that there ain't no ghosts and sich; can we, now?"

We agreed to that fact, and sat a little closer to Sam in the gathering gloom.

"Tell us about the Cap'n Brown house, Sam."

"Ye didn't never go over the Cap'n Brown house?"

No, we had not that advantage.

"Wal, yer see, Cap'n Brown he made all his money to sea, in furrin parts, and then come here to Oldtown to settle down.

"Now, there ain't no knowin' 'bout these 'ere old ship-masters, where they's ben, or what they's ben a doin', or how they got their money. Ask me no questions, and I'll tell ye no lies, is 'bout the best philosophy for them. Wal, it didn't do no good to ask Cap'n Brown questions too close, 'cause you didn't git no satisfaction. Nobody rightly knew 'bout who his folks was, or where they come from; and, ef a body asked him, he used to say that the very fust he know'd 'bout himself he was a young man walkin' the streets in London.

"But, yer see, boys, he hed money, and that is about all folks wanter know when a man comes to settle down. And he bought that 'are place, and built that 'are house. He built it all sea-cap'n fashion, so's to feel as much at home as he could. The parlor was like a ship's cabin. The table and chairs was fastened down to the floor, and the closets was made with holes to set the casters and the decanters and bottles in, jest's they be at sea; and there was stanchions to hold on by; and they say that blowy nights the cap'n used to fire up pretty well with his grog, till he hed about all he could carry, and then he'd set and hold on, and hear the wind blow, and kind o' feel out to sea right there to hum. There wasn't no Mis' Cap'n Brown, and there didn't seem likely to be none. And whether there ever hed been one, nobody know'd. He hed an old black Guinea nigger-woman, named Quassia, that did his work. She was shaped pretty much like one o' these 'ere great crookneck-squashes. She wa'n't no gret beauty, I can tell you; and she used to wear a gret red turban and a yaller short gown and red petticoat, and a gret string o' gold beads round her neck, and gret big gold hoops in her ears, made right in the middle o' Africa among the heathen there. For all she was black, she thought a heap o' herself, and was consid'able sort o' predominative over the cap'n. Lordy massy! boys, it's alius so. Get a man and a woman together, — any sort o' woman you're a mind to, don't care who 'tis, — and one way or another she gets the rule over him, and he jest has to train to her fife. Some does it one way, and some does it another; some does it by jawin' and some does it by kissin', and some does it by faculty and contrivance; but one way or another they allers does it. Old Cap'n Brown was a good stout, stocky kind o' John Bull sort o' fellow, and a good judge o' sperits, and allers kep' the best in them are cupboards o' his'n; but, fust and last, things in his house went pretty much as old Quassia said.

"Folks got to kind o' respectin' Quassia. She come to meetin' Sunday regular, and sot all fixed up in red and yaller and green, with glass beads and what not, lookin' for all the world like one o' them ugly Indian idols; but she was well-behaved as any Christian. She was a master hand at cookin'. Her bread and biscuits couldn't be beat, and no couldn't her pies, and there wa'n't no such pound-cake as she made nowhere. Wal, this 'ere story I'm a goin' to tell you was told me by Cinthy Pendleton. There ain't a more respectable gal, old or young, than Cinthy nowheres. She lives over to Sherburne now, and I hear tell she's sot up a manty-makin' business; but then she used to do tailorin' in Oldtown. She was a member o' the church, and a good Christian as ever was. Wal, ye see, Quassia she got Cinthy to come up and spend a week to the Cap'n Brown house, a doin' tailorin' and a fixin' over his close: 'twas along toward the fust o' March. Cinthy she sot by the fire in the front parlor with her goose and her press-board and her work: for there wa'n't no company callin', and the snow was drifted four feet deep right across the front door; so there wa'n't much danger o' anybody comin' in. And the cap'n he was a perlite man to wimmen; and Cinthy she liked it jest as well not to have company, 'cause the cap'n he'd make himself entertainin' tellin' on her sea-stories, and all about his adventures among the Ammonites, and Perresites, and Jebusites, and all sorts o' heathen people he'd been among.

"Wal, that 'are week there come on the master snow-storm. Of all the snow-storms that hed ben, that 'are was the beater; and I tell you the wind blew as if 'twas the last chance it was ever goin' to hev. Wal, it's kind o' scary like to be shet up in a lone house with all natur' a kind o' breakin' out, and goin' on so, and the snow a comin' down so thick ye can't see 'cross the street, and the wind a pipin' and a squeelin' and a rumblin' and a tumblin' fust down this chimney and then down that. I tell you, it sort o' sets a feller thinkin' o' the three great things, — death, judgment, and etarnaty; and I don't care who the folks is, nor how good they be, there's times when they must be feelin' putty consid'able solemn.

"Wal, Cinthy she said she kind o' felt so along, and she hed a sort o' queer feelin' come over her as if there was somebody or somethin' round the house more'n appeared. She said she sort o' felt it in the air; but it seemed to her silly, and she tried to get over it. But two or three times, she said, when it got to be dusk, she felt somebody go by her up the stairs. The front entry wa'n't very light in the daytime, and in the storm, come five o'clock, it was so dark that all you could see was jest a gleam o' somethin', and two or three times when she started to go up stairs she see a soft white suthin' that seemed goin' up before her, and she stopped with her heart a beatin' like a trip-hammer, and she sort o' saw it go up and along the entry to the cap'n's door, and then it seemed to go right through, 'cause the door didn't open.

"Wal, Cinthy says she to old Quassia, says she, 'Is there anybody lives in this house but us?'

"'Anybody lives here?' says Quassia: 'what you mean?' says she.

"Says Cinthy, 'I thought somebody went past me on the stairs last night and tonight.'

"Lordy massy! how old Quassia did screech and laugh. 'Good Lord!' says she, 'how foolish white folks is! Somebody went past you? Was't the capt'in?'

"'No, it wa'n't the cap'n,' says she: 'it was somethin' soft and white, and moved very still; it was like somethin' in the air,' says she. Then Quassia she haw-hawed louder. Says she, 'It's hysterikes, Miss Cinthy; that's all it is.'

"Wal, Cinthy she was kind o' 'shamed, but for all that she couldn't help herself. Sometimes evenin's she'd be a settin' with the cap'n, and she'd think she'd hear somebody a movin' in his room overhead; and she knowed it wa'n't Quassia, 'cause Quassia was ironin' in the kitchen. She took pains once or twice to find out that 'are.

"Wal, ye see, the cap'n's room was the gret front upper chamber over the parlor, and then right oppisite to it was the gret spare chamber where Cinthy slept. It was jest as grand as could be, with a gret four-post mahogany bedstead and damask curtains brought over from England; but it was cold enough to freeze a white bear solid, — the way spare chambers allers is. Then there was the entry between, run straight through the house: one side was old Quassia's room, and the other was a sort o' storeroom, where the old cap'n kep' all sorts o' traps.

"Wal, Cinthy she kep' a hevin' things happen and a seein' things, till she didn't railly know what was in it. Once when she come into the parlor jest at sundown, she was sure she see a white figure a vanishin' out o' the door that went towards the side entry. She said it was so dusk, that all she could see was jest this white figure, and it jest went out still as a cat as she come in.

"Wal, Cinthy didn't like to speak to the cap'n about it. She was a close woman, putty prudent, Cinthy was.

"But one night, 'bout the middle o' the week, this 'ere thing kind o' come to a crisis.

"Cinthy said she'd ben up putty late a sewin' and a finishin' off down in the parlor; and the cap'n he sot up with her, and was consid'able cheerful and entertainin', tellin' her all about things over in the Bermudys, and off to Chiny and Japan, and round the world ginerally. The storm that hed been a blowin' all the week was about as furious as ever; and the cap'n he stirred up a mess o' flip, and hed it for her hot to go to bed on. He was a good-natured critter, and allers had feelin's for lone women; and I s'pose he knew 'twas sort o' desolate for Cinthy.

"Wal, takin' the flip so right the last thing afore goin' to bed, she went right off to sleep as sound as a nut, and slep' on till somewhere about mornin', when she said somethin' waked her broad awake in a minute. Her eyes flew wide open like a spring, and the storm hed gone down and the moon come out; and there, standin' right in the moonlight by her bed, was a woman jest as white as a sheet, with black hair hangin' down to her waist, and the brightest, mourn fullest black eyes you ever see.

124

She stood there lookin' right at Cinthy; and Cinthy thinks that was what waked her up; 'cause, you know, ef anybody stands and looks steady at folks asleep it's apt to wake 'em.

"Any way, Cinthy said she felt jest as ef she was turnin' to stone. She couldn't move nor speak. She lay a minute, and then she shut her eyes, and begun to say her prayers; and a minute after she opened 'em, and it was gone.

"Cinthy was a sensible gal, and one that allers hed her thoughts about her; and she jest got up and put a shawl round her shoulders, and went first and looked at the doors, and they was both on 'em locked jest as she left 'em when she went to bed. Then she looked under the bed and in the closet, and felt all round the room: where she couldn't see she felt her way, and there wa'n't nothin' there.

"Wal, next mornin' Cinthy got up and went home, and she kep' it to herself a good while. Finally, one day when she was workin' to our house she told Hepsy about it, and Hepsy she told me."

"Well, Sam," we said, after a pause, in which we heard only the rustle of leaves and the ticking of branches against each other, "what do you suppose it was?"

"Wal, there 'tis: you know jest as much about it as I do. Hepsy told Cinthy it might 'a' ben a dream; so it might, but Cinthy she was sure it wa'n't a dream, 'cause she remembers plain hearin' the old clock on the stairs strike four while she had her eyes open lookin' at the woman; and then she only shet 'em a minute, jest to say 'Now I lay me,' and opened 'em and she was gone.

"Wal, Cinthy told Hepsy, and Hepsy she kep' it putty close. She didn't tell it to nobody except Aunt Sally Dickerson and the Widder Bije Smith and your Grandma Badger and the minister's wife; and they every one o' 'em 'greed it ought to be kep' close, 'cause it would make talk. Wal, come spring, somehow or other it seemed to 'a' got all over Oldtown. I heard on 't to the store and up to the tavern; and Jake Marshall he says to me one day, 'What's this 'ere about the cap'n's house?' And the Widder Loker she says to me, 'There's ben a ghost seen in the cap'n's house;' and I heard on 't clear over to Needham and Sherburne.

"Some o' the women they drew themselves up putty stiff and proper. Your Aunt Lois was one on 'em.

"'Ghost,' says she; 'don't tell me! Perhaps it would be best ef 'twas a ghost,' says she. She didn't think there ought to be no sich doin's in nobody's house; and your grandma she shet her up, and told her she didn't oughter talk so."

"Talk how?" said I, interrupting Sam with wonder. "What did Aunt Lois mean?"

"Why, you see," said Sam mysteriously, "there allers is folks in every town that's jest like the Sadducees in old times: they won't believe in angel nor sperit, no way you can fix it; and ef things is seen and done in a house, why, they say, it's 'cause there's somebody there; there's some sort o' deviltry or trick about it.

"So the story got round that there was a woman kep' private in Cap'n Brown's house, and that he brought her from furrin parts; and it growed and growed, till there was all sorts o' ways o' tellin on 't.

"Some said they'd seen her a settin' at an open winder. Some said that moonlight nights they'd seen her a walkin' out in the back garden kind o' in and out 'mong the bean-poles and squash-vines.

"You see, it come on spring and summer; and the winders o' the Cap'n Brown house stood open, and folks was all a watchin' on 'em day and night. Aunt Sally Dickerson told the minister's wife that she'd seen in plain daylight a woman a settin' at the chamber winder atween four and five o'clock in the mornin',— jist a settin' a lookin' out and a doin' nothin', like anybody else. She was very white and pale, and had black eyes.

"Some said that it was a nun the cap'n had brought away from a Roman Catholic convent in Spain, and some said he'd got her out o' the Inquisition.

"Aunt Sally said she thought the minister ought to call and inquire why she didn't come to meetin', and who she was, and all about her: 'cause, you see, she said it might be all right enough ef folks only know'd jest how things was; but ef they didn't, why, folks will talk."

"Well, did the minister do it?"

"What, Parson Lothrop? Wal, no, he didn't. He made a call on the cap'n in a regular way, and asked arter his health and all his family. But the cap'n he seemed jest as jolly and chipper as a spring robin, and he gin the minister some o' his old Jamaiky; and the minister he come away and said he didn't see nothin'; and no he didn't. Folks never does see nothin' when they aint' lookin' where 'tis. Fact is, Parson Lothrop wa'n't fond o' interferin'; he was a master hand to slick things over. Your grandma she used to mourn about it, 'cause she said he never gin no p'int to the doctrines; but 'twas all of a piece, he kind o' took everything the smooth way.

"But your grandma she believed in the ghost, and so did Lady Lothrop. I was up to her house t'other day fixin' a door-knob, and says she, 'Sam, your wife told me a strange story about the Cap'n Brown house.'

"'Yes, ma'am, she did,' says I.

"'Well, what do you think of it?' says she.

"'Wal, sometimes I think, and then agin I don't know,' says I. 'There's Cinthy she's a member o' the church and a good pious gal,' says I.

"'Yes, Sam,' says Lady Lothrop, says she; 'and Sam,' says she, 'it is jest like something that happened once to my grandmother when she was livin' in the old Province House in Bostin.' Says she, 'These 'ere things is the mysteries of Providence, and it's jest as well not to have 'em too much talked about.'

"'Jest so,' says I, — 'jest so. That 'are's what every woman I've talked with says; and I guess, fust and last, I've talked with twenty, — good, safe church-members, — and they's every one o' opinion that this 'ere oughtn't to be talked about. Why, over to the deakin's t'other night we went it all over as much as two or three hours, and we concluded that the best way was to keep quite still about it; and that's jest what they say over to Needham and Sherburne. I've been all round a hushin' this 'ere up, and I hain't found but a few people that hedn't the particulars one way or another. This 'ere was what I says to Lady Lothrop. The fact was, I never did see no report spread so, nor make sich sort o' sarchin's o' heart, as this 'ere. It railly did beat all; 'cause ef 'twas a ghost, why there was the p'int proved, ye see. Cinthy's a church-member, and she *see* it, and got right

127

up and sarched the room: but then agin, ef 'twas a woman, why that 'are was kind o' awful; it give cause, ye see, for thinkin' all sorts o' things. There was Cap'n Brown, to be sure, he wa'n't a church-member; but yet he was as honest and regular a man as any goin', as fur as any on us could see. To be sure, nobody know'd where he come from, but that wa'n't no reason agin' him: this 'ere might a ben a crazy sister, or some poor critter that he took out o' the best o' motives; and the Scriptur' says, 'Charity hopeth all things.' But then, ye see, folks will talk, — that 'are's the pester o' all these things, — and they did some on 'em talk consid'able strong about the cap'n; but somehow or other, there didn't nobody come to the p'int o' facin' on him down, and sayin' square out, 'Cap'n Brown, have you got a woman in your house, or hain't you? or is it a ghost, or what is it?' Folks somehow never does come to that. Ye see, there was the cap'n so respectable, a settin' up every Sunday there in his pew, with his ruffles round his hands and his red broadcloth cloak and his cocked hat. Why, folks' hearts sort o' failed 'em when it come to sayin' anything right to him. They thought and kind o' whispered round that the minister or the deakins oughter do it: but Lordy massy! ministers, I s'pose, has feelin's like the rest on us; they don't want to eat all the hard cheeses that nobody else won't eat. Anyhow, there wasn't nothin' said direct to the cap'n; and jest for want o' that all the folks in Oldtown kep' a bilin' and a bilin' like a kettle o' soap, till it seemed all the time as if they'd bile over.

"Some o' the wimmen tried to get somethin' out o' Quassy. Lordy massy! you might as well 'a' tried to get it out an old tom-turkey, that'll strut and gobble and quitter, and drag his wings on the ground, and fly at you, but won't say nothin'. Quassy she screeched her queer sort o' laugh; and she told 'em that they was a makin' fools o' themselves, and that the cap'n's matters wa'n't none o' their bisness; and that was true enough. As to goin' into Quassia's room, or into any o' the store-rooms or closets she kep' the keys of, you might as well hev gone into a lion's den. She kep' all her places locked up tight; and there was no gettin' at nothin' in the Cap'n Brown house, else I believe some o' the wimmen would 'a' sent a sarch-warrant."

"Well," said I, "what came of it? Didn't anybody ever find out?"

"Wal," said Sam, "it come to an end sort o', and didn't come to an end. It was jest this 'ere way. You see, along in October, jest in the cider-makin' time, Abel Flint he was took down with dysentery and died. You 'member the Flint house: it stood on a little rise o' ground jest lookin' over towards the Brown house. Wal, there was Aunt Sally Dickerson and the Widder Bije Smith, they set up with the corpse. He was laid out in the back chamber, you see, over the milk-room and kitchen; but there was cold victuals and sich in the front chamber, where the watchers sot. Wal, now, Aunt Sally she told me that between three and four o'clock she heard wheels a rumblin', and she went to the winder, and it was clear starlight; and she see a coach come up to the Cap'n Brown house; and she see the cap'n come out bringin' a woman all wrapped in a cloak, and old Quassy came arter with her arms full o' bundles; and he put her into the kerridge, and shet her in, and it driv off; and she see old Quassy stand lookin' over the fence arter it. She tried to wake up the widder, but 'twas towards mornin', and the widder allers was a hard sleeper; so there wa'n't no witness but her."

"Well, then, it wasn't a ghost," said I, "after all, and it *was* a woman."

"Wal, there 'tis, you see. Folks don't know that 'are yit, 'cause there it's jest as broad as 'tis long. Now, look at it. There's Cinthy, she's a good, pious gal: she locks her chamber-doors, both on 'em, and goes to bed, and wakes up in the night, and there's a woman there. She jest shets her eyes, and the woman's gone. She gits up and looks, and both doors is locked jest as she left 'em. That 'ere woman wa'n't flesh and blood now, no way, — not such flesh and blood as we knows on; but then they say Cinthy might hev dreamed it!

"Wal, now, look at it t'other way. There's Aunt Sally Dickerson; she's a good woman and a church-member: wal, she sees a woman in a cloak with all her bundles brought out o' Cap'n Brown's house, and put into a kerridge, and driv off, atween three and four o'clock in the mornin'. Wal, that 'ere shows there must 'a' ben a real live woman kep' there privately, and so what Cinthy saw wasn't a ghost.

"Wal, now, Cinthy says Aunt Sally might 'a' dreamed it, — that she got her head so full o' stories about the Cap'n Brown house, and watched it till she got asleep, and hed this 'ere dream; and, as there didn't nobody else see it, it might 'a' ben, you know. Aunt Sally's clear she didn't dream, and then agin Cinthy's clear *she* didn't dream; but which on 'em was awake, or which on 'em was asleep, is what ain't settled in Oldtown yet."

The Man with the Nose

Rhoda Broughton

[The details of this little story are of course imaginary, but the main incidents are, to the best of my belief, facts. They happened twenty, or more than twenty years ago.]

Chapter I.

"Let us get a map and see what places look pleasantest," says she.

"As for that," reply I, "on a map most places look equally pleasant."

"Never mind; get one!"

I obey.

"Do you like the seaside?" asks Elizabeth, lifting her little brown head and her small happy white face from the English sea-coast along which her forefinger is slowly travelling.

"Since you ask me, distinctly *no*," reply I, for once venturing to have a decided opinion of my own, which during the last few weeks of imbecility I can be hardly said to have had. "I broke my last wooden spade five and twenty years ago. I have but a poor opinion of cockles — sandy red-nosed things, are not they? and the air always makes me bilious."

"Then we certainly will not go there," says Elizabeth, laughing. "A bilious bridegroom! alliterative but horrible! None of our friends show the least eagerness to lend us their country house."

"Oh that God would put it into the hearts of men to take their wives straight home, as their fathers did!" say I with a cross groan.

"It is evident, therefore, that we must go somewhere," returns she, not heeding the aspiration contained in my last speech, making her forefinger resume its employment, and reaching Torquay.

"I suppose so," say I, with a sort of sigh; "for once in our lives we must resign ourselves to having the finger of derision pointed at us by waiters and landlords."

"You shall leave your new portmanteau at home, and I will leave all my best clothes, and nobody will guess that we are bride and bridegroom; they will think that we have been married — oh, ever since the world began" (opening her eyes very wide).

I shake my head. "With an old portmanteau and in rags we shall still have the mark of the beast upon us."

"Do you mind much? do you hate being ridiculous?" asks Elizabeth, meekly, rather depressed by my view of the case; "because if so, let us go somewhere out of the way, where there will be very few people to laugh at us."

"On the contrary," return I, stoutly, "we will betake ourselves to some spot where such as we do chiefly congregate — where we shall be swallowed up and lost in the multitude of our fellow-sinners." A pause devoted to reflection. "What do you say to Killarney?" say I cheerfully.

"There are a great many fleas there, I believe," replies Elizabeth, slowly; "flea-bites make large lumps on me; you would not like me if I were covered with large lumps."

At the hideous ideal picture thus presented to me by my little beloved I relapse into inarticulate idiocy; emerging from which by-and-by, I suggest, "The Lakes?" My arm is round her, and I feel her supple body shiver though it is mid-July and the bees are booming about in the still and sleepy noon garden outside.

"Oh — no — no — not *there!*"

"Why such emphasis?" I ask gaily; "more fleas? At this rate, and with this *sine quâ non*, our choice will grow limited."

"Something dreadful happened to me there," she says, with another shudder. "But indeed I did not think there was any harm in it — I never thought anything would come of it."

"What the devil was it?" cry I, in a jealous heat and hurry; "what the mischief *did* you do, and why have not you told me about it before?"

"I did not *do* much," she answers meekly, seeking for my hand, and when found kissing it in timid deprecation of my wrath; "but I was ill — very ill — there; I had a nervous fever. I was in a bed hung with a chintz with a red and green fernleaf pattern on it. I have always hated red and green fernleaf chintzes ever since."

"It would be possible to avoid the obnoxious bed, would it not?" say I, laughing a little. "Where does it lie? Windermere? Ulleswater? Wastwater? Where?"

"We were at Ulleswater," she says, speaking rapidly, while a hot colour grows on her small white cheeks — "Papa, mamma, and I; and there came a mesmeriser to Penrith, and we went to see him — everybody did — and he asked leave to mesmerise me — he said I should be such a good medium — and — and — I did not know what it was like. I thought it would be quite good fun — and — and — I let him."

She is trembling exceedingly; even the loving pressure of my arms cannot abate her shivering.

"Well?"

"And after that I do not remember anything — I believe I did all sorts of extraordinary things that he told me — sang and danced, and made a fool of myself — but when I came home I was very ill, very — I lay in bed for five whole weeks, and — and was off my head, and said odd and wicked things that you would not have expected me to say — that dreadful bed! shall I ever forget it?"

"We will *not* go to the Lakes," I say, decisively, "and we will not talk any more about mesmerism."

"That is right," she says, with a sigh of relief. "I try to think about it as little as possible; but sometimes, in the dead black of the night, when God seems a long way off, and the devil near, it comes back to me so strongly — I feel, do not you know, as if he were *there* somewhere in the room, and I *must* get up and follow him."

"Why should not we go abroad?" suggest I, abruptly turning the conversation.

"Why, indeed?" cries Elizabeth, recovering her gaiety, while her pretty blue eyes begin to dance. "How stupid of us not to have thought of it before; only *abroad* is a big word. *What* abroad?"

"We must be content with something short of Central Africa," I say, gravely, "as I think our one hundred and fifty pounds would hardly take us that far."

"Wherever we go, we must buy a dialogue book," suggests my little bride-elect, "and I will learn some phrases before we start."

"As for that, the Anglo-Saxon tongue takes one pretty well round the world," reply I, with a feeling of complacent British swagger, putting my hands in my breeches pockets.

"Do you fancy the Rhine?" says Elizabeth, with a rather timid suggestion; "I know it is the fashion to run it down nowadays, and call it a cocktail river; but — but — after all it cannot be so *very* contemptible, or Byron could not have said such noble things about it."

> *"The castled crag of Drachenfels*
> *Frowns o'er the wide and winding Rhine,*
> *Whose breast of waters broadly swells*
> *Between the banks which bear the vine,"*

say I, spouting. "After all, that proves nothing, for Byron could have made a silk purse out of a sow's ear."

"The Rhine will not do then?" says she resignedly, suppressing a sigh.

"On the contrary, it will do admirably: it *is* a cocktail river, and I do not care who says it is not," reply I, with illiberal positiveness; "but everybody should be able to say so from their own experience, and not from hearsay: the Rhine let it be, by all means."

So the Rhine it is.

Chapter II.

I have got over it; we have both got over it, tolerably, creditably; but after all, it is a much severer ordeal for a man than a woman, who, with a bouquet to occupy her hands, and a veil to gently shroud her features, need merely be prettily passive. I am alluding, I need hardly say, to the religious ceremony of marriage, which I flatter myself I have gone through with a stiff sheepishness not unworthy of my country. It is a three-days-old event now, and we are getting used to belonging to one another, though Elizabeth still takes off her ring twenty times a day to admire its bright thickness; still laughs when she hears herself called "Madame." Three days ago, we kissed all our friends, and left them to make themselves ill on our cake, and criticise our bridal behaviour, and now we are at Brussels, she and I feeling oddly, joyfully free from any chaperone. We have been mildly sight-seeing — very mildly most people would say, but we have resolved not to take our pleasure with the railway speed of Americans, or the hasty sadness of our fellow Britons. Slowly and gaily we have been taking ours. Today we have been to visit Wiertz's pictures. Have you ever seen them, oh reader? They are known to comparatively few people, but if you have a taste for the unearthly terrible — if you wish to sup full of horrors, hasten thither. We have been peering through the appointed peep-hole at the horrible cholera picture — the man buried alive by mistake, pushing up the lid of his coffin, and stretching a ghastly face and livid hands out of his winding sheet towards you, while awful grey-blue coffins are piled around, and noisome toads and giant spiders crawl damply about. On first seeing it, I have reproached myself for bringing one of so nervous a temperament as Elizabeth to see so haunting and hideous a spectacle; but she is less impressed than I expected — less impressed than I myself am.

"He is very lucky to be able to get his lid up," she says, with a half-laugh; "we should find it hard work to burst our brass nails, should not we? When you bury me, dear, fasten me down very slightly, in case there may be some mistake."

And now all the long and quiet July evening we have been prowling together about the streets — Brussels is the town of towns for *flâner*-ing — have been flattening our noses against the shop windows, and making each other imaginary presents. Elizabeth has not confined herself to imagination, however; she has made me buy her a little bonnet with feathers — "in order to look married," as she says, and the result is such a delicious picture of a child playing at being grown up, having practised a theft on its mother's wardrobe, that for the last two hours I have been in a foolish ecstasy of love and laughter over her and it. We are at the Bellevue, and have a fine suite of rooms, *au premier*, evidently specially devoted to the English, to the gratification of whose well-known loyalty the Prince and Princess of Wales are simpering from the walls. Is there anyone in the three kingdoms who knows his own face as well as he knows the faces of Albert Victor and Alexandra? The long evening has at last slidden into night — night far advanced — night melting into earliest day. All Brussels is asleep. One moment ago I also was asleep, soundly as any log. What is it that has made me take this sudden, headlong plunge out of sleep into wakefulness? Who is it that is clutching at and calling upon me? What is it that is making me struggle mistily up into a sitting posture, and try to revive my sleep-numbed senses? A summer night is never wholly dark; by the half light that steals through the closed *persiennes* and open windows I see my wife standing beside my bed; the extremity of terror on her face, and her fingers digging themselves with painful tenacity into my arm.

"Tighter, tighter!" she is crying, wildly. "What are you thinking of? You are letting me go!"

"Good heavens!" say I, rubbing my eyes, while my muddy brain grows a trifle clearer. "What is it? What has happened? Have you had a nightmare?"

"You saw him," she says, with a sort of sobbing breathlessness; "you know you did! You saw him as well as I."

"I!" cry I, incredulously — "not I! Till this second I have been fast asleep. *I* saw nothing."

"You did!" she cries, passionately. "You know you did. Why do you deny it? You were as frightened as I."

"As I live," I answer, solemnly, "I know no more than the dead what you are talking about; till you woke me by calling and catching hold of me, I was as sound asleep as the seven sleepers."

"Is it possible that it can have been a *dream*?" she says, with a long sigh, for a moment loosing my arm, and covering her face with her hands. "But no — in a dream I should have been somewhere else, but I was here — *here* — on that bed, and he stood *there*," pointing with her forefinger, "just *there*, between the foot of it and the window!"

She stops, panting.

"It is all that brute Wiertz," say I, in a fury. "I wish I had been buried alive myself before I had been fool enough to take you to see his beastly daubs."

"Light a candle," she says, in the same breathless way, her teeth chattering with fright. "Let us make sure he is not hidden somewhere in the room."

"How could he be?" say I, striking a match; "the door is locked."

"He might have got in by the balcony," she answers, still trembling violently.

"He would have had to have cut a very large hole in the *persiennes*," say I, half mockingly. "See, they are intact, and well fastened."

She sinks into an arm-chair, and pushes her loose soft hair from her white face.

"It *was* a dream then, I suppose?"

She is silent for a moment or two, while I bring her a glass of water, and throw a dressing-gown round her cold and shrinking form.

"Now tell me, my little one," I say coaxingly, sitting down at her feet, "what it was — what you thought you saw?"

"*Thought* I saw!" echoes she, with indignant emphasis, sitting upright, while her eyes sparkle feverishly. "I am as certain that I saw him standing there as I am that I see that candle burning — that I see this chair — that I see you."

"*Him!* but who is *him*?"

She falls forward on my neck, and buries her face in my shoulder.

"That — dreadful — man!" she says, while her whole body trembles.

"*What* dreadful man?" cry I impatiently.

She is silent.

"Who was he?"

"I do not know."

"Did you ever see him before?"

"Oh, no — no, never! I hope to God I may never see him again!"

"What was he like?"

"Come closer to me," she says, laying hold of my hand with her small and chilly fingers; "stay *quite* near me, and I will tell you," — after a pause — "he had a *nose!*"

"My dear soul," cry I, bursting out into a loud laugh in the silence of the night, "do not most people have noses? Would not he have been much more dreadful if he had had *none*?"

"But it was *such* a nose!" she says, with perfect trembling gravity.

137

"A bottle nose?" suggest I, still cackling.

"For heaven's sake, don't laugh!" she says nervously; "if you had seen his face, you would have been as little disposed to laugh as I."

"But his nose?" return I, suppressing my merriment, "what kind of nose was it? See, I am as grave as a judge."

"It was very prominent," she answers, in a sort of awe-struck half-whisper, "and very sharply chiselled; the nostrils very much cut out." A little pause. "His eyebrows were one straight black line across his face, and under them his eyes burnt like dull coals of fire, that shone and yet did not shine; they looked like dead eyes, sunken, half extinguished, and yet sinister."

"And what did he do?" asked I, impressed, despite myself, by her passionate earnestness; "when did you first see him?"

"I was asleep," she said — "at least, I thought so — and suddenly I opened my eyes, and he was *there* — *there*" — pointing again with trembling finger — "between the window and the bed."

"What was he doing? Was he walking about?"

"He was standing as still as stone — I never saw any live thing so still — *looking* at me; he never called or beckoned, or moved a finger, but his eyes *commanded* me to come to him, as the eyes of the mesmeriser at Penrith did." She stops, breathing heavily. I can hear her heart's loud and rapid beats.

"And you?" I say, pressing her more closely to my side, and smoothing her troubled hair.

"I *hated* it," she cries, excitedly; "I loathed it — abhorred it. I was ice-cold with fear and horror, but — I *felt* myself going to him."

"Yes?"

"And then I shrieked out to you, and you came running, and caught fast hold of me, and held me tight at first — quite tight — but presently I felt your hold slacken — slacken — and though I *longed* to stay with you, though I was *mad* with fright, yet I felt myself pulling strongly away from you — going to him; and he — he stood there always looking — looking — and then I gave one last loud shriek, and I suppose I awoke — and it was a dream!"

"I never heard of a clearer case of nightmare," say I, stoutly; "that vile Wiertz! I should like to see his whole *Musée* burnt by the hands of the hangman tomorrow."

She shakes her head. "It had nothing to say to Wiertz; what it meant I do not know, but —"

"It meant nothing," I answer, reassuringly, "except that for the future we will go and see none but good and pleasant sights, and steer clear of charnel-house fancies."

Chapter III.

Elizabeth is now in a position to decide whether the Rhine is a cocktail river or no, for she is on it, and so am I. We are sitting, with an awning over our heads, and little wooden stools under our feet. Elizabeth has a small sailor's hat and blue ribbon on her head. The river breeze has blown it rather awry; has tangled her plenteous hair; has made a faint pink stain on her pale cheeks. It is some fête day, and the boat is crowded. Tables, countless camp stools, volumes of black smoke pouring from the funnel, as we steam along. "Nothing to the Caledonian Canal!" cries a burly Scotchman in leggings, speaking with loud authority, and surveying with an air of contempt the eternal vine-clad slopes, that sound so well, and look so *sticky* in reality. "Cannot hold a candle to it!" A rival bride and bridegroom opposite, sitting together like love-birds under an umbrella, look into each other's eyes instead of at the Rhine scenery.

"They might as well have stayed at home, might not they?" says my wife with a little air of superiority. "Come, we are not so bad as that, are we?"

A storm comes on: hailstones beat slantwise and reach us — stone and sting us right under our awning. Everybody rushes down below, and takes the opportunity to feed ravenously. There are few actions more disgusting than eating *can* be made. A handsome girl close to us — her immaturity evidenced by the two long tails of black hair down her back — is thrusting her knife halfway down her throat.

"Come on deck again," says Elizabeth, disgusted and frightened at this last sight. "The hail was much better than this!"

So we return to our camp stools, and sit alone under one mackintosh in the lashing storm, with happy hearts and empty stomachs.

"Is not this better than any luncheon?" asks Elizabeth, triumphantly, while the rain-drops hang on her long and curled lashes.

"Infinitely better," reply I, madly struggling with the umbrella to prevent its being blown inside out, and gallantly ignoring a species of gnawing sensation at my entrails.

The squall clears off by-and-by, and we go steaming, steaming on past the unnumbered little villages by the water's edge with church spires and pointed roofs, past the countless rocks with their little pert castles perched on the top of them, past the tall, stiff poplar rows. The church bells are ringing gaily as we go by. A nightingale is singing from a wood. The black eagle of Prussia droops on the stream behind us, swish-swish through the dull green water. A fat woman who is interested in it leans over the back of the boat and, by some happy effect of crinoline, displays to her fellow-passengers two yards of thick white cotton legs. She is, fortunately for herself, unconscious of her generosity.

The day steals on; at every stopping place more people come on. There is hardly elbow room; and, what is worse, almost everybody is drunk. Rocks, castles, villages, poplars, slide by, while the paddles churn always the water, and the evening draws greyly on. At Bingen a party of big blue Prussian soldiers, very drunk, "glorious" as Tam o'Shanter, come and establish themselves close to us. They call for Lager Beer; talk at the tip-top of their strong voices; two of them begin to spar; all seem inclined to sing. Elizabeth is frightened. We are two hours late in arriving at Biebrich. It is half an hour more before we can get ourselves and our luggage into a carriage and set off along the winding road to Wiesbaden. "The night is chilly, but not dark." There is only a little shabby bit of a moon, but it shines as hard as it can. Elizabeth is quite worn out, her tired head droops in uneasy sleep on my shoulder. Once she wakes up with a start.

"Are you sure that it meant nothing?" she asks, looking me eagerly in my face; "do people often have such dreams?"

"Often, often," I answer, reassuringly.

"I am always afraid of falling asleep now," she says, trying to sit upright and keep her heavy eyes open, "for fear of seeing him standing there again. Tell me, do you think I shall? Is there any chance, any probability of it?"

"None, none!"

We reach Wiesbaden at last, and drive up to the Hôtel des Quatre Saisons. By this time it is full midnight. Two or three men are standing about the door. Morris, the maid, has got out — so have I, and I am holding out my hand to Elizabeth when I hear her give one piercing scream, and see her with ash-white face and starting eyes point with her forefinger —

"There he is! — there! — there!"

I look in the direction indicated, and just catch a glimpse of a tall figure standing half in the shadow of the night, half in the gas-light from the hotel. I have not time for more than one cursory glance, as I am interrupted by a cry from the bystanders, and turning quickly round, am just in time to catch my wife, who falls in utter insensibility into my arms. We carry her into a room on the ground floor; it is small, noisy, and hot, but it is the nearest at hand. In about an hour she re-opens her eyes. A strong shudder makes her quiver from head to foot.

"Where is he?" she says, in a terrified whisper, as her senses come slowly back. "He is somewhere about — somewhere near. I feel that he is!"

"My dearest child, there is no one here but Morris and me," I answer soothingly. "Look for yourself. See."

I take one of the candles and light up each corner of the room in succession.

"You saw him!" she says, in trembling hurry, sitting up and clenching her hands together. "I know you did — I pointed him out to you — you *cannot* say that it was a dream *this* time."

"I saw two or three ordinary-looking men as we drove up," I answer, in a commonplace, matter-of-fact tone. "I did not notice anything remarkable about any of them; you know, the fact is, darling, that you have had nothing to eat all day, nothing but a biscuit, and you are over-wrought, and fancy things."

"Fancy!" echoes she, with strong irritation. "How you talk! Was I ever one to fancy things? I tell you that as sure as I sit here — as sure as you stand there — I saw him — *him* — the man I saw in my dream, if it was a dream. There was not a hair's breadth of difference between them — and he was looking at me — looking —"

She breaks off into hysterical sobbing.

"My dear child!" say I, thoroughly alarmed, and yet half angry, "for God's sake do not work yourself up into a fever: wait till tomorrow, and we will find out who he is, and all about him; you yourself will laugh when we discover that he is some harmless bagman."

"Why not *now*?" she says, nervously; "why cannot you find out *now* — *this minute*?"

"Impossible! Everybody is in bed! Wait till tomorrow, and all will be cleared up."

The morrow comes, and I go about the hotel, inquiring. The house is so full, and the data I have to go upon are so small, that for some time I have great difficulty in making it understood to whom I am alluding. At length one waiter seems to comprehend.

"A tall and dark gentleman, with a pronounced and very peculiar nose? Yes; there has been such a one, certainly, in the hotel, but he left at 'grand matin' this morning; he remained only one night."

"And his name?"

The garçon shakes his head. "That is unknown, monsieur; he did not inscribe it in the visitors' book."

"What countryman was he?"

Another shake of the head. "He spoke German, but with a foreign accent."

"Whither did he go?"

That also is unknown. Nor can I arrive at any more facts about him.

Chapter IV.

A fortnight has passed; we have been hither and thither; now we are at Lucerne. Peopled with better inhabitants, Lucerne might well do for Heaven. It is drawing towards eventide, and Elizabeth and I are sitting hand in hand on a quiet bench, under the shady linden trees, on a high hill up above the lake. There is nobody to see us, so we sit peaceably hand in hand. Up by the still and solemn monastery we came, with its small and narrow windows, calculated to hinder the holy fathers from promenading curious eyes on the world, the flesh, and the devil, tripping past them in blue gauze veils: below us grass and green trees, houses with high-pitched roofs, little dormer-windows, and shutters yet greener than the grass; below us the lake in its rippleless peace, calm, quiet, motionless as Bethesda's pool before the coming of the troubling angel.

"I said it was too good to last," say I, doggedly, "did not I, only yesterday? Perfect peace, perfect sympathy, perfect freedom from nagging worries — when did such a state of things last more than two days?"

Elizabeth's eyes are idly fixed on a little steamer, with a stripe of red along its side, and a tiny puff of smoke from its funnel, gliding along and cutting a narrow white track on Lucerne's sleepy surface.

"This is the fifth false alarm of the gout having gone to his stomach within the last two years," continue I resentfully. "I declare to Heaven, that if it has not really gone there this time, I'll cut the whole concern."

Let no one cast up their eyes in horror, imagining that it is my father to whom I am thus alluding; it is only a great-uncle by marriage, in consideration of whose wealth and vague promises I have dawdled professionless through 28 years of my life.

"You *must* not go," says Elizabeth, giving my hand an imploring squeeze. "The man in the Bible said, 'I have married a wife, and therefore I cannot come'; why should it be a less valid excuse nowadays?"

"If I recollect rightly, it was considered rather a poor one even then," reply I, dryly.

Elizabeth is unable to contradict this; she therefore only lifts two pouted lips (Monsieur Taine objects to the redness of English women's mouths, but I do not) to be kissed, and says, "Stay." I am good enough to comply with her unspoken request, though I remain firm with regard to her spoken one.

"My dearest child," I say, with an air of worldly experience and superior wisdom, "kisses are very good things — in fact, there are few better — but one cannot live upon them."

"Let us try," she says coaxingly.

"I wonder which would get tired first?" I say, laughing. But she only goes on pleading, "Stay, stay."

"How *can* I stay?" I cry impatiently; "you talk as if I *wanted* to go! Do you think it is any pleasanter to me to leave you than to you to be left? But you know his disposition, his rancorous resentment of fancied neglects. For the sake of two days' indulgence, must I throw away what will keep us in ease and plenty to the end of our days?"

"I do not care for plenty," she says, with a little petulant gesture. "I do not see that rich people are any happier than poor ones. Look at the St. Clairs; they have £40,000 a year, and she is a miserable woman, perfectly miserable, because her face gets red after dinner."

"There will be no fear of *our* faces getting red after dinner," say I, grimly, "for we shall have no dinner for them to get red after."

A pause. My eyes stray away to the mountains. Pilatus on the right, with his jagged peak and slender snow-chains about his harsh neck; hill after hill rising silent, eternal, like guardian spirits standing hand in hand around their child, the lake. As I look, suddenly they have all flushed, as at some noblest thought, and over all their sullen faces streams an ineffable rosy joy — a solemn and wonderful effulgence, such as Israel saw reflected from the features of the Eternal in their prophet's transfigured eyes. The unutterable peace and stainless beauty of earth and sky seem to lie softly on my soul. "Would God I could stay! Would God all life could be like this!" I say, devoutly, and the aspiration has the reverent earnestness of a prayer.

"Why do you say, '*Would God!*'" she cries passionately, "when it lies with yourself? Oh my dear love," gently sliding her hand through my arm, and lifting wetly beseeching eyes to my face, "I do not know why I insist upon it so much — I cannot tell you myself — I dare say I seem selfish and unreasonable — but I feel as if your going now would be the end of all things — as if —" She breaks off suddenly.

"My child," say I, thoroughly distressed, but still determined to have my own way, "you talk as if I were going for ever and a day; in a week, at the outside, I shall be back, and then you will

144

thank me for the very thing for which you now think me so hard and disobliging."

"Shall I?" she answers, mournfully. "Well, I hope so."

"You will not be alone, either; you will have Morris."

"Yes."

"And every day you will write me a long letter, telling me every single thing that you do, say, and think."

"Yes."

She answers me gently and obediently; but I can see that she is still utterly unreconciled to the idea of my absence.

"What is it that you are afraid of?" I ask, becoming rather irritated. "What do you suppose will happen to you?"

She does not answer; only a large tear falls on my hand, which she hastily wipes away with her pocket handkerchief, as if afraid of exciting my wrath.

"Can you give me any good reason why I *should* stay?" I ask, dictatorially.

"None — none — only — stay — stay!"

But I am resolved *not* to stay. Early the next morning I set off.

Chapter V.

This time it is not a false alarm; this time it really has gone to his stomach, and, declining to be dislodged thence, kills him. My return is therefore retarded until after the funeral and the reading of the will. The latter is so satisfactory, and my time is so fully occupied with a multiplicity of attendant business, that I have no leisure to regret the delay. I write to Elizabeth, but receive no letters from her. This surprises and makes me rather angry, but does not alarm me. "If she had been ill, if anything had happened, Morris would have written. She never was great at writing, poor little soul. What dear little babyish notes she used to send me during our engagement! Perhaps she wishes to punish me for my disobedience to her wishes. Well, *now* she will see who was in the right." I am drawing near her now; I am walking up from the railway station in Lucerne. I am very joyful as I march along under an umbrella, in the grand broad shining of the summer afternoon. I think with pensive passion of the last glimpse I had of my beloved — her small and wistful face looking out from among the thick fair fleece of her long hair — winking away her tears and blowing kisses to me. It is a new sensation to me to have anyone looking tearfully wistful over my departure. I draw near the great glaring Schweizerhof, with its colonnaded tourist-crowded porch; here are all the pomegranates as I left them, in their green tubs, with their scarlet blossoms, and the dusty oleanders in a row. I look up at our windows; nobody is looking out from them; they are open, and the curtains are alternately swelled out and drawn in by the softly-playful wind. I run quickly upstairs and burst noisily into the sitting-room. Empty, perfectly empty! I open the adjoining door into the bedroom, crying, "Elizabeth! Elizabeth!" but I receive no answer. Empty too. A feeling of indignation creeps over me as I think, "Knowing the time of my return, she might have managed to be indoors." I have returned to the silent sitting-room, where the only noise is the wind still playing hide-and-seek with the curtains. As I look vacantly round my eye catches sight of a letter lying on the table. I pick it up mechanically and look at the address. Good heavens! what can this mean? It is my own, that I sent her two days ago, unopened, with the seal unbroken. Does she carry her resentment so far as not even to open my letters? I spring at the bell and violently ring it. It is answered by the waiter who has always specially attended us.

"Is madame gone out?"

The man opens his mouth and stares at me.

"Madame! Is monsieur then not aware that madame is no longer at the hotel?"

"*What?*"

"On the same day as monsieur, madame departed."

"*Departed!* Good God! what are you talking about?"

"A few hours after monsieur's departure — I will not be positive as to the exact time, but it must have been between one and two o'clock as the midday *table d'hôte* was in progress — a gentleman came and asked for madame —"

"Yes — be quick."

"I demanded whether I should take up his card, but he said no, that was unnecessary, as he was perfectly well known to

146

madame; and, in fact, a short time afterwards, without saying anything to anyone, she departed with him."

"And did not return in the evening?"

"No, monsieur; madame has not returned since that day."

I clench my hands in an agony of rage and grief. "So this is it! With that pure child-face, with that divine ignorance — only three weeks married — this is the trick she has played me!" I am recalled to myself by a compassionate suggestion from the garçon.

"Perhaps it was the brother of madame."

Elizabeth has no brother, but the remark brings back to me the necessity of self-command. "Very probably," I answer, speaking with infinite difficulty. "What sort of looking gentleman was he?"

"He was a very tall and dark gentleman with a most peculiar nose — not quite like any nose that I ever saw before — and most singular eyes. Never have I seen a gentleman who at all resembled him."

I sink into a chair, while a cold shudder creeps over me as I think of my poor child's dream — of her fainting fit at Wiesbaden — of her unconquerable dread of and aversion from my departure. And this happened twelve days ago! I catch up my hat, and prepare to rush like a madman in pursuit.

"How did they go?" I ask incoherently; "by train? — driving? —walking?"

"They went in a carriage."

"What direction did they take? Whither did they go?"

He shakes his head. "It is not known."

"It *must* be known," I cry, driven to frenzy by every second's delay. "Of course the driver could tell; where is he? — where can I find him?"

"He did not belong to Lucerne, neither did the carriage; the gentleman brought them with him."

"But madame's maid," say I, a gleam of hope flashing across my mind; "did she go with her?"

"No, monsieur, she is still here; she was as much surprised as monsieur at madame's departure."

"Send her at once," I cry eagerly; but when she comes I find that she can throw no light on the matter. She weeps noisily and says many irrelevant things, but I can obtain no information from her beyond the fact that she was unaware of her mistress's departure until long after it had taken place, when, surprised at not being rung for at the usual time, she had gone to her room and found it empty, and on inquiring in the hotel, had heard of her sudden departure; that, expecting her to return at night, she had sat up waiting for her till two o'clock in the morning, but that, as I knew, she had not returned, neither had anything since been heard of her.

Not all my inquiries, not all my cross-questionings of the whole staff of the hotel, of the visitors, of the railway officials, of nearly all the inhabitants of Lucerne and its environs, procure me a jot more knowledge. On the next few weeks I look back as on a hellish and insane dream. I can neither eat nor sleep; I am unable to remain one moment quiet; my whole existence, my nights and my days, are spent in seeking, seeking. Everything that human despair and frenzied love can do is done by me. I advertise, I communicate with the police, I employ detectives; but that fatal twelve days' start for ever baffles me. Only on one occasion do I obtain one tittle of information. In a village a few miles from Lucerne the peasants, on the day in question, saw a carriage driving rapidly through their little street. It was closed, but through the windows they could see the occupants — a dark gentleman, with the peculiar physiognomy which has so often been described, and on the opposite seat a lady lying apparently in a state of utter insensibility. But even this leads to nothing.

Oh, reader, these things happened twenty years ago; since then I have searched sea and land, but never have I seen my little Elizabeth again.

Seen in the Moonlight

Ellen Wood

"I tell you it is," repeated Tod. "One cannot mistake Temple, even at a distance."

"But this man looks so much older than he. And he has whiskers. Temple had none."

"And has not Temple grown older, do you suppose; and don't whiskers sprout and grow? You are always a muff, Johnny. That is Slingsby Temple."

We had gone by rail to Whitney Hall, and were walking up from the station. The Squire sent us to ask after Sir John's gout. It was a broiling hot day in the middle of summer. On the lawn before the house, with some of the Whitneys, stood a stranger; a little man, young, dark, and upright.

Tod was right, and I was wrong. It was Slingsby Temple. But I thought him much altered: older-looking than his years, which numbered close upon twenty-five, and more sedate and haughty than ever. We had neither seen nor heard of him since quitting Oxford.

"Oh, he's regularly in for it this time," said Bill Whitney, in answer to inquiries about his father, as they shook hands with us. "He has hardly ever had such a bout; can only lie in bed and groan. Temple, don't you remember Todhetley and Johnny Ludlow?"

"Yes, I do," answered Temple, holding out his hand to me first, and passing by Tod to do it. But that was Slingsby Temple's way. I was of no account, and therefore it did not touch his pride to notice me.

"I am glad to see you again," he said to Tod, cordially enough, as he turned to him; which was quite a gracious acknowledgment for Temple.

But it surprised us to see him there. The Whitneys had no acquaintance with the Temples; neither had he and Bill been special friends at college. Whitney explained it after luncheon, when we were sitting outside the windows in the shade, and Temple was pacing the shrubbery with Helen.

"I fancy it's a gone case," said Bill, nodding towards them.

"Oh, William, you should not say it," struck in Anna, in tones of remonstrance, and with her pretty blush. "It is not sure — and not right to Mr. Temple."

"Not say it to Tod and Johnny! Rubbish! Why, they are like ourselves, Anna. I say I think it is going to be a case."

"Helen with another beau!" cried free Tod. "How has it all come about?"

"The mother and Helen have been staying at Malvern, you know," said Whitney. "Temple turned up at the same hotel, the Foley Arms, and they struck up an intimacy. I went over for the last week, and was surprised to see how thick he was with them. The mother, who is more unsuspicious than a goose, told Temple, in her hospitable way, when they were saying good-bye, that she should be glad to see him if ever he found himself in these benighted parts: and I'll be shot if at the end of five days he was not here! If Helen's not the magnet, I don't know what else it can be."

"He appears to like her; but it may be only a temporary fancy that will pass away; it ought not to be talked about," reiterated Anna. "It may come to nothing."

"It may, or may not," persisted Bill.

"Will she consent to have him?" I asked.

"She'd be simple if she didn't," said Bill. "Temple would be a jolly fine match for any girl. Good in all ways. His property is large, and he himself is as sober and steady as any parson. Always has been."

I was not thinking of Temple's eligibility — that was undeniable; but of Helen's inclinations. Sometime before she had gone in for a love affair, which would not do at any price, caused some stir at the Hall, and came to signal grief: though I have not time to tell of it here. Whitney caught the drift of my thoughts.

"*That's* over and done with, Johnny. She'd never let its recollection spoil other prospects. You may trust Helen Whitney for that. She is as shallow-hearted as —"

"For shame, William!" remonstrated Anna.

"It's true," said he. "I didn't say *you* were. Helen would have twenty sweethearts to your one, and think nothing of it."

Tod looked at Anna, and laughed gently. Her cheeks turned the colour of the rose she was holding.

"What's this about a boating tour?" he inquired of Whitney. It had been alluded to at lunch-time.

"Temple's going in for one with some more fellows," was the reply. "He has asked me to join them. We mean to do some of the larger rivers; take our tent, and encamp on the bank at night."

"What a jolly spree!" cried Tod, his face flushing with delight. "How I should like it!"

"I wish to goodness you were coming. But Temple has made up his party. It is his affair, you know. He talks of staying out a month."

"One gets no chance in this slow place," cried Tod, fiercely. "I'll emigrate, I think, and go tiger-hunting. Is it a secret, this boating affair?"

"A secret! No."

"What made you kick me under the table, then, when I would have asked particulars at luncheon?"

"Because the mother was present. She has taken all sorts of queer notions into her head — mothers always have them — that the boat will be found bottom upwards someday, and we under it. Failing that, we are to catch colds and fevers and agues from the night encampments. So we say as little about it as possible before her."

"I see," nodded Tod. "Look here, Bill, I should like to get up a boating party myself; it sounds glorious. How do you set about it? — and where can you get a boat?"

"Temple knows," said Bill, "I don't. Let us go and ask him."

They went across the grass, leaving me alone with Anna. She and I were the best of friends, as the reader may remember, and exchanged many a little confidence with one another that the world knew nothing of.

"Should you like it for Helen?" I asked, indicating her sister and Slingsby Temple.

"Yes, I think I should," she answered. "But William had no warrant for speaking as he did. Mr. Temple will only be here a few days longer: when he leaves, we may never see him again."

"But he is evidently taken with Helen. He shows that he is. And when a man of Slingsby Temple's disposition allows himself to betray anything of the kind, rely upon it he means something."

"Did you like him at Oxford, Johnny?"

"Well — I did and did not," was my hesitating answer. "He was reserved, close, proud, and unsociable; and no man displaying those qualities can be very much liked. On the other hand, he was exemplary in conduct, deserving respect from all, and receiving it."

"I think he is religious," said Anna, her voice taking a lower tone.

"Yes, I always thought him that. I fancy their mother brought them up to be so. But Temple is the last man in the world to display it."

"What with papa's taking up two rooms to himself now he has the gout, and all of us being at home, mamma was a little at fault what chamber to give Mr. Temple. There was no time for much arrangement, for he came without notice; so she just turned Harry out of his room, which used to be poor John's, you know, and put Mr. Temple there. That night Harry chanced to go up to bed later than the rest of us. He forgot his room had been changed, and went straight into his own. Mr. Temple was kneeling down in prayer, and a Bible lay open on the table. Mamma says it is not all young men who say their prayers and read their Bible nowadays."

"Not by a good many, Anna. Yes, Temple is good, and I hope Helen will get him. She will have position, too, as his wife, and a large income."

"He comes into his estate this year, he told us; in September. He will be five-and-twenty then. But, Johnny, I don't like one thing: William says there was a report at Oxford that the Temples never live to be even middle-aged men."

"Some of them have died young, I believe. But, Anna, that's no reason why they all should."

"And — there's a superstition attaching to the family, is there not?" continued Anna. "A ghost that appears; or something of that sort?"

I hardly knew what to answer. How vividly the words brought back poor Fred Temple's communication to me on the subject, and his subsequent death.

"You don't speak," said she. "Won't you tell me what it is?"

"It is this, Anna: but I dare say it's all nonsense— all fancy. When one of the Temples is going to die, the spirit of the head of the family who last died is said to appear and beckon to him; a warning that his own death is near. Down in their neighbourhood people call it the Temple superstition."

"I don't quite understand," cried Anna, looking earnestly at me. "*Who* is it that is said to appear?"

"I'll give you an instance. When the late Mr. Temple, Slingsby's father, was walking home from shooting with his gamekeeper one September day, he thought he saw his father in the wood at a little distance: that is, his father's spirit, for he had been dead some years. It scared him very much at the moment, as the keeper testified. Well, Anna, in a day or two he, Mr. Temple, was dead— killed by an accident."

"I am glad I am not a Temple; I should be always fearing I might see the sight," observed Anna, a sad, thoughtful look on her gentle face.

"Oh no, you wouldn't, Anna. The Temples themselves don't think of it, and don't believe in it. Slingsby does not, at any rate. His brother Fred told me at Oxford that no one must presume to allude to it in Slingsby's presence."

"Fred? He died at Oxford, did he not?"

"Yes, he died there, poor fellow. Thrown from his horse. I saw it happen, Anna."

But I said nothing to her of that curious scene to which I had been a witness a night or two before the accident — when poor Fred, to Slingsby's intense indignation, fancied he saw his father on the college staircase; fancied his father beckoned to him. It was not a thing to talk of. After that time Slingsby had seemed to regard me with rather a special favour; I wondered whether it was because I had *not* talked of it.

The afternoon passed. We went up to see Sir John in his gouty room, and then said good-bye to them all, including Temple, and started for home again. Tod was surly and cross. He had come out in a temper and he was going back in one.

Tod liked his own way. No one in the world resented interference more than he: and just now he and the Squire were at war. Some twelve months before, Tod had dropped into a five-hundred-pound legacy from a distant relative. It was now ready to be paid to him. The Squire wished it paid over to himself, that he might take care of it; Tod wanted to be grand, and open a banking account of his own. For the past two days the argument had held out on both sides, and this morning Tod had lost his temper. Lost it was again now, but on another score.

"Slingsby Temple might as well have invited me to join the boating lot!" he broke out to me, as we drew near home. "He knows I am an old hand at it."

"But if his party is made up, Tod? Whitney said it was."

"Rubbish, Johnny. Made up! They could as well make room for another. And much good some of them are, I dare say! I can't remember that Slingsby ever took an oar in his hand at Oxford. All he went in for was star-gazing — and chapels — and lectures. And look at Bill Whitney! He hates rowing."

"Did you tell Temple you would like to join them?"

"He could see it. I didn't say in so many words, Will you have me? Of all things, I should enjoy a boating tour! It would be the most jolly thing on earth."

That night, after we got in, the subject of the money grievance cropped up again. The Squire was smoking his long church-warden pipe at the open window; Mrs. Todhetley sat by the centre table and the lamp, hemming a strip of muslin. Tod, open as the day on all subjects, abused Temple's "churlishness" for not inviting him to make one of the boating party, and declared he would organize one of his own, which he could readily do, now he was not tied for money. That remark set the Squire on.

"Ay, that's just where it would be, Joe," said he. "Let you keep the money in your own fingers, and we should soon see what it would end in."

"What would it end in?" demanded Tod.

"Ducks and drakes."

Tod tossed his head. "You think I am a child still, I believe, father."

"You are no better, where the spending of money's concerned," said the Squire, taking a long whiff. "Few young men are. Their fathers know that, and keep it from them as long as they can. And that's why so many are not let come into possession of their estates before they are five-and-twenty. This

154

young Temple, it seems, does not come into his; Johnny, here, does not."

"I should like to know what more harm it would do for the money to lie in my name in the Old Bank than if it lay in yours?" argued Tod. "Should I be drawing cheques on purpose to get rid of it? That's what you seem to suppose, father."

"You'd be drawing them to spend," said the pater.

"No, I shouldn't. It's my own money, after all. Being my own, I should take good care of it."

Old Thomas came in with some glasses, and the argument dropped. Tod began again as we were going upstairs together.

"You see, Johnny," he said, stepping inside my room on his way, and shutting the door for fear of eavesdroppers, "there's that hundred pounds I owe Brandon. The old fellow has been very good, never so much as hinting that he remembers it, and I shall pay him back the first thing. To do this, I must have absolute possession of the money. A fine bobbery the pater would make if he got to know of it. Besides, a man come to my age likes to have a banking account — if he can. Good-night, lad."

Tod carried his point. He turned so restive and obstinate over it as to surprise and vex the Squire, who of course knew nothing about the long-standing debt to Mr. Brandon. The Squire had no legal power to keep the money, if Tod insisted upon having it. And he did insist. The Squire put it down to boyish folly, self-assumption; and groaned and grumbled all the way to Worcester, when Tod was taking the five-hundred-pound cheque, paid to him free of duty, to the Old Bank.

"We shall have youngsters in their teens wanting to open a banking account next!" said the pater to Mr. Isaac, as Tod was writing his signature in the book. "The world's coming to something."

"I dare say young Mr. Todhetley will be prudent, and not squander it," observed Mr. Isaac, with one of his pleasant smiles.

"Oh, will he, though! You'll see. Look here," went on the Squire, tapping the banker on the arm, "couldn't you, if he draws too large a cheque at any time, refuse to cash it?"

"I fear we could not do that," laughed Mr. Isaac. "So long as he does not overdraw his account, we are bound to honour his cheques."

"And if you do overdraw it, Joe, I hope the bank will prosecute you! — I would, I know," was the Squire's last threat, as we left the bank and turned towards the Cross, Tod with a cheque-book in his pocket.

But Mr. Brandon could not be paid then. On going over to his house a day or two afterwards, we found him from home. The housekeeper thought he was on his way to one of the "water-cure establishments" in Yorkshire, she said, but he had not yet written to give his address.

"So it must wait," remarked Tod to me, as we went home. "I'm not sorry. How the bank would have stared at having to pay a hundred pounds down on the nail! Conclude, no doubt, that I was going to the deuce headlong."

"By Jove!" cried Tod, taking a leap in the air.

About a week had elapsed since the journey to the Old Bank, and Tod was opening a letter that had come addressed to him by the morning post.

"Johnny! will you believe it, lad? Temple asks me to be of the boating lot, after all."

It was even so. The letter was from Slingsby Temple, written from Templemore. It stated that he had been disappointed by some of those who were to have made up the number, and if Todhetley and Ludlow would supply their places, he should be glad.

Tod turned wild. You might have thought, as Mrs. Todhetley remarked, that he had been invited to Eden.

"The idea of Temple's asking you, Johnny!" he said. "You are of no good in a boat."

"Perhaps I had better decline?"

"No, don't do that, Johnny. It might upset the party altogether, perhaps. You must do your best."

"I have no boating-suit."

"I will treat you to one," said Tod, munificently. "We'll get it at Evesham. Pity but my things would fit you."

So it was, for he had loads of them.

The Squire, for a wonder, did not oppose the scheme. Mrs. Todhetley (like Lady Whitney) did, in her mild way. As Bill said, all mothers were alike — always foreseeing danger. And though she was not Tod's true mother, or mine either, she was just as anxious for us; and she looked upon it as nearly certain that one of us would come home drowned and the other with the ague.

"They won't sleep on the bare ground, of course," said Duffham, who chanced to call that morning, while Tod was writing his letter of acceptance to Slingsby Temple.

"Of course we shall," fired Tod, resenting the remark. "What harm could it do us?"

"Give some of you rheumatic-fever," said Duffham.

"Then why doesn't it give it to the gipsies?" retorted Tod.

"The gipsies are used to it — born to it, as one may say. You young men must have a waterproof sheet to lie upon, or a tarpaulin, or something of the sort."

Tod tossed his head, disdaining an answer, and wrote on.

"You will have plenty of rugs and great-coats with you, of course," went on Duffham. "And I'll give you a packet of quinine powders. It is as well to be prepared for contingencies. If you find any symptoms of unusual cold, or shivering, just take one or two of them."

"Look here, Mr. Duffham," said Tod, dashing his pen down on the table. "Don't you think you had better attend us yourself with a medicine-chest? Put up a cargo of rhubarb — and magnesia — and castor oil — and family pills. A few quarts of senna-tea might not come in amiss. My patience! I believe you take us for delicate infants."

"And I should recommend you to carry a small keg of whisky amongst the boat stores," continued Duffham, not in the least put out. "You'll want it. Take a nip of it neat when you first get up from the ground in the morning. It is necessary you should, and it will ward off some evils that might otherwise arise. Johnny Ludlow, I'll put the quinine into your charge: mind you don't forget it."

"Of all the old women!" muttered Tod to me. "Had the pater been in the room, this might have set him against our going."

On the following day we went over to Whitney Hall, intending to take Evesham on our way back, and buy what was wanted. Surprise the first. Bill Whitney was not at home, and was not to be of the boating party.

"You never saw anyone in such a way in your life," cried Helen, who could devote some time to us, now Temple was gone. "I must say it was too bad of papa. He never made any objection while Mr. Temple was here, but let poor William anticipate all the pleasure; and then he went and turned round afterwards."

"Did he get afraid for him?" cried Tod, in wonder. "I wouldn't have thought it of Sir John."

"Afraid! no," returned Helen, opening her eyes. "What he got was a fit of the gout. A relapse."

"What has the gout to do with Bill?"

"Why, old Featherston ordered papa to Buxton, and papa said he could not do without William to see to him there: mamma was laid up in bed with one of her bad colds — and she is not out of it yet. So papa went off, taking William — and you should just see how savage he was."

For William Whitney to be "savage" was something new. He had about the easiest temper in the world. I laughed, and said so.

"Savage for him, I mean," corrected Helen, who was given to talking at random. "Nothing puts him out. Some cross fellows would not have consented, and have told their fathers so to their faces. It is a shame."

"I don't suppose Bill cares much; he is no hand at rowing," remarked Tod. "Did he write to Temple and decline?"

"Of course he did," was Helen's resentfully spoken answer; and she seemed, to say the least, quite as much put out as Bill could have been. "What else could he do?"

"Well. I am sorry for this," said Tod. "Temple has asked me now. Johnny also."

"Has he!" exclaimed Helen, her eyes sparkling. "I hope you will go."

"Of course we shall go," said Tod. "Where's Anna?"

"Anna? Oh, sitting up with mamma. She likes a sick-room. I don't."

"You'd like a boat better — if Temple were in it," remarked Tod, with a saucy laugh.

"Just you be quiet," retorted Helen.

From Whitney Hall we went to Evesham, and hastily procured what we wanted. The next day but one was that fixed for our departure, and when it at last dawned, bright and hot, we started amidst the good wishes of all the house. Tod with a fishing-rod and line, in case the expedition should afford an opportunity for fishing, and I with Duffham's quinine powders in my pocket.

Templemore, the seat of the Temples, was on the Welsh borders. We were not going there, but to a place called Sanbury, which lay within a few miles of the mansion. Slingsby Temple and his brother Rupert were already there, with the boat and the tent and all the rest of the apparatus, making ready for our departure on the morrow. Our head-quarters, until the start, was at the Ship, a good, old-fashioned inn, and we found that we were expected to be Temple's guests there.

"I would have asked you to Templemore to dine and sleep," he observed, in cordial tones, "and my mother said she should have been pleased to see you; but to get down here in the morning would have been inconvenient. At least, it would take up the time that ought to be devoted to getting away. Will you come and see the boat?"

It was lying in a locked-up shed near the river. A tub-pair, large of its kind. Three of them were enough for it: and I saw that, in point of fact, I was not wanted for the working; but Temple either did not like to ask Tod without me, or else would not leave me out. The Temples might have more than their share of pride, but it was accompanied by an equal share of refined and considerate feeling.

"We shall make you useful, never fear," said he to me, with a smile. "And it will be capital boating experience for you."

"I am sure I shall like it," I answered. And I liked him better than I ever had in my life.

Numerous articles were lying ready with the boat. Temple seemed to have thought of every needful thing. A pot to boil water in, a pan for frying, a saucepan for potatoes, a mop and towing-rope, stone jugs for beer, milk, and fresh water, tins to hold our grog, and the like.

Amongst the stores were tea, sugar, candles, cheese, butter, a ham, some tinned provisions, a big jar of beer, and (Duffham should have seen it) a two-gallon keg of whisky.

"A doctor up with us said we ought to have whisky," remarked Tod. "He is nothing but an old woman. He put some quinine powders in Johnny's pocket, and talked of a waterproof sheet to sleep on."

"Quite right," said Temple. "There it lies."

And there it did lie, wrapped round the folded tent. A large waterproof tarpaulin to cover the ground, at night, and keep the damp from our limbs.

"Did you ever make a boating tour before, Temple?" asked Tod.

"Oh yes. I like it. I don't know any pleasure equal to that of camping out at night on a huge plain, where you may study all the stars in the heavens."

As Temple spoke, he glanced towards a small parcel in a corner. I guessed it was one of his night telescopes.

"Yes, it is," he assented; "but only a small one. The boat won't stretch, and we can only load it according to its limits."

Rupert Temple came up as we were leaving the shed. I had never seen him before. He was the only brother left, and Slingsby's heir presumptive. Why, I know not, but I had pictured Rupert as being like poor Fred — tall, fair, bright-looking as a man can be. But there existed not a grain of resemblance. Rupert was just a second edition of Slingsby: little, dark, plain, and proud. It was not an offensive pride — quite the contrary: and with those they knew well they were cordial and free.

Those originally invited by Temple were his cousin Arthur Slingsby; Lord Cracroft's son; Whitney; and a young Welshman named Pryce-Hughes. All had accepted, and intended to keep the engagement, knowing then of nothing to prevent them. But, curious to say, each one in succession wrote to decline it later. Whitney had to go elsewhere with his father; Pryce-Hughes hurt his arm, which disabled him from rowing: and Arthur Slingsby went off without ceremony in somebody's yacht to

Malta. As the last of the letters came, which was Whitney's, Mrs. Temple seemed struck with the coincidence of all refusing, or being compelled to refuse. "Slingsby, my dear," she said to her son, "it looks just as though you were not to go." "But I will go," answered Temple, who did not like to be baulked in a project more than anybody else likes it; "if these can't come, I'll get others who can." And he forthwith told his brother Rupert that there'd be room for him in the boat — he had refused him before; and wrote to Tod. After that, came another letter from Pryce-Hughes, saying his arm was better, and he could join the party at Bridgenorth or Bewdley. But it was too late: the boat was filled up. Temple meant to do the Severn, the Wye, and the Avon, with a forced interlude of canals, and to be out a month, taking it easily, and resting on Sundays.

"Catch Slingsby missing Sunday service if he can help it!" said Rupert aside to me.

We started in our flannel suits and red caps, and started well, but not until the afternoon, Temple steering, his brother and Tod taking the sculls. The water was very shallow: and by-and-by we ran aground. The stern of the boat swung round, and away went our tarpaulin; and it was carried off by the current before we could save it.

Well, that first afternoon there were difficulties to contend with, and one or other of the three was often in the water; but we made altogether some five or six miles. It was the hottest day I ever felt; and about seven o'clock, on coming to a convenient meadow, nearly level with the river, none of us were sorry to step ashore. Making fast the boat for the night, we landed the tent and other things, and looked about us. A coppice bounded the field on the left; right across, in a second field, stood a substantial farm-house, surrounded by its barns and ricks. Temple produced one of his cards, which was to be taken to the house, and the farmer's leave asked to encamp on the meadow. Rupert Temple and Tod made themselves decent to go on the errand.

"We shall want a bundle or two of straw," said Temple; "it won't do to lie on the bare ground. And some milk. You must ask if they will accommodate us, and pay what they charge."

They went off, carrying also the jar to beg for fresh water. Temple and I began to unfurl the tent, and to busy ourselves amongst the things generally.

"Halloa! what's to do here?"

We turned, and saw a stout, comely man, in white shirt-sleeves, an open waistcoat, knee-breeches and top-boots; no doubt the farmer himself. Temple explained. He and some friends were on a boating tour, and had landed there to encamp for the night.

"But who gave you leave to do it?" asked the farmer. "You are trespassing. This is my ground."

"I supposed it might be necessary to ask leave," said Temple, haughtily courteous; "and I have sent to yonder house — which I presume is yours — to solicit it. If you will kindly accord the permission, I shall feel obliged."

That Temple looked disreputable enough, there could be no denying. No shoes on, no stockings, trousers tucked up above the knee: for he had been several times in the water, and, as yet, had done nothing to himself. But two of our college-caps chanced to be lying exposed on the boat: and perhaps, Temple's tone and address had made their due impression. The farmer looked hard at him, as if trying to remember his face.

"It's not one of the young Mr. Temples, is it?" said he. "Of Templemore."

"I am Mr. Temple, of Templemore. I have sent my card to your house."

"Dash me!" cried the farmer, heartily. "Shake hands, sir. I fancied I knew the face. I've seen you out shooting, sir — and at Sanbury. I knew your father. I'm sure you are more than welcome to camp alongside here, and to any other accommodation I can give you. Will you shake hands, young gentleman?" giving his hand to me as he released Temple's.

"My brother and another of our party are gone to your house to beg some fresh water and buy some milk," said Temple, who did not seem at all to resent the farmer's familiarity, but rather to like it. "And we shall be glad of a truss or two of fresh straw, if you can either sell it to us or give it. We have had the misfortune to lose our waterproof sheet."

162

"Sell be hanged!" cried the farmer, with a jovial laugh. "Sell you a truss or two of straw! Sell you milk! Not if I know it, Mr. Temple. You're welcome, sir, to as much as ever you want of both. One of my men shall bring the straw down."

"You are very good."

"And anything else you please to think of. Don't scruple to ask, sir. Will you all come and take supper at my house? We've a rare round o' beef in cut, and I saw the missis making pigeon-pies this morning."

But Temple declined the invitation most decisively; and the farmer, perhaps noting that, did not press it. It was rare weather for the water, he observed.

"We could do with less heat," replied Temple.

"Ay," said the farmer, "I never felt it worse. But it's good for the corn."

And, with that, he left us. The other two came back with water and oceans of milk. Sticks were soon gathered from the coppice, and the fire made; the round pot, filled with water, was put on to boil for tea, and the tent was set up.

Often and often in my later life have I looked back to that evening. The meal over — and a jolly good one we made — we sat round the camp fire, then smouldering down to red embers, and watched the setting sun, Rupert Temple and Tod smoking. It was a glorious sunset, the west lighted up with gold and purple and crimson; the sky above us clear and dark-blue.

But oh, how hot it was! The moon came up as the sun went down, and the one, to our fancy, seemed to give out as much heat as the other. There we sat on, sipping our grog, and talking in the bright moonlight, Temple with his elbows on the grass, his face turned up towards the sky and the few stars that came out. The colours in the west gave place to a beautiful opal, stretching northwards.

It was singular — I shall always think so — that the conversation should turn on MacRae, the Scotchman who used to make our skin creep at Oxford with his tales of second-sight. We were *not* talking of Oxford, and I don't know how MacRae came up. Temple had been talking of astronomy; from that we got to astrology; so perhaps it was in that way. Up he came, however, he and his weird beliefs; and Rupert Temple, who had not enjoyed the honour of Mac's acquaintance, and had probably never heard his name before, got me to relate one or two of Mac's choice experiences.

"Was the man a fool?" asked Rupert.

"Not a bit of it."

"I'm sure I should say so. Making out that he could foresee people's funerals before they were dead, or likely to die."

"Poor Fred was three-parts of a believer in them," put in Temple, in a dreamy voice, as though his thoughts were buried in that past time.

"Fred was!" exclaimed Rupert, taking his brother up sharply. "Believer in what?"

"MacRae's superstitions."

"Nonsense, Slingsby!"

Temple made no rejoinder. In his eye, which chanced to catch mine at the moment, there sat a singular expression. I wondered whether he was recalling that other superstition of Fred's, that little episode a night or two before he died.

"We had better be turning in," said Temple, getting up. "It won't do to sit here too long; and we must be up betimes in the morning."

So we got to bed at last — if you can call it bed. The farmer's good straw was strewed thickly underneath us in the tent; we had our rugs; and the tent was fastened back at the entrance to admit air. But there was no air to admit, not a whiff of it; nothing came in but the moonlight. None of us remembered a lighter night, or a hotter one. I and Tod lay in the middle, the Temples on either side, Slingsby nearest the opening.

"I wonder who's got our sheet?" began Tod, breaking a silence that ensued when we had wished each other good-night.

No one answered.

"I say," struck in Rupert, by-and-by, "I've heard one ought not to go to sleep in the moonlight: it turns people luny. Do any of your faces catch it, outside there?"

"Go to sleep and don't talk," said Temple.

It might have been from the novelty of the situation, but the night was well on before any of us got to sleep. Tod and Rupert Temple went off first, and next (I thought) Temple did. *I* did not.

164

I dare say you've never slept four in a bed — and, that, one of littered straw. It's all very well to lie awake when you've a good wide mattress to yourself, and can toss and turn at will; but in the close quarters of a tent you can't do it for fear of disturbing the others. However, the longest watch has its ending; and I was just dropping off, when Temple, next to whom I lay, started hurriedly, and it aroused me.

"What's that?" he cried, in a half-whisper.

I lifted my head, startled. He was sitting up, his eyes fixed on the opening we had left in the tent.

"Who's there? — who is it?" he said again; and his low voice had a slow, queer sound, as though he spoke in fear.

"What is it, Temple?" I asked.

"There, standing just outside the tent, right in the moonlight," whispered he. "Don't you see?"

I could see nothing. The stir awoke Rupert. He called out to know what ailed us; and that aroused Tod.

"Some man looking in at us," explained Temple, in the same queer tone, half of abstraction, half of fear, his gaze still strained on the aperture. "He is gone now."

Up jumped Tod, and dashed outside the tent. Rupert struck a match and lighted the lantern. No one was to be seen but ourselves; and the only odd thing to be remarked was the white hue Temple's face had taken. Tod was marching round the tent, looking about him far and near, and calling out to all intruders to show themselves. But all that met his eye was the level plain we were encamped upon, lying pale and white under the moonlight, and all the sound he heard was the croaking of the frogs.

"What could have made you fancy it?" he asked of Temple.

"Don't think it was fancy," responded Temple. "Never saw any man plainer in my life."

"You were dreaming, Slingsby," said Rupert. "Let us get to sleep again."

Which we did. At least, I can answer for myself.

The first beams of the glorious sun awoke us, and we rose to the beginning of another day, and to the cold, shivery feeling that, in spite of the heat of the past night and of the coming day, attends the situation. I could understand now why the nip of whisky, as Duffham called it, was necessary. Tod served it out. Lighting the fire of sticks to boil our tea-kettle — or the round pot that served for a kettle — we began to get things in order to embark again, when breakfast should be over.

"I say, Slingsby," cried Rupert, to his brother, who seemed very sullen, "what on earth took you, that you should disturb us in the night for nothing?"

"It was not for nothing. Someone was there."

"It must have been a stray sheep."

"Nonsense, Rupert! Could one mistake a sheep for a man?"

"Some benighted ploughman then, 'plodding his weary way.'"

"If you could bring forward any ploughman to testify that it was he beyond possibility of doubt, I'd give him a ten-pound note."

"Look here," said Tod, after staring a minute at this odd remark of Temple's, "you may put all idea of ploughmen and everyone else away. No one was there. If there had been, I must have seen him: it was not possible he could betake himself out of sight in a moment."

"Have it as you like," said Temple; "I am going to take a bath. My head aches."

Stripping, he plunged into the river, which was very wide just there, and swam towards the middle of it.

"It seems to have put Slingsby out," observed Rupert, alluding to the night alarm. "Do you notice how thoughtful he is? Just look at that fire!"

The sticks had turned black, and began to smoke and hiss, giving out never a bit of blaze. Down knelt Rupert on one side and I on the other.

"Damp old obstinate things!" he ejaculated. And we set on to blow at them with all our might.

"Where's Temple?" I exclaimed presently; looking off, and not seeing him. Rupert glanced over the river.

"He must be diving, Johnny. Slingsby's fond of diving. Keep on blowing, lad, or we shall get no tea today."

So we kept on. But, I don't know why, a sort of doubtful feeling came over me, and while I blew I watched the water for Temple to come up. All in a moment he rose to the surface, gave one low, painful cry of distress, and disappeared again.

166

"Good Heavens!" cried Rupert, leaping up and overturning the kettle.

But Tod was the quickest, and jumped in to the rescue. A first-rate swimmer and diver was he, almost as much at home in the water as out of it. In no time, as it seemed, he was striking back, bearing Temple. It was fortunate for such a crisis that Temple was so small and slight — of no weight to speak of.

By dint of gently rubbing and rolling, we got some life into him and some whisky down his throat. But he remained in the queerest, faintest state possible; no exertion in him, no movement hardly, no strength; alive, and that was about all; and just able to tell us that he had turned faint in the water.

"What is to be done?" cried Rupert. "We must get a doctor to him: and he ought not to lie on the grass here. I wonder if that farmer would let him be taken to the house for an hour or two?"

I got into my boots, and ran off to ask; and met the farmer in the second field. He was coming towards us, curious perhaps to see whether we had started. Telling him what had happened, he showed himself alive with sympathy, called some of his men to carry Temple to the farm, and sent back to prepare his wife. Their name we found was Best: and most hospitable, good-hearted people they turned out to be.

Well, Temple was taken there and a doctor was called in. The doctor shook his head, looked grave, and asked to have another doctor. Then, for the first time, doubts stole over us that it might be more serious than we had thought for. A dreadful feeling of fear took possession of me, and, in spite of all I could do, that scene at Oxford, when poor Fred Temple had been carried into old Mrs. Golding's to die, would not go out of my mind.

We got into our reserve clothes, as if conscious that the boating flannels were done with for the present, left one of the farmer's men to watch our boat and things, and stayed with Temple. He continued very faint, and lay almost motionless. The doctors tried some remedies, but they did no good. He did not revive. One of them called it "syncope of the heart;" but the other said hastily, "No, no, that was not the right name." It struck me that perhaps they did not know what the right name was. At last they said Mrs. Temple had better be sent for.

"I was just thinking so," cried Rupert. "My mother ought to be here. Who will go for her?"

"Johnny can," said Tod. "He is of no good here."

For that matter, none of us were any good, for we could do nothing for Temple.

I did not relish the task: I did not care to tell a mother that her son, whom she believes is well and hearty, is lying in danger. But I had to go: Rupert seemed to take it as a matter of course.

"Don't alarm her more than you can help, Ludlow," he said. "Say that Slingsby turned faint in the water this morning, and the medical men seem anxious. But ask her not to lose time."

Mr. Best started me on his own horse — a fine hunter, iron-grey. The weather was broiling. Templemore lay right across country, about six miles off by road. It was a beautiful place; I could see that much, though I had but little time to look at it; and it stood upon an eminence, the last mile of the road winding gradually up to its gates.

As ill-luck had it, or perhaps good-luck — I don't know which — Mrs. Temple was at one of the windows, and saw me ride hastily in. Having a good memory of faces, she recollected mine. Knowing that I had started with her sons in the boat, she was seized with a prevision that something was wrong, and came out before I was well off the horse.

"It is Mr. Ludlow, I think," she said, her plain dark face (so much like Slingsby's) very pale. "What ill news have you brought?"

I told her in the best manner I was able, just in the words Rupert had suggested, speaking quietly, and not showing any alarm in my own manner.

"Is there danger?" she at once asked.

"I am not *sure* that there is," I said, hardly knowing how to frame my answer. "The doctors thought you had better come, in case — in case of danger arising; and Rupert sent me to ask you to do so."

She rang the bell, and ordered her carriage to be round instantly. "The bay horses," she added: "they are the fleetest. What will you take, Mr. Ludlow?"

I would not take anything. But a venerable old gentleman in black, with a powdered bald head — the butler, I concluded —

suggested some lemonade, after my hot ride: and that I was glad of.

I rode on first, piloting the way for the carriage, which contained Mrs. Temple. She came alone: her daughter was away on a visit — as I had learnt from Rupert.

Slingsby lay in the same state, neither better nor worse: perhaps the breathing was somewhat more difficult. He smiled when he saw his mother, and put out his hand.

The day dragged itself slowly on. We did not know what to do with ourselves; that was a fact. Temple was to be kept quiet, and we might not intrude into his room — one on the ground-floor that faced the east: not even Rupert. Mr. and Mrs. Best entertained us well as far as meals went, but one can't be eating for ever. Now down in the meadow by the boat — which seemed to have assumed a most forlorn aspect — and now hovering about the farm, waiting for the last report of Temple. In that way the day crept through.

"Is it here that Mr. Temple is lying?"

I was standing under the jessamine-covered porch, sheltering my head from the rays of the setting sun, when a stranger came up and put the question. An extraordinarily tall, thin man, with grey hair, clerical coat, and white neckcloth.

It was the Reverend Mr. Webster, perpetual curate of the parish around Templemore. And I seemed to know him before I heard his name, for he was the very image of his son, Long Webster, who used to be at Oxford.

"I am so grieved not to have been able to get here before," he said; "but I had just gone out for some hours when Mrs. Temple's message was brought to the Parsonage. Is he any better?"

"I am afraid not," I answered. "We don't know what to make of it; it all seems so sudden and strange."

"But what is it?" he asked in a whisper.

"I don't know, sir. The doctors have said something about the heart."

"I should like to see the doctors before I go in to Mrs. Temple. Are they here?"

"One of them is, I think. They have been going in and out all day."

I fetched the doctor out to him; and they talked together in low tones in the shaded and quiet porch. Not a ray of hope sat on the medical man's face: he as good as intimated that Temple was dying.

"Dear me!" cried the dismayed Mr. Webster.

"He seems to know it himself," continued the doctor. "At least, we fancy so, I and my brother-practitioner. Though we have been most cautious not to alarm him by any hint of the kind."

"I should like to see him," said the parson. "I suppose I can?"

He went in, and was shut up for some time alone with Temple. Yes, he said, when he came out again, Temple knew all about it, and was perfectly resigned and prepared.

You may be sure there was no bed for any of us that night. Temple's breathing grew worse; and at last we went in by turns, one of us at a time, to prop up the pillows behind, and keep them propped; it seemed to make it firmer and easier for him as he lay against them. Towards morning I was called in to replace Rupert. The shaded candle seemed to be burning dim.

"You can lie down, my dear," Mrs. Temple whispered to Rupert. "Should there be any change, I will call you."

He nodded, and left the room. Not to lie down. Only to sit over the kitchen fire with Tod, and so pass away the long hours of discomfort.

"Who is this now?" panted Slingsby, as I took my place.

"It is I. Johnny Ludlow. Do you feel any better?"

He made a little sound of dissent in answer.

"Nay, I think you look easier, my dear," said Mrs. Temple, gently.

"No, no," he said, just opening his eyes. "Do not grieve, mother. I shall be better off. I shall be with my father and Fred."

"Oh, my son, my son, don't lose heart!" she said, with a sob. "That will never do."

"I saw my father last night," said Temple.

The words seemed to strike her with a sort of shock. "No!" she exclaimed, perhaps thinking of the Temple superstition, and drawing back a step. "Pray, pray don't fancy that!"

"The tent was open to give us air," he said, speaking with difficulty. "I suddenly saw someone standing in the moonlight. I was next the opening; and I had not been able to get to sleep. For a moment I thought it was some man, some intruder passing by; but he took a strange likeness to my father, and I thought he beckoned —"

"We are not alone, Slingsby," interrupted Mrs. Temple, remembering me, her voice cold, not to say haughty.

"Ludlow knows. He knew the last time. Fred said he saw him, and I — I ridiculed it. Ludlow heard me. My father came for Fred, mother; he must have come for me."

"Oh, I can't — I can't believe this, Slingsby," she cried, in some excitement. "It was fancy — nervousness; nothing else. My darling, I cannot lose you! You have ever been dearer to me than my other children."

"Only for a little while, mother. It is God's will. That is our true home, you know; and then there will be no more parting. I am quite happy. I seem to be half there now. What is that light?"

Mrs. Temple looked round, and saw a faint streak coming in over the tops of the shutters. "It must be the glimmering of dawn in the east," she said. "The day is breaking."

"Ay," he answered: "my day. Where's Rupert? I should like to say good-bye to him. Yes, mother, that's the dawn of heaven."

And just as the sun rose, he went there.

That was the end of our boating tour. Ridicule has been cast on some of the facts, and will be again. It is a painful subject; and I don't know that I should have related it, but for its having led to another (and more lively) adventure, which I proceed to tell of.

The Secret Chamber

[Dedicated to the inquirers in the Norman Tower.]

Margaret Oliphant

Chapter I.

Castle Gowrie is one of the most famous and interesting in all Scotland. It is a beautiful old house, to start with, — perfect in old feudal grandeur, with its clustered turrets and walls that could withstand an army, — its labyrinths, its hidden stairs, its long mysterious passages — passages that seem in many cases to lead to nothing, but of which no one can be too sure what they lead to. The front, with its fine gateway and flanking towers, is approached now by velvet lawns, and a peaceful, beautiful old avenue, with double rows of trees, like a cathedral; and the woods out of which these grey towers rise, look as soft and rich in foliage, if not so lofty in growth, as the groves of the South. But this softness of aspect is all new to the place, — that is, new within the century or two which count for but little in the history of a dwelling-place, some part of which, at least, has been standing since the days when the Saxon Athelings brought such share of the arts as belonged to them to solidify and regulate the original Celtic art which reared incised stones upon rude burial-places, and twined mystic knots on its crosses, before historic days. Even of this primitive decoration there are relics at Gowrie, where the twistings and twinings of Runic cords appear still on some bits of ancient wall, solid as rocks, and almost as everlasting. From these to the graceful French turrets, which recall many a grey château, what a long interval of years! But these are filled with stirring chronicles enough, besides the dim, not always decipherable records, which different developments of architecture have left on the old house. The Earls of Gowrie had been in the heat of every commotion that took place on or about the Highland line for more generations than any but a Celtic pen could record. Rebellions, revenges, insurrections, conspiracies, nothing in which blood was shed and lands lost, took place in Scotland, in which they had not had a share; and the annals of the house are very full, and not without many a stain. They had been a bold and vigorous race — with much evil in them, and some good; never insignificant, whatever else they might be. It could not be said, however, that they are remarkable nowadays. Since the first Stuart rising, known in Scotland as "the Fifteen," they have not done much that has been worth recording; but yet their family history has always been of an unusual kind. The Randolphs could not be called eccentric in themselves: on the contrary, when you knew them, they were at bottom a respectable race, full of all the country-gentleman virtues; and yet their public career, such as it was, had been marked by the strange leaps and jerks of vicissitude. You would have said an impulsive, fanciful family — now making a grasp at some visionary advantage, now rushing into some wild speculation, now making a sudden sally into public life — but soon falling back into mediocrity, not able apparently, even when the impulse was purely selfish and mercenary, to keep it up. But this would not have been at all a true conception of the family character; their actual virtues were not of the imaginative order, and their freaks were a mystery to their friends. Nevertheless these freaks were what the general world was most aware of in the Randolph race. The late Earl had been a representative peer of Scotland (they had no English title), and had made quite a wonderful start, and for a year or two had seemed about to attain a very eminent place in Scotch affairs; but his ambition was found to have made use of some very equivocal modes of gaining influence, and he dropped accordingly at once and for ever from the political firmament. This was quite a common circumstance in the family. An apparently brilliant beginning, a discovery of evil means adopted for ambitious ends, a sudden subsidence, and the curious conclusion at the end of everything that this schemer, this unscrupulous speculator or politician, was a dull, good man after all — unambitious, contented, full of domestic kindness and benevolence. This family peculiarity made the history of the Randolphs a very strange one, broken by the oddest interruptions, and with no consistency in it. There was another circumstance, however, which attracted still more the wonder and observation of the public. For one who can appreciate such a recondite matter as family character, there are hundreds who are interested in a family secret, and this the house of Randolph possessed in perfection. It was a mystery which piqued the imagination and excited the interest of the entire country. The story went, that somewhere hid amid the massive walls and tortuous passages there was a secret chamber in Gowrie Castle. Everybody knew of its existence; but save the earl, his heir, and one other person, not of the family, but filling a confidential post in their service, no mortal knew where this mysterious hiding-place was. There had been countless guesses made at it, and expedients of all kinds invented to find it out. Every visitor who ever entered the old gateway, nay, even passing travellers who saw the turrets from the road, searched keenly for some trace of this mysterious chamber. But all guesses and researches were equally in vain.

I was about to say that no ghost-story I ever heard of has been so steadily and long believed. But this would be a mistake, for nobody knew even with any certainty that there was a ghost connected with it. A secret chamber was nothing wonderful in so old a house. No doubt they exist in many such old houses, and are always curious and interesting — strange relics, more moving than any history, of the time when a man was not safe in his own house, and when it might be necessary to secure a refuge beyond the reach of spies or traitors at a moment's notice. Such a refuge was a necessity of life to a great medieval noble. The peculiarity about this secret chamber, however, was that some secret connected with the very existence of the family was always understood to be involved in it. It was not only the secret hiding-place for an emergency, a kind of historical possession presupposing the importance of his race, of which a man might be honestly proud; but there was something hidden in it of which assuredly the race could not be proud. It is wonderful how easily a family learns to pique itself upon any distinctive possession. A ghost is a sign of importance not to be despised; a haunted room is worth as much as a small farm to the complacency of the family that owns it. And no doubt the younger branches of the Gowrie family — the lightminded portion of the race — felt this, and were proud of their unfathomable secret, and felt a thrill of agreeable awe and piquant suggestion go through them, when they remembered the mysterious something which they did not know in their familiar home. That thrill ran through the entire circle of visitors, and children, and servants, when the Earl peremptorily forbade a projected improvement, or stopped a reckless exploration. They looked at each other with a pleasurable shiver. "Did you hear?" they said. "He will not let Lady Gowrie have that closet she wants so much in that bit of wall. He sent the workmen about their business before they could touch it, though the wall is twenty feet thick if it is an inch; ah!" said the visitors, looking at each other; and this lively suggestion sent tinglings of excitement to their very finger-points; but even to his wife, mourning the commodious closet she had intended, the Earl made no explanations. For anything she knew, it might be there, next to her room, this mysterious lurking-place; and it may be supposed that this suggestion conveyed to Lady Gowrie's veins a thrill more keen and strange, perhaps too vivid to be pleasant. But she was not in the favoured or unfortunate number of those to whom the truth could be revealed.

I need not say what the different theories on the subject were. Some thought there had been a treacherous massacre there, and that the secret chamber was blocked by the skeletons of murdered guests, — a treachery no doubt covering the family with shame in its day, but so condoned by long softening of years as to have all the shame taken out of it. The Randolphs could not have felt their character affected by any such interesting historical record. They were not so morbidly sensitive. Some said, on the other hand, that Earl Robert, the wicked Earl, was shut up there in everlasting penance, playing cards with the devil for his soul. But it would have been too great a feather in the family cap to have thus got the devil, or even one of his angels, bottled up, as it were, and safely in hand, to make it possible that any lasting stigma could be connected with such a fact as this. What a thing it would be to know where to lay one's hand upon the Prince of Darkness, and prove him once for all, cloven foot and everything else, to the confusion of gainsayers!

So this was not to be received as a satisfactory solution, nor could any other be suggested which was more to the purpose. The popular mind gave it up, and yet never gave it up; and still everybody who visits Gowrie, be it as a guest, be it as a tourist, be it only as a gazer from a passing carriage, or from the flying railway train which just glimpses its turrets in the distance, daily and yearly spends a certain amount of curiosity, wonderment, and conjecture about the Secret Chamber — the most piquant and undiscoverable wonder which has endured unguessed and undeciphered to modern times.

This was how the matter stood when young John Randolph, Lord Lindores, came of age. He was a young man of great character and energy, not like the usual Randolph strain — for, as we have said, the type of character common in this romantically-situated family, notwithstanding the erratic incidents common to them, was that of dullness and honesty, especially in their early days. But young Lindores was not so. He was honest and honourable, but not dull. He had gone through almost a remarkable course at school and at the university — not perhaps in quite the ordinary way of scholarship, but enough to attract men's eyes to him. He had made more than one great speech at the Union. He was full of ambition, and force, and life, intending all sorts of great things, and meaning to make his position a stepping-stone to all that was excellent in public life. Not for him the country gentleman existence which was congenial to his father. The idea of succeeding to the family honours and becoming a Scotch peer, either represented or representative, filled him with horror; and filial piety in his case was made warm by all the energy of personal hopes when he prayed that his father might live, if not for ever, yet longer than any Lord Gowrie had lived for the last century or two. He was as sure of his election for the county the next time there was a chance, as anybody can be certain of anything; and in the meantime he meant to travel, to go to America, to go no one could tell where, seeking for instruction and experience, as is the manner of high-spirited young men with parliamentary tendencies in the present day. In former times he would have gone "to the wars in the Hie Germanie," or on a crusade to the Holy Land; but the days of the crusaders and

176

of the soldiers of fortune being over, Lindores followed the fashion of his time. He had made all his arrangements for his tour, which his father did not oppose. On the contrary, Lord Gowrie encouraged all those plans, though with an air of melancholy indulgence which his son could not understand. "It will do you good," he said, with a sigh. "Yes, yes, my boy; the best thing for you." This, no doubt, was true enough; but there was an implied feeling that the young man would require something to do him good — that he would want the soothing of change and the gratification of his wishes, as one might speak of a convalescent or the victim of some calamity. This tone puzzled Lindores, who, though he thought it a fine thing to travel and acquire information, was as scornful of the idea of being done good to as is natural to any fine young fellow fresh from Oxford and the triumphs of the Union. But he reflected that the old school had its own way of treating things, and was satisfied. All was settled accordingly for this journey, before he came home to go through the ceremonial performances of the coming of age, the dinner of the tenantry, the speeches, the congratulations, his father's banquet, his mother's ball. It was in summer, and the country was as gay as all the entertainments that were to be given in his honour. His friend who was going to accompany him on his tour, as he had accompanied him through a considerable portion of his life — Almeric Ffarrington, a young man of the same aspirations — came up to Scotland with him for these festivities. And as they rushed through the night on the Great Northern Railway, in the intervals of two naps, they had a scrap of conversation as to these birthday glories. "It will be a bore, but it will not last long," said Lindores. They were both of the opinion that anything that did not produce information or promote culture was a bore.

"But is there not a revelation to be made to you, among all the other things you have to go through?" said Ffarrington. "Have not you to be introduced to the secret chamber, and all that sort of thing? I should like to be of the party there, Lindores."

"Ah," said the heir, "I had forgotten that part of it," which, however, was not the case. "Indeed I don't know if I am to be told. Even family dogmas are shaken nowadays."

"Oh, I should insist on that," said Ffarrington, lightly. "It is not many who have the chance of paying such a visit — better than Home and all the mediums. I should insist upon that."

"I have no reason to suppose that it has any connection with Home or the mediums," said Lindores, slightly nettled. He was himself an *esprit fort*; but a mystery in one's own family is not like vulgar mysteries. He liked it to be respected.

"Oh, no offence," said his companion. "I have always thought that a railway train would be a great chance for the spirits. If one was to show suddenly in that vacant seat beside you, what a triumphant proof of their existence that would be! but they don't take advantage of their opportunities."

Lindores could not tell what it was that made him think at that moment of a portrait he had seen in a back room at the castle of old Earl Robert, the wicked Earl. It was a bad portrait — a daub — a copy made by an amateur of the genuine portrait, which, out of horror of Earl Robert and his wicked ways, had been removed by some intermediate lord from its place in the gallery. Lindores had never seen the original — nothing but this daub of a copy. Yet somehow this face occurred to him by some strange link of association — seemed to come into his eyes as his friend spoke. A slight shiver ran over him. It was strange. He made no reply to Ffarrington, but he set himself to think how it could be that the latent presence in his mind of some anticipation of this approaching disclosure, touched into life by his friend's suggestion, should have called out of his memory a momentary realisation of the acknowledged magician of the family. This sentence is full of long words; but unfortunately long words are required in such a case. And the process was very simple when you traced it out. It was the clearest case of unconscious cerebration. He shut his eyes by way of securing privacy while he thought it out; and being tired, and not at all alarmed by his unconscious cerebration, before he opened them again fell fast asleep.

And his birthday, which was the day following his arrival at Glenlyon, was a very busy day. He had not time to think of anything but the immediate occupations of the moment. Public and private greetings, congratulations, offerings, poured upon him. The Gowries were popular in this generation, which was far from being usual in the family. Lady Gowrie was kind and generous, with that kindness which comes from the heart, and which is the only kindness likely to impress the keen-sighted popular judgment; and Lord Gowrie had but little of the equivocal reputation of his predecessors. They could be splendid now and then on great occasions, though in general they were homely enough; all which the public likes. It was a bore, Lindores said; but yet the young man did not dislike the honours, and the adulation, and all the hearty speeches and good wishes. It is sweet to a young man to feel himself the centre of all hopes. It seemed very reasonable to him — very natural — that he should be so, and that the farmers should feel a pride of anticipation in thinking of his future speeches in Parliament. He promised to them with the sincerest good faith that he would not disappoint their expectations — that he would feel their interest in him an additional spur. What so natural as that interest and these expectations? He was almost solemnised by his own position — so young, looked up to by so many people — so many hopes depending on him; and yet it was quite natural. His father, however, was still more solemnised than Lindores — and this was strange, to say the least. His face grew graver and graver as the day went on, till it almost seemed as if he were dissatisfied with his son's popularity, or had some painful thought weighing on his mind. He was restless and eager for the termination of the dinner, and to get rid of his guests; and as soon as they were gone, showed an equal anxiety that his son should retire too. "Go to bed at once, as a favour to me," Lord Gowrie said. "You will have a great deal of fatigue — tomorrow." "You need not be afraid for me, sir," said Lindores, half affronted; but he obeyed, being tired. He had not once thought of the secret to be disclosed to him, through all that long day. But when he woke suddenly with a start in the middle of the night, to find the candles all lighted in his room, and his father standing by his bedside, Lindores instantly thought of it, and in a moment felt that the leading event — the chief incident of all that had happened — was going to take place now.

Chapter II.

Lord Gowrie was very grave, and very pale. He was standing with his hand on his son's shoulder to wake him; his dress was unchanged from the moment they had parted. And the sight of this formal costume was very bewildering to the young man as he started up in his bed. But next moment he seemed to know exactly how it was, and, more than that, to have known it all his life. Explanation seemed unnecessary. At any other moment, in any other place, a man would be startled to be suddenly woke up in the middle of the night. But Lindores had no such feeling; he did not even ask a question, but sprang up, and fixed his eyes, taking in all the strange circumstances, on his father's face.

"Get up, my boy," said Lord Gowrie, "and dress as quickly as you can; it is full time. I have lighted your candles, and your things are all ready. You have had a good long sleep."

Even now he did not ask, What is it? as under any other circumstances he would have done. He got up without a word, with an impulse of nervous speed and rapidity of movement such as only excitement can give, and dressed himself, his father helping him silently. It was a curious scene: the room gleaming with lights, the silence, the hurried toilet, the stillness of deep night all around. The house, though so full, and with the echoes of festivity but just over, was quiet as if there was not a creature within it — more quiet, indeed, for the stillness of vacancy is not half so impressive as the stillness of hushed and slumbering life.

Lord Gowrie went to the table when this first step was over, and poured out a glass of wine from a bottle which stood there, — a rich, golden-coloured, perfumy wine, which sent its scent through the room. "You will want all your strength," he said; "take this before you go. It is the famous Imperial Tokay; there is only a little left, and you will want all your strength."

Lindores took the wine; he had never drunk any like it before, and the peculiar fragrance remained in his mind, as perfumes so often do, with a whole world of association in them. His father's eyes dwelt upon him with a melancholy sympathy. "You are going to encounter the greatest trial of your life," he said; and taking the young man's hand into his, felt his pulse. "It is quick, but it is quite firm, and you have had a good long sleep." Then he did what it needs a great deal of pressure to induce an Englishman to do, — he kissed his son on the cheek. "God bless you!" he said, faltering. "Come, now, everything is ready, Lindores."

He took up in his hand a small lamp, which he had apparently brought with him, and led the way. By this time Lindores began to feel himself again, and to wake to the consciousness of all his own superiorities and enlightenments. The simple sense that he was one of the members of a family with a mystery, and that the moment of his personal encounter with this special power of darkness had come, had been the first thrilling, overwhelming thought. But now as he followed his father, Lindores began to remember that he himself was not altogether like other men; that there was that in him which would make it natural that he should throw some light, hitherto unthought of, upon this carefully-preserved darkness. What secret even there might be in it — secret of hereditary tendency, of psychic force, of mental conformation, or of some curious combination of circumstances at once more and less potent than these — it was for him to find out. He gathered all his forces about him, reminded himself of modern enlightenment, and bade his nerves be steel to all vulgar horrors. He, too, felt his own pulse as he followed his father. To spend the night perhaps amongst the skeletons of that old-world massacre, and to repent the sins of his ancestors — to be brought within the range of some optical illusion believed in hitherto by all the generations, and which, no doubt, was of a startling kind, or his father would not look so serious, — any of these he felt himself quite strong to encounter. His heart and spirit rose. A young man has but seldom the opportunity of distinguishing himself so early in his career; and his was such a chance as occurs to very few. No doubt it was something that would be extremely trying to the nerves and imagination. He called up all his powers to vanquish both. And along with this call upon himself to exertion, there was the less serious impulse of curiosity: he would see at last what the Secret Chamber was, where it was, how it fitted into the labyrinths of the old house. This he tried to put in its due place as a most interesting object. He said to himself that he would willingly have gone a long journey at any time to be present at such an exploration; and there is no doubt that in other circumstances a secret chamber, with probably some unthought-of historical interest in it, would have been a very fascinating discovery. He tried very hard to excite himself about this; but it was curious how fictitious he felt the interest, and how conscious he was that it was an effort to feel any curiosity at all on the subject. The fact was, that the Secret Chamber was entirely secondary — thrown back, as all accessories are, by a more pressing interest. The overpowering thought of what was in it drove aside all healthy, natural curiosity about itself.

It must not be supposed, however, that the father and son had a long way to go to have time for all these thoughts. Thoughts travel at lightning speed, and there was abundant leisure for this between the time they had left the door of Lindores' room and gone down the corridor, no further off than to Lord Gowrie's own chamber, naturally one of the chief rooms of the house. Nearly opposite this, a few steps further on, was a little neglected room devoted to lumber, with which Lindores had been familiar all his life. Why this nest of old rubbish, dust, and cob-webs should be so near the bedroom of the head of the house had been a matter of surprise to many people — to the guests who saw it while exploring, and to each new servant in succession who planned an attack upon its ancient stores, scandalised by finding it to have been neglected by their predecessors. All their attempts to clear it out had, however, been resisted, nobody could tell how, or indeed thought it worthwhile to inquire. As for Lindores, he had been used to the place from his childhood, and therefore accepted it as the most natural thing in the world. He had been in and out a hundred times in his play. And it was here, he remembered suddenly, that he had seen the bad picture of Earl Robert which had so curiously come into his eyes on his journeying here, by a mental movement which he had identified at once as unconscious cerebration. The first feeling in his mind, as his father went to the open door of this lumber-room, was a mixture of amusement and surprise. What was he going to pick up there? some old pentacle, some amulet or scrap of antiquated magic to act as armour against the evil one? But Lord Gowrie, going on and setting down the lamp on the table, turned round upon his son with a face of agitation and pain which barred all further amusement: he grasped him by the hand, crushing it between his own. "Now my boy, my dear son," he said, in tones that were scarcely audible. His countenance was full of the dreary pain of a looker-on — one who has no share in the excitement of personal danger, but has the more terrible part of watching those who are in deadliest peril. He was a powerful man, and his large form shook with emotion; great beads of moisture stood upon his forehead. An old sword with a cross handle lay upon a dusty chair among other dusty and battered relics. "Take this with you," he said, in the same inaudible, breathless way — whether as a weapon, whether as a religious symbol, Lindores could not guess. The young man took it mechanically. His father pushed open a door which it seemed to him he had never seen before, and led him into another vaulted chamber. Here even the limited powers of speech Lord Gowrie had retained seemed to forsake him, and his voice became a mere hoarse murmur in his throat. For want of speech he pointed to another door in the further corner of this small vacant room, gave him to understand by a gesture that he was to knock there, and then went back into the lumber-room. The door into this was left open, and a faint glimmer of the lamp shed light into this little intermediate place — this debatable land between the seen and the unseen. In spite of himself, Lindores' heart began to beat. He made a breathless pause, feeling his head go round. He held the old sword in his hand, not knowing what it was. Then, summoning all his courage, he went forward and knocked at the closed door. His knock was not loud, but it seemed to echo all over the silent house. Would everybody hear and wake, and rush to see what had happened? This caprice of imagination seized upon him, ousting all the firmer thoughts, the steadfast calm of mind with which he ought to have encountered the mystery. Would they all rush in, in wild *déshabille*, in terror and dismay, before the door opened? How long it was of opening! He touched the panel with his hand again. — This time there was no delay. In a moment, as if thrown suddenly open by someone within, the door moved. It opened just wide enough to let him enter, stopping half-way as if someone invisible held it, wide enough for welcome, but no more. Lindores stepped across the threshold with a beating heart. What was he about to see? the skeletons of the murdered victims? a ghostly charnel-house full of bloody traces of crime? He seemed to be hurried and pushed in as he made that step. What was this world of mystery into which he was plunged — what was it he saw?

He saw — nothing — except what was agreeable enough to behold, — an antiquated room hung with tapestry, very old tapestry of rude design, its colours faded into softness and harmony; between its folds here and there a panel of carved wood, rude too in design, with traces of half-worn gilding; a table covered with strange instruments, parchments, chemical tubes, and curious machinery, all with a quaintness of form and dimness of material that spoke of age. A heavy old velvet cover, thick with embroidery faded almost out of all colour, was on the table; on the wall above it, something that looked like a very old Venetian mirror, the glass so dim and crusted that it scarcely reflected at all, on the floor an old soft Persian carpet, worn into a vague blending of all colours. This was all that he thought he saw. His heart, which had been thumping so loud as almost to choke him, stopped that tremendous upward and downward motion like a steam piston; and he grew calm. Perfectly still, dim, unoccupied: yet not so dim either; there was no apparent source of light, no windows, curtains of tapestry drawn everywhere — no lamp visible, no fire — and yet a kind of strange light which made everything quite clear. He looked round, trying to smile at his terrors, trying to say to himself that it was the most curious place he had ever seen — that he must show Ffarrington some of that tapestry — that he must really bring away a panel of that carving, — when he suddenly saw that the door was shut by which he had entered — nay, more than shut, undiscernible, covered like all the rest of the walls by that strange tapestry. At this his heart began to beat again in spite of him. He looked round once more, and woke up to more vivid being with a sudden start. Had his eyes been incapable of vision on his first entrance? Unoccupied? Who was that in the great chair?

It seemed to Lindores that he had seen neither the chair nor the man when he came in. There they were, however, solid and unmistakable; the chair carved like the panels, the man seated in front of the table. He looked at Lindores with a calm and open gaze, inspecting him. The young man's heart seemed in his throat fluttering like a bird, but he was brave, and his mind made one final effort to break this spell. He tried to speak, labouring with a voice that would not sound, and with lips too parched to form a word. "I see how it is," was what he wanted to say. It was Earl Robert's face that was looking at him; and startled as he was, he dragged forth his philosophy to support him. What could it be but optical delusions, unconscious cerebration, occult seizure by the impressed and struggling mind of this one countenance? But he could not hear himself speak any word as he stood convulsed, struggling with dry lips and choking voice.

The Appearance smiled, as if knowing his thoughts — not unkindly, not malignly — with a certain amusement mingled with scorn. Then he spoke, and the sound seemed to breathe through the room not like any voice that Lindores had ever heard, a kind of utterance of the place, like the rustle of the air or the ripple of the sea. "You will learn better tonight: this is no phantom of your brain; it is I."

"In God's name," cried the young man in his soul; he did not know whether the words ever got into the air or not, if there was any air; — "in God's name, who are you?"

The figure rose as if coming to him to reply; and Lindores, overcome by the apparent approach, struggled into utterance. A cry came from him — he heard it this time — and even in his extremity felt a pang the more to hear the terror in his own voice. But he did not flinch, he stood desperate, all his strength concentrated in the act; he neither turned nor recoiled. Vaguely gleaming through his mind came the thought that to be thus brought in contact with the unseen was the experiment to be most desired on earth, the final settlement of a hundred questions; but his faculties were not sufficiently under command to entertain it. He only stood firm, that was all.

And the figure did not approach him; after a moment it subsided back again into the chair — subsided, for no sound, not the faintest, accompanied its movements. It was the form of a man of middle age, the hair white, but the beard only crisped with grey, the features those of the picture — a familiar face, more or less like all the Randolphs, but with an air of domination and power altogether unlike that of the race. He was dressed in a long robe of dark colour, embroidered with strange lines and angles. There was nothing repellent or terrible in his air — nothing except the noiselessness, the calm, the absolute stillness, which was as much in the place as in him, to keep up the involuntary trembling of the beholder. His expression was full of dignity and thoughtfulness, and not malignant or unkind. He might have been the kindly patriarch of the house, watching over its fortunes in a seclusion that he had chosen. The pulses that had been beating in Lindores were stilled. What was his panic for? A gleam even of self-ridicule took possession of him, to be standing there like an absurd hero of antiquated romance with the rusty, dusty sword — good for nothing, surely not adapted for use against this noble old magician — in his hand —

"You are right," said the voice, once more answering his thoughts; "what could you do with that sword against me, young Lindores? Put it by. Why should my children meet me like an enemy? You are my flesh and blood. Give me your hand."

A shiver ran through the young man's frame. The hand that was held out to him was large and shapely and white, with a straight line across the palm — a family token upon which the Randolphs prided themselves — a friendly hand; and the face smiled upon him, fixing him with those calm, profound, blue eyes. "Come," said the voice. The word seemed to fill the place, melting upon him from every corner, whispering round him with softest persuasion. He was lulled and calmed in spite of himself. Spirit or no spirit, why should not he accept this proffered courtesy? What harm could come of it? The chief thing that retained him was the dragging of the old sword, heavy and useless, which he held mechanically, but which some internal feeling — he could not tell what — prevented him from putting down. Superstition, was it?

"Yes, that is superstition," said his ancestor, serenely; "put it down and come."

"You know my thoughts," said Lindores; "I did not speak."

"Your mind spoke, and spoke justly. Put down that emblem of brute force and superstition together. Here it is the intelligence that is supreme. Come."

Lindores stood doubtful. He was calm; the power of thought was restored to him. If this benevolent venerable patriarch was all he seemed, why his father's terror? why the secrecy in which his being was involved? His own mind, though calm, did not seem to act in the usual way. Thoughts seemed to be driven across it as by a wind. One of these came to him suddenly now —

> "How there looked him in the face,
> An angel beautiful and bright,
> And how he knew it was a fiend."

The words were not ended, when Earl Robert replied suddenly with impatience in his voice, "Fiends are of the fancy of men; like angels and other follies. I am your father. You know me; and you are mine, Lindores. I have power beyond what you can understand; but I want flesh and blood to reign and to enjoy. Come, Lindores!"

He put out his other hand. The action, the look, were those of kindness, almost of longing, and the face was familiar, the voice was that of the race. Supernatural! was it supernatural that this man should live here shut up for ages? and why? and how? Was there any explanation of it? The young man's brain began to reel. He could not tell which was real — the life he had left half an hour ago, or this. He tried to look round him, but could not; his eyes were caught by those other kindred eyes, which seemed to dilate and deepen as he looked at them, and drew him with a strange compulsion. He felt himself yielding, swaying towards the strange being who thus invited him. What might happen if he yielded? And he could not turn away, he could not tear himself from the fascination of those eyes. With a sudden strange impulse which was half despair and half a bewildering half-conscious desire to try one potency against another, he thrust forward the cross of the old sword between him and those appealing hands. "In the name of God!" he said.

Lindores never could tell whether it was that he himself grew faint, and that the dimness of swooning came into his eyes after this violence and strain of emotion, or if it was his spell that worked. But there was an instantaneous change. Everything swam around him for the moment, a giddiness and blindness seized him, and he saw nothing but the vague outlines of the room, empty as when he entered it. But gradually his consciousness came back, and he found himself standing on the same spot as before, clutching the old sword, and gradually, as though a dream, recognised the same figure emerging out of the mist which — was it solely in his own eyes? — had enveloped everything. But it was no longer in the same attitude. The hands which had been stretched out to him were busy now with some of the strange instruments on the table, moving about, now in the action of writing, now as if managing the keys of a telegraph. Lindores felt that his brain was all atwist and set wrong; but he was still a human being of his century. He thought of the telegraph with a keen thrill of curiosity in the midst of his reviving sensations. What communication was this which was going on before his eyes? The magician worked on. He had his face turned towards his victim, but his hands moved with unceasing activity. And Lindores, as he grew accustomed to the position, began to weary — to feel like a neglected suitor waiting for an audience. To be wound up to such a strain of feeling, then left to wait, was intolerable; impatience seized upon him. What circumstances can exist, however horrible, in which a human being will not feel impatience? He made a great many efforts to speak before he could succeed. It seemed to him that his body felt more fear than he did — that his muscles were contracted, his throat parched, his tongue refusing its office, although his mind was unaffected and undismayed. At last he found an utterance in spite of all resistance of his flesh and blood.

"Who are you?" he said hoarsely. "You that live here and oppress this house?"

The vision raised its eyes full upon him, with again that strange shadow of a smile, mocking yet not unkind. "Do you remember me," he said, "on your journey here?"

"That was a delusion." The young man gasped for breath.

"More like that you are a delusion. You have lasted but one-and-twenty years, and I — for centuries."

"How? For centuries — and why? Answer me — are you man or demon?" cried Lindores, tearing the words as he felt out of his own throat. "Are you living or dead?"

The magician looked at him with the same intense gaze as before. "Be on my side, and you shall know everything, Lindores. I want one of my own race. Others I could have in plenty; but I want *you*. A Randolph, a Randolph! and *you*. Dead! do I seem dead? You shall have everything — more than dreams can give — if you will be on my side."

Can he give what he has not? was the thought that ran through the mind of Lindores. But he could not speak it. Something that choked and stifled him was in his throat.

"Can I give what I have not? I have everything — power, the one thing worth having; and you shall have more than power, for you are young — my son! Lindores!"

To argue was natural, and gave the young man strength. "Is this life," he said, "here? What is all your power worth — here? To sit for ages, and make a race unhappy?"

A momentary convulsion came across the still face. "You scorn me", he cried, with an appearance of emotion, "because you do not understand how I move the world. Power! 'Tis more than fancy can grasp. And you shall have it!" said the wizard, with what looked like a show of enthusiasm. He seemed to come nearer, to grow larger. He put forth his hand again, this time so close that it seemed impossible to escape. And a crowd of wishes seemed to rush upon the mind of Lindores. What harm to try if this might be true? To try what it meant — perhaps nothing, delusions, vain show, and then there could be no harm; or perhaps there was knowledge to be had, which was power. Try, try, try! the air buzzed about him. The room seemed full of voices urging him. His bodily frame rose into a tremendous whirl of excitement, his veins seemed to swell to bursting, his lips seemed to force a yes, in spite of him, quivering as they came apart. The hiss of the *s* seemed in his ears. He changed it into the name which was a spell too, and cried, "Help me, God!" not knowing why.

Then there came another pause — he felt as if he had been dropped from something that had held him, and had fallen, and was faint. The excitement had been more than he could bear.

Once more everything swam around him, and he did not know where he was. Had he escaped altogether? was the first waking wonder of consciousness in his mind. But when he could think and see again, he was still in the same spot, surrounded by the old curtains and the carved panels — but alone. He felt, too, that he was able to move, but the strangest dual consciousness was in him throughout all the rest of his trial. His body felt to him as a frightened horse feels to a traveller at night — a thing separate from him, more frightened than he was — starting aside at every step, seeing more than its master. His limbs shook with fear and weakness, almost refusing to obey the action of his will, trembling under him with jerks aside when he compelled himself to move. The hair stood upright on his head — every finger trembled as with palsy — his lips, his eyelids, quivered with nervous agitation. But his mind was strong, stimulated to a desperate calm. He dragged himself round the room, he crossed the very spot where the magician had been — all was vacant, silent, clear. Had he vanquished the enemy? This thought came into his mind with an involuntary triumph. The old strain of feeling came back. Such efforts might be produced, perhaps, only by imagination, by excitement, by delusion —

Lindores looked up, by a sudden attraction he could not tell what: and the blood suddenly froze in his veins that had been so boiling and fermenting. Someone was looking at him from the old mirror on the wall. A face not human and life-like, like that of the inhabitant of this place, but ghostly and terrible, like one of the dead; and while he looked, a crowd of other faces came behind, all looking at him, some mournfully, some with a menace in their terrible eyes. The mirror did not change, but within its small dim space seemed to contain an innumerable company, crowded above and below, all with one gaze at him. His lips dropped apart with a gasp of horror. More and more and more! He was standing close by the table when this crowd came. Then all at once there was laid upon him a cold hand. He turned; close to his side, brushing him with his robe, holding him fast by the arm, sat Earl Robert in his great chair. A shriek came from the young man's lips. He seemed to hear it echoing away into unfathomable distance. The cold touch penetrated to his very soul.

"Do you try spells upon me, Lindores? That is a tool of the past. You shall have something better to work with. And are you so sure of whom you call upon? If there is such a one, why should He help you who never called on Him before?"

Lindores could not tell if these words were spoken; it was a communication rapid as the thoughts in the mind. And he felt as if something answered that was not all himself. He seemed to stand passive and hear the argument. "Does God reckon with a man in trouble, whether he has ever called to Him before? I call now" (now he felt it was himself that said): "go, evil spirit! — go, dead and cursed! — go, in the name of God!"

He felt himself flung violently against the wall. A faint laugh, stifled in the throat, and followed by a groan, rolled round the room; the old curtains seemed to open here and there, and flutter, as if with comings and goings. Lindores leaned with his back against the wall, and all his senses restored to him. He felt blood trickle down his neck; and in this contact once more with the physical, his body, in its madness of fright, grew manageable. For the first time he felt wholly master of himself. Though the magician was standing in his place, a great, majestic, appalling figure, he did not shrink. "Liar!" he cried, in a voice that rang and echoed as in natural air — "clinging to miserable life like a worm — like a reptile; promising all things, having nothing, but this den, unvisited by the light of day. Is this your power — your superiority to men who die? is it for this that you oppress a race, and make a house unhappy? I vow, in God's name, your reign is over! You and your secret shall last no more."

There was no reply. But Lindores felt his terrible ancestor's eyes getting once more that mesmeric mastery over him which had already almost overcome his powers. He must withdraw his own, or perish. He had a human horror of turning his back upon that watchful adversary: to face him seemed the only safety; but to face him was to be conquered. Slowly, with a pang indescribable, he tore himself from that gaze: it seemed to drag his eyes out of their sockets, his heart out of his bosom. Resolutely, with the daring of desperation, he turned round to the spot where he entered — the spot where no door was, — hearing already in anticipation the step after him — feeling the grip that would crush and smother his exhausted life — but too desperate to care.

Chapter III.

How wonderful is the blue dawning of the new day before the sun! not rosy-fingered, like that Aurora of the Greeks who comes later with all her wealth; but still, dreamy, wonderful, stealing out of the unseen, abashed by the solemnity of the new birth. When anxious watchers see that first brightness come stealing upon the waiting skies, what mingled relief and renewal of misery is in it! another long day to toil through — yet another sad night over! Lord Gowrie sat among the dust and cobwebs, his lamp flaring idly into the blue morning. He had heard his son's human voice, though nothing more; and he expected to have him brought out by invisible hands, as had happened to himself, and left lying in long deathly swoon outside that mystic door. This was how it had happened to heir after heir, as told from father to son, one after another, as the secret came down. One or two bearers of the name Lindores had never recovered; most of them had been saddened and subdued for life. He remembered sadly the freshness of existence which had never come back to himself; the hopes that had never blossomed again; the assurance with which never more he had been able to go about the world. And now his son would be as himself — the glory gone out of his living — his ambitions, his aspirations wrecked. He had not been endowed as his boy was — he had been a plain, honest man, and nothing more; but experience and life had given him wisdom enough to smile by times at the coquetries of mind in which Lindores indulged. Were they all over now, those freaks of young intelligence, those enthusiasms of the soul? The curse of the house had come upon him — the magnetism of that strange presence, ever living, ever watchful, present in all the family history. His heart was sore for his son; and yet along with this there was a certain consolation to him in having henceforward a partner in the secret — someone to whom he could talk of it as he had not been able to talk since his own father died. Almost all the mental struggles which Gowrie had known had been connected with this mystery; and he had been obliged to hide them in his bosom — to conceal them even when they rent him in two. Now he had a partner in his trouble. This was what he was thinking as he sat through the night. How slowly the moments passed! He was not aware of the daylight coming in. After a while even thought got suspended in listening. Was not the time nearly over? He rose and began to pace about the encumbered space, which was but a step or two in extent. There was an old cupboard in the wall, in which there were restoratives — pungent essences and cordials, and fresh water which he had himself brought — everything was ready; presently the ghastly body of his boy, half dead, would be thrust forth into his care.

But this was not how it happened. While he waited, so intent that his whole frame seemed to be capable of hearing, he heard the closing of the door, boldly shut with a sound that rose in muffled echoes through the house, and Lindores himself appeared, ghastly indeed as a dead man, but walking upright and firmly, the lines of his face drawn, and his eyes staring. Lord Gowrie uttered a cry. He was more alarmed by this unexpected return than by the helpless prostration of the swoon which he had expected. He recoiled from his son as if he too had been a spirit. "Lindores!" he cried; was it Lindores, or someone else in his place? The boy seemed as if he did not see him. He went straight forward to where the water stood on the dusty table, and took a great draught, then turned to the door. "Lindores!" said his father, in miserable anxiety; "don't you know me?" Even then the young man only half looked at him, and put out a hand almost as cold as the hand that had clutched himself in the Secret Chamber; a faint smile came upon his face. "Don't stay here," he whispered; "come! come!"

Lord Gowrie drew his son's arm within his own, and felt the thrill through and through him of nerves strained beyond mortal strength. He could scarcely keep up with him as he stalked along the corridor to his room, stumbling as if he could not see, yet swift as an arrow. When they reached his room he turned and closed and locked the door, then laughed as he staggered to the bed. "That will not keep him out, will it?" he said.

"Lindores," said his father, "I expected to find you unconscious. I am almost more frightened to find you like this. I need not ask if you have seen him —"

"Oh, I have seen him. The old liar! Father, promise to expose him, to turn him out — promise to clear out that accursed old nest! It is our own fault. Why have we left such a place shut out from the eye of day? Isn't there something in the Bible about those who do evil hating the light?"

"Lindores! you don't often quote the Bible."

"No, I suppose not; but there is more truth in — many things than we thought."

"Lie down," said the anxious father. "Take some of this wine — try to sleep."

"Take it away; give me no more of that devil's drink. Talk to me — that's better. Did you go through it all the same, poor papa? — and hold me fast. You are warm — you are honest!" he cried. He put forth his hands over his father's, warming them with the contact. He put his cheek like a child against his father's arm. He gave a faint laugh, with the tears in his eyes. "Warm and honest," he repeated. "Kind flesh and blood! and did you go through it all the same?"

"My boy!" cried the father, feeling his heart glow and swell over the son who had been parted from him for years by that development of young manhood and ripening intellect which so often severs and loosens the ties of home. Lord Gowrie had felt that Lindores half despised his simple mind and duller imagination; but this childlike clinging overcame him, and tears stood in his eyes. "I fainted, I suppose. I never knew how it ended. They made what they liked of me. But you, my brave boy, you came out of your own will."

Lindores shivered. "I fled!" he said. "No honour in that. I had not courage to face him longer. I will tell you by-and-by. But I want to know about you."

What an ease it was to the father to speak! For years and years this had been shut up in his breast. It had made him lonely in the midst of his friends.

"Thank God," he said, "that I can speak to you, Lindores. Often and often I have been tempted to tell your mother. But why should I make her miserable? She knows there is something; she knows when I see him, but she knows no more."

"When you see him?" Lindores raised himself, with a return of his first ghastly look, in his bed. Then he raised his clenched fist wildly, and shook it in the air. "Vile devil, coward, deceiver!"

"Oh hush, hush, hush, Lindores! God help us! what troubles you may bring!"

"And God help me, whatever troubles I bring," said the young man. "I defy him, father. An accursed being like that must be less, not more powerful, than we are — with God to back us. Only stand by me: stand by me —"

"Hush, Lindores! You don't feel it yet — never to get out of hearing of him all your life! He will make you pay for it — if not now, after; when you remember he is there; whatever happens, knowing everything! But I hope it will not be so bad with you as with me, my poor boy. God help you indeed if it is, for you have more imagination and more mind. I am able to forget him sometimes when I am occupied — when in the hunting-field, going across country. But you are not a hunting man, my poor boy," said Lord Gowrie, with a curious mixture of a regret, which was less serious than the other. Then he lowered his voice. "Lindores, this is what has happened to me since the moment I gave him my hand."

"I did not give him my hand."

"You did not give him your hand? God bless you, my boy! You stood out?" he cried, with tears again rushing to his eyes; "and they say — they say — but I don't know if there is any truth in it." Lord Gowrie got up from his son's side, and walked up and down with excited steps. "If there should be truth in it! Many people think the whole thing is a fancy. If there should be truth in it, Lindores!"

"In what, father?"

"They say, if he is once resisted his power is broken — once refused. *You* could stand against him — you! Forgive me, my boy, as I hope God will forgive me, to have thought so little of His best gifts," cried Lord Gowrie, coming back with wet eyes; and stooping, he kissed his son's hand. "I thought you would be more shaken by being more mind than body," he said, humbly.

"I thought if I could but have saved you from the trial; and *you* are the conqueror!"

"Am I the conqueror? I think all my bones are broken, father — out of their sockets," said the young man, in a low voice. "I think I shall go to sleep."

"Yes, rest, my boy. It is the best thing for you," said the father, though with a pang of momentary disappointment.

Lindores fell back upon the pillow. He was so pale that there were moments when the anxious watcher thought him not sleeping but dead. He put his hand out feebly, and grasped his father's hand. "Warm — honest," he said, with a feeble smile about his lips, and fell asleep.

The daylight was full in the room, breaking through shutters and curtains and mocking at the lamp that still flared on the table. It seemed an emblem of the disorders, mental and material, of this strange night; and, as such, it affected the plain imagination of Lord Gowrie, who would have fain got up to extinguish it, and whose mind returned again and again, in spite of him, to this symptom of disturbance. By-and-by, when Lindores' grasp relaxed, and he got his hand free, he got up from his son's bedside, and put out the lamp, putting it carefully out of the way. With equal care he put away the wine from the table, and gave the room its ordinary aspect, softly opening a window to let in the fresh air of the morning. The park lay fresh in the early sunshine, still, except for the twittering of the birds, refreshed with dews, and shining in that soft radiance of the morning which is over before mortal cares are stirring. Never, perhaps, had Gowrie looked out upon the beautiful world around his house without a thought of the weird existence which was going on so near to him, which had gone on for centuries, shut up out of sight of the sunshine. The Secret Chamber had been present with him since ever he saw it. He had never been able to get free of the spell of it. He had felt himself watched, surrounded, spied upon, day after day, since he was of the age of Lindores, and that was thirty years ago. He turned it all over in his mind, as he stood there and his son slept. It had been on his lips to tell it all to his boy, who had now come to inherit the enlightenment of his race. And it was a disappointment to him to have it all forced back again, and silence imposed upon him once more. Would he care to hear it when he woke? would he not rather, as Lord Gowrie remembered to have done himself, thrust the thought as far as he could away from him, and endeavour to forget for the moment — until the time came when he would not be permitted to forget? He had been like that himself, he recollected now. He had not wished to hear his own father's tale. "I remember," he said to himself; "I remember" — turning over everything in his mind — if Lindores might only be willing to hear the story when he woke! But then he himself had not been willing when he was Lindores, and he could understand his son, and could not blame him; but it would be a disappointment. He was thinking this when he heard Lindores' voice calling him. He went back hastily to his bedside. It was strange to see him in his evening dress with his worn face, in the fresh light of the morning, which poured in at every crevice. "Does my mother know?" said Lindores; "what will she think?"

"She knows something; she knows you have some trial to go through. Most likely she will be praying for us both; that's the way of women," said Lord Gowrie, with the tremulous tenderness which comes into a man's voice sometimes when he speaks of a good wife. "I'll go and ease her mind, and tell her all is well over —"

"Not yet. Tell me first," said the young man, putting his hand upon his father's arm.

What an ease it was! "I was not so good to my father," he thought to himself, with sudden penitence for the long-past, long-forgotten fault, which, indeed, he had never realised as a fault before. And then he told his son what had been the story of his life — how he had scarcely ever sat alone without feeling, from some corner of the room, from behind some curtain, those eyes upon him; and how, in the difficulties of his life, that secret inhabitant of the house had been present, sitting by him and advising him. "Whenever there has been anything to do: when there has been a question between two ways, all in a moment I have seen him by me: I feel when he is coming. It does not matter where I am — here or anywhere — as soon as ever there is a question of family business; and always he persuades me to the wrong way, Lindores. Sometimes I yield to him, how can I help it? He makes everything so clear; he makes wrong seem right. If I have done unjust things in my day —"

"You have not, father."

"I have: there were these Highland people I turned out. I did not mean to do it, Lindores; but he showed me that it would be better for the family. And my poor sister that married Tweedside and was wretched all her life. It was his doing, that marriage; he said she would be rich, and so she was, poor thing, poor thing! and died of it. And old Macalister's lease — Lindores, Lindores! when there is any business it makes my heart sick. I know he will come, and advise wrong, and tell me — something I will repent after."

"The thing to do is to decide beforehand, that, good or bad, you will not take his advice."

Lord Gowrie shivered. "I am not strong like you, or clever; I cannot resist. Sometimes I repent in time and don't do it; and then! But for your mother and you children, there is many a day I would not have given a farthing for my life."

"Father," said Lindores, springing from his bed. "two of us together can do many things. Give me your word to clear out this cursed den of darkness this very day."

"Lindores, hush, hush, for the sake of heaven!"

"I will not, for the sake of heaven! Throw it open — let everybody who likes see it — make an end of the secret — pull down everything, curtains, walls. What do you say? — sprinkle holy water? Are you laughing at me?"

"I did not speak," said Earl Gowrie, growing very pale, and grasping his son's arm with both his hands. "Hush, boy; do you think he does not hear?"

And then there was a low laugh close to them — so close that both shrank; a laugh no louder than a breath.

"Did you laugh — father?"

"No, Lindores." Lord Gowrie had his eyes fixed. He was as pale as the dead. He held his son tight for a moment; then his gaze and his grasp relaxed, and he fell back feebly in a chair.

"You see!" he said; "whatever we do it will be the same; we are under his power."

And then there ensued the blank pause with which baffled men confront a hopeless situation. But at that moment the first faint stirrings of the house — a window being opened, a bar undone, a movement of feet, and subdued voices — became audible in the stillness of the morning. Lord Gowrie roused himself at once. "We must not be found like this," he said; "we must not show how we have spent the night. It is over, thank God! and oh, my boy, forgive me! I am thankful there are two of us to bear it; it makes the burden lighter — though I ask your pardon humbly for saying so. I would have saved you if I could, Lindores."

"I don't wish to have been saved; but I will not bear it. I will end it," the young man said, with an oath out of which his emotion took all profanity. His father said, "Hush, hush." With a look of terror and pain, he left him; and yet there was a thrill of tender pride in his mind. How brave the boy was! even after he had been there. Could it be that this would all come to nothing, as every other attempt to resist had done before?

"I suppose you know all about it now, Lindores," said his friend Ffarrington, after breakfast; "luckily for us who are going over the house. What a glorious old place it is!"

"I don't think that Lindores enjoys the glorious old place today," said another of the guests under his breath. "How pale he is! He doesn't look as if he had slept."

"I will take you over every nook where I have ever been," said Lindores. He looked at his father with almost command in his eyes. "Come with me, all of you. We shall have no more secrets here."

"Are you mad?" said his father in his ear.

"Never mind," cried the young man. "Oh, trust me; I will do it with judgment. Is everybody ready?" There was an excitement about him that half frightened, half roused the party. They all rose, eager, yet doubtful. His mother came to him and took his arm.

"Lindores! you will do nothing to vex your father; don't make him unhappy. I don't know your secrets, you two; but look, he has enough to bear."

"I want you to know our secrets, mother. Why should we have secrets from you?"

"Why, indeed?" she said, with tears in her eyes. "But, Lindores, my dearest boy, don't make it worse for *him*."

"I give you my word, I will be wary," he said; and she left him to go to his father, who followed the party, with an anxious look upon his face.

"Are you coming, too?" he asked.

"I? No; I will not go: but trust him — trust the boy, John."

"He can do nothing; he will not be able to do anything," he said.

And thus the guests set out on their round — the son in advance, excited and tremulous, the father anxious and watchful behind. They began in the usual way, with the old state-rooms and picture-gallery; and in a short time the party had half forgotten that there was anything unusual in the inspection. When, however, they were half-way down the gallery, Lindores stopped short with an air of wonder. "You have had it put back then?" he said. He was standing in front of the vacant space where Earl Robert's portrait ought to have been. "What is it?" they all cried, crowding upon him, ready for any marvel. But as there was nothing to be seen, the strangers smiled among themselves. "Yes, to be sure, there is nothing so suggestive as a vacant place," said a lady who was of the party. "Whose portrait ought to be there, Lord Lindores?"

He looked at his father, who made a slight assenting gesture, then shook his head drearily.

"Who put it there?" Lindores said, in a whisper.

"It is not there; but you and I see it," said Lord Gowrie, with a sigh.

Then the strangers perceived that something had moved the father and the son, and, notwithstanding their eager curiosity, obeyed the dictates of politeness, and dispersed into groups looking at the other pictures. Lindores set his teeth and clenched his hands. Fury was growing upon him — not the awe that filled his father's mind. "We will leave the rest of this to another time," he cried, turning to the others, almost fiercely. "Come, I will show you something more striking now." He made no further pretence of going systematically over the house. He turned and went straight up-stairs, and along the corridor. "Are we going over the bedrooms?" someone said. Lindores led the way straight to the old lumber-room, a strange place for such a gay party. The ladies drew their dresses about them. There was not room for half of them. Those who could get in began to handle the strange things that lay about, touching them with dainty fingers, exclaiming how dusty they were. The window was half blocked up by old armour and rusty weapons; but this did not hinder the full summer daylight from penetrating in a flood of light. Lindores went in with fiery determination on his face. He went straight to the wall, as if he would go through, then paused with a blank gaze. "Where is the door?" he said.

"You are forgetting yourself," said Lord Gowrie, speaking over the heads of the others. "Lindores! you know very well there never was any door there; the wall is very thick; you can see by the depth of the window. There is no door there."

The young man felt it over with his hand. The wall was smooth, and covered with the dust of ages. With a groan he turned away. At this moment a suppressed laugh, low, yet distinct, sounded close by him. "You laughed?" he said, fiercely, to Ffarrington, striking his hand upon his shoulder.

"I — laughed! Nothing was farther from my thoughts," said his friend, who was curiously examining something that lay upon an old carved chair. "Look here! what a wonderful sword, cross-hilted! Is it an Andrea? What's the matter, Lindores?"

Lindores had seized it from his hands; he dashed it against the wall with a suppressed oath. The two or three people in the room stood aghast.

"Lindores!" his father said, in a tone of warning. The young man dropped the useless weapon with a groan. "Then God help us!" he said; "but I will find another way."

"There is a very interesting room close by," said Lord Gowrie, hastily — "this way! Lindores has been put out by — some changes that have been made without his knowledge," he said, calmly. "You must not mind him. He is disappointed. He is perhaps too much accustomed to have his own way."

But Lord Gowrie knew that no one believed him. He took them to the adjoining room, and told them some easy story of an apparition that was supposed to haunt it. "Have you ever seen it?" the guests said, pretending interest. "Not I; but we don't mind ghosts in this house," he answered, with a smile. And then they resumed their round of the old noble mystic house.

I cannot tell the reader what young Lindores has done to carry out his pledged word and redeem his family. It may not be known, perhaps, for another generation, and it will not be for me to write that concluding chapter: but when, in the ripeness of time, it can be narrated, no one will say that the mystery of Gowrie Castle has been a vulgar horror, though there are some who are disposed to think so now.

The Open Door

Charlotte Riddell

Some people do not believe in ghosts. For that matter, some people do not believe in anything. There are persons who even affect incredulity concerning that open door at Ladlow Hall. They say it did not stand wide open — that they could have shut it; that the whole affair was a delusion; that they are sure it must have been a conspiracy; that they are doubtful whether there is such a place as Ladlow on the face of the earth; that the first time they are in Meadowshire they will look it up.

That is the manner in which this story, hitherto unpublished, has been greeted by my acquaintances. How it will be received by strangers is quite another matter. I am going to tell what happened to me exactly as it happened, and readers can credit or scoff at the tale as it pleases them. It is not necessary for me to find faith and comprehension in addition to a ghost story, for the world at large. If such were the case, I should lay down my pen.

Perhaps, before going further, I ought to premise there was a time when I did not believe in ghosts either. If you had asked me one summer's morning years ago when you met me on London Bridge if I held such appearances to be probable or possible, you would have received an emphatic 'No' for answer.

But, at this rate, the story of the Open Door will never be told; so we will, with your permission, plunge into it immediately.

"Sandy!"

"What do you want?"

"Should you like to earn a sovereign?"

"Of course I should."

A somewhat curt dialogue, but we were given to curtness in the office of Messrs Frimpton, Frampton and Fryer, auctioneers and estate agents, St. Benet's Hill, City.

(My name is not Sandy or anything like it, but the other clerks so styled me because of a real or fancied likeness to some character, an ill-looking Scotchman, they had seen at the theatre. From this it may be inferred I was not handsome. Far from it.

The only ugly specimen in my family, I knew I was very plain; and it chanced to be no secret to me either that I felt grievously discontented with my lot.

I did not like the occupation of clerk in an auctioneer's office, and I did not like my employers.

We are all of us inconsistent, I suppose, for it was a shock to me to find they entertained a most cordial antipathy to me.)

"Because," went on Parton, a fellow, my senior by many years — a fellow who delighted in chaffing me, "I can tell you how to lay hands on one."

"How?" I asked, sulkily enough, for I felt he was having what he called his fun.

"You know that place we let to Carrison, the tea-dealer?" Carrison was a merchant in the China trade, possessed of fleets of vessels and towns of warehouses; but I did not correct Parton's expression, I simply nodded.

"He took it on a long lease, and he can't live in it; and our governor said this morning he wouldn't mind giving anybody who could find out what the deuce is the matter, a couple of sovereigns and his travelling expenses."

"Where is the place?" I asked, without turning my head; for the convenience of listening I had put my elbows on the desk and propped up my face with both hands.

"Away down in Meadowshire, in the heart of the grazing country."

"And what *is* the matter?" I further enquired.

"A door that won't keep shut."

"What?"

"A door that will keep open, if you prefer that way of putting it," said Parton.

"You are jesting."

"If I am, Carrison is not, or Fryer either. Carrison came here in a nice passion, and Fryer was in a fine rage; I could see he was, though he kept his temper outwardly. They have had an active correspondence it appears, and Carrison went away to talk to his lawyer. Won't make much by that move, I fancy."

"But tell me," I entreated, "why the door won't keep shut?"

"They say the place is haunted."

"What nonsense!" I exclaimed.

"Then you are just the person to take the ghost in hand. I thought so while old Fryer was speaking."

"If the door won't keep shut," I remarked, pursuing my own train of thought, "why can't they let it stay open?"

"I have not the slightest idea. I only know there are two sovereigns to be made, and that I give you a present of the information."

And having thus spoken, Parton took down his hat and went out, either upon his own business or that of his employers.

There was one thing I can truly say about our office, we were never serious in it. I fancy that is the case in most offices nowadays; at all events, it was the case in ours. We were always chaffing each other, playing practical jokes, telling stupid stories, scamping our work, looking at the clock, counting the weeks to next St. Lubbock's Day, counting the hours to Saturday.

For all that we were all very earnest in our desire to have our salaries raised, and unanimous in the opinion no fellows ever before received such wretched pay. I had twenty pounds a year, which I was aware did not half provide for what I ate at home. My mother and sisters left me in no doubt on the point, and when new clothes were wanted I always hated to mention the fact to my poor worried father.

We had been better off once, I believe, though I never remember the time. My father owned a small property in the country, but owing to the failure of some bank, I never could understand what bank, it had to be mortgaged; then the interest was not paid, and the mortgages foreclosed, and we had nothing left save the half-pay of a major, and about a hundred a year which my mother brought to the common fund.

We might have managed on our income, I think, if we had not been so painfully genteel; but we were always trying to do something quite beyond our means, and consequently debts accumulated, and creditors ruled us with rods of iron.

Before the final smash came, one of my sisters married the younger son of a distinguished family, and even if they had been disposed to live comfortably and sensibly she would have kept her sisters up to the mark. My only brother, too, was an officer, and of course the family thought it necessary he should see we preserved appearances.

It was all a great trial to my father, I think, who had to bear the brunt of the dunning and harass, and eternal shortness of money; and it would have driven me crazy if I had not found a happy refuge when matters were going wrong at home at my aunt's. She was my father's sister, and had married so "dreadfully below her" that my mother refused to acknowledge the relationship at all.

For these reasons and others, Parton's careless words about the two sovereigns stayed in my memory.

I wanted money badly — I may say I never had sixpence in the world of my own — and I thought if I could earn two sovereigns I might buy some trifles I needed for myself, and present my father with a new umbrella. Fancy is a dangerous little jade to flirt with, as I soon discovered.

She led me on and on. First I thought of the two sovereigns; then I recalled the amount of the rent Mr. Carrison agreed to pay for Ladlow Hall; then I decided he would gladly give more than two sovereigns if he could only have the ghost turned out of possession. I fancied I might get ten pounds — twenty pounds. I considered the matter all day, and I dreamed of it all night, and when I dressed myself next morning I was determined to speak to Mr. Fryer on the subject.

I did so — I told that gentleman Parton had mentioned the matter to me, and that if Mr. Fryer had no objection, I should like to try whether I could not solve the mystery. I told him I had been accustomed to lonely houses, and that I should not feel at all nervous; that I did not believe in ghosts, and as for burglars, I was not afraid of them.

"I don't mind your trying," he said at last. "Of course you understand it is no cure, no pay. Stay in the house for a week; if at the end of that time you can keep the door shut, locked, bolted, or nailed up, telegraph for me, and I will go down — if not, come back. If you like to take a companion there is no objection."

I thanked him, but said I would rather not have a companion.

"There is only one thing, sir, I should like," I ventured.

"And that   ?" he interrupted.

"Is a little more money. If I lay the ghost, or find out the ghost, I think I ought to have more than two sovereigns."

"How much more do you think you ought to have?" he asked.

His tone quite threw me off my guard, it was so civil and conciliatory, and I answered boldly: "Well, if Mr. Carrison cannot now live in the place perhaps he wouldn't mind giving me a ten-pound note."

Mr. Fryer turned, and opened one of the books lying on his desk. He did not look at or refer to it in any way — I saw that.

"You have been with us how long, Edlyd?" he said.

"Eleven months tomorrow," I replied.

"And our arrangement was, I think, quarterly payments, and one month's notice on either side?"

"Yes, sir." I heard my voice tremble, though I could not have said what frightened me.

"Then you will please to take your notice now. Come in before you leave this evening, and I'll pay you three months' salary, and then we shall be quits."

"I don't think I quite understand," I was beginning, when he broke in:

"But I understand, and that's enough. I have had enough of you and your airs, and your indifference, and your insolence here. I never had a clerk I disliked as I do you. Coming and dictating terms, forsooth! No, you shan't go to Ladlow. Many a poor chap" — (he said, "devil") — "would have been glad to earn half a guinea, let alone two sovereigns; and perhaps you may be before you are much older."

"Do you mean that you won't keep me here any longer, sir?" I asked in despair. "I had no intention of offending you. I —"

"Now you need not say another word,' he interrupted, 'for I won't bandy words with you. Since you have been in this place you have never known your position, and you don't seem able to realize it. When I was foolish enough to take you, I did it on the strength of your connections, but your connections have done nothing for me. I have never had a penny out of any one of your friends — if you have any. You'll not do any good in business for yourself or anybody else, and the sooner you go to Australia' — (here he was very emphatic) — 'and get off these premises, the better I shall be pleased."

I did not answer him — I could not. He had worked himself to a white heat by this time, and evidently intended I should leave his premises then and there. He counted five pounds out of his cash-box, and, writing a receipt, pushed it and the money across the table, and bade me sign and be off at once.

My hand trembled so I could scarcely hold the pen, but I had presence of mind enough left to return one pound ten in gold, and three shillings and fourpence I had, quite by the merest good fortune, in my waistcoat pocket.

"I can't take wages for work I haven't done," I said, as well as sorrow and passion would let me. "Good-morning," and I left his office and passed out among the clerks.

I took from my desk the few articles belonging to me, left the papers it contained in order, and then, locking it, asked Parton if he would be so good as to give the key to Mr. Fryer.

"What's up?" he asked "Are you going?"

I said, "Yes, I am going".

"Got the sack?"

"That is exactly what has happened."

"Well, I'm —!" exclaimed Mr. Parton.

I did not stop to hear any further commentary on the matter, but bidding my fellow-clerks goodbye, shook the dust of Frimpton's Estate and Agency Office from off my feet.

I did not like to go home and say I was discharged, so I walked about aimlessly, and at length found myself in Regent Street. There I met my father, looking more worried than usual.

"Do you think, Phil," he said (my name is Theophilus), "you could get two or three pounds from your employers?"

Maintaining a discreet silence regarding what had passed, I answered: "No doubt I could."

"I shall be glad if you will then, my boy," he went on, "for we are badly in want of it."

I did not ask him what was the special trouble. Where would have been the use? There was always something — gas, or water, or poor-rates, or the butcher, or the baker, or the bootmaker.

Well, it did not much matter, for we were well accustomed to the life; but, I thought, "if ever I marry, we will keep within our means". And then there rose up before me a vision of Patty, my cousin — the blithest, prettiest, most useful, most sensible girl that ever made sunshine in poor man's house.

My father and I had parted by this time, and I was still walking aimlessly on, when all at once an idea occurred to me. Mr. Fryer had not treated me well or fairly. I would hoist him on his own petard. I would go to headquarters, and try to make terms with Mr. Carrison direct.

No sooner thought than done. I hailed a passing omnibus, and was ere long in the heart of the city. Like other great men, Mr. Carrison was difficult of access — indeed, so difficult of access, that the clerk to whom I applied for an audience told me plainly I could not see him at all. I might send in my message if I liked, he was good enough to add, and no doubt it would be attended to. I said I should not send in a message, and was then asked what I would do. My answer was simple. I meant to wait till I did see him. I was told they could not have people waiting about the office in this way.

I said I supposed I might stay in the street. "Carrison didn't own that," I suggested.

The clerk advised me not to try that game, or I might get locked up.

I said I would take my chance of it.

After that we went on arguing the question at some length, and we were in the middle of a heated argument, in which several of Carrison's "young gentlemen", as they called themselves, were good enough to join, when we were all suddenly silenced by a grave-looking individual, who authoritatively enquired:

"What is all this noise about?"

Before anyone could answer I spoke up: "I want to see Mr. Carrison, and they won't let me."

"What do you want with Mr. Carrison?"

"I will tell that to himself only."

"Very well, say on — I am Mr. Carrison."

For a moment I felt abashed and almost ashamed of my persistency; next instant, however, what Mr. Fryer would have called my "native audacity" came to the rescue, and I said, drawing a step or two nearer to him, and taking off my hat:

"I wanted to speak to you about Ladlow Hall, if you please, sir."

In an instant the fashion of his face changed, a look of irritation succeeded to that of immobility; an angry contraction of the eyebrows disfigured the expression of his countenance.

"Ladlow Hall!" he repeated; "and what have you got to say about Ladlow Hall?"

"That is what I wanted to tell you, sir," I answered, and a dead hush seemed to fall on the office as I spoke.

The silence seemed to attract his attention, for he looked sternly at the clerks, who were not using a pen or moving a finger.

"Come this way, then," he said abruptly; and next minute I was in his private office.

"Now, what is it?" he asked, flinging himself into a chair, and addressing me, who stood hat in hand beside the great table in the middle of the room.

I began — I will say he was a patient listener — at the very beginning, and told my story straight through. I concealed nothing. I enlarged on nothing. A discharged clerk I stood before him, and in the capacity of a discharged clerk I said what I had to say. He heard me to the end, then he sat silent, thinking.

At last he spoke.

"You have heard a great deal of conversation about Ladlow, I suppose?" he remarked.

"No sir; I have heard nothing except what I have told you."

"And why do you desire to strive to solve such a mystery?"

"If there is any money to be made, I should like to make it, sir."

"How old are you?"

"Two-and-twenty last January."

"And how much salary had you at Frimpton's?"

"Twenty pounds a year."

"Humph! More than you are worth, I should say."

"Mr. Fryer seemed to imagine so, sir, at any rate," I agreed, sorrowfully.

"But what do you think?" he asked, smiling in spite of himself.

"I think I did quite as much work as the other clerks," I answered.

"That is not saying much, perhaps," he observed. I was of his opinion, but I held my peace.

"You will never make much of a clerk, I am afraid," Mr. Carrison proceeded, fitting his disparaging remarks upon me as he might on a lay figure. "You don't like desk work?"

"Not much, sir."

"I should judge the best thing you could do would be to emigrate," he went on, eyeing me critically.

"Mr. Fryer said I had better go to Australia or —" I stopped, remembering the alternative that gentleman had presented.

"Or where?" asked Mr. Carrison.

"The —, sir" I explained, softly and apologetically.

He laughed — he lay back in his chair and laughed — and I laughed myself, though ruefully.

After all, twenty pounds was twenty pounds, though I had not thought much of the salary till I lost it.

We went on talking for a long time after that; he asked me all about my father and my early life, and how we lived, and where we lived, and the people we knew; and, in fact, put more questions than I can well remember.

"It seems a crazy thing to do," he said at last; "and yet I feel disposed to trust you. The house is standing perfectly empty. I can't live in it, and I can't get rid of it; all my own furniture I have removed, and there is nothing in the place except a few old-fashioned articles belonging to Lord Ladlow. The place is a loss to me. It is of no use trying to let it, and thus, in fact, matters are at a deadlock. You won't be able to find out anything, I know, because, of course, others have tried to solve the mystery ere now; still, if you like to try you may. I will make this bargain with you. If you like to go down, I will pay your reasonable expenses for a fortnight; and if you do any good for me, I will give you a ten-pound note for yourself. Of course I must be satisfied that what you have told me is true and that you are what you represent. Do you know anybody in the city who would speak for you?"

I could think of no one but my uncle. I hinted to Mr. Carrison he was not grand enough or rich enough, perhaps, but I knew nobody else to whom I could refer him.

"What!" he said, "Robert Dorland, of Cullum Street. He does business with us. If he will go bail for your good behaviour I shan't want any further guarantee. Come along."

And to my intense amazement, he rose, put on his hat, walked me across the outer office and along the pavements till we came to Cullum Street.

"Do you know this youth, Mr. Dorland?" he said, standing in front of my uncle's desk, and laying a hand on my shoulder.

"Of course I do, Mr. Carrison," answered my uncle, a little apprehensively; for, as he told me afterwards, he could not imagine what mischief I had been up to. "He is my nephew."

"And what is your opinion of him — do you think he is a young fellow I may safely trust?"

My uncle smiled, and answered, "That depends on what you wish to trust him with."

"A long column of addition, for instance."

"It would be safer to give that task to somebody else."

"Oh, uncle!" I remonstrated; for I had really striven to conquer my natural antipathy to figures — worked hard, and every bit of it against the collar.

My uncle got off his stool, and said, standing with his back to the empty fire-grate:

"Tell me what you wish the boy to do, Mr. Carrison, and I will tell you whether he will suit your purpose or not. I know him, I believe, better than he knows himself."

In an easy, affable way, for so rich a man, Mr. Carrison took possession of the vacant stool, and nursing his right leg over his left knee, answered:

"He wants to go and shut the open door at Ladlow for me. Do you think he can do that?"

My uncle looked steadily back at the speaker, and said, "I thought, Mr. Carrison, it was quite settled no one could shut it?"

Mr. Carrison shifted a little uneasily on his seat, and replied: "*I* did not set your nephew the task he fancies he would like to undertake."

"Have nothing to do with it, Phil," advised my uncle, shortly.

"You don't believe in ghosts, do you, Mr. Dorland?" asked Mr. Carrison, with a slight sneer.

"Don't you, Mr. Carrison?" retorted my uncle.

There was a pause — an uncomfortable pause — during the course of which I felt the ten pounds, which, in imagination, I had really spent, trembling in the scale. I was not afraid. For ten pounds, or half the money, I would have faced all the inhabitants of spirit land. I longed to tell them so; but something in the way those two men looked at each other stayed my tongue.

"If you ask me the question here in the heart of the city, Mr. Dorland," said Mr. Carrison, at length, slowly and carefully, "I answer 'No'; but if you were to put it to me on a dark night at Ladlow, I should beg time to consider. I do not believe in supernatural phenomena myself, and yet — the door at Ladlow is as much beyond my comprehension as the ebbing and flowing of the sea."

"And you can't live at Ladlow?" remarked my uncle.

"I can't live at Ladlow, and what is more, I can't get anyone else to live at Ladlow."

"And you want to get rid of your lease?"

"I want so much to get rid of my lease that I told Fryer I would give him a handsome sum if he could induce anyone to solve the mystery. Is there any other information you desire, Mr. Dorland? Because if there is, you have only to ask and have. I feel I am not here in a prosaic office in the city of London, but in the Palace of Truth."

My uncle took no notice of the implied compliment. When wine is good it needs no bush. If a man is habitually honest in his speech and in his thoughts, he desires no recognition of the fact.

"I don't think so," he answered; "it is for the boy to say what he will do. If he be advised by me he will stick to his ordinary work in his employers' office, and leave ghost-hunting and spirit-laying alone."

Mr. Carrison shot a rapid glance in my direction, a glance which, implying a secret understanding, might have influenced my reply could I have stooped to deceive my uncle.

"I can't stick to my work there any longer," I said. "I got my marching orders today."

"What *had* you been doing, Phil?" asked my uncle.

"I wanted ten pounds to go and lay the ghost!" I answered, so dejectedly, that both Mr. Carrison and my uncle broke out laughing.

"Ten pounds!" cried my uncle, almost between laughing and crying. "Why, Phil boy, I had rather, poor man though I am, have given thee ten pounds than that thou should'st go ghost-hunting or ghostlaying."

When he was very much in earnest my uncle went back to thee and thou of his native dialect. I liked the vulgarism, as my mother called it, and I knew my aunt loved to hear him use the caressing words to her. He had risen, not quite from the ranks it is true, but if ever a gentleman came ready born into the world it was Robert Dorland, upon whom at our home everyone seemed to look down.

"What will you do, Edlyd?" asked Mr. Carrison; "you hear what your uncle says, 'Give up the enterprise', and what I say; I do not want either to bribe or force your inclinations."

"I will go, sir," I answered quite steadily. "I am not afraid, and I should like to show you —" I stopped. I had been going to say, "I should like to show you I am not such a fool as you all take me for", but I felt such an address would be too familiar, and refrained.

Mr. Carrison looked at me curiously. I think he supplied the end of the sentence for himself, but he only answered:

"I should like you to show me that door fast shut; at any rate, if you can stay in the place alone for a fortnight, you shall have your money."

"I don't like it, Phil," said my uncle: "I don't like this freak at all."

"I am sorry for that, uncle," I answered, "for I mean to go."

"When?" asked Mr. Carrison.

"Tomorrow morning," I replied.

"Give him five pounds, Dorland, please, and I will send you my cheque. You will account to me for that sum, you understand," added Mr. Carrison, turning to where I stood.

"A sovereign will be quite enough," I said.

"You will take five pounds, and account to me for it," repeated Mr. Carrison, firmly; "also, you will write to me every day, to my private address, and if at any moment you feel the thing too much for you, throw it up. Good afternoon," and without more formal leave-taking he departed.

"It is of no use talking to you, Phil, I suppose?" said my uncle.

"I don't think it is," I replied; "you won't say anything to them at home, will you?"

"I am not very likely to meet any of them, am I?" he answered, without a shade of bitterness — merely stating a fact.

"I suppose I shall not see you again before I start," I said, "so I will bid you goodbye now."

"Goodbye, my lad; I wish I could see you a bit wiser and steadier."

I did not answer him; my heart was very full, and my eyes too. I had tried, but office-work was not in me, and I felt it was just as vain to ask me to sit on a stool and pore over writing and figures as to think a person born destitute of musical ability could compose an opera.

Of course I went straight to Patty; though we were not then married, though sometimes it seemed to me as if we never should be married, she was my better half then as she is my better half now.

She did not throw cold water on the project; she did not discourage me. What she said, with her dear face aglow with excitement, was, "I only wish, Phil, I was going with you." Heaven knows, so did I.

Next morning I was up before the milkman. I had told my people overnight I should be going out of town on business. Patty and I settled the whole plan in detail. I was to breakfast and dress there, for I meant to go down to Ladlow in my volunteer garments. That was a subject upon which my poor father and I never could agree; he called volunteering child's play, and other things equally hard to bear; whilst my brother, a very carpet warrior to my mind, was never weary of ridiculing the force, and chaffing me for imagining I was "a soldier".

Patty and I had talked matters over, and settled, as I have said, that I should dress at her father's.

A young fellow I knew had won a revolver at a raffle, and willingly lent it to me. With that and my rifle I felt I could conquer an army.

It was a lovely afternoon when I found myself walking through leafy lanes in the heart of Meadowshire. With every vein of my heart I loved the country, and the country was looking its best just then: grass ripe for the mower, grain forming in the ear, rippling streams, dreamy rivers, old orchards, quaint cottages.

"Oh that I had never to go back to London," I thought, for I am one of the few people left on earth who love the country and hate cities. I walked on, I walked a long way, and being uncertain as to my road, asked a gentleman who was slowly riding a powerful roan horse under arching trees — a gentleman accompanied by a young lady mounted on a stiff white pony — my way to Ladlow Hall.

"That is Ladlow Hall," he answered, pointing with his whip over the fence to my left hand. I thanked him and was going on, when he said: "No one is living there now."

"I am aware of that," I answered.

He did not say anything more, only courteously bade me good-day, and rode off. The young lady inclined her head in acknowledgement of my uplifted cap, and smiled kindly. Altogether I felt pleased, little things always did please me. It was a good beginning — half-way to a good ending!

When I got to the Lodge I showed Mr. Carrison's letter to the woman, and received the key.

"You are not going to stop up at the Hall alone, are you, sir?" she asked.

"Yes, I am," I answered, uncompromisingly, so uncompromisingly that she said no more.

The avenue led straight to the house; it was uphill all the way, and bordered by rows of the most magnificent limes I ever beheld. A light iron fence divided the avenue from the park, and between the trunks of the trees I could see the deer browsing and cattle grazing. Ever and anon there came likewise to my ear the sound of a sheep-bell.

It was a long avenue, but at length I stood in front of the Hall — a square, solid-looking, old-fashioned house, three stories high, with no basement; a flight of steps up to the principal entrance; four windows to the right of the door, four windows to the left; the whole building flanked and backed with trees; all the blinds pulled down, a dead silence brooding over the place: the sun westering behind the great trees studding the park. I took all this in as I approached, and afterwards as I stood for a moment under the ample porch; then, remembering the business which had brought me so far, I fitted the great key in the lock, turned the handle, and entered Ladlow Hall.

For a minute — stepping out of the bright sunlight — the place looked to me so dark that I could scarcely distinguish the objects by which I was surrounded; but my eyes soon grew accustomed to the comparative darkness, and I found I was in an immense hall, lighted from the roof, a magnificent old oak staircase conducted to the upper rooms.

The floor was of black and white marble. There were two fireplaces, fitted with dogs for burning wood; around the walls hung pictures, antlers, and horns, and in odd niches and corners stood groups of statues, and the figures of men in complete suits of armour.

To look at the place outside, no one would have expected to find such a hall. I stood lost in amazement and admiration, and then I began to glance more particularly around.

Mr. Carrison had not given me any instructions by which to identify the ghostly chamber — which I concluded would most probably be found on the first floor.

I knew nothing of the story connected with it — if there were a story. On that point I had left London as badly provided with mental as with actual luggage — worse provided, indeed, for a hamper, packed by Patty, and a small bag were coming over from the station; but regarding the mystery I was perfectly unencumbered. I had not the faintest idea in which apartment it resided. Well, I should discover that, no doubt, for myself ere long.

I looked around me — doors — doors — doors I had never before seen so many doors together all at once. Two of them stood open — one wide, the other slightly ajar.

"I'll just shut them as a beginning," I thought, "before I go upstairs."

The doors were of oak, heavy, well-fitting, furnished with good locks and sound handles. After I had closed I tried them. Yes, they were quite secure. I ascended the great staircase feeling curiously like an intruder, paced the corridors, entered the many bed-chambers — some quite bare of furniture, others containing articles of an ancient fashion, and no doubt of considerable value — chairs, antique dressing-tables, curious wardrobes, and such like. For the most part the doors were closed, and I shut those that stood open before making my way into the attics.

I was greatly delighted with the attics. The windows lighting them did not, as a rule, overlook the front of the Hall, but commanded wide views over wood, and valley, and meadow. Leaning out of one, I could see, that to the right of the Hall the ground, thickly planted, shelved down to a stream, which came out into the daylight a little distance beyond the plantation, and meandered through the deer park. At the back of the Hall the windows looked out on nothing save a dense wood and a portion of the stable-yard, whilst on the side nearest the point from whence I had come there were spreading gardens surrounded by thick yew hedges, and kitchen-gardens protected by high walls; and further on a farmyard, where I could perceive cows and oxen, and, further still, luxuriant meadows, and fields glad with waving corn.

"What a beautiful place!" I said. "Carrison must have been a duffer to leave it." And then I thought what a great ramshackle house it was for anyone to be in all alone.

Getting heated with my long walk, I suppose, made me feel chilly, for I shivered as I drew my head in from the last dormer window, and prepared to go downstairs again.

In the attics, as in the other parts of the house I had as yet explored, I closed the doors, when there were keys locking them; when there were not, trying them, and in all cases, leaving them securely fastened.

When I reached the ground floor the evening was drawing on apace, and I felt that if I wanted to explore the whole house before dusk I must hurry my proceedings.

"I'll take the kitchens next," I decided, and so made my way to a wilderness of domestic offices lying to the rear of the great hall. Stone passages, great kitchens, an immense servants'-hall, larders, pantries, coal-cellars, beer-cellars, laundries, brewhouses, housekeeper's room — it was not of any use lingering over these details.

The mystery that troubled Mr. Carrison could scarcely lodge amongst cinders and empty bottles, and there did not seem much else left in this part of the building. I would go through the living-rooms, and then decide as to the apartments I should occupy myself.

The evening shadows were drawing on apace, so I hurried back into the hall, feeling it was a weird position to be there all alone with those ghostly hollow figures of men in armour, and the statues on which the moon's beams must fall so coldly. I would just look through the lower apartments and then kindle a fire. I had seen quantities of wood in a cupboard close at hand, and felt that beside a blazing hearth, and after a good cup of tea, I should not feel the solitary sensation which was oppressing me.

The sun had sunk below the horizon by this time, for to reach Ladlow I had been obliged to travel by cross lines of railway, and wait besides for such trains as condescended to carry third-class passengers; but there was still light enough in the hail to see all objects distinctly. With my own eyes I saw that one of the doors I had shut with my own hands was standing wide!

I turned to the door on the other side of the hall. It was as I had left it — closed. *This, then, was the room — this with the open door.* For a second I stood appalled; I think I was fairly frightened.

That did not last long, however. There lay the work I had desired to undertake, the foe I had offered to fight; so without more ado I shut the door and tried it.

"Now I will walk to the end of the hall and see what happens," I considered. I did so. I walked to the foot of the grand staircase and back again, and looked.

The door stood wide open.

I went into the room, after just a spasm of irresolution — went in and pulled up the blinds: a good-sized room, twenty by twenty (I knew, because I paced it afterwards), lighted by two long windows.

The floor, of polished oak, was partially covered with a Turkey carpet. There were two recesses beside the fireplace, one fitted up as a bookcase, the other with an old and elaborately caned cabinet. I was astonished also to find a bedstead in an apartment so little retired from the traffic of the house; and there were also some chairs of an obsolete make, covered, so far as I could make out, with faded tapestry. Beside the bedstead, which stood against the wall opposite to the door, I perceived another door. It was fast locked, the only locked door I had as yet met with in the interior of the house. It was a dreary, gloomy room: the dark panelled walls; the black, shining floor; the windows high from the ground; the antique furniture; the dull four-poster bedstead, with dingy velvet curtains; the gaping chimney; the silk counterpane that looked like a pall

"Any crime might have been committed in such a room," I thought pettishly; and then I looked at the door critically.

Someone had been at the trouble of fitting bolts upon it, for when I passed out I not merely shut the door securely, but bolted it as well.

"I will go and get some wood, and then look at it again," I soliloquized. When I came back it stood wide open once more.

"Stay open, then!" I cried in a fury. "I won't trouble myself any more with you tonight!"

Almost as I spoke the words, there came a ring at the front door. Echoing through the desolate house, the peal in the then state of my nerves startled me beyond expression.

It was only the man who had agreed to bring over my traps. I bade him lay them down in the hall, and, while looking out some small silver, asked where the nearest post-office was to be found. Not far from the park gates, he said; if I wanted any letter sent, he would drop it in the box for me; the mail-cart picked up the bag at ten o'clock.

I had nothing ready to post then, and told him so. Perhaps the money I gave was more than he expected, or perhaps the dreariness of my position impressed him as it had impressed me, for he paused with his hand on the lock, and asked:

"Are you going to stop here all alone, master?"

"All alone," I answered, with such cheerfulness as was possible under the circumstances.

"That's the room, you know," he said, nodding in the direction of the open door, and dropping his voice to a whisper.

"Yes, I know," I replied.

"What, you've been trying to shut it already, have you? Well, you are a game one!" And with this complementary if not very respectful comment he hastened out of the house. Evidently he had no intention of proffering his services towards the solution of the mystery.

I cast one glance at the door — it stood wide open. Through the windows I had left bare to the night, moonlight was beginning to stream cold and silvery. Before I did aught else I felt I must write to Mr. Carrison and Patty, so straightway I hurried to one of the great tables in the hall, and lighting a candle my thoughtful little girl had provided, with many other things, sat down and dashed off the two epistles.

Then down the long avenue, with its mysterious lights and shades, with the moonbeams glinting here and there, playing at hide-and-seek round the boles of the trees and through the tracery of quivering leaf and stem, I walked as fast as if I were doing a match against time.

It was delicious, the scent of the summer odours, the smell of the earth; if it had not been for the door I should have felt too happy. As it was — "Look here, Phil," I said, all of a sudden; "life's not child's play, as uncle truly remarks. That door is just the trouble you have now to face, and you must face it! But for that door you would never have been here. I hope you are not going to turn coward the very first night. Courage! — that is your enemy — conquer it."

"I will try," my other self answered back. "I can but try. I can but fail."

The post-office was at Ladlow Hollow, a little hamlet through which the stream I had remarked dawdling on its way across the park flowed swiftly, spanned by an ancient bridge.

As I stood by the door of the little shop, asking some questions of the postmistress, the same gentleman I had met in the afternoon mounted on his roan horse, passed on foot. He wished me goodnight as he went by, and nodded familiarly to my companion, who curtseyed her acknowledgements.

"His lordship ages fast," she remarked, following the retreating figure with her eyes.

"His lordship," I repeated. 'Of whom are you speaking?'

"Of Lord Ladlow," she said.

"Oh! I have never seen him," I answered, puzzled.

"Why, *that* was Lord Ladlow!" she exclaimed.

You may be sure I had something to think about as I walked back to the Hall — something beside the moonlight and the sweet night-scents, and the rustle of beast and bird and leaf, that make silence seem more eloquent than noise away down in the heart of the country. Lord Ladlow! my word, I thought he was hundreds, thousands of miles away; and here I find him — he walking in the opposite direction from his own home — I an inmate of his desolate abode. Hi! — what was that? I heard a noise in a shrubbery close at hand, and in an instant I was in the thick of the underwood. Something shot out and darted into the cover of the further plantation. I followed, but I could catch never a glimpse of it. I did not know the lie of the ground sufficiently to course with success, and I had at length to give up the hunt — heated, baffled, and annoyed.

When I got into the house the moon's beams were streaming down upon the hall; I could see every statue, every square of marble, every piece of armour. For all the world it seemed to me like something in a dream; but I was tired and sleepy, and decided I would not trouble about fire or food, or the open door, till the next morning: I would go to sleep.

With this intention I picked up some of my traps and carried them to a room on the first floor I had selected as small and habitable. I went down for the rest, and this time chanced to lay my hand on my rifle.

It was wet. I touched the floor — it was wet likewise.

I never felt anything like the thrill of delight which shot through me. I had to deal with flesh and blood, and I would deal with it, heaven helping me.

The next morning broke clear and bright. I was up with the lark — had washed, dressed, breakfasted, explored the house before the postman came with my letters.

One from Mr. Carrison, one from Patty, and one from my uncle. I gave the man half a crown, I was so delighted, and said I was afraid my being at the Hall would cause him some additional trouble.

"No, sir," he answered, profuse in his expressions of gratitude; "I pass here every morning on my way to her ladyship's."

"Who is her ladyship?" I asked.

"The Dowager Lady Ladlow," he answered — "the old lord's widow."

"And where is her place?" I persisted.

"If you keep on through the shrubbery and across the waterfall, you come to the house about a quarter of a mile further up the stream."

He departed, after telling me there was only one post a day; and I hurried back to the room in which I had breakfasted, carrying my letters with me.

I opened Mr. Carrison's first. The gist of it was, 'Spare no expense; if you run short of money telegraph for it.'

I opened my uncle's next. He implored me to return; he had always thought me hair-brained, but he felt a deep interest in and affection for me, and thought he could get me a good berth if I would only try to settle down and promise to stick to my work. The last was from Patty. O Patty, God bless you! Such women, I fancy, the men who fight best in battle, who stick last to a sinking ship, who are firm in life's struggles, who are brave to resist temptation, must have known and loved. I can't tell you more about the letter, except that it gave me strength to go on to the end.

I spent the forenoon considering that door. I looked at it from within and from without. I eyed it critically. I tried whether there was any reason why it should fly open, and I found that so long as I remained on the threshold it remained closed; if I walked even so far away as the opposite side of the hall, it swung wide.

Do what I would, it burst from latch and bolt. I could not lock it because there was no key.

Well, before two o'clock I confess I was baffled.

At two there came a visitor — none other than Lord Ladlow himself. Sorely I wanted to take his horse round to the stables, but he would not hear of it.

"Walk beside me across the park, if you will be so kind," he said; "I want to speak to you."

We went together across the park, and before we parted I felt I could have gone through fire and water for this simple-spoken nobleman.

"You must not stay here ignorant of the rumours which are afloat," he said. "Of course, when I let the place to Mr. Carrison I knew nothing of the open door."

"Did you not, sir? — my lord, I mean," I stammered.

He smiled. "Do not trouble yourself about my title, which, indeed, carries a very empty state with it, but talk to me as you might to a friend. I had no idea there was any ghost story connected with the Hall, or I should have kept the place empty."

I did not exactly know what to answer, so I remained silent.

"How did you chance to be sent here?" he asked, after a pause.

I told him. When the first shock was over, a lord did not seem very different from anybody else. If an emperor had taken a morning canter across the park, I might, supposing him equally affable, have spoken as familiarly to him as to Lord Ladlow. My mother always said I entirely lacked the bump of veneration!

Beginning at the beginning, I repeated the whole story, from Parton's remark about the sovereign to Mr. Carrison's conversation with my uncle. When I had left London behind in the narrative, however, and arrived at the Hall, I became somewhat more reticent. After all, it was *his* Hall people could not live in — *his* door that would not keep shut; and it seemed to me these were facts he might dislike being forced upon his attention.

But he would have it. What had *I* seen? What did *I* think of the matter? Very honestly I told him I did not know what to say. The door certainly would not remain shut, and there seemed no human agency to account for its persistent opening; but then, on the other hand, ghosts generally did not tamper with firearms, and my rifle, though not loaded, had been tampered with — I was sure of that.

My companion listened attentively. "You are not frightened, are you?" he enquired at length.

"Not now," I answered. "The door did give me a start last evening, but I am not afraid of that since I find someone else is afraid of a bullet."

He did not answer for a minute; then he said: "The theory people have set up about the open door is this: as in that room my uncle was murdered, they say the door will never remain shut till the murderer is discovered."

"Murdered!" I did not like the word at all; it made me feel chill and uncomfortable.

"Yes — he was murdered sitting in his chair, and the assassin has never been discovered. At first many persons inclined to the belief that I killed him; indeed, many are of that opinion still."

"But you did not, sir — there is not a word of truth in that story, is there?"

He laid his hand on my shoulder as he said:

"No, my lad; not a word. I loved the old man tenderly. Even when he disinherited me for the sake of his young wife, I was sorry, but not angry; and when he sent for me and assured me he had resolved to repair that wrong, I tried to induce him to leave the lady a handsome sum in addition to her jointure. 'If you do not, people may think she has not been the source of happiness you expected,' I added.

"'Thank you, Hal,' he said. 'You are a good fellow; we will talk further about this tomorrow.' And then he bade me goodnight.

"Before morning broke — it was in the summer two years ago — the household was aroused by a fearful scream. It was his death-cry. He had been stabbed from behind in the neck. He was seated in his chair writing — writing a letter to me. But for that I might have found it harder to clear myself than was in the case; for his solicitors came forward and said he had signed a will leaving all his personalty to me — he was very rich — unconditionally, only three days previously. That, of course, supplied the motive, as my lady's lawyer put it. She was very vindictive, spared no expense in trying to prove my guilt, and said openly she would never rest till she saw justice done, if it cost her the whole of her fortune. The letter lying before the dead man, over which blood had spurted, she declared must have been placed on his table by me; but the coroner saw there was an animus in this, for the few opening lines stated my uncle's desire to confide in me his reasons for changing his will — reasons, he said, that involved his honour, as they had destroyed his peace. 'In the statement you will find sealed up with my will in —' At that point he was dealt his death-blow. The papers were never found, and the will was never proved. My lady put in the former will, leaving her everything. Ill as I could afford to go to law, I was obliged to dispute the matter, and the lawyers are at it still, and very likely will continue at it for years.

"When I lost my good name, I lost my good health, and had to go abroad; and while I was away Mr. Carrison took the Hall. Till I returned, I never heard a word about the open door. My solicitor said Mr. Carrison was behaving badly; but I think now I must see them or him, and consider what can be done in the affair. As for yourself, it is of vital importance to me that this mystery should be cleared up, and if you are really not timid, stay on. I am too poor to make rash promises, but you won't find me ungrateful."

"Oh, my lord!" I cried — the address slipped quite easily and naturally off my tongue — "I don't want any more money or anything, if I can only show Patty's father I am good for something —"

"Who is Patty?" he asked.

He read the answer in my face, for he said no more.

"Should you like to have a good dog for company?" he enquired after a pause.

I hesitated; then I said: "No, thank you. I would rather watch and hunt for myself."

And as I spoke, the remembrance of that "something" in the shrubbery recurred to me, and I told him I thought there had been someone about the place the previous evening.

"Poachers," he suggested; but I shook my head.

"A girl or a woman I imagine. However, I think a dog might hamper me."

He went away, and I returned to the house. I never left it all day. I did not go into the garden, or the stable-yard, or the shrubbery, or anywhere; I devoted myself solely and exclusively to that door.

If I shut it once, I shut it a hundred times, and always with the same result. Do what I would, it swung wide. Never, however, when I was looking at it. So long as I could endure to remain, it stayed shut — the instant I turned my back, it stood open.

About four o'clock I had another visitor; no other than Lord Ladlow's daughter — the Honourable Beatrice, riding her funny little white pony.

She was a beautiful girl of fifteen or thereabouts, and she had the sweetest smile you ever saw.

"Papa sent me with this," she said; "he would not trust any other messenger," and she put a piece of paper in my hand.

> "Keep your food under lock and key; buy what you require yourself.
> Get your water from the pump in the stable-yard.
> I am going from home; but if you want anything, go or send to my daughter."

"Any answer?" she asked, patting her pony's neck.

"Tell his lordship, if you please, I will 'keep my powder dry!'" I replied.

"You have made papa look so happy," she said, still patting that fortunate pony.

"If it is in my power, I will make him look happier still, Miss —" and I hesitated, not knowing how to address her.

"Call me Beatrice," she said, with an enchanting grace; then added, slyly, "Papa promises me I shall be introduced to Patty ere long," and before I could recover from my astonishment, she had tightened the bit and was turning across the park.

"One moment, please," I cried. "You can do something for me."

"What is it?" and she came back, trotting over the great sweep in front of the house.

"Lend me your pony for a minute."

She was off before I could even offer to help her alight — off, and gathering up her habit dexterously with one hand, led the docile old sheep forward with the other.

I took the bridle — when I was with horses I felt amongst my own kind — stroked the pony, pulled his ears, and let him thrust his nose into my hand.

Miss Beatrice is a countess now, and a happy wife and mother; but I sometimes see her, and the other night she took me carefully into a conservatory and asked:

"Do you remember Toddy, Mr. Edlyd?"

"Remember him!" I exclaimed; "I can never forget him!"

"He is dead!" she told me, and there were tears in her beautiful eyes as she spoke the words.

"Mr. Edlyd, *I loved Toddy!*"

Well, I took Toddy up to the house, and under the third window to the right hand. He was a docile creature, and let me stand on the saddle while I looked into the only room in Ladlow Hall I had been unable to enter.

It was perfectly bare of furniture, there was not a thing in it — not a chair or table, not a picture on the walls, or ornament on the chimney-piece.

"That is where my grand-uncle's valet slept," said Miss Beatrice. "It was he who first ran in to help him the night he was murdered."

"Where is the valet?" I asked.

"Dead," she answered. "The shock killed him. He loved his master more than he loved himself."

I had seen all I wished, so I jumped off the saddle, which I had carefully dusted with a branch plucked from a lilac tree; between jest and earnest pressed the hem of Miss Beatrice's habit to my lips as I arranged its folds; saw her wave her hand as she went at a hand-gallop across the park; and then turned back once again into the lonely house, with the determination to solve the mystery attached to it or die in the attempt.

Why, I cannot explain, but before I went to bed that night I drove a gimlet I found in the stables hard into the floor, and said to the door:

"Now *I* am keeping you open."

When I went down in the morning the door was close shut, and the handle of the gimlet, broken off short, lying in the hall.

I put my hand to wipe my forehead; it was dripping with perspiration. I did not know what to make of the place at all! I went out into the open air for a few minutes; when I returned the door again stood wide.

If I were to pursue in detail the days and nights that followed, I should weary my readers.

I can only say they changed my life. The solitude, the solemnity, the mystery, produced an effect I do not profess to understand, but that I cannot regret.

I have hesitated about writing of the end, but it must come, so let me hasten to it.

Though feeling convinced that no human agency did or could keep the door open, I was certain that some living person had means of access to the house which *I* could not discover. This was made apparent in trifles which might well have escaped unnoticed had several, or even two people occupied the mansion, but that in my solitary position it was impossible to overlook. A chair would be misplaced, for instance; a path would be visible over a dusty floor; my papers I found were moved; my clothes touched — letters I carried about with me, and kept under my pillow at night; still, the fact remained that when I went to the post-office, and while I was asleep, someone did wander over the house. On Lord Ladlow's return I meant to ask him for some further particulars of his uncle's death, and I was about to write to Mr. Carrison and beg permission to have the door where the valet had slept broken open, when one morning, very early indeed, I spied a hairpin lying close beside it.

What an idiot I had been! If I wanted to solve the mystery of the open door, of course I must keep watch in the room itself. The door would not stay wide unless there was a reason for it, and most certainly a hairpin could not have got into the house without assistance.

I made up my mind what I should do — that I would go to the post early, and take up my position about the hour I had hitherto started for Ladlow Hollow. I felt on the eve of a discovery, and longed for the day to pass, that the night might come.

It was a lovely morning; the weather had been exquisite during the whole week, and I flung the hall-door wide to let in the sunshine and the breeze. As I did so, I saw there was a basket on the top step — a basket filled with rare and beautiful fruit and flowers.

Mr. Carrison had let off the gardens attached to Ladlow Hall for the season — he thought he might as well save something out of the fire, he said, so my fare had not been varied with delicacies of that kind. I was very fond of fruit in those days, and seeing a card addressed to me, I instantly selected a tempting peach, and ate it a little greedily perhaps.

I might say I had barely swallowed the last morsel, when Lord Ladlow's caution recurred to me. The fruit had a curious flavour — there was a strange taste hanging about my palate. For a moment, sky, trees and park swam before my eyes; then I made up my mind what to do.

I smelt the fruit — it had all the same faint odour; then I put some in my pocket — took the basket and locked it away — walked round to the farmyard — asked for the loan of a horse that was generally driven in a light cart, and in less than half an hour was asking in Ladlow to be directed to a doctor.

Rather cross at being disturbed so early, he was at first inclined to pooh-pooh my idea; but I made him cut open a pear and satisfy himself the fruit had been tampered with.

"It is fortunate you stopped at the first peach," he remarked, after giving me a draught, and some medicine to take back, and advising me to keep in the open air as much as possible. "I should like to retain this fruit and see you again tomorrow."

We did not think then on how many morrows we should see each other!

Riding across to Ladlow, the postman had given me three letters, but I did not read them till I was seated under a great tree in the park, with a basin of milk and a piece of bread beside me.

Hitherto, there had been nothing exciting in my correspondence. Patty's epistles were always delightful, but they could not be regarded as sensational; and about Mr. Carrison's there was a monotony I had begun to find tedious. On this occasion, however, no fault could be found on that score. The contents of his letter greatly surprised me. He said Lord Ladlow had released him from his bargain — that I could, therefore, leave the Hall at once. He enclosed me ten pounds, and said he would consider how he could best advance my interests; and that I had better call upon him at his private house when I returned to London.

"I do not think I shall leave Ladlow yet awhile," I considered, as I replaced his letter in its envelope. "Before I go I should like to make it hot for whoever sent me that fruit; so unless Lord Ladlow turns me out I'll stay a little longer."

Lord Ladlow did not wish me to leave. The third letter was from him.

"I shall return home tomorrow night," he wrote, "and see you on Wednesday. I have arranged satisfactorily with Mr. Carrison, and as the Hall is my own again, I mean to try to solve the mystery it contains myself. If you choose to stop and help me to do so, you would confer a favour, and I will try to make it worth your while."

"I will keep watch tonight, and see if I cannot give you some news tomorrow," I thought. And then I opened Patty's letter — the best, dearest, sweetest letter any postman in all the world could have brought me.

If it had not been for what Lord Ladlow said about his sharing my undertaking, I should not have chosen that night for my vigil. I felt ill and languid — fancy, no doubt, to a great degree inducing these sensations. I had lost energy in a most unaccountable manner. The long, lonely days had told upon my spirits — the fidgety feeling which took me a hundred times in the twelve hours to look upon the open door, to close it, and to count how many steps I could take before it opened again, had tried my mental strength as a perpetual blister might have worn away my physical. In no sense was I fit for the task I had set myself, and yet I determined to go through with it. Why had I never before decided to watch in that mysterious chamber? Had I been at the bottom of my heart afraid? In the bravest of us there are depths of cowardice that lurk unsuspected till they engulf our courage.

The day wore on — the long, dreary day; evening approached — the night shadows closed over the Hall. The moon would not rise for a couple of hours more. Everything was still as death. The house had never before seemed to me so silent and so deserted.

I took a light, and went up to my accustomed room, moving about for a time as though preparing for bed; then I extinguished the candle, softly opened the door, turned the key, and put it in my pocket, slipped softly downstairs, across the hall, through the open door. Then I knew I had been afraid, for I felt a thrill of terror as in the dark I stepped over the threshold. I paused and listened — there was not a sound — the night was still and sultry, as though a storm were brewing. Not a leaf seemed moving — the very mice remained in their holes! Noiselessly I made my way to the other side of the room. There was an old-fashioned easy-chair between the bookshelves and the bed; I sat down in it, shrouded by the heavy curtain.

The hours passed — were ever hours so long? The moon rose, came and looked in at the windows, and then sailed away to the west; but not a sound, no, not even the cry of a bird. I seemed to myself a mere collection of nerves. Every part of my body appeared twitching. It was agony to remain still; the desire to move became a form of torture. Ah! a streak in the sky; morning at last, Heaven be praised! Had ever anyone before so welcomed the dawn? A thrush began to sing — was there ever heard such delightful music? It was the morning twilight, soon the sun would rise; soon that awful vigil would be over, and yet I was no nearer the mystery than before. Hush! what was that? *It had come.* After the hours of watching and waiting; after the long night and the long suspense, it came in a moment.

The locked door opened — so suddenly, so silently, that I had barely time to draw back behind the curtain, before I saw a woman in the room. She went straight across to the other door and closed it, securing it as I saw with bolt and lock. Then just glancing around, she made her way to the cabinet, and with a key she produced shot back the wards. I did not stir, I scarcely breathed, and yet she seemed uneasy. Whatever she wanted to do she evidently was in haste to finish, for she took out the drawers one by one, and placed them on the floor; then, as the light grew better, I saw her first kneel on the floor, and peer into every aperture, and subsequently repeat the same process, standing on a chair she drew forward for the purpose. A slight, lithe woman, not a lady, clad all in black — not a bit of white about her. What on earth could she want? In a moment it flashed upon me — THE WILL AND THE LETTER! SHE IS SEARCHING FOR THEM.

I sprang from my concealment — I had her in my grasp; but she tore herself out of my hands, fighting like a wild-cat: she hit, scratched, kicked, shifting her body as though she had not a bone in it, and at last slipped herself free, and ran wildly towards the door by which she had entered.

If she reached it, she would escape me. I rushed across the room and just caught her dress as she was on the threshold. My blood was up, and I dragged her back: she had the strength of twenty devils, I think, and struggled as surely no woman ever did before.

"I do not want to kill you," I managed to say in gasps — "but I will if you do not keep quiet."

"Bah!" she cried; and before I knew what she was doing she had the revolver out of my pocket and fired.

She missed: the ball just glanced off my sleeve. I fell upon her — I can use no other expression, for it had become a fight for life, and no man can tell the ferocity there is in him till he is placed as I was then — fell upon her, and seized the weapon. She would not let it go, but I held her so tight she could not use it. She bit my face; with her disengaged hand she tore my hair. She turned and twisted and slipped about like a snake, but I did not feel pain or anything except a deadly horror lest my strength should give out.

Could I hold out much longer? She made one desperate plunge, I felt the grasp with which I held her slackening; she felt it too, and seizing her advantage tore herself free, and at the same instant fired again blindly, and again missed.

Suddenly there came a look of horror into her eyes — a frozen expression of fear.

"See!" she cried; and flinging the revolver at me, fled.

I saw, as in a momentary flash, that the door I had beheld locked stood wide — that there stood beside the table an awful figure, with uplifted hand — and then I saw no more. I was struck at last; as she threw the revolver at me she must have pulled the trigger, for I felt something like red-hot iron enter my shoulder, and I could but rush from the room before I fell senseless on the marble pavement of the hall.

When the postman came that morning, finding no one stirring, be looked through one of the long windows that flanked the door; then he ran to the farmyard and called for help.

"There is something wrong inside," he cried. "That young gentleman is lying on the floor in a pool of blood."

As they rushed round to the front of the house they saw Lord Ladlow riding up the avenue, and breathlessly told him what had happened.

"Smash in one of the windows," he said; "and go instantly for a doctor."

They laid me on the bed in that terrible room, and telegraphed for my father. For long I hovered between life and death, but at length I recovered sufficiently to be removed to the house Lord Ladlow owned on the other side of the Hollow.

Before that time I had told him all I knew, and begged him to make instant search for the will.

"Break up the cabinet if necessary," I entreated, "I am sure the papers are there."

And they were. His lordship got his own, and as to the scandal and the crime, one was hushed up and the other remained unpunished. The dowager and her maid went abroad the very morning I lay on the marble pavement at Ladlow Hall — they never returned.

My lord made that one condition of his silence.

Not in Meadowshire, but in a fairer county still, I have a farm which I manage, and make both ends meet comfortably.

Patty is the best wife any man ever possessed — and I — well, I am just as happy if a trifle more serious than of old; but there are times when a great horror of darkness seems to fall upon me, and at such periods I cannot endure to be left alone.

In the Dark

Mary E. Penn

"It is the strangest, most unaccountable thing I ever knew! I don't think I am superstitious, but I can't help fancying that —"

Ethel left the sentence unfinished, wrinkling her brows in a thoughtful frown as she gazed into the depths of her empty tea-cup.

"What has happened?" I enquired, glancing up from the Money Article of the *Times* at my daughter's pretty, puzzled face. "Nothing uncanny, I hope? You haven't discovered that a 'ghost' is included among the fixtures of our new house?"

This new house, The Cedars, was a pretty old-fashioned riverside villa between Richmond and Kew, which I had taken furnished, as a summer residence, and to which we had only just removed.

Let me state, in parenthesis, by way of introducing myself to the reader, that I, John Dysart, am a widower with one child: the blue-eyed, fair-haired young lady who sat opposite to me at the breakfast table that bright June morning: and that I have been for many years the manager of an old-established Life Insurance Company in the City.

"What is the mystery?" I repeated, as Ethel did not reply.

She came out of her brown study, and looked at me impressively.

"It really is a mystery, papa, and the more I think of it the more puzzled I am."

"I am in the dark at present as to what 'it' may be," I reminded her.

"Something that happened last night. You know that adjoining my bedroom there is a large, dark closet, which can be used as a box or store-room?"

"I had forgotten the fact, but I will take your word for it. Well, Ethel?"

"Well, last night I was restless, and it was some hours before I could sleep. When at last I did so, I had a strange dream about that closet. It seemed that as I lay in bed I heard a noise within, as if someone were knocking at the door, and a child's voice, broken by sobs, crying piteously 'Let me out, let me out!' I thought that I got out of bed and opened the door, and there, crouching all in a heap against the wall, was a little boy; a pretty, pale little fellow of six or seven, looking half wild with fright. At the same moment I woke."

"And lo, it was a dream!" I finished. "If that is all Ethel — "

"But it is not," she interposed. "The strangest part of the story has to come. The dream was so vivid that when I woke I sat up in bed, and looked towards the closet door, almost expecting to hear the sounds again. Papa, you may believe me or not, but it is a fact that I *did* hear them, the muffled knocking, and the pitiful cry. As I listened, it grew fainter and fainter and at length ceased altogether. Then I summoned courage to get out of bed and open the door. There was no living creature in the place. Was it not mysterious?" she concluded. "What can it mean?"

I glanced at her with a smile, as I refolded the paper and rose from my chair.

"It means, my dear, that you had night-mare last night. Let me recommend you for the future not to eat cucumber at dinner."

"No, papa," she interrupted. "I was broad awake, and I heard the child's voice as plainly as I ever heard a sound in my life."

"Why didn't you call me?"

"I was afraid to stir till the sound had ceased; but if I ever hear it again, I will let you know at once."

"Be sure you do. Meantime, suppose you come into the garden," I continued, throwing open the French windows; "the morning air will blow all these cobwebs from your brain."

Ethel complied, and for the present I heard no more of the subject.

Some days passed away, and we began to feel quite at home in our new quarters.

A more delightful summer retreat than The Cedars could hardly be imagined, with its cool, dusky rooms, from which the sunlight was excluded by the screen of foliage outside; its trellised veranda, overgrown with creepers, and its smooth lawn, shaded by the rare old cedar-trees which gave the place its name.

Our friends soon discovered its attractions and took care that we should not stagnate for want of society. We kept open house; lawn-tennis, garden-parties, and boating excursions were the order of the day. It was glorious summer weather, the days warm and golden, the nights starlit and still.

One night, having important letters to finish, I sat up writing after all the household were in bed. The window was open, and at intervals I glanced up from my paper across the moonlit lawn, where the shadows of the cedars lay dark and motionless. Now and then a great downy moth would flutter in and hover round the shaded lamp; now and then the swallows under the eaves uttered a faint, sleepy chirp. For all other signs and sounds of life I might have been the only watcher in all the sleeping world.

I had finished my task and was just closing my writing-case when I heard a hurried movement in the room above — Ethel's. Footsteps descended the stairs, and the next moment the dining-room door opened, and Ethel appeared, in a long, white dressing-gown, with a small night-lamp in her hand.

There was a look on her face which made me start up and exclaim:

"What is the matter? What has happened?"

She set down the lamp and came towards me.

"I have heard it again," she breathed, laying her hand on my wrist.

"You have heard — what?"

"The noise in the box-room."

I stared at her a moment in bewilderment, and then half smiled.

"Oh, is that it?" I exclaimed, in a tone of relief. "You have been dreaming again, it seems."

"I have not been asleep at all," she replied. "The sounds have kept me awake. They are louder than the first time; the child seems to be sobbing and crying as if his heart would break. It is miserable to hear it."

"Have you looked inside?" I asked, impressed in spite of myself by her manner.

"No, I dared not tonight. I was afraid of seeing — something," she returned with a shiver.

"Come, we must get to the bottom of this mystery," I said cheerfully, and taking up the lamp I led the way upstairs to her room.

As the door of the mysterious closet was level with the wall, and papered like it, I did not perceive it till Ethel pointed it out. I listened with my ear close to it, but heard not the faintest sound, and after waiting a moment, threw it open and looked in, holding the lamp so that every corner was lighted. It was a cramped, close, airless place, the ceiling (which was immediately below the upper staircase) sloping at an acute angle to the floor. A glance showed me that it contained nothing but a broken chair and a couple of empty boxes.

Slightly shrugging my shoulders, I closed the door.

"Your ghost is 'vox et præterea nihil,' it seems," I remarked drily. "Don't you think, Ethel, you may have been —"

Ethel held up her hand, motioning me to silence.

"Hark," she whispered, "there it is again! But it is dying away now. Listen —"

I complied, half infected by her excitement, but within and without the house all was profoundly still.

"There — it has ceased," she said at length, drawing a deep breath. "You heard it, did you not?"

I shook my head. "My dear Ethel, there was nothing to hear."

She opened her blue eyes to their widest.

"Papa — am I not to believe the evidence of my own senses?"

"Not when they are affected by nervous excitement. If you give way to this fancy, you will certainly make yourself ill. See how you tremble! Come, lie down again, and try to sleep."

"Not here," she returned, glancing round with a shudder. "I shall go to the spare chamber. Nothing would induce me to spend another night in this room."

I said no more, but I felt perplexed and uneasy. It was so unlike Ethel to indulge in superstitious fancies that I began to fear she must be seriously out of health, and I resolved for my own satisfaction to have a doctor's opinion regarding her. It happened that our nearest neighbour was a physician, whom I knew by repute, though not personally acquainted with him. After breakfast, without mentioning my intention to my daughter, I sent a note to Dr. Cameron, requesting him to call at his earliest convenience.

He came without delay: a tall, grey-bearded man of middle age, with a grave, intelligent face, observant eyes and sympathetic manner.

His patient received him with undisguised astonishment, and on learning that he had called at my request she gave me a look of mute reproach.

"I am sorry that papa troubled you, Dr. Cameron. There is really nothing whatever the matter with me," she said.

And indeed at that moment, with flushed cheeks, and eyes even brighter than usual, she looked as little like an invalid as could well be imagined.

"My dear Ethel," I interposed, "when people take to dreaming startling dreams, and hearing supernatural sounds, it is a sign of something wrong with either mind or body — as I am sure Dr. Cameron will tell you."

The doctor started perceptibly. "Ah — is that Miss Dysart's case?" he enquired, turning to her with a sudden look of interest.

She coloured and hesitated. "I have had a strange — experience, which papa considers a delusion. I daresay you will be of the same opinion."

"Suppose you tell me what it was?" he suggested.

She was silent, trifling with one of her silver bangles.

"Please excuse me," she said hurriedly, at length. "I don't care to speak of it; but papa will tell you." And before I could detain her, she had hurriedly left the room.

When we were alone he turned to me enquiringly, and in a few words I related to him what the reader already knows. He listened without interruption, and when I had finished, sat for some moments without speaking, thoughtfully stroking his beard.

He was evidently impressed by what he had heard, and I waited anxiously for his opinion. At length he looked up.

"Mr. Dysart," he said, gravely, "you will be surprised to learn that your daughter is not the first who has had this strange 'experience.' Previous tenants of The Cedars have heard exactly the sounds which she describes."

I pushed my chair back half-a-yard in my astonishment.

"Impossible!"

He nodded emphatically.

"It is a fact, though I don't pretend to explain it. These strange manifestations have been noticed at intervals for the last three or four years; ever since the house was occupied by a Captain Vandeleur, whose orphan nephew —"

"Vandeleur?" I interrupted; "why, he was a client of ours. He insured his nephew's life in our office for a large amount, and —"

"And a few months afterwards, the child suddenly and mysteriously died?" my companion put in. "A singular coincidence, to say the least of it."

"So singular," I acquiesced, "that we thought it a case for enquiry, particularly as the ex-captain did not bear the best of characters, and was known to be over head and ears in debt. But I am bound to say that after the closest investigation nothing was discovered to suggest a suspicion of foul play."

"Nevertheless there *had* been foul play," was the doctor's reply.

"You don't mean that he murdered the boy! that pretty, fragile-looking little fellow —"

"No, he did not murder him, but he let him die," Dr. Cameron rejoined. "Perhaps you were not aware," he continued, "that the little lad was somewhat feeble in mind as well as body? I attended him more than once, at Vandeleur's request, and found that among other strange fears and antipathies he had a morbid dread of darkness. To be left alone in a dark room for only a few minutes was enough to throw him into a paroxysm of nervous excitement. His uncle — who by the way, professed more affection for him than I could quite believe in, when I noticed how the child shrank from him — consulted me as to the best means of overcoming this weakness. I strongly advised him to humour it for the present, warning him that any mental shock might endanger the boy's reason, or even his life. I little thought those words of mine would prove his death warrant."

"What do you mean?"

"Only a few days afterwards, Vandeleur locked him up all night in a dark closet, where he was found the next morning, crouching against the wall; his hands clenched, his eyes fixed and staring — dead."

"Good heavens, how horrible! But no word of this was mentioned at the inquest?"

"No; and I did not hear of it myself till long afterwards, from a woman who had been Vandeleur's housekeeper, but was too much afraid of him to betray him at the time. From her, too, I learnt by what refined cruelty the poor little lad's nerves had been shaken and his health undermined. If 'the intention makes the deed,' James Vandeleur was a murderer."

I was silent a moment, thinking, with an uncomfortable thrill, of Ethel's dream. "I wish I had never entered this ill-omened house!" I exclaimed at length. "I dread the effect of this revelation on my daughter's mind."

"Why need you tell her?" he questioned. "My advice is to say nothing more about it. The sooner she forgets the subject the better. Send her away to the sea-side; change of air and scene will soon efface it from her memory."

He rose as he spoke, and took up his hat.

"What has become of Vandeleur?" I enquired. "I have heard nothing of him since we paid the policy."

"He has been living abroad, I believe — going to the dogs, no doubt. But he is in England now," the doctor added: "or else it was his 'fetch' which I saw at your gate the other night."

"At our gate!" I echoed in astonishment. "What the deuce was he doing there?"

"He seemed to be watching the house. It was last Sunday evening. I had been dining with friends at Richmond, and on my way back, between eleven and twelve o'clock, I noticed a man leaning over the gate of The Cedars. On hearing footsteps he turned and walked away, but not before I had caught a glimpse of his face in the moonlight."

"And you are sure it was he?"

"Almost certain — though he was greatly altered for the worse. I have a presentiment do you know, that you will see or hear of him yourself before long," he added thoughtfully, as he shook hands and went his way.

I lost no time in following his advice with regard to Ethel, whom I despatched to Scarborough, in charge of my married sister, a few days later.

I had taken a hearty dislike to The Cedars, and resolved to get it off my hands as soon as might be.

Until another tenant could be found however, I continued to occupy it, going to and from town as before.

One evening I was sitting on the lawn, smoking an after-dinner cigar, and re-reading Ethel's last letter, which quite reassured me as to her health and spirits, when our sedate old housekeeper presented herself with the information that "a party" had called to see the house.

"A gentleman or a lady?" I enquired.

"A gentleman, sir, but he didn't give his name."

I found the visitor standing near the open window of the drawing-room; a tall, gaunt man of thirty-five or thereabouts, with handsome but haggard features, and restless dark eyes. His lips were covered by a thick moustache, which he was nervously twisting as he stood looking out at the lawn.

"This house is to be let, I believe; will you allow me to look over it?" he asked, turning towards me as I entered.

His voice seemed familiar; I looked at him more closely, and then, in spite of the change in his appearance, I recognised Captain Vandeleur.

What could have brought him here, I wondered. Surely he would not care to return to the house, even if he were in a position to do so — which, judging from the shabbiness of his appearance, seemed very doubtful.

Half-a-dozen vague conjectures flashed through my mind, as I glanced at his face, and noticed the restless, "hunted" look which told of some wearing dread or anxiety.

After a moment's hesitation I assented to his request, and resolved to conduct him myself on his tour of inspection.

"I think I have met you before," I said, feeling curious to know whether he recollected me.

He glanced at me absently.

"Possibly — but not of late years; for I have been living abroad," was his reply.

Having shown him the apartments on the ground-floor, I led the way upstairs. He followed me from room to room in an absent, listless fashion, till we came to the chamber which Ethel had occupied. Then his interest seemed to revive all at once.

He glanced quickly round the walls, his eyes resting on the door of the box-closet.

"That is a bath or dressing-room, I suppose," he said, nodding towards it.

"No, only a place for lumber. Perhaps I ought to tell you that it is said to be haunted," I added, affecting to speak carelessly, while I kept my eyes on his face.

He started and turned towards me.

"Haunted — by what?" he enquired, with a faint sneer. "Nothing worse than rats or mice, I expect."

"There is a tragical story connected with that place," I answered, deliberately. "It is said that an unfortunate child was shut up there to die of fear, in the dark."

The colour rushed to his face, then retreated, leaving it deadly white.

"Indeed!" he faltered; "and do you mean to say that he — the child — has been seen?"

"No, but he has been heard, knocking within, and crying to be let out. The fact is confirmed by every tenant who has occupied the house since —"

I stopped short, startled by the effect of my revelation.

My companion was gazing at me with a blank stare of horror which banished all other expression from his face.

"Good heavens!" I heard him mutter; "can it be true? Can this be the reason why I was drawn back to the place in spite of myself?"

Recollecting himself, however, he turned to me, and forced his white lips into a smile.

"A mysterious story!" he commented, drily. "I don't believe a word of it, myself, but I should hardly care to take a house with such an uncanny reputation. I think I need not trouble you any further."

As he turned towards the door, I saw his figure sway as if he were falling. He put his hand to his side, with a gasp of pain, a bluish shade gathering over his face.

"Are you ill?" I exclaimed, in alarm.

"I — it is nothing. I have a weakness of the heart, and I am subject to these attacks. May I ask you for a glass of water?"

I left the room to procure it. When I returned I found that he had fallen upon the bed in a dead swoon.

I hastily despatched a servant for Dr. Cameron, who happened to be at home, and came immediately.

He recognised my visitor at once, and glanced at me significantly. I rapidly explained what had happened, while he bent over the unconscious man, and bared his chest to listen to the heart-beats.

When he raised himself his face was ominously grave.

"Is he in danger?" I asked, quickly.

"Not in immediate danger, but the next attack will probably be his last. His heart is mortally diseased."

It was nearly an hour before Vandeleur awoke, and then only to partial consciousness. He lay in a sort of stupor, his limbs nerveless, his hands damp and cold.

"It is impossible to remove him in this condition," the doctor remarked; "I fear he must stay here for the night. I will send you someone to watch him."

"Don't trouble — I intend to sit up with him myself," I replied, speaking on an impulse I could hardly explain.

He looked at me keenly over his spectacles.

"Should you like me to share your watch?" he enquired, after a moment.

"I shall be only too glad of your company, if you can come without inconvenience."

He nodded.

"I must leave you now, but I will return in an hour," he responded.

Three hours had passed away; it was nearly midnight. The night was oppressively close, and profoundly still. The bedroom window stood wide open, but not a breath of air stirred the curtains. Outside, all was vague and dark, for neither moon nor stars were visible.

Vandeleur still lay, half-dressed, on the bed, but now asleep. His deep, regular breathing sounded distinctly in the silence. Dr. Cameron sat near the dressing-table, reading by the light of a shaded lamp. I, too, had a book, but found it impossible to keep my attention fixed upon it. My mind was possessed by an uneasy feeling, half dread, half expectation. I found myself listening nervously to fancied sounds, and starting when the doctor turned a leaf.

At length, overcome by the heat and stillness, I closed my eyes, and unconsciously sank into a doze. How long it lasted I cannot tell, but I woke abruptly, and looked round with a sense of vague alarm. I glanced at the doctor. He had laid down his book, and was leaning forward with one arm on the dressing-table, looking intently towards the door of the box-room. Instinctively I held my breath and listened.

Never shall I forget the thrill that ran through my nerves when I heard from within a muffled knocking sound, and a child's voice, distinct, though faint, and broken by sobs, crying piteously: "Let me out — let me out!"

"Do you hear?" I whispered, bending forward to my companion.

He inclined his head in assent and motioned me to be silent, pointing towards the bed. Its occupant moved uneasily, as if disturbed, muttering some incoherent phrases. Suddenly he pushed back his covering and sat upright, gazing round with a wild, bewildered stare.

The pitiful entreaty was repeated more violently, more passionately than before. "Let me out, let me out!"

With a cry that rang through the room, Vandeleur sprang from the bed, reached the closet door in two strides and tore it open.

It was empty. Empty at least to our eyes, but it was evident that our companion beheld what we could not.

For a few breathless seconds he stood as if frozen, his eyes fixed with the fascination of terror on something just within the threshold; then, as if retreating before it, he recoiled step by step across the room till he was stopped by the opposite wall, where he crouched in an attitude of abject fear.

The sight was so horrible that I could bear it no longer.

"Are you dreaming? Wake up!" I exclaimed, and shook his shoulder.

He raised his eyes, and looked at me vacantly. His lips moved, but no sound came from them. Suddenly a convulsive shudder ran through him and he fell heavily forward at my feet.

"He has swooned again," I said turning to my companion, who stooped and lifted the drooping head on to his knee.

After one glance, he laid it gently down again.

"He is dead," was his grave reply.

And with Vandeleur's death my story ends, for after that night the sounds were heard no more. The forlorn little ghost was at rest.

The Story of the Rippling Train

A True Ghost Story

Mary Louisa Molesworth

"Let's tell ghost stories, then," said Gladys.

"Aren't you tired of them? One hears nothing else nowadays. And they're all 'authentic,' really vouched for, only you never see the person who saw or heard or felt the ghost. It is always somebody's sister or cousin, or friend's friend," objected young Mrs. Snowdon, another of the guests at the Quarries.

"I don't know that that is quite a reasonable ground for discrediting them *en masse*," said her husband. "It is natural enough, indeed inevitable, that the principal or principals in such cases should be much more rarely come across than the stories themselves. A hundred people can repeat the story, but the author, or rather hero, of it, can't be in a hundred places at once. You don't disbelieve in any other statement or narrative merely because you have never seen the prime mover in it?"

"But I didn't say I discredited them on that account," said Mrs. Snowdon. "You take one up so, Archie. I'm not logical and reasonable; I don't pretend to be. If I meant anything, it was that a ghost story would have a great pull over other ghost stories if one could see the person it happened to. One does get rather provoked at *never* coming across him or her," she added a little petulantly.

She was tired; they were all rather tired, for it was the first evening since the party had assembled at the large country house known as "the Quarries" on which there was not to be dancing, with the additional fatigue of "ten miles there and ten back again"; and three or four evenings of such doings without intermission tell even on the young and vigorous.

Tonight various less energetic ways of passing the evening had been proposed, — music, games, reading aloud, recitation, — none had found favour in everybody's sight, and now Gladys Lloyd's proposal that they should "tell ghost stories" seemed likely to fall flat also.

For a moment or two no one answered Mrs. Snowdon's last remarks. Then, somewhat to everybody's surprise, the young daughter of the house turned to her mother.

"Mamma," she said, "don't be vexed with me — I know you warned me once to be careful how I spoke of it; but *wouldn't* it be nice if Uncle Paul would tell us his ghost story? And then, Mrs. Snowdon," she went on, "you could always say you had heard *one* ghost story at or from — which should I say? — headquarters."

Lady Denholme glanced round half nervously before she replied.

"Locally speaking, it would not be *at* headquarters, Nina," she said. "The Quarries was not the scene of your uncle's ghost story. But I almost think it is better not to speak about it — I am not sure that he would like it mentioned, and he will be coming in a moment. He had only a note to write."

"I do wish he would tell it to us," said Nina regretfully. "Don't you think, mamma, I might just run to the study and ask him, and if he did not like the idea he might say so to me, and no one would seem to know anything about it? Uncle Paul is so kind — I'm never afraid of asking him any favour."

"Thank you, Nina, for your good opinion of me; you see there is no rule without exceptions; listeners do sometimes hear pleasant things of themselves," said Mr. Marischal, as he at that moment came round the screen which half concealed the doorway. "What is the special favour you were thinking of asking me?"

Nina looked rather taken aback.

"How softly you opened the door, Uncle Paul," she said. "I would not have spoken of you if I had known you were there."

"But after all you were saying no harm," observed her brother Michael. "And for my part I don't believe Uncle Paul would mind our asking him what we were speaking of."

"What was it?" asked Mr. Marischal. "I think, as I have heard so much, you may as well tell me the whole."

"It was only —" began Nina, but her mother interrupted her.

"I have told Nina not to speak of it, Paul," she said anxiously; "but — it was only that all these young people are talking about ghost stories, and they want you to tell them your own strange experience. You must not be vexed with them."

"Vexed!" said Mr. Marischal, "not in the least." But for a moment or two he said no more, and even pretty, spoilt Mrs. Snowdon looked a little uneasy.

"You shouldn't have persisted, Nina," she whispered.

Mr. Marischal must have had unusually quick ears. He looked up and smiled.

"I really don't mind telling you all there is to hear," he said. "At one time I had a sort of dislike to mentioning the story, for the sake of others. The details would have led to its being recognised — and it might have been painful. But there is no one now living to whom it would matter — you know," he added, turning to his sister; "her husband is dead too."

Lady Denholme shook her head.

"No," she said, "I did not hear."

"Yes," said her brother, "I saw his death in the papers last year. He had married again, I believe. There is not now, therefore, any reason why I should not tell the story, if it will interest you," he went on, turning to the others. "And there is not very much to tell. Not worth making such a preamble about. It was — let me see — yes, it must be nearly fifteen years ago."

"Wait a moment, Uncle Paul," said Nina. "Yes, that's all right, Gladys. You and I will hold each other's hands, and pinch hard if we get very frightened."

"Thank you," Miss Lloyd replied. "On the whole I should prefer for you not to hold my hand."

"But I won't pinch you so as to hurt," said Nina reassuringly; "and it isn't as if we were in the dark."

"Shall I turn down the lamps?" asked Mr. Snowdon.

"No, no," exclaimed his wife.

"There really is nothing frightening — scarcely even 'creepy,' in my story at all," said Mr. Marischal, half apologetically. "You make me feel like an impostor."

"Oh no, Uncle Paul, don't say that. It is all my fault for interrupting," said Nina. "Now go on, please. I have Gladys's hand all the same," she added *sotto voce*, "it's just as well to be prepared."

"Well, then," began Mr. Marischal once more, "it must be nearly fifteen years ago; and I had not seen her for fully ten years before that again! I was not thinking of her in the least; in a sense I had really forgotten her: she had quite gone out of my life; that has always struck me as a very curious point in the story," he added parenthetically.

"Won't you tell us who 'she' was, Uncle Paul?" asked Nina half shyly.

"Oh yes, I was going to do so. I am not skilled in story-telling, you see. She was, at the time I first knew her — at the only time, indeed, that I knew her — a very sweet and attractive girl, named Maud Bertram. She was very pretty — more than pretty, for she had remarkably regular features — her profile was always admired, and a tall and graceful figure. And she was a bright and happy creature too; that, perhaps, was almost her greatest charm. You will wonder — I see the question hovering on your lips, Miss Lloyd, and on yours too, Mrs. Snowdon — why, if I admired her and liked her so much, I did not go further. And I will tell you frankly that I did not because I dared not. I had then no prospect of being able to marry for years to come, and I was not very young. I was already nearly thirty, and Maud was quite ten years younger. I was wise enough and old enough to realise the situation thoroughly, and to be on my guard."

"And Maud?" asked Mrs. Snowdon.

"She was surrounded by admirers; it seemed to me then that it would have been insufferable conceit to have even asked myself if it could matter to her. It was only in the light of after events that the possibility of my having been mistaken occurred to me. And I don't even now see that I could have acted otherwise —" Here Uncle Paul sighed a little. "We were the best of friends. She knew that I admired her, and she seemed to take a frank pleasure in its being so. I had always hoped that she really liked and trusted me as a friend, but no more. The last time I saw her was just before I started for Portugal, where I remained three years. When I returned to London Maud had been married for two years, and had gone straight out to India on her marriage, and except by some few friends who had known us both intimately, I seldom heard her mentioned. And time passed. I cannot say I had exactly forgotten her, but she was not much or often in my thoughts. I was a busy and much-absorbed man, and life had proved a serious matter to me. Now and then some passing resemblance would recall her to my mind — once especially when I had been asked to look in to see the young wife of one of my cousins in her court-dress; something in her figure and bearing brought back Maud to my memory, for it was thus, in full dress, that I had last seen her, and thus perhaps, unconsciously, her image had remained photographed on my brain. But as far as I can recollect at the time when the occurrence I am going to relate to you happened, I had not been thinking of Maud Bertram for months. I was in London just then, staying with my brother, my eldest brother, who had been married for several years, and lived in our own old town-house in — Square. It was in April, a clear spring day, with no fog or half-lights about, and it was not yet four o'clock in the afternoon — not very ghost-like circumstances, you will admit. I had come home early from my club — it was a sort of holiday-time with me just then for a few weeks — intending to get some letters written which had been on my mind for some days, and I had sauntered into the library, a pleasant, fair-sized room lined with books, on the first-floor. Before setting to work I sat down for a moment or two in an easy-chair by the fire, for it was still cool enough weather to make a fire desirable, and began thinking over my letters. No thought, no shadow of a thought of my old friend Miss Bertram was present with me; of that I am perfectly certain. The door was on the same side of the room as the fireplace; as I sat there, half facing the fire, I also half faced the door. I had not shut it properly on coming in — I had only closed it without turning the handle — and I did not feel surprised when it slowly and noiselessly swung open, till it stood right out into the room, concealing the actual doorway from my view. You will perhaps understand the position better if you think of the door as just then acting like a screen to the doorway. From where I sat I could not have seen anyone entering the room till he or she had got beyond the door itself. I glanced up, half expecting to see someone come in, but there was no one; the door had swung open of itself. For the moment

I sat on, with only the vague thought passing through my mind, 'I must shut it before I begin to write.'

"But suddenly I found my eyes fixing themselves on the carpet; something had come within their range of vision, compelling their attention in a mechanical sort of way. What was it?

"'Smoke,' was my first idea. 'Can there be anything on fire?' But I dismissed the notion almost as soon as it suggested itself. The something, faint and shadowy, that came slowly rippling itself in as it were beyond the dark wood of the open door, was yet too material for 'smoke.' My next idea was a curious one. 'It looks like soapy water,' I said to myself; 'can one of the housemaids have been scrubbing, and upset a pail on the stairs?' For the stair to the next floor almost faced the library door. But — no; I rubbed my eyes and looked again; the soapy water theory gave way. The wavy something that kept gliding, rippling in, gradually assumed a more substantial appearance. It was — yes, I suddenly became convinced of it — it was ripples of soft silken stuff, creeping in as if in some mysterious way unfolded or unrolled, not jerkily or irregularly, but glidingly and smoothly, like little wavelets on the sea-shore.

"And I sat there and gazed. 'Why did you not jump up and look behind the door to see what it was?' you may reasonably ask. That question I cannot answer. Why I sat still, as if bewitched, or under some irresistible influence, I cannot tell, but so it was.

"And it — came always rippling in, till at last it began to rise as it still came on, and I saw that a figure — a tall, graceful woman's figure — was slowly advancing, backwards of course, into the room, and that the waves of pale silk — a very delicate shade of pearly grey I think it must have been — were in fact the lower portion of a long court-train, the upper part of which hung in deep folds from the lady's waist. She moved in — I cannot describe the motion, it was not like ordinary walking or stepping backwards — till the whole of her figure and the clear profile of her face and head were distinctly visible, and when at last she stopped and stood there full in my view just, but only just beyond the door, I saw — it came upon me like a flash — that she was no stranger to me, this mysterious visitant! I recognised, unchanged it seemed to me since the day, ten years ago, when I had last seen her, the beautiful features of Maud Bertram."

Mr. Marischal stopped a moment. Nobody spoke. Then he went on again.

"I should not have said 'unchanged.' There was one great change in the sweet face. You remember my telling you that one of my girl-friend's greatest charms was her bright sunny happiness — she never seemed gloomy or depressed or dissatisfied, seldom even pensive. But in this respect the face I sat there gazing at was utterly unlike Maud Bertram's. Its expression, as she — or 'it' — stood there looking, not towards me, but out beyond, as if at someone or something outside the doorway, was of the profoundest sadness. Anything *so* sad I had never seen in a human face, and I trust I never may. But I sat on, as motionless almost as she, gazing at her fixedly, with no desire, no power perhaps, to move or approach more nearly to the phantom. I was not in the least frightened. I knew it *was* a phantom, but I felt paralysed, and as if I myself had somehow got outside of ordinary conditions. And there I sat — staring at Maud, and there she stood, gazing before her with that terrible, unspeakable sadness in her face, which, even though I felt no *fear*, seemed to freeze me with a kind of unutterable pity.

"I don't know how long I had sat thus, or how long I might have continued to sit there, almost as if in a trance, when suddenly I heard the front-door bell ring. It seemed to awaken me. I started up and glanced round, half-expecting that I should find the vision dispelled. But no; she was still there, and I sank back into my seat just as I heard my brother coming quickly upstairs. He came towards the library, and seeing the door wide open walked in, and I, still gazing, saw his figure *pass through that of the woman in the doorway* as you may walk through a wreath of mist or smoke — only, don't misunderstand me, the figure of Maud till that moment had had nothing unsubstantial about it. She had looked to me, as she stood there, literally and exactly like a living woman — the shade of her dress, the colour of her hair, the few ornaments she wore, all were as defined and clear as yours, Nina, at the present moment, and remained so, or perhaps became so again as soon as my brother was well within the room. He came forward addressing me by name, but I answered him in a whisper, begging him to be silent and to sit down on the seat opposite me for a moment or two. He did so, though he was taken aback by my strange manner, for I still kept my eyes fixed on the door. I had a queer consciousness that if I looked away *it* would fade, and I wanted to keep cool and see what would happen. I asked Herbert in a low voice if *he* saw nothing, but though he mechanically followed the direction of my eyes, he shook his head in bewilderment. And for a moment or two he remained thus. Then I began to notice that the figure was growing less clear, as if it were receding, yet without growing smaller to the sight; it grew fainter and vaguer, the colours grew hazy. I rubbed my eyes once or twice with a half idea that my long watching was making them misty, but it was not so. My eyes were not at fault — slowly but surely Maud Bertram, or her ghost, melted away, till all trace of her had gone. I saw again the familiar pattern of the carpet where she had stood and the objects of the room that had been hidden by her draperies — all again in the most commonplace way, but she was gone, quite gone.

"Then Herbert, seeing me relax my intense gaze, began to question me. I told him exactly what I have told you. He answered, as every "common-sensible" person of course would, that it was strange, but that such things did happen sometimes and were classed by the wise under the head of 'optical delusions.' I was not well, perhaps, he suggested. Been overworking? Had I not better see a doctor? But I shook my head. I was quite well, and I said so. And perhaps he was right, it might be an optical delusion only. I had never had any experience of such things.

"'All the same,' I said, 'I shall mark down the date.'

"Herbert laughed and said that was what people always did in such cases. If he knew where Mrs. — then was he would write to her, just for the fun of the thing, and ask her to be so good as to look up her diary, if she kept one, and let us know what she had been doing on that particular day — 'the 6th of April, isn't it?' he said — when I would have it her wraith had paid me a visit. I let him talk. It seemed to remove the strange painful impression — painful because of that terrible sadness in the sweet face. But we neither of us knew where she was, we scarcely remembered her married name! And so there was nothing to be done — except, what I did at once in spite of Herbert's rallying, to mark down the day and hour with scrupulous exactness in *my* diary.

"Time passed. I had not forgotten my strange experience, but of course the impression of it lessened by degrees till it seemed more like a curious dream than anything more real, when one day I *did* hear of poor Maud again. 'Poor' Maud I cannot help calling her. I heard of her indirectly, and probably, but for the sadness of her story, I should never have heard it at all. It was a friend of her husband's family who had mentioned the circumstances in the hearing of a friend of mine, and one day something brought round the conversation to old times, and he startled me by suddenly inquiring if I remembered Maud Bertram. I said, of course I did. Did he know anything of her? And then he told me.

"She was dead — she had died some months ago after a long and trying illness, the result of a terrible accident. She had caught fire one evening when dressed for some grand entertainment or other, and though her injuries did not seem likely to be fatal at the time, she had never recovered the shock.

"'She was so pretty,' my friend said, 'and one of the saddest parts of it was that I hear she was terrifically disfigured, and she took this most sadly to heart. The right side of her face was utterly ruined, and the sight of the right eye lost, though, strange to say, the left side entirely escaped, and seeing her in profile one would have had no notion of what had happened. Was it not sad? She was such a sweet, bright creature.'

"I did not tell him *my* story, for I did not want it chattered about, but a strange sort of shiver ran through me at his words. *It was the left side of her face only* that the wraith of my poor friend had allowed me to see."

"Oh, Uncle Paul!" exclaimed Nina.

"And — as to the dates?" inquired Mr. Snowdon.

"I never knew the exact date of the accident," said Mr. Marischal, "but that of her death was fully six months after I had seen her. And in my own mind, I have never made any doubt that it was at or about, probably a short time after, the accident, that she came to me. It seemed a kind of appeal for sympathy — and — a farewell also, poor child."

They all sat silent for some little time, and then Mr. Marischal got up and went off to his own quarters, saying something vaguely about seeing if his letters had gone.

"What a touching story!" said Gladys Lloyd. "I am afraid, after all, it has been more painful than he realised for Mr. Marischal to tell it. Did you know anything of Maud's husband, dear Lady Denholme? Was he kind to her? Was she happy?"

"We never heard much about her married life," her hostess replied. "But I have no reason to think she was unhappy. Her husband married again two or three years after her death, but that says nothing."

"N — no," said Nina. "All the same, mamma, I am sure she really did love Uncle Paul very much, — much more than he had any idea of. Poor Maud!"

"And he has never married," added Gladys.

"No," said Lady Denholme, "but there have been many practical difficulties in the way of his doing so. He has had a most absorbingly busy life, and now that he is more at leisure he feels himself too old to form new ties."

"But," persisted Nina, "if he had had any idea at the time that Maud cared for him so?"

"Ah well," Lady Denholme allowed, "in that case, in spite of the practical difficulties, things would probably have been different."

And again Nina repeated softly, "Poor Maud!"

A Wicked Voice

Vernon Lee

To M.W., IN REMEMBRANCE OF THE LAST SONG AT PALAZZO
BARBARO, *Chi ha inteso, intenda.*

They have been congratulating me again today upon being the
only composer of our days — of these days of deafening
orchestral effects and poetical quackery — who has despised the
new-fangled nonsense of Wagner, and returned boldly to the
traditions of Handel and Gluck and the divine Mozart, to the
supremacy of melody and the respect of the human voice.

O cursed human voice, violin of flesh and blood, fashioned
with the subtle tools, the cunning hands, of Satan! O execrable
art of singing, have you not wrought mischief enough in the
past, degrading so much noble genius, corrupting the purity of
Mozart, reducing Handel to a writer of high-class singing-
exercises, and defrauding the world of the only inspiration
worthy of Sophocles and Euripides, the poetry of the great poet
Gluck? Is it not enough to have dishonoured a whole century in
idolatry of that wicked and contemptible wretch the singer,
without persecuting an obscure young composer of our days,
whose only wealth is his love of nobility in art, and perhaps
some few grains of genius?

And then they compliment me upon the perfection with
which I imitate the style of the great dead masters; or ask me
very seriously whether, even if I could gain over the modern
public to this bygone style of music, I could hope to find singers
to perform it. Sometimes, when people talk as they have been
talking today, and laugh when I declare myself a follower of
Wagner, I burst into a paroxysm of unintelligible, childish rage,
and exclaim, "We shall see that some day!"

Yes; some day we shall see! For, after all, may I not recover
from this strangest of maladies? It is still possible that the day
may come when all these things shall seem but an incredible
nightmare; the day when *Ogier the Dane* shall be completed, and
men shall know whether I am a follower of the great master of

the Future or the miserable singing-masters of the Past. I am but half-bewitched, since I am conscious of the spell that binds me. My old nurse, far off in Norway, used to tell me that were-wolves are ordinary men and women half their days, and that if, during that period, they become aware of their horrid transformation they may find the means to forestall it. May this not be the case with me? My reason, after all, is free, although my artistic inspiration be enslaved; and I can despise and loathe the music I am forced to compose, and the execrable power that forces me.

Nay, is it not because I have studied with the doggedness of hatred this corrupt and corrupting music of the Past, seeking for every little peculiarity of style and every biographical trifle merely to display its vileness, is it not for this presumptuous courage that I have been overtaken by such mysterious, incredible vengeance?

And meanwhile, my only relief consists in going over and over again in my mind the tale of my miseries. This time I will write it, writing only to tear up, to throw the manuscript unread into the fire. And yet, who knows? As the last charred pages shall crackle and slowly sink into the red embers, perhaps the spell may be broken, and I may possess once more my long-lost liberty, my vanished genius.

It was a breathless evening under the full moon, that implacable full moon beneath which, even more than beneath the dreamy splendour of noon-tide, Venice seemed to swelter in the midst of the waters, exhaling, like some great lily, mysterious influences, which make the brain swim and the heart faint — a moral malaria, distilled, as I thought, from those languishing melodies, those cooing vocalizations which I had found in the musty music-books of a century ago. I see that moonlight evening as if it were present. I see my fellow-lodgers of that little artists' boarding-house. The table on which they lean after supper is strewn with bits of bread, with napkins rolled in tapestry rollers, spots of wine here and there, and at regular intervals chipped pepper-pots, stands of toothpicks, and heaps of those huge hard peaches which nature imitates from the marble-shops of Pisa. The whole *pension*-full is assembled, and examining stupidly the engraving which the American etcher has just brought for me, knowing me to be mad about eighteenth century music and musicians, and having noticed, as he turned over the heaps of penny prints in the square of San Polo, that the portrait is that of a singer of those days.

Singer, thing of evil, stupid and wicked slave of the voice, of that instrument which was not invented by the human intellect, but begotten of the body, and which, instead of moving the soul, merely stirs up the dregs of our nature! For what is the voice but the Beast calling, awakening that other Beast sleeping in the depths of mankind, the Beast which all great art has ever sought to chain up, as the archangel chains up, in old pictures, the demon with his woman's face? How could the creature attached to this voice, its owner and its victim, the singer, the great, the real singer who once ruled over every heart, be otherwise than wicked and contemptible? But let me try and get on with my story.

I can see all my fellow-boarders, leaning on the table, contemplating the print, this effeminate beau, his hair curled into *ailes de pigeon*, his sword passed through his embroidered pocket, seated under a triumphal arch somewhere among the clouds, surrounded by puffy Cupids and crowned with laurels by a bouncing goddess of fame. I hear again all the insipid exclamations, the insipid questions about this singer: — "When did he live? Was he very famous? Are you sure, Magnus, that this is really a portrait," &c. &c. And I hear my own voice, as if in the far distance, giving them all sorts of information, biographical and critical, out of a battered little volume called *The Theatre of Musical Glory; or, Opinions upon the most Famous Chapel-masters and Virtuosi of this Century*, by Father Prosdocimo Sabatelli, Barnalite, Professor of Eloquence at the College of Modena, and Member of the Arcadian Academy, under the pastoral name of Evander Lilybaean, Venice, 1785, with the approbation of the Superiors. I tell them all how this singer, this Balthasar Cesari, was nick-named Zaffirino because of a sapphire engraved with cabalistic signs presented to him one evening by a masked stranger, in whom wise folk recognized that great cultivator of the human voice, the devil; how much more wonderful had been this Zaffirino's vocal gifts than those of any singer of ancient or modern times; how his brief life had been but a series of triumphs, petted by the greatest kings, sung by the most famous poets, and finally, adds Father Prosdocimo, "courted (if the grave Muse of history may incline her ear to the gossip of gallantry) by the most charming nymphs, even of the very highest quality."

My friends glance once more at the engraving; more insipid remarks are made; I am requested — especially by the American young ladies — to play or sing one of this Zaffirino's favourite songs — "For of course you know them, dear Maestro Magnus, you who have such a passion for all old music. Do be good, and sit down to the piano." I refuse, rudely enough, rolling the print in my fingers. How fearfully this cursed heat, these cursed moonlight nights, must have unstrung me! This Venice would certainly kill me in the long-run! Why, the sight of this idiotic engraving, the mere name of that coxcomb of a singer, have made my heart beat and my limbs turn to water like a love-sick hobbledehoy.

After my gruff refusal, the company begins to disperse; they prepare to go out, some to have a row on the lagoon, others to saunter before the *cafés* at St. Mark's; family discussions arise, gruntings of fathers, murmurs of mothers, peals of laughing from young girls and young men. And the moon, pouring in by the wide-open windows, turns this old palace ballroom, nowadays an inn dining-room, into a lagoon, scintillating, undulating like the other lagoon, the real one, which stretches out yonder furrowed by invisible gondolas betrayed by the red prow-lights. At last the whole lot of them are on the move. I shall be able to get some quiet in my room, and to work a little at my opera of *Ogier the Dane*. But no! Conversation revives, and, of all things, about that singer, that Zaffirino, whose absurd portrait I am crunching in my fingers.

The principal speaker is Count Alvise, an old Venetian with dyed whiskers, a great check tie fastened with two pins and a chain; a threadbare patrician who is dying to secure for his lanky son that pretty American girl, whose mother is intoxicated by all his mooning anecdotes about the past glories of Venice in general, and of his illustrious family in particular. Why, in Heaven's name, must he pitch upon Zaffirino for his mooning, this old duffer of a patrician?

"Zaffirino, — ah yes, to be sure! Balthasar Cesari, called Zaffirino," snuffles the voice of Count Alvise, who always repeats the last word of every sentence at least three times. "Yes, Zaffirino, to be sure! A famous singer of the days of my forefathers; yes, of my forefathers, dear lady!" Then a lot of rubbish about the former greatness of Venice, the glories of old music, the former Conservatoires, all mixed up with anecdotes of Rossini and Donizetti, whom he pretends to have known intimately. Finally, a story, of course containing plenty about his illustrious family: — "My great grand-aunt, the Procuratessa Vendramin, from whom we have inherited our estate of Mistrà, on the Brenta" — a hopelessly muddled story, apparently, fully of digressions, but of which that singer Zaffirino is the hero. The narrative, little by little, becomes more intelligible, or perhaps it is I who am giving it more attention.

"It seems," says the Count, "that there was one of his songs in particular which was called the 'Husbands' Air' — *L'Aria dei Marit* — because they didn't enjoy it quite as much as their better-halves…. My grand-aunt, Pisana Renier, married to the Procuratore Vendramin, was a patrician of the old school, of the style that was getting rare a hundred years ago. Her virtue and her pride rendered her unapproachable. Zaffirino, on his part, was in the habit of boasting that no woman had ever been able to resist his singing, which, it appears, had its foundation in fact — the ideal changes, my dear lady, the ideal changes a good deal from one century to another! — and that his first song could make any woman turn pale and lower her eyes, the second make her madly in love, while the third song could kill her off on the spot, kill her for love, there under his very eyes, if he only felt inclined. My grand-aunt Vendramin laughed when this story was told her, refused to go to hear this insolent dog, and added that it might be quite possible by the aid of spells and infernal pacts to kill a *gentildonna*, but as to making her fall in love with a lackey — never! This answer was naturally reported to Zaffirino, who piqued himself upon always getting the better of anyone who was wanting in deference to his voice. Like the ancient Romans, *parcere subjectis et debellare superbos*. You American ladies, who are so learned, will appreciate this little quotation from the divine Virgil. While seeming to avoid the Procuratessa Vendramin, Zaffirino took the opportunity, one evening at a large assembly, to sing in her presence. He sang and sang and sang until the poor grand-aunt Pisana fell ill for love. The most skilful physicians were kept unable to explain the mysterious malady which was visibly killing the poor young lady; and the Procuratore Vendramin applied in vain to the most venerated Madonnas, and vainly promised an altar of silver, with massive gold candlesticks, to Saints Cosmas and Damian, patrons of the art of healing. At last the brother-in-law of the Procuratessa, Monsignor Almorò Vendramin, Patriarch of Aquileia, a prelate famous for the sanctity of his life, obtained in a vision of Saint Justina, for whom he entertained a particular devotion, the information that the only thing which could benefit the strange illness of his sister-in-law was the voice of Zaffirino. Take notice that my poor grand-aunt had never condescended to such a revelation.

"The Procuratore was enchanted at this happy solution; and his lordship the Patriarch went to seek Zaffirino in person, and carried him in his own coach to the Villa of Mistrà, where the Procuratessa was residing.

"On being told what was about to happen, my poor grand-aunt went into fits of rage, which were succeeded immediately by equally violent fits of joy. However, she never forgot what was due to her great position. Although sick almost unto death, she had herself arrayed with the greatest pomp, caused her face to be painted, and put on all her diamonds: it would seem as if she were anxious to affirm her full dignity before this singer. Accordingly she received Zaffirino reclining on a sofa which had been placed in the great ballroom of the Villa of Mistrà, and beneath the princely canopy; for the Vendramins, who had intermarried with the house of Mantua, possessed imperial fiefs and were princes of the Holy Roman Empire. Zaffirino saluted her with the most profound respect, but not a word passed between them. Only, the singer inquired from the Procuratore whether the illustrious lady had received the Sacraments of the Church. Being told that the Procuratessa had herself asked to be given extreme unction from the hands of her brother-in-law, he declared his readiness to obey the orders of His Excellency, and sat down at once to the harpsichord.

"Never had he sung so divinely. At the end of the first song the Procuratessa Vendramin had already revived most extraordinarily; by the end of the second she appeared entirely cured and beaming with beauty and happiness; but at the third air — the *Aria dei Mariti*, no doubt — she began to change frightfully; she gave a dreadful cry, and fell into the convulsions of death. In a quarter of an hour she was dead! Zaffirino did not wait to see her die. Having finished his song, he withdrew instantly, took post-horses, and travelled day and night as far as Munich. People remarked that he had presented himself at Mistrà dressed in mourning, although he had mentioned no death among his relatives; also that he had prepared everything for his departure, as if fearing the wrath of so powerful a family. Then there was also the extraordinary question he had asked before beginning to sing, about the Procuratessa having confessed and received extreme unction…. No, thanks, my dear lady, no cigarettes for me. But if it does not distress you or your charming daughter, may I humbly beg permission to smoke a cigar?"

And Count Alvise, enchanted with his talent for narrative, and sure of having secured for his son the heart and the dollars of his fair audience, proceeds to light a candle, and at the candle one of those long black Italian cigars which require preliminary disinfection before smoking.

… If this state of things goes on I shall just have to ask the doctor for a bottle; this ridiculous beating of my heart and disgusting cold perspiration have increased steadily during Count Alvise's narrative. To keep myself in countenance among the various idiotic commentaries on this cock-and-bull story of a vocal coxcomb and a vaporing great lady, I begin to unroll the engraving, and to examine stupidly the portrait of Zaffirino, once so renowned, now so forgotten. A ridiculous ass, this singer, under his triumphal arch, with his stuffed Cupids and the great fat winged kitchen-maid crowning him with laurels. How flat and vapid and vulgar it is, to be sure, all this odious eighteenth century!

But he, personally, is not so utterly vapid as I had thought. That effeminate, fat face of his is almost beautiful, with an odd smile, brazen and cruel. I have seen faces like this, if not in real life, at least in my boyish romantic dreams, when I read Swinburne and Baudelaire, the faces of wicked, vindictive women. Oh yes! he is decidedly a beautiful creature, this Zaffirino, and his voice must have had the same sort of beauty and the same expression of wickedness....

"Come on, Magnus," sound the voices of my fellow-boarders, "be a good fellow and sing us one of the old chap's songs; or at least something or other of that day, and we'll make believe it was the air with which he killed that poor lady."

"Oh yes! the *Aria dei Mariti*, the 'Husbands' Air,'" mumbles old Alvise, between the puffs at his impossible black cigar. "My poor grand-aunt, Pisana Vendramin; he went and killed her with those songs of his, with that *Aria dei Mariti*."

I feel senseless rage overcoming me. Is it that horrible palpitation (by the way, there is a Norwegian doctor, my fellow-countryman, at Venice just now) which is sending the blood to my brain and making me mad? The people round the piano, the furniture, everything together seems to get mixed and to turn into moving blobs of colour. I set to singing; the only thing which remains distinct before my eyes being the portrait of Zaffirino, on the edge of that boarding-house piano; the sensual, effeminate face, with its wicked, cynical smile, keeps appearing and disappearing as the print wavers about in the draught that makes the candles smoke and gutter. And I set to singing madly, singing I don't know what. Yes; I begin to identify it: 'tis the *Biondina in Gondoleta*, the only song of the eighteenth century which is still remembered by the Venetian people. I sing it, mimicking every old-school grace; shakes, cadences, languishingly swelled and diminished notes, and adding all manner of buffooneries, until the audience, recovering from its surprise, begins to shake with laughing; until I begin to laugh myself, madly, frantically, between the phrases of the melody, my voice finally smothered in this dull, brutal laughter.... And then, to crown it all, I shake my fist at this long-dead singer, looking at me with his wicked woman's face, with his mocking, fatuous smile.

"Ah! you would like to be revenged on me also!" I exclaim. "You would like me to write you nice roulades and flourishes, another nice *Aria dei Mariti*, my fine Zaffirino!"

That night I dreamed a very strange dream. Even in the big half-furnished room the heat and closeness were stifling. The air seemed laden with the scent of all manner of white flowers, faint and heavy in their intolerable sweetness: tuberoses, gardenias, and jasmines drooping I know not where in neglected vases. The moonlight had transformed the marble floor around me into a shallow, shining, pool. On account of the heat I had exchanged my bed for a big old-fashioned sofa of light wood, painted with little nosegays and sprigs, like an old silk; and I lay there, not attempting to sleep, and letting my thoughts go vaguely to my opera of *Ogier the Dane*, of which I had long finished writing the words, and for whose music I had hoped to find some inspiration in this strange Venice, floating, as it were, in the stagnant lagoon of the past. But Venice had merely put all my ideas into hopeless confusion; it was as if there arose out of its shallow waters a miasma of long-dead melodies, which sickened but intoxicated my soul. I lay on my sofa watching that pool of whitish light, which rose higher and higher, little trickles of light meeting it here and there, wherever the moon's rays struck upon some polished surface; while huge shadows waved to and fro in the draught of the open balcony.

I went over and over that old Norse story: how the Paladin, Ogier, one of the knights of Charlemagne, was decoyed during his homeward wanderings from the Holy Land by the arts of an enchantress, the same who had once held in bondage the great Emperor Caesar and given him King Oberon for a son; how Ogier had tarried in that island only one day and one night, and yet, when he came home to his kingdom, he found all changed, his friends dead, his family dethroned, and not a man who knew his face; until at last, driven hither and thither like a beggar, a poor minstrel had taken compassion of his sufferings and given him all he could give — a song, the song of the prowess of a hero dead for hundreds of years, the Paladin Ogier the Dane.

The story of Ogier ran into a dream, as vivid as my waking thoughts had been vague. I was looking no longer at the pool of moonlight spreading round my couch, with its trickles of light and looming, waving shadows, but the frescoed walls of a great saloon. It was not, as I recognized in a second, the dining-room of that Venetian palace now turned into a boarding-house. It was a far larger room, a real ballroom, almost circular in its octagon shape, with eight huge white doors surrounded by stucco mouldings, and, high on the vault of the ceiling, eight little galleries or recesses like boxes at a theatre, intended no doubt for musicians and spectators. The place was imperfectly lighted by only one of the eight chandeliers, which revolved slowly, like huge spiders, each on its long cord. But the light struck upon the gilt stuccoes opposite me, and on a large expanse of fresco, the sacrifice of Iphigenia, with Agamemnon and Achilles in Roman helmets, lappets, and knee-breeches. It discovered also one of the oil panels let into the mouldings of the roof, a goddess in lemon and lilac draperies, foreshortened over a great green peacock. Round the room, where the light reached, I could make out big yellow satin sofas and heavy gilded consoles; in the shadow of a corner was what looked like a piano, and farther in the shade one of those big canopies which decorate the anterooms of Roman palaces. I looked about me, wondering where I was: a heavy, sweet smell, reminding me of the flavour of a peach, filled the place.

Little by little I began to perceive sounds; little, sharp, metallic, detached notes, like those of a mandolin; and there was united to them a voice, very low and sweet, almost a whisper, which grew and grew and grew, until the whole place was filled with that exquisite vibrating note, of a strange, exotic, unique quality. The note went on, swelling and swelling. Suddenly there was a horrible piercing shriek, and the thud of a body on the floor, and all manner of smothered exclamations. There, close by the canopy, a light suddenly appeared; and I could see, among the dark figures moving to and fro in the room, a woman lying on the ground, surrounded by other women. Her blond hair, tangled, full of diamond-sparkles which cut through the half-darkness, was hanging dishevelled; the laces of her bodice had been cut, and her white breast shone among the sheen of jewelled brocade; her face was bent forwards, and a thin white arm trailed, like a broken limb, across the knees of one of the women who were endeavouring to lift her. There was a sudden splash of water against the floor, more confused exclamations, a hoarse, broken moan, and a gurgling, dreadful sound…. I awoke with a start and rushed to the window.

Outside, in the blue haze of the moon, the church and belfry of St. George loomed blue and hazy, with the black hull and rigging, the red lights, of a large steamer moored before them. From the lagoon rose a damp sea-breeze. What was it all? Ah! I began to understand: that story of old Count Alvise's, the death of his grand-aunt, Pisana Vendramin. Yes, it was about that I had been dreaming.

I returned to my room; I struck a light, and sat down to my writing-table. Sleep had become impossible. I tried to work at my opera. Once or twice I thought I had got hold of what I had looked for so long…. But as soon as I tried to lay hold of my theme, there arose in my mind the distant echo of that voice, of that long note swelled slowly by insensible degrees, that long note whose tone was so strong and so subtle.

There are in the life of an artist moments when, still unable to seize his own inspiration, or even clearly to discern it, he becomes aware of the approach of that long-invoked idea. A mingled joy and terror warn him that before another day, another hour have passed, the inspiration shall have crossed the threshold of his soul and flooded it with its rapture. All day I had felt the need of isolation and quiet, and at nightfall I went for a row on the most solitary part of the lagoon. All things seemed to tell that I was going to meet my inspiration, and I awaited its coming as a lover awaits his beloved.

I had stopped my gondola for a moment, and as I gently swayed to and fro on the water, all paved with moonbeams, it seemed to me that I was on the confines of an imaginary world. It lay close at hand, enveloped in luminous, pale blue mist, through which the moon had cut a wide and glistening path; out to sea, the little islands, like moored black boats, only accentuated the solitude of this region of moonbeams and wavelets; while the hum of the insects in orchards hard by merely added to the impression of untroubled silence. On some such seas, I thought, must the Paladin Ogier, have sailed when about to discover that during that sleep at the enchantress's knees centuries had elapsed and the heroic world had set, and the kingdom of prose had come.

While my gondola rocked stationary on that sea of moonbeams, I pondered over that twilight of the heroic world. In the soft rattle of the water on the hull I seemed to hear the rattle of all that armour, of all those swords swinging rusty on the walls, neglected by the degenerate sons of the great champions of old. I had long been in search of a theme which I called the theme of the "Prowess of Ogier;" it was to appear from time to time in the course of my opera, to develop at last into that song of the Minstrel, which reveals to the hero that he is one of a long-dead world. And at this moment I seemed to feel the presence of that theme. Yet an instant, and my mind would be overwhelmed by that savage music, heroic, funereal.

Suddenly there came across the lagoon, cleaving, checkering, and fretting the silence with a lacework of sound even as the moon was fretting and cleaving the water, a ripple of music, a voice breaking itself in a shower of little scales and cadences and trills.

I sank back upon my cushions. The vision of heroic days had vanished, and before my closed eyes there seemed to dance multitudes of little stars of light, chasing and interlacing like those sudden vocalizations.

"To shore! Quick!" I cried to the gondolier.

But the sounds had ceased; and there came from the orchards, with their mulberry-trees glistening in the moonlight, and their black swaying cypress-plumes, nothing save the confused hum, the monotonous chirp, of the crickets.

I looked around me: on one side empty dunes, orchards, and meadows, without house or steeple; on the other, the blue and misty sea, empty to where distant islets were profiled black on the horizon.

A faintness overcame me, and I felt myself dissolve. For all of a sudden a second ripple of voice swept over the lagoon, a shower of little notes, which seemed to form a little mocking laugh.

Then again all was still. This silence lasted so long that I fell once more to meditating on my opera. I lay in wait once more for the half-caught theme. But no. It was not that theme for which I was waiting and watching with baited breath. I realized my delusion when, on rounding the point of the Giudecca, the murmur of a voice arose from the midst of the waters, a thread of sound slender as a moonbeam, scarce audible, but exquisite, which expanded slowly, insensibly, taking volume and body, taking flesh almost and fire, an ineffable quality, full, passionate, but veiled, as it were, in a subtle, downy wrapper. The note grew stronger and stronger, and warmer and more passionate, until it burst through that strange and charming veil, and emerged beaming, to break itself in the luminous facets of a wonderful shake, long, superb, triumphant.

There was a dead silence.

"Row to St. Mark's!" I exclaimed. "Quick!"

The gondola glided through the long, glittering track of moonbeams, and rent the great band of yellow, reflected light, mirroring the cupolas of St. Mark's, the lace-like pinnacles of the palace, and the slender pink belfry, which rose from the lit-up water to the pale and bluish evening sky.

In the larger of the two squares the military band was blaring through the last spirals of a *crescendo* of Rossini. The crowd was dispersing in this great open-air ballroom, and the sounds arose which invariably follow upon out-of-door music. A clatter of spoons and glasses, a rustle and grating of frocks and of chairs, and the click of scabbards on the pavement. I pushed my way among the fashionable youths contemplating the ladies while sucking the knob of their sticks; through the serried ranks of respectable families, marching arm in arm with their white frocked young ladies close in front. I took a seat before Florian's, among the customers stretching themselves before departing, and the waiters hurrying to and fro, clattering their empty cups and trays. Two imitation Neapolitans were slipping their guitar and violin under their arm, ready to leave the place.

"Stop!" I cried to them; "don't go yet. Sing me something — sing *La Camesella* or *Funiculì, funiculà* — no matter what, provided you make a row;" and as they screamed and scraped their utmost, I added, "But can't you sing louder, d—n you! — sing louder, do you understand?"

I felt the need of noise, of yells and false notes, of something vulgar and hideous to drive away that ghost-voice which was haunting me.

Again and again I told myself that it had been some silly prank of a romantic amateur, hidden in the gardens of the shore or gliding unperceived on the lagoon; and that the sorcery of moonlight and sea-mist had transfigured for my excited brain mere humdrum roulades out of exercises of Bordogni or Crescentini.

But all the same I continued to be haunted by that voice. My work was interrupted ever and anon by the attempt to catch its imaginary echo; and the heroic harmonies of my Scandinavian legend were strangely interwoven with voluptuous phrases and florid cadences in which I seemed to hear again that same accursed voice.

To be haunted by singing-exercises! It seemed too ridiculous for a man who professedly despised the art of singing. And still, I preferred to believe in that childish amateur, amusing himself with warbling to the moon.

One day, while making these reflections the hundredth time over, my eyes chanced to light upon the portrait of Zaffirino, which my friend had pinned against the wall. I pulled it down and tore it into half a dozen shreds. Then, already ashamed of my folly, I watched the torn pieces float down from the window, wafted hither and thither by the sea-breeze. One scrap got caught in a yellow blind below me; the others fell into the canal, and were speedily lost to sight in the dark water. I was overcome with shame. My heart beat like bursting. What a miserable, unnerved worm I had become in this cursed Venice, with its languishing moonlights, its atmosphere as of some stuffy boudoir, long unused, full of old stuffs and potpourri!

That night, however, things seemed to be going better. I was able to settle down to my opera, and even to work at it. In the intervals my thoughts returned, not without a certain pleasure, to those scattered fragments of the torn engraving fluttering down to the water. I was disturbed at my piano by the hoarse voices and the scraping of violins which rose from one of those music-boats that station at night under the hotels of the Grand Canal. The moon had set. Under my balcony the water stretched black into the distance, its darkness cut by the still darker outlines of the flotilla of gondolas in attendance on the music-boat, where the faces of the singers, and the guitars and violins, gleamed reddish under the unsteady light of the Chinese-lanterns.

"*Jammo, jammo; jammo, jammo jà,*" sang the loud, hoarse voices; then a tremendous scrape and twang, and the yelled-out burden, "*Funiculi, funiculà; funiculi, funiculà; jammo, jammo, jammo, jammo, jammo jà.*"

Then came a few cries of "*Bis, Bis!*" from a neighbouring hotel, a brief clapping of hands, the sound of a handful of coppers rattling into the boat, and the oar-stroke of some gondolier making ready to turn away.

"Sing the Camesella," ordered some voice with a foreign accent.

"No, no! *Santa Lucia.*"

"I want the *Camesella.*"

"No! *Santa Lucia.* Hi! sing *Santa Lucia* — d'you hear?"

The musicians, under their green and yellow and red lamps, held a whispered consultation on the manner of conciliating these contradictory demands. Then, after a minute's hesitation, the violins began the prelude of that once famous air, which has remained popular in Venice — the words written, some hundred years ago, by the patrician Gritti, the music by an unknown composer — *La Biondina in Gondoleta.*

That cursed eighteenth century! It seemed a malignant fatality that made these brutes choose just this piece to interrupt me.

At last the long prelude came to an end; and above the cracked guitars and squeaking fiddles there arose, not the expected nasal chorus, but a single voice singing below its breath.

My arteries throbbed. How well I knew that voice! It was singing, as I have said, below its breath, yet none the less it sufficed to fill all that reach of the canal with its strange quality of tone, exquisite, far-fetched.

They were long-drawn-out notes, of intense but peculiar sweetness, a man's voice which had much of a woman's, but more even of a chorister's, but a chorister's voice without its limpidity and innocence; its youthfulness was veiled, muffled, as it were, in a sort of downy vagueness, as if a passion of tears withheld.

There was a burst of applause, and the old palaces re-echoed with the clapping. "Bravo, bravo! Thank you, thank you! Sing again — please, sing again. Who can it be?"

And then a bumping of hulls, a splashing of oars, and the oaths of gondoliers trying to push each other away, as the red prow-lamps of the gondolas pressed round the gaily lit singing-boat.

But no one stirred on board. It was to none of them that this applause was due. And while everyone pressed on, and clapped and vociferated, one little red prow-lamp dropped away from the fleet; for a moment a single gondola stood forth black upon the black water, and then was lost in the night.

For several days the mysterious singer was the universal topic. The people of the music-boat swore that no one besides themselves had been on board, and that they knew as little as ourselves about the owner of that voice. The gondoliers, despite their descent from the spies of the old Republic, were equally unable to furnish any clue. No musical celebrity was known or suspected to be at Venice; and everyone agreed that such a singer must be a European celebrity. The strangest thing in this strange business was, that even among those learned in music there was no agreement on the subject of this voice: it was called by all sorts of names and described by all manner of incongruous adjectives; people went so far as to dispute whether the voice belonged to a man or to a woman: everyone had some new definition.

In all these musical discussions I, alone, brought forward no opinion. I felt a repugnance, an impossibility almost, of speaking about that voice; and the more or less commonplace conjectures of my friend had the invariable effect of sending me out of the room.

Meanwhile my work was becoming daily more difficult, and I soon passed from utter impotence to a state of inexplicable agitation. Every morning I arose with fine resolutions and grand projects of work; only to go to bed that night without having accomplished anything. I spent hours leaning on my balcony, or wandering through the network of lanes with their ribbon of blue sky, endeavouring vainly to expel the thought of that voice, or endeavouring in reality to reproduce it in my memory; for the more I tried to banish it from my thoughts, the more I grew to thirst for that extraordinary tone, for those mysteriously downy, veiled notes; and no sooner did I make an effort to work at my opera than my head was full of scraps of forgotten eighteenth century airs, of frivolous or languishing little phrases; and I fell to wondering with a bitter-sweet longing how those songs would have sounded if sung by that voice.

At length it became necessary to see a doctor, from whom, however, I carefully hid away all the stranger symptoms of my malady. The air of the lagoons, the great heat, he answered cheerfully, had pulled me down a little; a tonic and a month in the country, with plenty of riding and no work, would make me myself again. That old idler, Count Alvise, who had insisted on accompanying me to the physician's, immediately suggested that I should go and stay with his son, who was boring himself to death superintending the maize harvest on the mainland: he could promise me excellent air, plenty of horses, and all the peaceful surroundings and the delightful occupations of a rural life — "Be sensible, my dear Magnus, and just go quietly to Mistrà."

Mistrà — the name sent a shiver all down me. I was about to decline the invitation, when a thought suddenly loomed vaguely in my mind.

"Yes, dear Count," I answered; "I accept your invitation with gratitude and pleasure. I will start tomorrow for Mistrà."

The next day found me at Padua, on my way to the Villa of Mistrà. It seemed as if I had left an intolerable burden behind me. I was, for the first time since how long, quite light of heart. The tortuous, rough-paved streets, with their empty, gloomy porticoes; the ill-plastered palaces, with closed, discoloured shutters; the little rambling square, with meagre trees and stubborn grass; the Venetian garden-houses reflecting their crumbling graces in the muddy canal; the gardens without gates and the gates without gardens, the avenues leading nowhere; and the population of blind and legless beggars, of whining sacristans, which issued as by magic from between the flag-stones and dust-heaps and weeds under the fierce August sun, all this dreariness merely amused and pleased me. My good spirits were heightened by a musical mass which I had the good fortune to hear at St. Anthony's.

Never in all my days had I heard anything comparable, although Italy affords many strange things in the way of sacred music. Into the deep nasal chanting of the priests there had suddenly burst a chorus of children, singing absolutely independent of all time and tune; grunting of priests answered by squealing of boys, slow Gregorian modulation interrupted by jaunty barrel-organ pipings, an insane, insanely merry jumble of bellowing and barking, mewing and cackling and braying, such as would have enlivened a witches' meeting, or rather some mediaeval Feast of Fools. And, to make the grotesqueness of such music still more fantastic and Hoffmannlike, there was, besides, the magnificence of the piles of sculptured marbles and gilded bronzes, the tradition of the musical splendour for which St. Anthony's had been famous in days gone by. I had read in old travellers, Lalande and Burney, that the Republic of St. Mark had squandered immense sums not merely on the monuments and decoration, but on the musical establishment of its great cathedral of Terra Firma. In the midst of this ineffable concert of impossible voices and instruments, I tried to imagine the voice of Guadagni, the soprano for whom Gluck had written *Che faru senza Euridice,* and the fiddle of Tartini, that Tartini with whom the devil had once come and made music. And the delight in anything so absolutely, barbarously, grotesquely, fantastically incongruous as such a performance in such a place was heightened by a sense of profanation: such were the successors of those wonderful musicians of that hated eighteenth century!

The whole thing had delighted me so much, so very much more than the most faultless performance could have done, that I determined to enjoy it once more; and towards vesper-time, after a cheerful dinner with two bagmen at the inn of the Golden Star, and a pipe over the rough sketch of a possible cantata upon the music which the devil made for Tartini, I turned my steps once more towards St. Anthony's.

The bells were ringing for sunset, and a muffled sound of organs seemed to issue from the huge, solitary church; I pushed my way under the heavy leathern curtain, expecting to be greeted by the grotesque performance of that morning.

I proved mistaken. Vespers must long have been over. A smell of stale incense, a crypt-like damp filled my mouth; it was already night in that vast cathedral. Out of the darkness glimmered the votive-lamps of the chapels, throwing wavering lights upon the red polished marble, the gilded railing, and chandeliers, and plaqueing with yellow the muscles of some sculptured figure. In a corner a burning taper put a halo about the head of a priest, burnishing his shining bald skull, his white surplice, and the open book before him. "Amen" he chanted; the book was closed with a snap, the light moved up the apse, some dark figures of women rose from their knees and passed quickly towards the door; a man saying his prayers before a chapel also got up, making a great clatter in dropping his stick.

The church was empty, and I expected every minute to be turned out by the sacristan making his evening round to close the doors. I was leaning against a pillar, looking into the greyness of the great arches, when the organ suddenly burst out into a series of chords, rolling through the echoes of the church: it seemed to be the conclusion of some service. And above the organ rose the notes of a voice; high, soft, enveloped in a kind of downiness, like a cloud of incense, and which ran through the mazes of a long cadence. The voice dropped into silence; with two thundering chords the organ closed in. All was silent. For a moment I stood leaning against one of the pillars of the nave: my hair was clammy, my knees sank beneath me, an enervating heat spread through my body; I tried to breathe more largely, to suck in the sounds with the incense-laden air. I was supremely happy, and yet as if I were dying; then suddenly a chill ran through me, and with it a vague panic. I turned away and hurried out into the open.

The evening sky lay pure and blue along the jagged line of roofs; the bats and swallows were wheeling about; and from the belfries all around, half-drowned by the deep bell of St. Anthony's, jangled the peel of the *Ave Maria*.

"You really don't seem well," young Count Alvise had said the previous evening, as he welcomed me, in the light of a lantern held up by a peasant, in the weedy back-garden of the Villa of Mistrà. Everything had seemed to me like a dream: the jingle of the horse's bells driving in the dark from Padua, as the lantern swept the acacia-hedges with their wide yellow light; the grating of the wheels on the gravel; the supper-table, illumined by a single petroleum lamp for fear of attracting mosquitoes, where a broken old lackey, in an old stable jacket, handed round the dishes among the fumes of onion; Alvise's fat mother gabbling dialect in a shrill, benevolent voice behind the bullfights on her fan; the unshaven village priest, perpetually fidgeting with his glass and foot, and sticking one shoulder up above the other. And now, in the afternoon, I felt as if I had been in this long, rambling, tumble-down Villa of Mistrà — a villa three-quarters of which was given up to the storage of grain and garden tools, or to the exercise of rats, mice, scorpions, and centipedes — all my life; as if I had always sat there, in Count Alvise's study, among the pile of undusted books on agriculture, the sheaves of accounts, the samples of grain and silkworm seed, the ink-stains and the cigar-ends; as if I had never heard of anything save the cereal basis of Italian agriculture, the diseases of maize, the peronospora of the vine, the breeds of bullocks, and the iniquities of farm labourers; with the blue cones of the Euganean hills closing in the green shimmer of plain outside the window.

After an early dinner, again with the screaming gabble of the fat old Countess, the fidgeting and shoulder-raising of the unshaven priest, the smell of fried oil and stewed onions, Count Alvise made me get into the cart beside him, and whirled me along among clouds of dust, between the endless glister of poplars, acacias, and maples, to one of his farms.

In the burning sun some twenty or thirty girls, in coloured skirts, laced bodices, and big straw-hats, were threshing the maize on the big red brick threshing-floor, while others were winnowing the grain in great sieves. Young Alvise III. (the old one was Alvise II.: everyone is Alvise, that is to say, Lewis, in that family; the name is on the house, the carts, the barrows, the very pails) picked up the maize, touched it, tasted it, said something to the girls that made them laugh, and something to the head farmer that made him look very glum; and then led me into a huge stable, where some twenty or thirty white bullocks were stamping, switching their tails, hitting their horns against the mangers in the dark. Alvise III. patted each, called him by his name, gave him some salt or a turnip, and explained which was the Mantuan breed, which the Apulian, which the Romagnolo, and so on. Then he bade me jump into the trap, and off we went again through the dust, among the hedges and ditches, till we came to some more brick farm buildings with pinkish roofs smoking against the blue sky. Here there were more young women threshing and winnowing the maize, which made a great golden Danaë cloud; more bullocks stamping and lowing in the cool darkness; more joking, fault-finding, explaining; and thus through five farms, until I seemed to see the rhythmical rising and falling of the flails against the hot sky, the shower of golden grains, the yellow dust from the winnowing-sieves on to the bricks, the switching of innumerable tails and plunging of innumerable horns, the glistening of huge white flanks and foreheads, whenever I closed my eyes.

"A good day's work!" cried Count Alvise, stretching out his long legs with the tight trousers riding up over the Wellington boots. "Mamma, give us some aniseed-syrup after dinner; it is an excellent restorative and precaution against the fevers of this country."

"Oh! You've got fever in this part of the world, have you? Why, your father said the air was so good!"

"Nothing, nothing," soothed the old Countess. "The only thing to be dreaded are mosquitoes; take care to fasten your shutters before lighting the candle."

"Well," rejoined young Alvise, with an effort of conscience, "of course there *are* fevers. But they needn't hurt you. Only, don't go out into the garden at night, if you don't want to catch them. Papa told me that you have fancies for moonlight rambles. It won't do in this climate, my dear fellow; it won't do. If you must stalk about at night, being a genius, take a turn inside the house; you can get quite exercise enough."

After dinner the aniseed-syrup was produced, together with brandy and cigars, and they all sat in the long, narrow, half-furnished room on the first floor; the old Countess knitting a garment of uncertain shape and destination, the priest reading out the newspaper; Count Alvise puffing at his long, crooked cigar, and pulling the ears of a long, lean dog with a suspicion of mange and a stiff eye. From the dark garden outside rose the hum and whirr of countless insects, and the smell of the grapes which hung black against the starlit, blue sky, on the trellis. I went to the balcony. The garden lay dark beneath; against the twinkling horizon stood out the tall poplars. There was the sharp cry of an owl; the barking of a dog; a sudden whiff of warm, enervating perfume, a perfume that made me think of the taste of certain peaches, and suggested white, thick, wax-like petals. I seemed to have smelt that flower once before: it made me feel languid, almost faint.

"I am very tired," I said to Count Alvise. "See how feeble we city folk become!"

But, despite my fatigue, I found it quite impossible to sleep. The night seemed perfectly stifling. I had felt nothing like it at Venice. Despite the injunctions of the Countess I opened the solid wooden shutters, hermetically closed against mosquitoes, and looked out.

The moon had risen; and beneath it lay the big lawns, the rounded tree-tops, bathed in a blue, luminous mist, every leaf glistening and trembling in what seemed a heaving sea of light.

Beneath the window was the long trellis, with the white shining piece of pavement under it. It was so bright that I could distinguish the green of the vine-leaves, the dull red of the catalpa-flowers. There was in the air a vague scent of cut grass, of ripe American grapes, of that white flower (it must be white) which made me think of the taste of peaches all melting into the delicious freshness of falling dew. From the village church came the stroke of one: Heaven knows how long I had been vainly attempting to sleep. A shiver ran through me, and my head suddenly filled as with the fumes of some subtle wine; I remembered all those weedy embankments, those canals full of stagnant water, the yellow faces of the peasants; the word malaria returned to my mind. No matter! I remained leaning on the window, with a thirsty longing to plunge myself into this blue moon-mist, this dew and perfume and silence, which seemed to vibrate and quiver like the stars that strewed the depths of heaven…. What music, even Wagner's, or of that great singer of starry nights, the divine Schumann, what music could ever compare with this great silence, with this great concert of voiceless things that sing within one's soul?

As I made this reflection, a note, high, vibrating, and sweet, rent the silence, which immediately closed around it. I leaned out of the window, my heart beating as though it must burst. After a brief space the silence was cloven once more by that note, as the darkness is cloven by a falling star or a firefly rising slowly like a rocket. But this time it was plain that the voice did not come, as I had imagined, from the garden, but from the house itself, from some corner of this rambling old villa of Mistrà.

Mistrà — Mistrà! The name rang in my ears, and I began at length to grasp its significance, which seems to have escaped me till then. "Yes," I said to myself, "it is quite natural." And with this odd impression of naturalness was mixed a feverish, impatient pleasure. It was as if I had come to Mistrà on purpose, and that I was about to meet the object of my long and weary hopes.

Grasping the lamp with its singed green shade, I gently opened the door and made my way through a series of long passages and of big, empty rooms, in which my steps re-echoed as in a church, and my light disturbed whole swarms of bats. I wandered at random, farther and farther from the inhabited part of the buildings.

This silence made me feel sick; I gasped as under a sudden disappointment.

All of a sudden there came a sound — chords, metallic, sharp, rather like the tone of a mandolin — close to my ear. Yes, quite close: I was separated from the sounds only by a partition. I fumbled for a door; the unsteady light of my lamp was insufficient for my eyes, which were swimming like those of a drunkard. At last I found a latch, and, after a moment's hesitation, I lifted it and gently pushed open the door. At first I could not understand what manner of place I was in. It was dark all round me, but a brilliant light blinded me, a light coming from below and striking the opposite wall. It was as if I had entered a dark box in a half-lighted theatre. I was, in fact, in something of the kind, a sort of dark hole with a high balustrade, half-hidden by an up-drawn curtain. I remembered those little galleries or recesses for the use of musicians or lookers-on — which exist under the ceiling of the ballrooms in certain old Italian palaces. Yes; it must have been one like that. Opposite me was a vaulted ceiling covered with gilt mouldings, which framed great time-blackened canvases; and lower down, in the light thrown up from below, stretched a wall covered with faded frescoes. Where had I seen that goddess in lilac and lemon draperies foreshortened over a big, green peacock? For she was familiar to me, and the stucco Tritons also who twisted their tails round her gilded frame. And that fresco, with warriors in Roman cuirasses and green and blue lappets, and knee-breeches — where could I have seen them before? I asked myself these questions without experiencing any surprise. Moreover, I was very calm, as one is calm sometimes in extraordinary dreams — could I be dreaming?

I advanced gently and leaned over the balustrade. My eyes were met at first by the darkness above me, where, like gigantic spiders, the big chandeliers rotated slowly, hanging from the ceiling. Only one of them was lit, and its Murano-glass pendants, its carnations and roses, shone opalescent in the light of the guttering wax. This chandelier lighted up the opposite wall and that piece of ceiling with the goddess and the green peacock; it illumined, but far less well, a corner of the huge room, where, in the shadow of a kind of canopy, a little group of people were crowding round a yellow satin sofa, of the same kind as those that lined the walls. On the sofa, half-screened from me by the surrounding persons, a woman was stretched out: the silver of her embroidered dress and the rays of her diamonds gleamed and shot forth as she moved uneasily. And immediately under the chandelier, in the full light, a man stooped over a harpsichord, his head bent slightly, as if collecting his thoughts before singing.

He struck a few chords and sang. Yes, sure enough, it was the voice, the voice that had so long been persecuting me! I recognized at once that delicate, voluptuous quality, strange, exquisite, sweet beyond words, but lacking all youth and clearness. That passion veiled in tears which had troubled my brain that night on the lagoon, and again on the Grand Canal singing the *Biondina*, and yet again, only two days since, in the deserted cathedral of Padua. But I recognized now what seemed to have been hidden from me till then, that this voice was what I cared most for in all the wide world.

The voice wound and unwound itself in long, languishing phrases, in rich, voluptuous *rifioriituras*, all fretted with tiny scales and exquisite, crisp shakes; it stopped ever and anon, swaying as if panting in languid delight. And I felt my body melt even as wax in the sunshine, and it seemed to me that I too was turning fluid and vaporous, in order to mingle with these sounds as the moonbeams mingle with the dew.

Suddenly, from the dimly lighted corner by the canopy, came a little piteous wail; then another followed, and was lost in the singer's voice. During a long phrase on the harpsichord, sharp and tinkling, the singer turned his head towards the dais, and there came a plaintive little sob. But he, instead of stopping, struck a sharp chord; and with a thread of voice so hushed as to be scarcely audible, slid softly into a long *cadenza*. At the same moment he threw his head backwards, and the light fell full upon the handsome, effeminate face, with its ashy pallor and big, black brows, of the singer Zaffirino. At the sight of that face, sensual and sullen, of that smile which was cruel and mocking like a bad woman's, I understood — I knew not why, by what process — that his singing *must* be cut short, that the accursed phrase *must* never be finished. I understood that I was before an assassin, that he was killing this woman, and killing me also, with his wicked voice.

I rushed down the narrow stair which led down from the box, pursued, as it were, by that exquisite voice, swelling, swelling by insensible degrees. I flung myself on the door which must be that of the big saloon. I could see its light between the panels. I bruised my hands in trying to wrench the latch. The door was fastened tight, and while I was struggling with that locked door I heard the voice swelling, swelling, rending asunder that downy veil which wrapped it, leaping forth clear, resplendent, like the sharp and glittering blade of a knife that seemed to enter deep into my breast. Then, once more, a wail, a death-groan, and that dreadful noise, that hideous gurgle of breath strangled by a rush of blood. And then a long shake, acute, brilliant, triumphant.

The door gave way beneath my weight, one half crashed in. I entered. I was blinded by a flood of blue moonlight. It poured in through four great windows, peaceful and diaphanous, a pale blue mist of moonlight, and turned the huge room into a kind of submarine cave, paved with moonbeams, full of shimmers, of pools of moonlight. It was as bright as at midday, but the brightness was cold, blue, vaporous, supernatural. The room was completely empty, like a great hayloft. Only, there hung from the ceiling the ropes which had once supported a chandelier; and in a corner, among stacks of wood and heaps of Indian-corn, whence spread a sickly smell of damp and mildew, there stood a long, thin harpsichord, with spindle-legs, and its cover cracked from end to end.

I felt, all of a sudden, very calm. The one thing that mattered was the phrase that kept moving in my head, the phrase of that unfinished cadence which I had heard but an instant before. I opened the harpsichord, and my fingers came down boldly upon its keys. A jingle-jangle of broken strings, laughable and dreadful, was the only answer.

Then an extraordinary fear overtook me. I clambered out of one of the windows; I rushed up the garden and wandered through the fields, among the canals and the embankments, until the moon had set and the dawn began to shiver, followed, pursued for ever by that jangle of broken strings.

People expressed much satisfaction at my recovery.

It seems that one dies of those fevers.

Recovery? But have I recovered? I walk, and eat and drink and talk; I can even sleep. I live the life of other living creatures. But I am wasted by a strange and deadly disease. I can never lay hold of my own inspiration. My head is filled with music which is certainly by me, since I have never heard it before, but which still is not my own, which I despise and abhor: little, tripping flourishes and languishing phrases, and long-drawn, echoing cadences.

O wicked, wicked voice, violin of flesh and blood made by the Evil One's hand, may I not even execrate thee in peace; but is it necessary that, at the moment when I curse, the longing to hear thee again should parch my soul like hell-thirst? And since I have satiated thy lust for revenge, since thou hast withered my life and withered my genius, is it not time for pity? May I not hear one note, only one note of thine, O singer, O wicked and contemptible wretch?

The Trainer's Ghost

Lettice Galbraith

The Cat and Compass was shut in for the night. The front of the house was dark and silent, for it was long past closing time, but from one of the rear ground-floor windows a thin shaft of yellow light gleamed through the failing rain, and indicated that behind the shutters of the snug bar-parlour, in a cheerful atmosphere of tobacco smoke and the odorous steam of hot "Scotch" Mr. Samuel Vicary, licensed victualler, and two other congenial spirits, were "making a night of it".

"It's too late for Downey now," the landlord remarked, with a glance at the clock, as he leaned forward to knock out his pipe on the hob. "Twenty past twelve, and raining like blazes. Damn the weather, if it holds on like this, 'The Ghoul' will have his work cut out to get round the old course on Thursday with 8 stone 9."

"Not with that lot behind him," rejoined a seedy individual who sat on the farther side of the table. "I've watched them pretty careful. The race lies between us and the favourite, and with Downey up, she's safe enough. It's real jam this time — eh, Mr. Davis?"

The gentleman indicated drained his glass with an unctuous smile. His exterior suggested the prosperous undertaker. As a matter of fact he was a bookmaker in a big way of business, and suspected, moreover, of having considerable interest in a stable notorious for the in and out running of its horses.

"That's about the size of it," he answered, drawing in his thick lips with a gentle, sucking sound, expressive of inward satisfaction.

"Prime whisky this, Vicary! I'll take another tot. Yes, it is a big thing, and, after this, Davis, Smiles, and Co. must lie quiet for a bit. There'll be plenty of fools to cry over burnt fingers by Monday, and what with stewards meddling where they've no cause to interfere, and the press writing up a lot of rot about 'rings' and such like, and the Jockey Club holding inquiries, a man must mind his Ps and Qs in these days. Racing is going to the dogs, and soon there'll be no making a decent living on the turf. How it does rain to be sure! I shouldn't care to find myself abroad tonight."

"Here's some poor devil as has got to face it," said the tout, as the sound of horse-hoofs echoed down the quiet road. "Ain't he coming a lick, too! He's not afraid of bustling his cattle."

"Small blame to him either in weather like this," grunted the landlord, removing his pipe to listen. "Why, that's Downey's hack. I'd swear to her gallop among a thousand. To think, now, of his turning up at this time of night!"

The clatter of hoofs ceased, and the men sprang to their feet. In the silence that followed they heard the muffled slam of a closing gate, and the clink of shoes on the stones of the yard outside. Vicary snatched up the lamp and hurried to the door, while the visitors looked at each other.

"'Tis Downey sure enough," said the bookmaker, spitting energetically into the fire. "Now, what brings him here so late? He hasn't pelted over from Hawkhurst in the teeth of this storm for the pleasure of our company, I'll go bail."

The newcomer had swung himself off his horse before the landlord could unfasten the door.

"Yes, it's me — Downey," was his answer to that worthy's cautious challenge. "Look sharp with that chain and let me get under cover. I'm stiff with the cold, I can tell you, and the mare is about beat."

The chain fell with a clank, and Vicary flung back the door.

"Come in, come in," he cried, holding the lamp above his head to get a better view of his visitor. "Lord! how it do rain! Get out of that coat and put a tot of whisky inside you, while I see to the mare. 'Tis all right," he added, as the other jerked his head interrogatively in the direction of the bar-parlour, "there's only me and Slimmy and Davis. Go right in and help yourself."

Thus assured, the fresh arrival went forward, the water dripping from his soaked hat and covert coat, and trickling in little black streams over the well-stoned passage; while Vicary, flinging a rug across his shoulders, led the tired horse round to the stables. When he returned to the parlour Downey was drying himself before the fire, a smoking tumbler in his hand, and a good cigar between his lips.

"Well?" inquired the landlord, setting down the lamp with a keen glance at the disturbed countenances of the three men. "I take it, you did not come through this rain for nothing. Is aught the matter?"

"Matter enough," ejaculated Slimmy. "Here's Coulson got a rod in pickle that is going to upset our pot."

Vicary laughed.

"Go on with you," he said derisively, "they've nothing at Malton as can collar the Ghoul."

"Don't you be so precious sharp," the tout retorted. "Wait till you hear what Downey's got to say."

The jockey shifted his cigar to the other side of his mouth. "It is this way," he began. "One of Coulson's lads was at our place this afternoon, and he let on to me in confidence that they have a colt over there they think a real good thing for the Ebor. It is entered in Berkeley's name — the Captain, him as sold the Malton place to Coulson."

"The Captain's been stony broke this three year," put in Vicary. "How did he come by the colt?"

"Picked him up in the dales, from what I gather (he'd always a rare eye for a horse had the Captain), and fancied him so that he got young Alick to take half-share, and lend the purchase-money into the bargain, I reckon. The Coulsons always thought a lot of the old family. It wouldn't be the first time one of them had helped a Berkeley out of a tight place."

"That's true," assented the landlord. "Markham told me old Alick held enough of the squire's paper to cover a room. There wasn't anything he'd have stuck at to keep him on his legs. I remember him saying once in that very bar there, 'I'd come from hell,' he says, 'to stand by one of the old stock.' Fifteen years ago this very day it was, just before the Ebor, and the last time I ever saw the old chap alive, for Blue Ruin kicked the life out of him in his box at Malton on the morning of the race. Nothing would serve the squire but the horse must be shot the same night — lord, what a shindy there was! And if it weren't like one of old Berkeley's fool's-tricks to 'blue' twelve hundred pounds that way, and him not knowing where to turn for the ready! But about this colt; if he's such a clipper, how is it nobody's heard of him before this?"

286

"Coulson has kept him dark. He's been trained at Beverley, and they only brought him to Malton three weeks back. The lad tells me he has been doing very good work, and he is to be tried in the morning with Cream Cheese — that is schoolmaster to the Leger crack. Now look here, if the colt can beat Cream Cheese at a stone, he's a mortal for the Ebor. On a heavy course he'll walk right away from the Ghoul, and put us in the cart."

The landlord whistled.

"You are sure the lad's square?"

"I'd peel the flesh off his bones if I thought he was putting the double on me; but he daren't try it. Coulson as good as swore the boys over to hold their tongues, but Tom says the stable is that sweet on his chance, they'll put their shirts on the colt at starting-price."

"Who's to ride him?"

"Alick's head lad. The brute has a temper, and won't stand much 'footling' about; but Jevons and he understand each other, and his orders are to get him off well, and sit still."

"I suppose now," suggested the bookmaker, "this Jevons ain't a reasonable sort of chap?"

Downey grinned. "As well try to square Coulson himself. He is one of your Sunday-school-and-ten-commandments sort, is Jevons. Besides, his father was the old squire's second horseman, and the lad was brought up in the stables. He swears by the Berkeleys, and would never lend a hand to put a spoke in the Captain's wheel."

"Do you know what time the trial is to come off?"

"About six. I reckoned on Slimmy's being within call, for there is precious little time to lose. It is light by four."

"I'm game," said the tout, "if Mr. Vicary will lend me something to take me over."

The landlord consulted his watch. "Half-past one," he said. "Let's see; it's close on fifteen mile to Coulson's. I'll drop you at the Pig and Whistle. You can get over the fields from Gunny's corner in twenty minutes."

"You know your way?" queried Davis, uneasily.

"Every yard of it, guv'nor. Coulson and me is old friends so long as we don't happen to meet. There is a nice bit of cover at the end of the ground where I can lie snug. Will you wait for me, Mr. Vicary?"

"Aye, I'll be on the road by Gunny's at seven. What for you, Downey can we give you a shakedown here?"

"No thank you; I'm off," answered the jockey, laughing, "you're altogether too warm in this corner for a nice young man like me. I'm putting up at the Great Northern, and shall see you and Davis for the first time on the course, and not more than I can help of you then."

The rain had cleared off, and the first pale rifts in the eastern sky were broadening into grey dawn before Slimmy, from the convenient elevation of a friendly elder-bush, caught sight of a line of dark specks moving across the wold, and gradually resolving themselves into a string of horses.

"Here they come," he murmured, pocketing the flat bottle from which he had been refreshing his inner man, and working himself cautiously forward on the stout bough, while he parted the leaves with his left hand to command a better view. "And here's young Alick and the Captain. I thought as much," he added, triumphantly, for the trainer and Berkeley had cantered up and reined in their hacks within ten paces of his hiding-place.

In a very few minutes the horses were stripped and got into line. "They will start themselves," said Coulson, "and take it easy for the first half mile. Then you'll see, Captain, that there is very little fear but what the colt will give a good account of himself tomorrow. There they go, and a good start too."

The horses jumped off together, a big chestnut, which even in the half light Slimmy had recognized as Cream Cheese, coming to the front, with a clear lead. The soft drum of the hoof on the moist ground died away, and the two men stood up in their stirrups, following with keen eyes the dim outline of the horses as they rounded the curve and swept into the straight, the chestnut still showing the way, with his stable companion and a powerful-looking bay in close attendance. "There he goes!" was the tout's mental ejaculation, for, at the bend for home, a dark horse crept up on the inside, and, taking up the running at half distance, came on and finished easily with a couple of lengths to spare.

Coulson turned to his companion with a smile.

"He'll do, Captain. The money is as good as banked. You can put on his clothes, Jevons, and take him home. He's a clipper, and no mistake. He came up the straight like a —"

"Rocket," suggested Berkeley. "How's that for a name? By Gunpowder out of Falling Star — not bad, I think."

"Couldn't be better," was the hearty answer.

"A few more of his sort, and we'll soon have you back at the Hall, Master Charles. I shall live to lead in a Derby winner for you yet Lord! I think it would almost bring the old man out of his grave to know the Berkeleys had their own again."

The words were hardly past his lips when a crack, like the report of a pistol, close behind them, made both men jump as if they had been shot.

Mr. Slimmy, who, having heard and seen all he wanted, was in the act of beating a masterly retreat, had unfortunately set his foot on a rotten branch, which instantly snapped beneath his weight. Taken by surprise, the tout lost his foothold and his balance at the same time, made an ineffectual grab at the swinging boughs, pitched forward, and, despite his wild endeavours to recover himself, descended precipitately in a shower of leaves and dry twigs on the wrong side of the hedge.

"Where the deuce did the fellow come from?" ejaculated Berkeley, as he gazed blankly at the heap on the ground. Coulson's only answer was to swing himself off his horse and fling the bridle to his companion. The quick-witted trainer had reckoned up the situation in a moment, and before the luckless Slimmy could gather himself together Coulson's hand was on his collar, and Coulson's "crop" was cracking and curling about his person, picking out the tenderest parts with a scientific precision that made him writhe and twist in frantic efforts to free himself from that iron grip. But the trainer stood six feet in his socks, and was well built. He held his victim like a rat, while his strong right arm brought the lash whistling down again and again with a force that cut through the tout's seedy clothing like a knife.

"For God's sake, Coulson," cried Captain Berkeley, "hold hard, or you will kill the man."

"And a good thing, too," said the trainer, relinquishing his hold on Slimmy with a suddenness that sent him sprawling into the muddy ditch. "I know him, and I'll have no touting on my place. If he shows his face here again, he'll find himself in the horse pond. Stop that row," he went on, turning to where Slimmy lay in the ditch, crying and cursing alternately, "and get off my ground before I chuck you over the fence."

White with rage and pain, the tout picked himself up and scrambled through the gap in the hedge as fast as his aching limbs could carry him. But when he had put a safe distance between himself and Coulson, he turned and shook his fist at the trainer's retreating figure.

"Curse you," he said, with a horrible imprecation. "I'll pay you out for this. I'll be even with you, if I swing for it, so help me if I ain't."

Owner and trainer rode home in silence.

Coulson was a good deal upset by the discovery that his horse was being watched. He had recognized Slimmy, and Slimmy was known to be in the employ of a party popularly supposed to stick at nothing, and quite capable of trying to get at a horse that threatened to upset their game. Then, again, the arrangements and time of the trial had been kept so quiet that it seemed impossible the tout could get wind of it, except from one directly connected with the stables. Altogether Coulson felt uneasy, and, after some consideration, he mentioned his suspicions to his head lad, in whom he had the most implicit confidence. Jevons thought things over for a bit. Then he suggested the colt's box should be changed, and that he should sit up with him.

"Put him in the end box next the saddle-room, sir; it is so seldom used that an outsider would not think of trying it, and there isn't many of the lads as would like to rux about in there tonight, leastways not one as has a bad conscience."

Coulson knew what he meant. In the box next the saddle-room his father, old Alick Coulson, had come by his end, kicked to death by the Ebor favourite on the very eve of the race. A training-stable is not exactly a hot-bed of superstition, but, without doubt, a feeling did exist in connection with that particular box, and, as Jevons had said, it was very rarely used.

"Shall you like to sit up there yourself?" the trainer asked bluntly.

Jevons did not mind at all. He said he did not hold with ghosts and such like, and he was sure a sportsman like the old master would know better than to come upsetting the colt and spoiling his, Jevons's, nerve just before the race. Still, as there was gas in the saddle-room and a fire, if Mr. Coulson had no objection, he might as well sit there, and look in every now and again to see his charge next door was getting on all right.

The trainer readily agreed. He had a high opinion of the lad's coolness and common sense, but he also felt that to pass the night alone and without a light in a place which, however undeservedly, had the reputation of being haunted, and that, too, on the very anniversary of the tragedy from which the superstition took its rise, was a performance calculated to try the strongest nerves, and he preferred that Jevons should not face the ordeal.

Indeed, it struck him as he left the lad for the night that he would scarcely have cared to undertake the watch himself. It might be fancy, but there was a queer feel about the place.

"Fifteen years ago tonight," thought Coulson, "since an Ebor crack stood in that box. It was a dark horse, too, and owned by the squire. It is a coincidence anyway. No, I shouldn't care to take on Jevons's job."

Nor was he alone in his conclusions. Several other people expressed a similar conviction, notably Jevons's subordinate, who had heard of the arrangement in the morning.

"I wouldn't be in Bill's shoes tonight — no, not for fifty down," he said, and slipped off unobserved to the nearest box to post a letter.

The communication he despatched was addressed to "S. Downey, Esq., Great Northern Hotel, York," and was marked "immediate". The lad was going over to the races in the afternoon, and felt tolerably certain of getting speech with the jockey, but he was a careful young man, and wisely left nothing to chance.

It wanted fifteen minutes to midnight. Outside, the night was as black as your hat, not a vestige of a moon, not a single star to break the uniform darkness of the sky. With sunset a noisy blustering wind had sprung up, rattling about the chimneys, clashing the wet branches, and deadening the sound of cautious footfalls creeping across the paddock in the direction of the stables. Jevons was sitting over the saddle-room fire, with his pipe and the *Sporting Life* for company, and the remains of his supper-beer on the table beside him. From time to time he took a lantern and went to look at his charge. The colt had been quiet enough all the earlier part of the evening, but for the last half-hour Jevons fancied he could hear him fidgeting about on the other side of the wall.

"What ails the brute?" he said to himself, laying down his pipe to listen.

The wind dropped suddenly, making the silence all the more intense by contrast with the previous roar; and through the stillness Jevons heard the clink of a bucket, and the sound of someone moving about in the loose-box.

He sprang to his feet and snatched up the lantern. His sole idea was that someone was trying to get at the horse, and his hand was on the revolver in his breast-pocket when he opened the door. So strong was the impression that he was positively surprised to find no sign of an intruder. The colt was lying in the farthest corner and perfectly quiet. Jevons looked all round. There was certainly nothing to see, but it struck him that the air felt very cold, and he shut the door. The instant it closed behind him, a dark shadow fell across the square of light issuing from the entrance to the saddle-room.

"Now's your time, Slimmy," whispered Mr. Vicary. "Nip in and doctor his liquor. This is getting precious slow."

The beer stood on a table barely two paces from the door. Stretching out his arm, the tout emptied the contents of a small bottle into the jug, and crept noiselessly back to his hiding-place.

"There's a deuce of a draught in here," said Jevons to himself, "and where it comes from fairly beats me."

He held up his hand at different heights, trying to test the direction of the chill current of air. But it seemed to come from every quarter at once, and shifted continually.

The lad struck a lucifer, and held it level with his shoulder. To his utter astonishment the flame burned clear and steady, though he could feel the cold draught blowing on his face, and even stirring the hair on his closely cropped head.

"That's a rum go," he said, staring at the match as it died out. He backed a few steps towards the wall, the draught was fainter; when he came level with the horse it ceased altogether.

"You are wise, my lad, to stick to this corner," Jevons remarked as he looked at the colt, "it's enough to blow your head off on the other side. Well, it must have been the wind I heard, for there ain't nothing here."

He locked the door and went back to the saddle-room. The hands of the American clock on the narrow mantelpiece pointed to twelve. Jevons loaded his pipe, poured out the rest of the beer, and took a long pull. Then he kicked the fire together, and looked about for a match.

"Now, where did I put that box," he said, staring stupidly round. "Where did I put that — what is it I'm looking for? What's got my head? It's all of a swim."

He felt for a chair and sat down, holding his hand to his heavy eyes. The lids felt as if they were weighted with lead. The gas danced in a golden mist that blinded him, and the whole room was spinning round and round. Then the pipe dropped from his nerveless fingers, and his head forward on the table.

"He's safe," muttered Vicary, as he softly pushed the door ajar and surveyed the unconscious lad. "That's prime stuff to keep the baby quiet. Here's the key, Slimmy; I'll bring the light. When we've damped the powder in that there rocket, Coulson will wish he hadn't been so handy with his crop this morning."

Slimmy turned the key in the lock and looked into the box; then he gave a slight start, and drew quickly back.

"What's up?" inquired the landlord. "Go on, it's all right"

"Sh!" whispered the tout, "he might hear you."

"Hear us? not he, nor the last day neither, if it come now."

He was thinking of Jevons, but Slimmy pulled to the door and held it "There's someone in there," he muttered, "an old chap. He's sitting on a bucket right in front of the horse."

"Did he see you?"

"I don't know, his back was turned and he looked asleep like."

He leaned forward, listening intently, but not a sound came from behind the dosed door.

"Coulson didn't mean to be caught napping," said Vicary, under his breath. "Is it a stable hand?"

"A cut above that," returned the other, in the same tone. "'Tis queer he should keep so quiet."

They waited a few minutes, but everything was still.

"See here," whispered Slimmy, untwisting the muffler he wore round his neck, "there ain't no manner of use standing here all night. Give me the stick. If I can get past him quiet, I will but if he moves, you be ready to slip the handkerchief over his head. He can't make much of a fight against the two of us, and we ain't got this far to be stalled off by an old crock like him; keep well behind him. Never mind the lantern. He's got a light inside."

There was a light inside, but where it came from would have been difficult to say. It fell clear as a limelight over half the box, and beyond the shadow lay black and impenetrable, a wall of darkness.

As he crossed the threshold Slimmy felt a blast of cold air sweep towards him, striking a strange chill into his very bones.

Straight opposite stood a horse, and before him an old man was sitting on a reversed bucket, his elbow resting on his knee, his head on his hand. To all appearances he was asleep. But even in that intense stillness the tout could catch no sound of breathing. His own heart was thumping against his ribs with the force of a sledge-hammer. He felt his flesh creeping with a sensation of fear that was almost sickening. Fear? Yes, that was the word; he was horribly afraid. And of what? Of a weak old man, for whom he would have been more than a match single-handed, and they were two to one. What a fool he was, to be sure! With desperate effort he pulled himself together and went forward, his eye warily fixed on the silent figure. Neither man nor horse moved. Slimmy thrust his hand into his pocket and felt for the bottle which was to settle the Rocket's chances for the Ebor! His fingers were on the cork, when the silence was broken by a sound that brought a cold sweat out on his forehead and lifted the hair on his head. It was a low chuckling laugh. The man on the bucket was looking at him. The gleaming eyes fixed on him with a sort of mesmeric power, and the bottle fell from his trembling fingers.

"Quick with the rag, Sam," he gasped, "he's seen me." But Vicary stood like one turned to stone. His gaze fastened on the seated figure, taking in every item of the quaint dress, the high gill collar and ample bird's-eye stock, the drab coat and antiquated breeches and gaiters. His mouth was open, but for the life of him he could not speak. He was waiting in the helpless fascination of horror to see the face of a man who had been dead and buried for fifteen years.

Slowly, like an automaton, that strange watcher turned his head. The square, resolute mouth was open as if to speak, the shrunken skin was a greenish yellow colour, like the skin of a corpse; along the temple ran a dull blue mark in the shape of a horse's hoof but the eyes burned like two living coals, as they fixed themselves on the face of the terrified publican.

With a single yell of "Lord ha' mercy on us! 'tis old Alick himself!"

Vicary turned and fled.

Slimmy heard the crash of the lantern on the stones and the sound of his flying feet, and an awful terror came upon him, a great fear, which made his teeth chatter in his head and curdled the blood in his veins.

The place seemed full of an unnatural light — the blue flames that dance at night over deserted graveyards. The air was foul with the horrible odours of decay. Above all, he felt the fearful presence of that which was neither living nor dead — the semblance of a man whose human body had for fifteen years been rotting in the grave. It was not living, but it moved. Its cold, shining eyes were looking into his, were coming nearer. Now they were close to him. With the energy of despair, Slimmy grasped his stick by the thin end and struck with his full force at the horror before him. The loaded knob whistled through empty air, and, overbalanced by the force of his own blow, the wretched tout pitched forward, and with one piercing shriek fell prone on the straw.

"Did you hear that?"

"What the deuce was it?"

The two men, who were sitting over the fire in the comfortable smoking-room, sprang to their feet. Coulson put down his pipe and went into the hall. Someone was moving about in the kitchen.

"Is that you, Martin?" he called. "What was that row?"

The man came out at once.

"Did you hear it too, sir? It made me jump, it came so sudden. Sounded like someone hollering out in the stables."

"Get a lantern. I must go across and see what it was. Are you coming, too, Captain? Then bring that shillelagh in your hand. It might be useful."

Martin unbolted the side door, which opened on the garden, and the three men crossed the gravel path and went through the yard. Here they saw the gleam of another lantern. Someone was running towards them. It was one of the lads, half dressed, and evidently just out of bed.

"Is that you, Mr. Coulson?" he said breathlessly. "Did you hear that scream? It woke us all up. Bryant can see the saddle-room from his window, and he says the door is wide open."

"Come on," was Coulson's answer, as they hurried across to the stables. The square of light from the saddle-room showed clearly through the darkness.

"Here's Jevons," said the trainer, who was the first to enter. "He is only asleep," he added, as he lifted the lad's head and listened to the regular breathing. He shook him roughly, trying to arouse him, but Jevons was beyond being awakened by any ordinary method; he made an inarticulate grunt, and dropped back into his former attitude.

"Drunk?" ejaculated Martin, blankly.

"Drugged, by gad!" Captain Berkeley had taken the empty jug from the table and smelt it. The sickly odour of the powerful opiate clung about the pitcher and told its own tale.

"Then," cried the trainer, "as I'm a living man, they've got at the colt." His face was white and set as he seized the lantern and ran to the loose-box. The door was open; the key was in the lock. The men crowded up. There was scarcely a doubt in their minds but that the mischief was already done. Coulson held up the lantern and looked round. The colt was standing up in the corner, snorting and sniffing the air. He, too, had been startled by that terrible cry.

On the ground, straight in front of the door, a man lay prone on his face. There was no mistaking the look of that helpless body, the limp flaccidity of those outstretched arms.

"He's dead, sir," said Martin, as he turned up the white face; "hold the light down, his coat's all wet with — something."

It was not blood, only a sticky, dark-coloured fluid, the contents of a broken bottle lying underneath the body. Just beyond the reach of the clenched right hand was a heavy loaded-stick, and near the door they found a thick woollen handkerchief. Berkeley bent down and looked at the drawn features.

"Surely," he said, in a low voice, "it is the same man you thrashed this morning?"

Coulson nodded. "He meant squaring accounts with me and he has had to settle his own instead. It is strange that there should be no marks of violence about him, and yet he looks as if he had died hard."

And truly, the dead man's face was terrible in its fixed expression of mortal fear. The eyes were staring and wide open, the teeth clenched, a little froth hung about the blue lips. It was a horrid sight. They satisfied themselves that life was absolutely extinct. Then Coulson gave orders for the colt to be taken back to his old box, locked the door on the corpse until the police could arrive, and spent the remainder of the night in the saddle-room, waiting until Jevons should have slept off the effects of the opiate.

But when the lad awoke he could throw very little light on the matter. He swore positively there was no one in the box when he paid his last visit at five minutes to twelve, and he could remember nothing after returning to the saddle-room. How the tout had effected an entrance, by what means his purpose had been frustrated and his life destroyed, remained for ever a mystery. The only living man who knew the truth held his tongue, and the dead can tell no tales. But Mr. Vicary, as he watched Captain Berkeley's colt walk away from his field next day, and, cleverly avoiding a collision with the favourite on the rails, pass the post a winner by three lengths, was struck by the fact that the "Rocket" had grown smaller during the night, and he could have sworn the horse he saw in the loose-box had some white about him somewhere.

"He's one o' raight sort," exclaimed a stalwart Yorkshireman who stood at Vicary's elbow. "When an seed him i' t' paddock, an said aa'l hev a pound on th' squoire's 'oss for t' sake of ould toimes, for he's strange and loike Blue Ruin, as won th' Ebor in seventy-foive. 'Twas fust race as aver aa'd clapped eyes on, and aa'd backed him for ivery penny aa'd got."

The publican turned involuntarily to the speaker, "Did you say yon colt was like Blue Ruin?" he asked hoarsely.

"The very moral of him, barring he ain't quite so thick, and ain't got no white stocking. I reckon you'll remember Blue Ruin," added the farmer, referring to a friend on the other side, "him as killed ould Coulson?"

Vicary was a strong man, but at the mention of that name a strange, sickly sensation crept over him. The colour forsook his face, and when, a few minutes later he called for a brandy "straight", the hand he stretched out for the glass was shaking visibly.

Once, and once only, did the landlord allude to the events of that fatal night. It was when Mr. David, loudly deploring his losses, expressed an opinion that Slimmy was "a clumsy fool, and matters would have come out very differently if he had been there."

"You may thank your stars," was Vicary's energetic rejoinder, "that you never set foot in the cursed place. The poor chap is dead, and there ain't no call for me to get myself mixed up in the business. Least said, soonest mended, say I; but you mind the story I told you the night Downey brought the news of that blooming colt, about ould Coulson swearing he'd come back from the dead, if need be, to do a Berkeley a good turn."

"I remember right enough. What's that got to do with it?"

The landlord glanced nervously over his shoulder. "Only this," he answered, sinking his voice to a whisper, *"he kept his word!"*

How He Left the Hotel

Louisa Baldwin

I used to work the passenger-lift in the Empire Hotel, that big block of building in lines of red and white brick like streaky bacon, that stands at the corner of —— Street. I'd served my time in the army, and got my discharge with good-conduct stripes; and how I got the job was in this way. The hotel was a big company affair with a managing committee of retired officers and such-like; gentlemen with a bit o' money in the concern, and nothing to do but fidget about it, and my late Colonel was one of 'em. He was as good-tempered a man as ever stepped when his will wasn't crossed, and when I asked him for a job, "Mole," says he, "you're the very man to work the lift at our big hotel. Soldiers are civil and business-like, and the public like 'em only second best to sailors. We've had to give our last man the sack, and you can take his place."

I liked my work well enough and my pay, and kept my place a year, and I should have been there still if it hadn't been for a circumstance — But don't let me anticipate. Ours was a hydraulic lift. None o' them rickety things swung up like a poll parrot's cage in a well staircase that I shouldn't care to trust my neck to. It ran as smooth as oil, a child might have worked it, and safe as standing on the ground. Instead of being stuck full of advertisements like an omnibus, we'd mirrors in it, and the ladies would look at themselves, and pat their hair, and set their mouths when I was taking 'em downstairs dressed of an evening. It was a little sitting-room, with red velvet cushions to sit down on, and you'd nothing to do but get into it, and it 'ud float you up or float you down light as a bird.

All the visitors used the lift one time or another, going up or coming down. Some of them was French, and they called the lift the "*assenser*," and good enough for them in their language, no doubt; but why the Americans, that can speak English when they choose, and are always finding out ways of doing things quicker than other folks, should waste time and breath calling a lift an elevator, I can't make out.

I was in charge of the lift from noon till midnight. By that time the theatre and dining-out folks had come in, and anyone returning late walked upstairs, for my day's work was done. One of the porters worked the lift till I come on duty in the morning; but before twelve there was nothing particular going on, and not much till after two o'clock. Then it was pretty hot work with visitors going up and down constant, and the electric bell ringing you from one floor to another like a house on fire. Then came a quiet spell while dinner was on, and I'd sit down comfortable in the lift and read my paper, only I mightn't smoke. But nobody else might neither, and I had to ask furren gentlemen to please not smoke in it, it was against the rule. I hadn't so often to tell English gentlemen, they're not like furreners that seem as if their cigars was glued to their lips.

I always noticed faces as folks got into the lift, for I've sharp sight and a good memory, and none of the visitors needed to tell me twice where to take them. I knew them and I knew their floor as well as they did themselves.

It was in November that Colonel Saxby came to the Empire Hotel. I noticed him particularly, because you could see at once that he was a soldier. He was a tall, thin man about fifty, with a hawk nose, keen eyes, and a grey moustache, and walked stiff from a gun-shot wound in the knee. But what I noticed most was the scar of a sabre-cut across the right side of the face. As he got into the lift to go to his room on the fourth floor, I thought what a difference there is among officers. Colonel Saxby put me in mind of a telegraph-post for height and thinness; and my old Colonel was like a barrel in uniform, but a brave soldier and a gentleman all the same. Colonel Saxby's room was number 210, just opposite the glass door leading to the lift, and every time I stopped on the fourth floor number 210 stared me in the face. The Colonel used to go up in the lift every day regular, though he never came down in it till — But I'm coming to that presently. Sometimes, when he was alone in the lift, he'd speak to me. He asked me in what regiment I'd served, and said he knew the officers in it. But I can't say he was comfortable to talk to. There was something stand-off about him, and he always seemed deep in his own thoughts. He never sat down in the lift.

Whether it was empty or full he stood bolt upright under the lamp, where the light fell on his pale face and scarred cheek.

One day in February I didn't take the Colonel up in the lift, and as he was regular as clockwork I noticed it, but I supposed he'd gone away for a few days, and I thought no more about it. Whenever I stopped on the fourth floor the door of 210 was shut, and as he often left it open, I made sure the Colonel was away. At the end of a week I heard a chambermaid say that Colonel Saxby was ill; so, thinks I, that's why he hasn't been in the lift lately.

It was a Tuesday night, and I'd had an uncommonly busy time of it. It was one stream of traffic up and down, and so it went on the whole evening. It was on the strike of midnight, and I was about to put out the light in the lift, lock the door, and leave the key in the office for the man in the morning, when the electric bell rang out sharp; I looked at the dial, and saw I was wanted on the fourth floor. It struck twelve as I stepped into the lift. As I passed the second and third floors, I wondered who it was that had rung so late, and thought it must be a stranger that didn't know the rule of the house. But when I stopped at the fourth floor and flung open the door of the lift, Colonel Saxby was standing there wrapped in a military cloak. The door of his room was shut behind him, for I read the number on it. I thought he was ill in his bed, and ill enough he looked, but he had his hat on, and what could a man that had been in bed ten days want with going out on a winter midnight? I don't think he saw me, but when I'd set the lift in motion, I looked at him standing under the lamp, with the shadow of his hat hiding his eyes, and the light full on the lower part of his face, that was deadly pale, the scar on his cheek showing still paler.

"Glad to see you're better, sir," said I; but he said nothing, and I didn't like to look at him again. He stood like a statue with his cloak about him, and I was downright glad when I opened the door of the lift for him to step out in the hall. I saluted as he got out, and he went past me towards the front door.

"The Colonel wants to go out," I said to the porter who stood staring, and he opened the door and Colonel Saxby walked out into the snow.

"That's a queer go!" he said.

"It is," said I. "I don't like the Colonel's looks, he doesn't seem himself at all. He's ill enough to be in his bed, and there he is gone out on a night like this."

"Anyhow he's got a famous cloak to keep him warm. I say, supposing he's gone to a fancy ball, and got that cloak on to hide his dress," said the porter, laughing uneasily, for we both felt queerer than we cared to say, and as we spoke there came a loud ring at the door-bell.

"No more passengers for me!" I said; and I was really putting the light out this time, when Joe opened the door, and two gentlemen entered that I knew at a glance were doctors. One was tall, and the other was short and stout, and they both came to the lift.

"Sorry, gentlemen, but it's against the rule for the lift to go up after, midnight."

"Nonsense!" said the stout gentleman; "it's only just past twelve, and a matter of life and death. Take us up at once to the fourth floor," and they were in the lift like a shot; so up we went, and when I opened the door, they walked straight to number 210. A nurse came out to meet them, and the stout doctor said: "No change for the worse, I hope?"

And I heard her reply: "The patient died five minutes ago, sir."

Though I'd no business to speak, that was more than I could stand. I followed the doctors to the door and said: "There's some mistake here, gentlemen, I took the Colonel down in the lift since the clock struck twelve, and he went out."

The stout doctor said sharply: "A case of mistaken identity. It was someone else you took for the Colonel."

"Begging your pardon, gentlemen, it was the Colonel himself, and the night porter that opened the front door for him knew him as well as me. He was dressed for a night like this, with his military cloak wrapped round him."

"Step in and see for yourself," said the nurse.

I followed the doctor into the room, and there lay Colonel Saxby looking just as I had seen him a few minutes before. There he lay, dead as his forefathers, and the great cloak spread over the bed to keep him warm that would feel heat and cold no more. I never slept that night. I sat up with Joe, expecting every minute to hear the Colonel ring the front door bell. Next day, every time the bell for the lift rang sharp and sudden, the sweat broke out on me and I shook again. I felt as bad as I did the first time I was in action. Me and Joe told the manager all about it, and he said we'd been dreaming; but, said he, "Mind you don't talk about it, or the house'll be empty in a week."

The Colonel's coffin was smuggled into the house the next night. Me and the manager and the undertaker's men took it up in the lift, and it lay right across it, and not an inch to spare. They carried it into number 210, and while I waited for them to come out again, a queer feeling came over me. Then the door opened softly, and four men carried out the long coffin straight across the passage, and set it down with its foot towards the door of the lift, and the manager looked round for me.

"I can't do it, sir," I said. "I can't take the Colonel down *again.* I took him down at midnight yesterday, and that was enough for me."

"Push it in," said the manager, speaking short and sharp, and they ran the coffin into the lift without a sound. The manager got in last, and before he closed the door he said, "Mole, you've worked this lift for the last time, it strikes me." And I had, for I wouldn't have stayed on at the Empire Hotel after what had happened, not if they'd doubled my wages; and me and the night porter left together.

The Picture on the Wall

Katharine Tynan

"Upon my word, Millicent" — with an impatient laugh — "there are times I could swear your heart wasn't in it; times when, for all your child-like transparency, I could almost believe there was another man somewhere to whom you had given all that ought to be mine."

"Oh, hush, hush!" answered a soft voice; "don't say such things, my darling; they are treason against our love."

"Poor little woman," said the man repentantly. "I oughtn't to have said that, for I know it is not true. But you are cold-blooded, little girl — deucedly cold-blooded. Here have I been talking about our honeymoon — our honeymoon that you seem so determined to postpone — and cheating myself by talking of it into a half-belief that it had arrived, and yet, when I look in those milky eyes of yours to see if I have put a spark of fire into them, I find only a wandering look of alarm. Is it any wonder you baffle and distress me?"

The girl lifted up the eyes he had called milky. The unusual epithet was the right one in her case. The wide, innocent-looking eyes were of a curious pale-blue, nearer the colour of spilt milk than anything else one could think of. There was a slightly scared expression about them, and the sensitive lines of the mouth, the fineness of the silky hair, the frequent movements of the slender hands, all spoke of a highly strung, nervous organisation.

"I am afraid," she said, "with me, love means fear. You are so strong and confident. While I, since I have known and loved you, I have realised with anguish the thousand and one chances that may snatch us away from each other for ever."

"The more reason for hastening our marriage. If I had your shadowy fears, Millicent — as I have not, for you are healthy, my white rose, despite your too active imagination — I should scarcely breathe till we belonged to each other. After that the deluge."

The girl trembled violently within his arms, murmuring his name half-inaudibly.

"'Geoffrey, Geoffrey,'" he repeated after her. "But what have I said to frighten you, my sweetheart? Nothing can separate us. It is only your timidity that delays our heaven. Why, Millicent, why? Do you know sometimes I could crush you to bend your will to mine? What a will, little girl, though you look so soft and yielding!"

"I will yield everything once we are married, Geoffrey."

"Yes, darling," said the man, suddenly mollified; "but when is that to be?"

"Let us forget about it, Geoffrey, for a little while. Let us be lovers. Marriage so often means the end of love, or, at least, the end of romance."

"It shall not with us, you foolish child. I promise you that, if that is all you fear."

She gave a little tired sigh as of one who gives in out of weariness.

"Poor Geoffrey," she said, stroking his cheek. "It is hard that you should be worried with my inexplicable whims. Wait a little longer patiently. When you come to Dormer Court next month I promise you that then I will fix the date — if you still desire it."

The man laughed.

"If I still desire it, sweetheart! Well, thanks for so much grace. I have had visions of your perpetual unwillingness that should land us somehow into old age unmarried."

The girl crept close to him and they were silent — the silence of lovers that means so much satisfaction. After a time they stood up and sauntered easily down the garden-path. It was September, and the late roses were out in bloom, and now and again a bird trilled sweetly, a little song very different from the full rapture of early summer.

> "The latest of late warblers sings as one
> That trolls at random when the feast is over,"

quoted Millicent Gray.

The homely red house came into sight, with its verandah, and the many garden paths diverging from it into winding walk and shrubbery. There was a lady in the verandah, comfortably seated in a rocking-chair, her eyes bent on the novel in her hand, and a pretty tea equipage drawn within reach of her. She looked up as the lovers approached.

"Dear people," she said gaily, "I am glad you have thought at last of me and the tea. I have had some difficulty in restraining Jones's impatience. Though, indeed, if I had taken my tea a quarter of an hour ago, and given you the tannin, I don't suppose you would be a whit the wiser."

She tinkled a little bell at her elbow, and in a minute or two the spruce Jones arrived with the tea-pot. Mrs. Evelyn drew herself up from her languid position and poured out the tea. She was an exceedingly pretty woman, nut-brown and with flashing white teeth, this cousin of Geoffrey Annesley, and school-friend of his betrothed.

"Well, Helen," said Annesley, "we haven't been idle. Millicent has at least named a time for naming the time for our marriage. Most men mightn't think it a tremendous concession, but I am grateful for small favours."

"She's a shy bird, Geoffrey," Mrs. Evelyn answered, getting up to kiss her friend. "So I think you have gained a concession. And Millicent is well worth waiting for. But here comes my great boy!" she cried, as the house-door was opened by a smiling nurse, and a delightful brown-faced youngster toddled on to the verandah, and ran to his mother.

"Thank you, Nurse," she said. "Now you go to your tea while I take care of Master John."

The boy trotted from his mother to Millicent, and stood by her knee, leaning his chubby arms upon her dress. Presently the two went down on the lawn for a romp — a delightful romp — with a ball and a puppy, which was accompanied by peals of laughter.

"She will make an exquisite mother someday," said Mrs. Evelyn, translating into words something of the look in the man's eyes.

He gave her a swift glance, which had a shy gratitude in it.

"I am nearly tired waiting, Helen," he said. "She is in no great hurry to give me my happiness."

"But she has promised something now?"

"She has promised to fix a date when I go down next month to their place. Have you ever been there, Helen?"

"Never. For all our staunch friendship, Millicent has always had her reserves with me. I know little about her family except that they are poor and proud."

"The father's letter to me was stiff enough. I suppose they live in a kind of feudal atmosphere in their Northumbrian woods. I might have resented the tone of it, only I feel so unworthy of my girl. After all, if the old fellow writes as if he were of the blood royal, I, Millicent's lover, should be the last to complain."

"You have the ideal temper for a lover."

"It has been sorely tried, Helen, I assure you. You women wear well through an indefinite engagement. For some incredible reason you make your heyday of it; while with us it is a time that stirs the sleeping savage in us more than any other set of circumstances in which we could be placed."

"Poor Geoffrey! But here comes your pretty lady-love. And my young savage has pulled down all the gold-silver of her hair. How delightful she looks dishevelled!"

It was indeed a charming face that looked at them as Millicent came towards them, vainly endeavouring to twist up the coil the child had pulled about her shoulders.

September passed goldenly, and the trees were in full pomp when there came in wild weather with the October new moon. The storms very soon made havoc of garden and woodland, and every day brought tidings of destruction by land and sea. It was on one of those wild days that Geoffrey Annesley and Millicent Gray left King's Cross for the long journey northwards. It was murky in the great station, and without in the yellow streets there was a fog of rain, and a sodden plashing under foot where the miserable ranks of pedestrians trudged stolidly.

The lovers were undismayed by the weather. Millicent for once seemed to have pitched care to the winds, and her eyes had a brighter light, her cheeks a rosier flush than usual.

When the train had steamed out, and they were rushing through grey sheets of water, past ghosts of warehouses, and ranges of dingy dwellings, dimly seen through the mist,

Geoffrey leant forward and took the two little hands, warm from the muff. They were alone in the compartment.

"This might be our honeymoon, little woman," he said, fondling the slim fingers.

"In this weather?" she asked.

"Yes; why not? I should have no eyes for the weather."

"Nor I," she said, softly audacious.

"No, sweet?" he cried delightedly. "So you wish for the dreaded time, after all?"

"*Wish* for it! Ah, that is a poor way of putting it."

He had not often seen her in this mood, and was enchanted.

"You are making up to me now for being so cold sometimes. You have starved me, Millicent. You women don't know what it is never to meet with an answering ardour."

"I have never felt cold even when I seemed so. I have been afraid to show you all I felt. Believe this, my dear. But today I am done with fear. No matter what comes you must believe in the fullness of my love for you."

The rain lasted all day till late evening, when the lights of a little wayside station shone blurred through the mist.

They drove to Dormer Court through a heavily wooded country. The place looked ancient, and did, indeed, date back some hundreds of years. The dining-hall was panelled with fine old oak, and the fire-places on each side massively carved. A gallery ran round it, from which corridors diverged each side to the sleeping apartments. There was a good deal of armour in shadowy corners, and on the high dresser there was a show of heavy silver plate, the sale of which might have turned the poverty of the Gray family to affluence. But Sir Roland Gray would as soon have thought of selling one of his daughters, perhaps sooner, as of reducing the heritage that had come to him by turning the slightest portion of it into hard cash.

He was a frosty old gentleman, with a haughty air which Annesley did not find reassuring. Dormer Court seemed to him a rather chilly place, and glancing at Millicent as they entered, he thought she looked suddenly nervous and depressed. Those great fireplaces would have needed roaring cressets of wood in them to make the place human, but they showed only polished brass dogs, evidently quite innocent of use — for some time, at least.

Annesley noticed these things as he passed through the hall on his way to the drawing-room, an apartment as stately as the dining-hall, and more chilly. There Millicent's sister and his hostess awaited them. She was a rather unhappy-looking woman, past her first youth, and delicate-looking.

His room, to which he followed a man-servant carrying his portmanteau, was gloomy. The bed had huge testers hung with heavy curtains; the shuttered windows were also heavily draped; the dark mahogany furniture was of the most massive build. But as soon as the servant had left the room, and Annesley had an opportunity to notice these things, he observed a portrait above the fireplace which seemed to dominate the room, and which drew his own gaze to it with a curious sense of fascination.

The portrait was that of a handsome man, dressed according to the period of the second Charles. His skin had the peculiarly warm ruddy tinge we associate with Vandyck's portraits, and out of this setting his eyes looked startlingly blue. His love-locks straying over a steel corselet were golden brown, and altogether he looked a most gallant cavalier. But the painting of the eyes was the painter's great achievement. As Annesley stood looking at the picture with a candle lighted the better to see it, he could have sworn the eyes looked back at him like those of a living man. He turned to the dressing-table with a half-uneasy laugh at his own delusion. He had laughed out unconsciously, and as he did so he thought the laugh was faintly echoed within the room. He looked around him sharply. No, the room looked harmless enough, and it was not likely to be anything but imagination. Yet the eyes of the portrait seemed to gaze towards him, and he fancied now that they had a saturnine gleam in them.

"Nerves, my friend," he muttered to himself. "This is a new development. You'll be looking under the bed and prodding the window-curtains for burglars next, like any hysterical woman."

But he could not shake off the sense of being watched. He made a resolution not to yield to his folly by looking at the portrait, but as he went to and fro he felt assured that the eyes were following him.

"Confound you, Sir," he said at last, half jocosely, "I wish you'd keep your eyes out of my back."

He could have sworn again that he heard the faint, malicious laugh.

"Well," he said as he finished his toilet, "if Dormer Court possesses such a thing as a haunted room, I'm in it. It would make a nice little case for the Psychical Society."

At dinner the conversation somewhat flagged. Annesley did his best valiantly to keep it going, but reflected within himself that certainly Dormer Court was not cheerful. Millicent had become very quiet since she entered her home, and Sir Roland, though he treated his guest with very punctilious courtesy, had apparently little to say; the elder Miss Gray scarcely spoke, and once when Annesley addressed her directly, started violently.

"Poor little Millicent!" said the lover to himself. "No wonder she is a little strange sometimes. She will be different in a happier atmosphere."

Presently, in the search for a subject of conversation, he remembered the portrait.

"That is a very fine portrait over the fireplace in my bed-room. A genuine Vandyck, is it not, Sir Roland?"

The baronet bent his frosty brows upon him.

"It is not a Vandyck," he said coldly.

Millicent had turned quite pale when the picture was mentioned. She now leant forward, and said in a shocked voice—

"You have not put him in *that* room, father?"

"Why not?" said the old man sharply. "Guests of honour have slept in that room many a time."

The girl sank back in her seat very pale. Annesley had no opportunity later of asking the meaning of this odd little scene. He guessed, indeed, that the room had some ill name, but was not perturbed. The man in the portrait was a decent looking fellow, he thought, and if he chose to walk, why, one might have worse company. He was not at all likely to be afraid of a ghost; indeed, to see one was an experience he rather coveted, for he had had most other adventures that can fall to a civilised man.

The evening was no improvement on the dinner. Millicent sat silent and scared-looking. Her sister played melancholy music at the grand piano, and Sir Roland, having detained the young man inordinately long in the dining-room, discussing some dry aspect of politics which happened to interest him, continued the discussion till ten o'clock, at which hour everyone was expected to retire. By ten o'clock Annesley was indeed in rather a bad temper. He didn't like his future father-in-law, with his bushy eyebrows, his pursed, opinionated mouth, and his light eyes, with their suggestion of evil temper.

"Once I carry off my girl," he said to himself, "'tis precious little Dormer Court will see of us."

He had nothing but a handshake of her at parting for the night. Into that, however, he managed to infuse as much loving reassurance as he could under her father's discouraging glance. When he went up to his room he again examined the portrait. The life-likeness of the eyes was so pronounced that he reached up to feel the painted canvas, and so make sure. He was reminded of a story he had once read, in which someone had been spied upon by living eyes gazing through the holes where the painted eyes of the portrait had been.

"Only harmless canvas!" he said to himself; "but the painter of those eyes, if he wasn't Vandyck, must have had an uncanny sort of genius of his own."

He determined to look no more at the portrait, but blew out his candle and jumped into bed. He was soon sleeping soundly, in spite of the rain that beat against the windows, and the blast that howled in the chimney.

He could not have told how long he had slept when he was awakened by a cold breath on his forehead. He opened his eyes in thick darkness, and thrust out his hands; they met only the air, though that struck strangely chill. Then from the dark into which he gazed a face shaped itself, an evil face, swollen, distorted, malignant; the eyes, with a red gleam in them, looked furiously into his. Annesley was a brave man, but the hair of his head stood up, and the sweat came in drops on his forehead. He pushed both hands against the face, and felt nothing, but it seemed to recede a little into the darkness. Then, still watching it, he felt for the box of matches which had stood beside his bed. He scarcely knew how he was able to see the face, because he felt the darkness of the room to be intense; the light seemed to come in some strange way from the apparition itself, and to illumine only that.

He struck a match sharply, and the flame sputtered a little, and then stood up steadily. The face was gone now. He jumped out of bed, and lit the candles on his dressing-table. Then he peered about him into the dark corners. There was nothing. He opened the great wardrobe, looked behind curtains, lifted the valance of the bed. There was nothing anywhere. He sat down on the side of his bed and wiped his face.

"By Jove!" he said; "that was a nasty experience!"

He lifted his eyes to the portrait. The eyes were still watching him, and he had the delusion that their expression had changed. They looked like the eyes of an enemy. The eyes of the apparition — he shuddered recalling them — had the expression of a tiger before he springs. Annesley felt with a sick horror that another minute of darkness, and the creature would have grappled with him.

He was struck now by a certain likeness between the eyes of the portrait and those tiger-eyes. And the face — yes, there had been a shadowy likeness. If the handsome face there on the wall had been battered, bruised, beaten out of human likeness, it might be something like that face in the dark.

Annesley looked at his watch: one o'clock. The room was very cold, and smelt damp. He was determined not to lie down again in the canopied bed, where he had seemed so horribly at the mercy of the evil thing. He looked around for materials to make a fire. There were none. A fire would have been companionable in his vigil. He looked at his two candles. They were tall and solid, and would last till daylight. He wished he had had a book to keep him company, for he was determined not to sleep again; but the most diligent search in the room brought him nothing, and he remembered, with an impatient exclamation, that he had left his big parcel of newspapers in the hall as he entered.

He dressed himself fully, and then threw himself in an arm-chair to get through the hours as best he could. He had deliberately turned the chair so that he should not see the portrait. How he wished for some companionship in his dreary vigil; if only he had Jim, his bull-dog, whom he had left forlorn behind him in London! He gazed at the candles steadily while the slow minutes passed. When he thought half an hour had gone he looked at his watch. It was only ten minutes past one. If he had been more at home in the house he would have left that unpleasant room, and betaken himself anywhere, out in the storm even. But he had the English dislike of doing anything out of the ordinary, and when he contemplated an escape from the house he imagined a midnight alarm, and all the consequent rumpus.

He must have dozed in his chair, for he awoke in a cold sweat suddenly, with that clammy breath lifting the hair on his forehead, and an ice-cold hand on his throat. When he sprang into wakefulness the hand slowly relaxed its grasp. There was nothing to be seen, except that the candles were guttering in the wind from the chimney.

He flung back the window shutters and opened the windows. He thought now of the room as of a grave. The fresh air rushing in seemed to steady him. His heart was beating fast, and he could not rid himself of a conviction that those fingers had meant to strangle him. The rest of the night and during the grey dawn he walked up and down his room.

The morning brought relief, and also anger. He was in no state of mind to unravel the things that had happened to him, but he was furious at the house and the people. That old devil, as he mentally called Sir Roland, must have known what guests that infernal room of his harboured, and yet had put him there to sleep. And Millicent — she had let him sleep there.

His anger became cold, but none the less steady, at the thought of her.

But the bitter things he could have said in his first brief anger froze on his lips when they met. He was early in the breakfast-room, and had packed his portmanteau for his departure before coming downstairs. But she was waiting for him. A great rush of pity flowed into his heart as he saw her. She looked so pale, so forlorn, so utterly hopeless and wretched. And he had been thinking of her as sleeping well!

He went towards her with a half-articulate expression of tenderness.

"No," she said, waving him back, "not now. Come this way, we shall be disturbed here, and I must speak to you."

She led the way to a little room that opened off the hall.

"This is my own room, where no one comes unless I ask them," she said. "We are safe here. Now tell me, my dear, how did the night go?"

Her voice was full of tenderness, but it was a tenderness that repelled rather than attracted. He felt that she wanted no lover-like demonstrations, and that the few feet of space between them might have been as wide as the sea, so effectually did she seem to set him apart.

"You know," he said awkwardly, by way of answer, "I did not sleep well."

"You saw *it*?" she asked, her eyes dilating.

"I certainly fancied I saw something very unpleasant."

"Don't try to describe it," she said. "Go back to the room. Lift the picture over the fireplace and look at the reverse side. Then come back here and tell me if that is what you saw."

He obeyed dumbly. The portrait was a heavy one to lift, but his arms were strong, and he swung it around on its cord. When it turned into the light he almost cried out. On the back of the portrait was painted the face he had seen in the night.

He hurried from the room with a shudder. He felt that he never wanted to enter it again, and his repugnance to the house was so strong that he could hardly breathe within its four walls. He returned to where he had left her.

"Well?" she said.

"I don't know what devilry is at the root of it, but the face on the back of the portrait is the face that came to me in the night."

For a minute she hid her eyes. Then she spoke in a voice which pain had made apathetic.

"It is the end of our love."

He would have uttered a fierce protest, but she silenced him with a commanding gesture.

"It is the end, and nothing you can ever say or do will make it otherwise. The man on the wall, whose evil spirit still haunts that room, was an ancestor — Sir Anthony Gray. He was a bad man, and after a wicked life he died raving mad. Whether the second portrait of him in his madness was painted cynically or seriously, none of us know. Its existence is only known to ourselves. Unhappily, Sir Anthony left us his madness. Now and then it skips a generation; my father escaped, but our only brother is a dangerous madman, and at any time the curse may seize upon Alison or me. I was wicked when I thought I could marry you and keep this from you, but not wicked enough to do it with a light heart. You will someday be grateful for the night of terror that saved you from a worse thing. I shall never marry now, and I only hope that you will be able to forgive me, because I loved you and was sorely tempted."

"I will not give you up," said the man with an oath.

"You will," she said sadly. "You will be sad for a little while, but presently you will realise what an escape you have had, and be glad."

"Millicent, Millicent, are you in earnest? Am I really to go away out of your life, and you out of mine?"

There was despair in his cry, but there was also acquiescence, and she caught the sound. She looked at his imploring face with a maternal pity.

"It must be, my dear," she said.

"I will wait for you," he cried. "I shall never marry, and I shall always be ready to come to you. Oh, Millicent, Millicent, is there no help?"

But even as he said it he knew there was none. The reeling shock of the thing, coming upon him after his night of terror, had scarcely left him the power of thinking clearly, but somewhere at the back of his mind he was conscious that what she had told him was irrevocable. However his wounded passion cried out for her, he felt that her most unhappy doom had set her as far beyond man's love as though she were already dead.

"Good-bye," she said mournfully; but she did not offer to kiss him or to touch his hand. "The carriage will be round for you presently, and you will wait here till it comes. I shall explain to my father, for you will not care to see him."

She left him standing there, dumb, and glided like a ghost from the room. A few minutes later the servant brought him his coffee on a tray, with a message that the carriage was ready. He drank the coffee half-consciously, thinking to himself that she had not been so lost in her bitter trouble as to forget his material wants. Millicent had always been kind; he remembered that her kindness was one of the qualities he had loved in her.

A minute later the carriage had swept him into the depths of the forest. Millicent Gray, unseen herself, watched it depart, and noticed that his head was bowed and his shoulders drooped. It was her last sight of him. As the forest took him she turned away to accept the burden of her lonely life, and the terrible possibilities it held.

The Woodley Lane Ghost

Madeleine Vinton Dahlgren

It was the afternoon of the longest day of the year, the 21ˢᵗ of June, and jogging along over the splendid sweep of Massachusetts Avenue, whose picturesque homes are grouped around the statues of historic men, past Thomas Circle, past Scott Circle, reaching Dupont Circle, then by way of Connecticut Avenue and over the city boundary line, Dr. Rawle's buggy finally turned into that lovely stretch of circling drive called Woodley Lane. The doctor was a young man, a newly-married man, just starting into a meagre practice, and quite disposed, while waiting for more patients, to take life as easily as very limited means would permit. His comely, girlish wife was seated at his side, an embroidered linen lap-robe deftly tucked around her. Such is the inconsequence of youth that these two were as happy, perhaps more so, than another two who whirled past them in a grand equipage. In fact, the foolish doctor was even as content as if he were plodding around town with his hired boy visiting patients and coining dollars.

"Ah, my Cynthia," said he, "what an Eden Washington would be were it not so detestably healthy. Why, my sweet moon-flower (a pet name of his, in allusion to hers of Cynthia), with more money, you, too, would bloom forth in a stylish victoria."

"Pray, dear Rufus," she laughed, cheerily, "don't wish it, for in such case *you* would not be my driver."

"Wise words fallen from fragrant lips," was the approving answer. Strange how all men, lover and husband alike, are magnetized by the electric stroke of flattery!

At this moment, turning a sharp corner of the winding road, they perceived an oldish man coming toward them with slow and feeble step. Although his scanty locks were white, he gave the impression of one rather bending under the weight of a settled sadness than as if oppressed by years. Notwithstanding his stooping gait, it was evident that he was tall of stature, and his bearing was that of a man concentered upon himself, forced back into a brooding introspection by the strong pressure of a stormy past. As thus he tottered on, with eyes fixed upon the ground, all unobservant, a flashing wheel of glittering steel, noiseless and swift, hurtled past them. There was, as one might hold their breath, a forceful clash, a sudden outcry, a horror-stricken scream from Cynthia, and the doctor with a quick spring stood beside two fallen men. The reckless bicyclist had struck the ground with such jarring whirl as partially to stun him, but the old man who had been thus ruthlessly run over, lay limp, moaning and helpless.

"I trust that you are not much hurt, sir," said the doctor, stooping over him, as with careful precision he made an examination. "Oh, yes, here it is; a compound fracture of the hip, and, it is to be feared, internal injuries."

Meantime, Cynthia ran to the little brook nearby, and filling her straw hat with water, poured it over the head of the youthful wheelman, who, reviving, did not pause to thank her, but, picking himself up, as best he could, remounted his wheel and was off; doubtless fearing arrest, should he remain and assist.

"An imp of Satan," groaned the wounded. "By the Highest One, the Spirit of Bad has prevailed."

The doctor looked significantly at his wife, as much as to say, "Poor man, his mind wanders."

"Can you tell me where to take you, sir?" inquired the doctor, in a compassionate voice. "We will lift you as gently as possible into my buggy, and not leave you. Have courage."

"Courage," gasped the old man, "comes of force of will. It is a subtle essence, it penetrates and overcomes, I WILL, to endure — I will point the way."

Cynthia helped her husband, and together they succeeded in placing the unfortunate, leaning against and supported by her, in the buggy, the doctor leading the horse very slowly. The transfer, the motion, were torture to the hurt man, whose pallid brow was bathed with great beaded drops, such was his agony.

"By Siva!" muttered he, grinding his teeth, "my cycle is closing."

Cynthia shivered, but she firmly upheld the sufferer amid all his delirious ravings. Yet, incoherent as were his utterances, he retained sufficient consciousness to point out the way exactly.

By his direction they had turned off from Woodley Lane into the Tenleytown road, when presently he called out: "Turn in there," and they entered unkempt grounds through a shackly gate. With what a masterful command over himself, tortured and almost swooning as he was, had he guided their progress. The doctor, who had had a season of training in the hospital wards, understood the force of will this man had exerted, saying, as if to himself: "Most men would lie in the stupor of a dead swoon who had borne this nervous shock and endured his awful pain. This is no common man." They were now slowly ascending a hill by a narrow, serpentine and undulating road. The season, as we have said, was leafy June, and these grounds, neglected as they were, gloried in the majestic growth of a magnificent oak forest. So entirely was the house hidden by their dark and towering branches that one came upon it as a surprise, so unexpectedly, and yet it was a substantial, well-built brick house, of ample proportions. There was no attempt at architectural lines, except, perhaps, in a square tower that was projected from the center of the house, forming a hall of entrance below, and a small room, as if of observation, above. Otherwise, the structure was a plain red-brick dwelling of two spacious rooms, one on each side of a wide hall below, and on the second floor were precisely corresponding rooms, with the addition of the tower apartment. Directly in front of the building was a knoll of horseshoe shape crowned by an immense red Virginia oak. It stood a very sentinel tree, shooting a skyward shaft some seventy feet, its finely-veined oblong leaves of a vivid green, framed in and screened the house in umbrageous beauty. As they passed under its protecting boughs, the hurt man, who seemed to have grown very faint during the hard jolting of the winding ascent, instantly revived, as if through some mysterious accession of strength, and uplifting an ardent gaze of yearning tenderness, he extended wide his arms, upraising them as if to embrace the sighing leaves that bent over him. "I come, I come!" he almost shouted with a fierce eagerness; then, as if his very soul had gone forth in the supreme effort, he sank back in a dead swoon of pain.

There was not a soul to greet them. No, not even yelping cur, or mewing cat, or singing bird. This strange man, then, lived alone, yes, literally all alone. The doctor entered the unlocked door, and ascending to the tower room brought forth a small mattress, upon which he laid the now insensible form. As the doctor's fair young wife zealously helped him, he said to her caressingly, "My Cynthia, how good and brave you are." The momentary glance he had given the tower room amazed him. It was evident, as he had said, that his patient was no common man. Here was the den of a natural philosopher, a chemist, an astronomer, in fact, of a wide student of nature. This was his laboratory, his workshop. Here, undoubtedly, he performed various experiments with scientific precision, and through his well-planted telescope that pierced a small opening adjusted to its use, the heavens were nightly read. And what, at that time, was of vital consequence, was the existence of a carefully labeled pharmacy, evidently supplementing extensive investigations in chemistry.

"It is wonderful, simply wonderful!" said the doctor. "Here are all appliances needed for treatment. Have you rubbed Aladdin's lamp and sent a geni hither, my moon-flower?" queried he.

"'Tis the Pitris," murmured the patient. They both started. He must have heard and measured the doctor's words in his seeming syncope. Meantime Dr. Rawle made strenuous and successful efforts to revive his patient, preparatory to the more serious operation that he knew must be attempted. It was not long before the old man spoke again.

"Do not torture me," he said; "all surgery is useless. I shall soon be dissolved. My work in this transition is at an end. All that now remains is to disintegrate the earth-bound ties. Leave me — go quickly, and bring hither one learned in the law. But hearken. No jugglery, no priestcraft. Do as you are bid. Now hasten."

The doctor looked inquiringly at his wife. "Do you dare to stay, Cynthia, until I come back?" asked he.

"I dare," said the brave little woman, "but hasten, Rufus, for the night closes in." Her words were calmly spoken, but her heart beat violently

"Daughter of Eve," said the sick man, looking kindly upon her, "you do well — stay!"

Some two hours later — it seemed an endless age to Cynthia, as she watched in profound silence, amid the gathering gloom — her husband returned, bringing with him his friend, Mr. Albright, a well-known Washington lawyer. Already the face of the dying man had taken on that ashen hue that precedes approaching dissolution, and the mildew of death had gathered on his humid brow. But now, as if collecting himself for a last effort, his faculties were clear.

"You are two men, and strong," said he, "lift me to my Edris. Be quick!" and he pointed his gaunt finger upward.

They carried him gently on the mattress and laid it upon the narrow couch in the tower room. The motion, slight as it was, was exhaustive of a fast ebbing life. He pointed to a shelf whispering as he did so, "The nameless amphora," adding, as it was touched, "Open!" The doctor silently obeyed, and the delicious perfume of some aromatic volatile essence filled the air. All felt the subtle and penetrating effect of this exhilarating aroma.

"Write! write!" cried the dying man with a momentary force.

The lawyer wrote as dictated —

"I, the Java Aleim, being of sound disposing mind, do hereby devise, give, and bequeath all that I possess, both of real estate and personal, to —," he paused and looked impatiently at the doctor — "Quick your name!"

"My name?" muttered the dazed doctor, "my name?"

The lawyer smiled and wrote "to Rufus Rawle, of the city of Washington, D. C."

"We must have three signatures to this will," said the lawyer.

The Java Aleim listened intently for a moment, or rather shrank within himself by some inward act of volition, then gasped —

"Two men approach! I hear the footsteps of the Silent Brothers! Hasten to meet them!"

Five minutes later and the doctor, who had left the room in a bewildered way, returned with two men, whom he had met at the gate. They glanced at the Java Aleim, who became so agitated that he drew his breath convulsively; but speedily controlling himself, he took the pen and signed his name. Then the lawyer and the two men appended their signatures, when, without comment, the two latter disappeared. Were these sentient, living forms, or were they merely the astral souls of 'Silent Brothers', evoked by one of their number to serve his purpose? Or was it a dream, a mere figment of the imagination? Verily, there were the names, fairly written in good black ink of the "Idra Rabba" and "Adam Ferio."

The Brahman, for such he was, wearily joined his thin hands above his head, then marking his forehead with the sign sacred to Vishnu, his lips moved as if in prayer. The moribund, fixed and rigid as one in a trance, now spoke rapidly and continuously in a hoarse, cavernous whisper that seemed to issue from his body as from a half-closed vault.

"My soul escapes, oh, Triad! The expiatory hour is at hand. My life has failed in abnegation and the taint of selfishness must be expurged. Gross emanations have passed like a murky cloud over the spirit, shutting out Nirvana. I must traverse eons of cyclic arcs ere I can once again reach the ascending cosmic scale. Oh, woe is me! I must be absorbed in the universal whole!"

He paused and seemed to listen, then seizing the triple cord that girded his loins, the invocations were renewed.

"O, Brahma! O, Vishnu! O, Siva! Triad of Triads! Help my return to nature — when this aching clod, this husk of the outer shell shall be evolved and absorbed into the heart and essence of yon far-spreading oak, when my clogged veins shall run along its deep-reaching roots in rivulets of fire, when with heavy lateral pressure, my pent-up thoughts shall scintillate and strike deep the flinty rocks, taking wide and wider range, pressing down into the bowels of Mother Earth; then, with fierce upspringing power, remount in juicy sap, flushing with incarnadine splendor its autumn leaves, or dropping its purifying tears that fill the sacred viscum's pearly coronals; then, partially released, forming true essence of Virgil's golden bough, I shall arise a fluidic spectre of transcendent brightness, permeate the opalescent moonlit rays — a glorious astral shape! Ugh! The way is blinding dark — oh, this confusing present — but the end is luminous — I know it — I feel it!" Partially arousing himself, he fixed his burning eyes upon the three.

322

"Mystic Triad — children groping in the outer darkness, heed — this, my last injunction — failing which, beware! Bury with me the seven knotted bamboo rod, the Gurugave — rest my bones, that they may mingle with the roots of the cabalistic oak that shoots its sacred shaft aloft within the triple circle of the horse shoe knoll. Thus shall my essence be infused in it, and the virtue from out the oak be effused to me, and thus I shall be transformed into a dual life. But beware!" and his face grew livid and distorted, "violate not this sacred tree, touch it not, handle it not! Let the holy lustration that shall proceed as we two become one in cosmic scale continue undisturbed." His bony finger, still fixed and rigid like a note of warning, amid convulsive shudderings terrible to behold, with one long outcry of *A. U. M.*, he gave up the ghost.

Silence and darkness intervened, only broken now and then by the nervous, spasmodic sobs of Cynthia.

"Poor wife," said the doctor; "the strain was awful."

The Java Aliem was buried as he had requested. Did the process of a metempsychosis then and there commence!

Dr. Rawle found himself suddenly a rich man. No need now of troubling himself about the health of Washington. With a pleasant home, that commanded a splendid view, with a goodly store of bonds, securities, and rare coins and curios; and for his wife, gold chains of fine filigree work, filmy taffeties embroidered in silver; tortoise shell combs set with plates of gold, and girdles enriched with pearls, sapphires and diamonds; rings and necklaces of ruby, blue topaz, yellow tourmalines, blood stones, cat's eyes, and amethyst; *etuis* of aquamarine and cinnamon stone, and of various devices to charm a woman's eye. The doctor loved books, and was an enthusiast in his profession. There were various works in chemistry and medical books, but others not a few, filled with hieroglyphics and strangely illuminated, besides rolls of palimpsests covered with secret Arabic symbols bearing evidence of successive ages, and one, most precious of all, steeped in a musky, dankish odor, inscribed in Candian sanscrit and bound in thick, lacquered ivory boards, encrusted with gems, framing the enigmatic abraxas. Happily for the doctor, he was a matter-of-fact man, or he surely would have sworn by the Vedas, yielded to the fascination of his surroundings, and become a Buddhist. As it was he only sighed and said: "What a pity that I am not an Oriental scholar!" But already he was to a degree imbued with the influences pressing upon him, smoking a superb chibouk with amber mouthpiece the while, lazily immersed in vague speculations and day-dreams.

Now and then his friend the lawyer came to see him, drawn by curiosity he could not resist to revisit a spot of such weird memories. But Dr. Rawle never left this idlewild of Woodley Lane, nor, strange to say, did Cynthia wish for change. Was the spirit of the old seer and Brahman permeating the atmosphere with an oriental repose at the very outset of their occupancy? Some energy had been displayed in transforming the house into a more cheerful home, and in building a verandah over the front door, whence the superb view could be more fully enjoyed. They had found the two lower rooms unfurnished, and the one nearest the mystic oak-tree was fitted up as a kitchen, while the room across the hall was pleasantly adorned as a drawing-room and dining-room as well. Here Cynthia, presided, spending happy, quiet hours, quite content, as she imagined, and yet not knowing why or wherefore, subdued and gradually toned into a half-drooping melancholy.

"How can gladness and sadness be one, dear Rufus?" asked she puzzled to understand herself.

"'Tis the spirit of the place, pale moon-flower," he answered, smiling, yet sighing.

It was strange, but various little mishaps, too trifling to notice, attended the building of that part of the verandah nearest the horseshoe knoll. If so much as a chip fell upon that spot it rebounded, inflicting some hurt, and the mechanic, not knowing why, declared it an unlucky thing to work on that side.

There came to be a tacit understanding between the doctor and his wife to avoid all allusion to that deathbed scene, and after the verandah was finished it began to be unpleasant to sit upon it on a moonlight night, and even the sun's rays glinted with a sickly glare through the umbrageous screen. At all times there was never a surcease of low, humming, busy sound, a shadowy play of leaves, and when the droning summer faded into autumn, and the coruscant foliage threw out vivid flashes of light, the blood-red veins became swelled and tinged, tracing mystic imagery against the blue of Heaven, and the grand old tree communed with nature, rustling with a sad susurrus.

"Passing strange," softly said the doctor.

"Uncanny," whispered Cynthia.

The first positive discomfort was experienced when, one evening in the early winter, the two Irish domestics, a man and woman servant, were seated in the kitchen at dusk, their hands folded at the close of a day's work, and they resting in that inert way that marks the repose succeeding manual labor. The open-mouthed fireplace was all aglow with the hot coals of oak-wood cinders, when, almost imperceptibly at first, the burning mass became astir. Presently odd and fierce flashes leaped forth from out the incandescent heat, accompanied by the constant popping of exploding fragments, when, as if gaining a rapid aggressive force, a lurid light appeared, out of which sprang forth an impalpable shape that advanced into the room. Scream after scream called Dr. Rawle and his wife to the scene just as the woman fainted, and the man rushing out, hatless and distracted, never stopped until he reached Swampoodle, crossing himself under the shadow of the Jesuit church in Washington, vociferating all the way, "Spooks! spooks!" Nor would the woman stay one hour after she was revived, declaring that "a say of howly wather" was not enough "to clane that fiery divil out." "It must have been the knotted heart of oak that split and frightened those fools out of their shallow wits," cried the doctor, much irritated. "Oh, no, Rufus," said Cynthia, mildly, "It was a dead bough that fell from *the* oak. Katy told me that she picked it up from off the knoll where it had fallen, and tripped with it in her arms, nearly tumbling into the fire as she threw it on, and then it burned savagely into that dreadful mass of coals."

"Old women's tales, forsooth," muttered the doctor. But be that as it may, after this incident, with that freemasonry of signals that exists among the Ishmallites, it was understood that the house was haunted, and no one would hire out to live at that place. This event also seemed to mark a distinct epoch, as if that baptism of fire had liberated an astral soul. Henceforth there was a shadowy shade, an indefinable *something* in that room that took possession. So the door was closed and the doctor took the key thereof.

"D—n it," said he, "what's the use of a kitchen, Cynthia, if there's no cook?"

"Don't swear, Rufus," she shudderingly answered. "I love to cook, dear. With our little oil-stove in the drawing-room it's like playing at housekeeping. Yes, positively, I prefer it, dear. Then, it is so nice for us to be alone; just we two."

"Moon-flower, how sweetly you expand!" cried the doctor, enfolding her in his arms and kissing her.

If a wife wishes to make her husband a radiant lover let her try cooking for him; that is, if she knows how!

And thus the winter closed in upon these two, who lived in the old house without other occupants. Dr. Rawle soon became so deeply interested in the occult investigations into which he was led through the books left him by the Java Aleim that he did not feel the weariness of their solitary life; but it was not so with his wife. She, poor lady, had entered that strange house a gay and laughing bride, in good health and fine spirits. It was not long before she moved about silently, growing each day paler and paler, like some tender plant that requires sunshine and wilts in cheerless shade. She was not unhappy, because she led a life apart from the world, with her husband, for she loved him too fondly to pine for other society, still less did she care for the dissipation of gayety. But her nervous system had received a serious shock. The terrifying accident and harrowing death-bed scene, succeeded by the horror of that spectral fire, phantasmal as it undoubtedly was, had left an impression, not to be shaken off, that the place was haunted. She would constantly repeat to herself that it was a mere hallucination, and yet the feeling wore upon her, and she became exceedingly sensitive to all sounds. A vague distrust and fear took possession of her. Upon the eminence where they lived the winter storms oft and again held wildest revelry. To her morbid imagination the rude blasts had human voices that sighed, moaned, groaned, wailed, howled and shrieked, and during the blackness of the long winter nights all these voices of nature were a thousand-fold intensified to her acute perceptions. Oh, how she dreaded the prolonged swirl of the tempest, with its tumultuous onset, the swift-recurring waves of direful sound of these viewless legions of the air, when her timid soul shrank shrivelled and aghast within its shell. During that dismal winter they slept in the chamber directly above the now-closed room, which she felt sure had a nightly occupant. One thing Cynthia became aware of. Only *her* ears were opened to these preternatural sounds. She had, it is true, an increasing consciousness that they might be evoked at any time; but she never heard, or thought she heard, the plaintive sighs, the stealthy tread, nor the slamming of a door she knew was closed, or even, oh, hideous feeling, that she was being breathed upon, unless she was alone, or her husband's spirit locked in sleep. The something, whatever it was, that had access to that house, had not the force to impress itself upon the stronger organization of the doctor. At moments she became overwhelmed with a creeping fear, that if she slept, when her willpower was dormant would it not then oppress her, and could not the ghoul live from her life and gloat upon her vitality? All that she had read about the ravening vampire would then recur to her disturbed fancy and afright her. And thus, month after month, poor Cynthia, half distraught, communed within herself. At first, whenever she would strive to express her impressions, they were brusquely repelled by her husband as silly dreams, and he thus quite unwittingly condemned this woman, whom he loved, to untold torture.

But at last the dreary winter passed away, and the budding of spring cast a more cheerful atmosphere upon the gloomy spot. Then the doctor aroused himself somewhat from the long hibernation over the books from which he had derived sustenance. Opening his eyes to things around him, he began to notice how wan and thin his wife was. All the while his love had never abated, but in the strange existence he had led, absorbing thoughts had occupied him. Had he been dreaming? He was vexed with himself. He feared, indeed, he felt sure, that he must have neglected his darling while leading this visionary life. Like one who returns from a foreign land, where, deeply interested in the new scenes around him, he, for the moment, forgets loved ones at home, yet rekindles his devotion on his return, so it was with this student of the occult. Once awakened, he again recognizes all that had made a part of his former life, and he was uneasy about his wife. "My pale moon-flower!" he would say tenderly, and Cynthia was revived by this delicate attention, finding relief in tears. Oh, if man could only understand how inexpressibly it comforts the heart of a woman to cry! Tears, consoling tears, are the one special, delicious, feminine luxury. They fertilize and revivify the arid wastes of a woman's heart. The affectionate care the doctor now bestowed upon his wife was quite oppressive, for he was always thinking what healing influences would be most beneficial. He besought her to live more in the open air, but such was her morbid dread of passing the tree that she would actually stay indoors from the dread of going out. Then he began to think seriously of leaving the place, and reproached himself anew for past obliviousness.

"Better far," thought he, "to go back to the city. I have been a fool indeed to burrow in the old wizard's den, immersed in the mystical so-called black arts that occupied him, while the very essence of a being dearer than my own life was fading away. A thousand times rather be the poor man, the struggling young practitioner of a year ago." With a sigh of regret he pictured to himself the joyousness, the lightheartedness of that time, and in the retrospect, the past months, during nearly a year, seemed to be in dismal shadow, in unwholesome dreariness, as compared with the sunshine and bright cheeriness of the healthful effort then made. It's strange that young people never can realize what a bracing, wholesome life those lead who begin with merely a competence, and how much pleasure is involved in the eagerness of pursuit, stimulated by hopes elate of the future. In youth uncertainty lends a zest to the present, and makes a constant incentive for action. All the little daily plans that grow out of such situations form, as it were, a series of plots and counterplots of a drama, where no one can foresee the ending. "I worried then," sadly mused the doctor, "because we were poor; I know now that we were very happy."

Thus the summer days succeeded each other, finding Cynthia more and more prostrated, and her husband more and more irresolute. Was it the enervating atmosphere in which they lived? The omened old oak, had the brunt bravely borne, of the wild, wintry winds, fiercely flinging its bared, brawny arms aloft, as one bereft and bestraught; or, sullenly standing aloof, besprent of the vested beauty of its foliage, an image of statuesque despair. But with the renaissant spring came the mystery of its revivification, when coursing through all its gaunt length of frame mounted the renewing vital sap. Then the sere, crackling branches put on a semblance of youth, and innumerous tiny leaflets that burgeoned from out its frowning wrinkles thrilled with the joy of new-born living, until the hot embrace of June completed its glorious expansion, and the dull splendor of its resurgence. Oh, touching symbols of the mysteries of life and death that nature ever and ever exhibits! Oh, dullard eyes that scan so illy the clear mirror ever held forth to view! Yes, a perpetual pageant is unfolded of birth, growth, maturity, decay, decline to dissolution, out of which the endless circling cycles bring forth fruition. But in the midst of this great joy of living, drinking in this wine of life, so freely offered, we grow riotous of language, and forget to face our facts solemnly.

To recall a coincidence of time, it will be remembered that the tragic opening of this story occurred on the 21st day of June. As this anniversary drew near, Cynthia became really ill. She was in an unceasing state of agitation, so that the doctor grew seriously alarmed. It was the eve of that day that Cynthia, weak and prostrated, retired early. The isolated place was, as usual, very still, and the doctor, wearied with apprehension, also retired and was soon soundly sleeping. Not so with Cynthia. Insomnia had become a dreaded condition, and she solaced her waking hours wistfully looking at the handsome face of her sleeping spouse, upon which, even in sleep, a certain sadness rested under the closed lips and expressed itself in the drooping lines around the mouth. Then it occurred to her that if she gazed upon him when his will-power was relaxed, it might infuse some mesmeric state not well for him, so she silently arose, and impelled by a vague desire she could not resist, gently opened her window and leaned forward. The young moon, with clear and beaming crescent, lazily drifted on a bed of lightest amber cloudlets, diffusing that faint, mysterious light so grateful to her questioning soul. Before her stood the mystic oak, now so very near, in its far-spreading branches of vivid green, that were softened and exquisitely tinted by the opalescent rays that shone upon it, so that its splendid noon-tide beauty was etherealized.

"Oh, translucent image," sighed Cynthia, "art thou in very truth, as the Druids would have thee, a sacred form to worship — or" — and as she paused in her unconscious invocation, as if responsive to her call, and effused from out the deep-planted roots of the tree, a mild radiance played with swaying motion, to and fro, over the horse-shoe knoll. At one moment swinging slowly, hovering with a phosphorescent glow, rising a little, then sinking again as if about to die out, but all the while steadily gaining force to remount higher.

Eagerly bending toward the witching glimmer, stretching forth her hand in supplication, she adjured the aura, "Oh, elemental, arise; disengage thyself from these painful, earth-bound ties!"

She had scarcely spoken when, as if awaiting the summons to arise, and by it permeated with a force it had hitherto vainly sought, it suddenly streamed upward with a clear and steady flame until it touched the lower sweep of the oak tree branches when, forming instantaneously into definite shape, the aural soul of Java Aleim stood before her.

As Cynthia uttered an agonized cry it extended toward her a skeleton arm, with gestures of pleading entreaty; then slowly sinking downward, as if repelled by want of attractive power, and casting upon her a lowering look of fierce hatred, it disappeared just as the doctor was aroused by the shriek of his wife. In another moment he bore, with tenderest care, her fainting form back to bed. He had not seen the vision, but he knew what it all meant.

"This, this is too dreadful!" he cried, in a transport of rage. "The old demon gave me a true devil's gift, fair to the seeming, illusory in the holding, and fatal in reality. Tomorrow, the anniversary of this cursed existence here, shall witness my return to the busy scenes of the outer world. I shall have done with this infernal nonsense. I shall end it all."

"Shall end it all!" slowly re-echoed a phantom voice. Unnerved and horrified, the doctor hastened to close the window, with averted eyes, and applied himself to the restoration of his poor wife.

"Darling, sweetest, dearest, best!" he implored, "revive, awake! Tomorrow there shall come a new life, for tomorrow shall end it all."

"Shall end it all," was the weird warning whispered in his ear.

The doctor started, then collected himself defiantly. "This way lies madness," he muttered. "The time has come to be up and doing. Tomorrow —"

The morrow of that predestined day, forewarned by the entombed, now dawned. There are good hours, and there are evil hours, that appear in the horoscope of life, and from the Chaldeans of remote ages to the soothsayers and Buddhists of the present time the starry hosts have been compelled to give up their secrets. Have they found true interpreters?

What happened on this recurring 21st day of June — this day of seven times three and three times seven? The day found Cynthia too ill to rise. The doctor saw the danger of brain fever, and tried to calm himself and quiet her.

"Rest today, dearest wife," he said to her. "You need rest. But tomorrow, when you are stronger, we will leave this lonely place. Forgive me, darling, that I have let you pine away in these dark shadows so long —"

She made no reply other than to mutter: "Too late! too late!"

The doctor sadly turned to the window, from whence the night before he had borne his swooning wife. Through the exquisite screen of the lofty oak, he caught glimpses here and there of a ravishing landscape. The peerless city of liberty stretched out at his feet in graceful repose, then a vista of the rounded dome of the capitol, or of the sinuous line of the meandering Potomac sparkling in the sunlight, beautified by its island oasis, dotted here and there and encrusted by its gem-like environment of undulating verdure-clad hills.

"Oh, paradisaical earth! why, why should the trail of the serpent rest on thy fair bosom! Why should the malign glance of the evil eye empoison thy fairest scenes!" groaned the wretched man. His mind was filled with the rich imagery of that hidden lore, over which he had been listlessly dreaming during this past year. But he had received a rude awakening, as he at last fully realized the critical condition of his beloved wife. Cynthia's fever rose as the hot June sun heated the air with its vertical rays, and as the day wore slowly on the doctor saw that she was no better.

Was it a psychic effect that influenced Mr. Albright and attracted him to such a degree that putting aside a mass of papers claiming his careful attention, he yielded to the power that impelled him to revisit his friends? "It is the anniversary," he thought, "of one of the strangest events I have ever witnessed, and many hidden aspects of life have been laid open to me in the course of the practice of my profession. I have not seen Rawle for months, for both he and his pretty wife are positively buried." Thus it came to pass that just as the sun set gorgeous cloud masses transfigured into ethereal shapes, the two friends met, and they walked together in the oak forest, not far distant from the house. Cynthia continued very ill, too ill to be moved, and the doctor was in a state of agitation and grief difficult to describe. It was indeed a welcome relief to grasp the friendly hand of Albright thus unexpectedly extended to him, and to unburthen his heart. The lawyer listened with that precise and patient attention which was his habit.

The story of the two apparitions, of the dismal winter, filled with its imaginary terrors, and the frantic fright of the previous night, culminating in the present delirium of Cynthia, was all told.

When the doctor had finished, his friend said: "Of course, Rawle, the weird part, and it is weird, must be all fustian and fancy. The serious part comes in the effect produced."

Dr. Rawle was about to reply, "effect produced from a cause" — but he shrank from making the open avowal. The bravest men are apt to be moral cowards in the face of ridicule, so he merely said with an assumed assent he did not feel — "Of course."

They were silent, but after a moment's pause the doctor remarked:

"Please excuse me an instant. I wish to see if my wife still sleeps."

Left alone in this lone forest, as the light of day was rapidly yielding to the gathering twilight, even the incredulous lawyer felt a creeping sensation, a thrill of the nerves, that was, to say the least, uncomfortable; but he resolutely battled against the influence, and retired within his triple armor of incredulity, materialism and logical sequence, thus defying the visionary. For all that, he found the hour that he was thus left alone both tedious and uncomfortable. But at last the doctor came striding forward. Cynthia was awake and raving about a bough of the oak that, she declared, had waved over her, assuming the grinning aspect of a death's head.

"Albright," said Rawle, "I must try the effect of heroic treatment. I mean to ascend to that devilish bough and cut it off. I wish I could destroy the whole infernal tree, root and branch. We have lived too long under its deadly upas shade. I hope, old fellow, that the sudden revulsion when Cynthia sees it crashing down will help her to overcome these diabolical illusions. Promise me, my dear friend," he added, with emotion, "that while I am doing this thing you will watch over my darling, so that no harm can befall her in some frenzied mood." The obscurity of the early dusk was now giving way to the glimmering pallor of the newly-risen moon as the two friends approached the house.

Suddenly Albright exclaimed, "Look!" A flickering, uncertain, shadowy, lambent light played above the grave that these two men had dug one year ago that very night. Then, as if condensing, casting a sickly sheen around, it hovered here and there, at one moment darting upward fiercely, as a thin pillar of fire, then subsiding, trailing along near the ground, gradually sinking, and finally its flamboyant curving line was lost to sight!

It was a somewhat varied repetition of the phantom flights that had horrified Cynthia, but neither the doctor nor the lawyer had ever before seen a visible shape thus defined from the invisible. They were students and thinkers, not disposed to accept an illusory semblance, and both men declared that it must be an optical illusion. But Dr. Rawle was under a strong and fierce excitement on account of the sickness of his wife. "My God!" groaned he, "what if Cynthia has seen it!"

He hastened past the horse-shoe knoll, up to her room. She was still reclining as he had left her, muttering inarticulate sounds — her hands tightly clasped and her eyelids half open. It was evident that she had not stirred. In a few minutes the doctor returned, carrying a saw.

"Go, watch her, Albright," said he, hoarsely. "The time has come for me to ascend this accursed tree. I will lop off these hellish branches. I will hack and hew" —

He strode fiercely forward, stamping heavily over the horse-shoe knoll.

"Ha! ha!" he laughed, strangely moved. "To molest my Cynthia; mine, with its tricksy images, its impish delusions, its uncanny spectacular shows!"

He now commenced to ascend the gnarled trunk of the knotted oak. Climbing and clinging to every inequality. The doctor was a practiced athlete, and this was child's play for him.

Up! up! and the fated branch is reached! The sharp teeth of the saw had made its first deep, grinding incision, when —

As Albright entered the room Cynthia had risen and stood beside the open window, enveloped in a fleecy flowing robe of some light India stuff; a gray cashmere shawl of richest oriental design was carelessly thrown over her fair shoulders, and her wealth of pale, ashen-colored hair, fell, unheeded, in tangled masses, around her person. Albright, wishing to protect, but not to disturb her, approached with noiseless step. She did not see him, or, seeing, heeded not. With the palms of her thin hands closely pressed against the blue-veined temples, the large orbs of her wide-opened eyes gazing fixedly, she stood in speechless affright. Albright could not resist the impulse. He advanced and stood beside her, and he, too, gazed outwardly intently. The doctor had commenced his work, and with sure and swift motion the pitiless saw ground through the twisted bark. Already the huge branch swayed and rocked to and fro. The air was filled with the sharp clicking resonance of the breaking branches; they moved backward and forward; they crackle; they oscillate; they swing; they sway — when — "Oh God! my God!" shrieked Cynthia, for now the flickering light arose from out the grave, the emanation rapidly gathering force, when sheeted with encircling flames, the fierce phantom arose in might and with an awful swirl enveloped the daring iconoclast in its skeleton ribs of furious fire, bearing downward in one crushing mass the crashing bough and the crushed man.

Cynthia had swooned away, but the horror-stricken Albright heard distinctly, in vibratory sepulchral tones — "Dead! All is at an end!"

And poor Cynthia?

"Dead! All is at an end!"

The Ghost of the Belle-Alliance Plantation

Lilian Giffen

The Natchez swung her gang-plank over the *levee* to allow a passenger to land in the Parish of St. James, and the moment he stepped on the bank, with the ringing of her bells, and the rapid swishing of backing water under her wheel-house, the great steamer rapidly continued her trip up the Mississippi.

A middle-aged colored man was waiting to meet the boat, and his round, shining, black face had looked troubled as he lounged up and down, while his little eyes wandered uneasily in the direction of a great square white house some half mile away, that loomed up shadow-like in the night; but he brightened when the passenger landed, and baring his woolly head, took his valise, saying — "Howdy, Boss."

The newcomer nodded pleasantly — "All well, Peter?" he asked.

The man hesitated. "I'se kinder wor'ied," he answered at last. "I don't like de way tings seems a-goin'."

"Any trouble at the Sugar House?"

"No, sah."

"Trouble among the '*hands*'?"

"No, Boss."

"Then what is it?"

Peter walked on sturdily as though he had not heard the question, but there was evidently a struggle going on within him, and his thick lips twitched a little.

"You'se not goin' tuh de 'Big House' tuh night, is you?" he inquired, after a pause.

"Why not?"

The servant's black face became ashy. "For de Lawd's sake Missah Allise don't sleep der!"

"Is there going to be any rising over there, that you do not want me to go to the 'Big House'?" asked Mr. Allise in a low tone, glancing closely at his companion, and indicating the "*Quarters*" of the "*hands*" with a slight gesture.

"No! No! not dat!" replied Peter, still more gloomily. Then edging nearer he whispered "Der's Ghosses in de 'Big House'!"

His companion burst out laughing. "Is that all?" he asked.

Peter shuddered in dread of the punishment, by an offended spiritual world, of such untimely mirth. "You kin laugh," he objected stubbornly, "but dey's der!"

"Since when, Peter, and what do they want?"

The negro did not deign to answer, but from the furtive glances of his bead-like eyes, it was easy to see that he, at least, did not find this a jesting matter.

The two men had by this time reached a branch in the path, and as they turned into the one leading to the house, Peter made another effort.

"Missah Allise," he commenced, but seeing determination on the other's face, his objections sank to mutterings, while his lagging steps seemed to invite his companion to gain some distance ahead of him in the path.

Mr. Allise, however, apparently recognizing that this maneuver meant desertion, wheeled briskly, and put his servant before him.

Peter gave up opposition, but his teeth were commencing to chatter. "You won't believe what I says," he warned, "but what you a-goin' tuh say, ef de Ghoss comes tuh you dis evenin'?"

With a shrug of his shoulders, Mr. Allise abandoned an effort to reason. "What will I say?" he answered, "Why, I will ask him to take a chair, and keep me company. It is rather lonely now over at the house, and I would like to have someone to talk to."

Peter literally gasped, and before he could collect his startled senses sufficiently to speak, his tormentor, who was beginning to enjoy the situation, continued — "By the way, whose Ghost is it?"

The negro's horror was too great to permit him reflection on the tone in which the inquiry was made. All he heard was the interrogation, and in obedience to it, he ejaculated, "It's de ole Missis' husban'!"

"Peter," said his companion, sternly, "You never saw the old Missis' husband; he never lived in this house — it was built after his death, when the river ate in so far on this side of the bank that, in the survey, the line for the new *levee* passed through the spot where the old house stood, and so this one had to be built some distance back of it."

"I don't care 'bout dat," Peter insisted stubbornly, "He could come here ef he had a mind tuh. Lots of de new house was made from de ole. Dis is de home place anyway, an' dis house would a bin his ef he had a lived, so he kin come home jes' when he like."

"Logically proved," laughed the other, "But why are you afraid of him? If you were doing your work properly he would not trouble you."

Peter shook his head dubiously. "Most ever sence you an' dat Chinee 'hand' done bin up in de garret de Ghosses bin oneasy-like; off and on a-howlin' an' a-howlin' till you' blood jes' run cold," he said fearfully. "An' Hannah was a-comin' down stairs yesterday evenin' wid a candle, and she say as how de ole Missis' husban' done meet her on de landin', and he was a-carryin' his head in his hands, and when he seed her a-comin', she 'low as how he jes' blow her candle right out."

"Peter, Peter," objected the other severely. "If the Ghost was carrying his own head in his hands, how could he blow Hannah's candle out?"

"Yes, sah, he done so," affirmed Peter, emphatically.

"What else, Peter?"

"You'se a-laughin' now Missah Allise," said his servant in a gloomily prophetic tone, "But I tells you it's mighty bad luck fur dem Ghosses tuh be a-walkin' round like dat, an' cryin' an' howlin' — it's mighty bad luck — you see ef somethin' ain't goin' tuh happen." He paused, and the two men walked on silently till they stood in front of the old house. All around it ran broad verandahs, supported by huge white columns, whose solid bases were but a few feet off the ground, while their capitals reached to the second story; the tall pillars making monster shadows in the moonlight.

Nothing but habitual obedience to his master's commands, aided by the pressure of the latter's hand on his shoulder induced Peter to move forward, and ascend the huge white steps leading to the front door.

Mr. Allise put his latch-key in the lock, pushed the door open, and they entered a tremendous hall, whose inky blackness the faint light of the lantern made, if possible, deeper, as it glanced on the polished floor and furniture.

Over the echoing boards the two men went past the closed doors of apartments on either side of the hall, directing their steps towards the stairway more through familiarity than sight.

The heavy atmosphere of an empty house, and the intense stillness, now that even the faint noises of the crickets and the night were shut out by the great doors, fell oppressively over all, making the steps of the two men ascending the broad, square staircase sound followed by other footfalls, while reverberation seemed to echo the negro's hurried breathing mockingly.

Silently they gained the upper hall, and entered one of the large front rooms. In a few moments the broad flame of a lamp illuminated the lofty ceiling and gigantic four-post bed, bare now of curtains and draperies, whose great, gaunt shadow thrown against the wall, looked like the skeleton of some prehistoric monster.

Peter moved about arranging things in the room for a while, then he turned to his companion, "Kin I go over tuh de '*Quarters*' tuh night?" he asked.

Mr. Allise nodded, and the negro moved towards the door. Suddenly, he almost dropped his lantern, and his trembling limbs refusing to uphold him, he grasped at the wall for support, paralyzed with fear; while even his companion started and looked around strangely.

A long, low cry like a wail of agony, echoed through the empty house. Following it came a succession of sobbing moans, weird and far reaching, now in fading tones as though the faintness of exhaustion was overtaking their author, now rising as with a last despairing agony.

Through and through the empty house the unearthly noise sounded, echoing back after each prolonged cry, until the whole air seemed filled with voices.

Shaking himself free from the impression that had held him spell-bound, Mr. Allise sprang for the stairs leading to the upper stories, whence the strange plaints seemed to come, dragging after him his half unconscious servant, whom, for the moment, fear had deprived of the power of resistance.

As they rushed up, the unearthly cries ceased, and the men paused, appalled by the succeeding silence. Suddenly, again the hideous sobs rang out still above and above the listeners, only to cease as they stumbled up the dark stairway into the garret, and stood, breathless, gazing on the streak of pale light the lantern threw on two dormer windows that looked out to the river and the night. With a quick movement Mr. Allise lifted the lantern he had taken from his companion's shaking fingers, and advanced. Beside him was a door leading into what he knew was used as a sort of lumber room. But as his steps sounded on the floor, apparently through the very panels burst a series of the unearthly howls and cries, whilst the barrier itself seemed to tremble with a frenzied effort for freedom.

His hand was on the knob, when extremity of fear roused the negro from his passive obedience. Mad with terror, he stayed the other's movements, pleading hoarsely — "Fur Gawd's sake don't let de Ghoss loose on us — he'll kill us! Oh! my Gawd, Missah Allise, don't, don't do dat!"

With an exclamation Mr. Allise threw off the detaining hand, and flung open the door.

A shrill, piercing yell rang out, as something rushed through the opening. Instantly there was a noise of falling as Peter, beside himself, half raced, half rolled down the steps to escape. Two glistening, green, glass-like eyes danced around Mr. Allise, a small body struck against him, and the deep moans changed to half snarling yelps. A small, miserable, half starved, white dog, frightened almost into convulsions was running about wildly, sniffing the floor curiously, as though every now and then detecting a well-known trace.

It was the little dog of the Chinese "*hand*" who had gone up into the garret with him two days before, Mr. Allise afterwards told Peter; and neither man noticing that the dog had followed them, it had inadvertently been closed up in the lumber room. But though this explanation was carefully pointed out to him as an illustration of the nonexistence of Ghosts, Peter continued to shake his head solemnly, and his own interpretation of the affair was that the Ghost, disturbed in his nocturnal peregrinations, and for reasons of his own not wishing to expose these to his descendant, though compelled by the laws of the spiritual world to appear in visible form on earth at that hour, had purposely assumed the shape of the Chinaman's little dog, in order to mislead those who were blind enough to occult forces to hold explained, things for which material reasons were evident.

"But," Peter wound up impressively in telling the story in the '*Quarters*,' "Dat Ghoss can't fool me!" And from that time forward, from the moment the sun went down, not a negro would stay alone in the 'Big House,' and after nightfall no power on earth would have made one approach the haunted portals, and risk meeting the Ghost of the Belle-Alliance Plantation.

Made in the USA
Las Vegas, NV
15 October 2022

57376741R00204